L. ?

October 13, 2021

Augusta's Daughter

Life in Nineteenth Century Sweden

by
Judit Martin

A typical nineteenth century Swedish peasant cottage

Penfield
BOOKS

My thanks to Eva Lambert, Don Thomas, Bill Mitchell, Joan Morrison, Jan Smedh, and Diane Hurst for taking the time to read and comment on the manuscript, and to Anna Molander, Maja Ridell, and Urban and Elisabeth Flodström for their willing help with practical matters.

Cover design by: M. A. Cook Design
Front cover photo by: Judit Martin
Back cover author photo by: Barbara Brady Conn

Edited by: Miriam Canter, Whitney Pope, Deb Schense, Mary Sharp, and David Wright.

AUTHOR'S NOTE

Well into the first years of the twentieth century Swedes spoke in a manner which sounds awkward to English-speaking ears. Instead of addressing each other in the second person ("Are you tired, Carl?" or "It's time for you to get up, Carl,") they used the third person ("Is Carl [or he] tired?" or "It's time for Carl [or him] to get up,") when speaking directly to each other. In the middle of the century the use of the Swedish equivalent of 'you' in its more formal plural form began to take over when one spoke with strangers and acquaintances, while 'you' in its more informal singular form was reserved for family and friends. Finally, by the end of the 1960s, there was a campaign to encourage people to use the informal singular 'you' with everyone. For the sake of authenticity and atmosphere, I have written as people spoke at the time in which the story takes place.

Also by Judit Martin is, "Kajsa," the sequel to "Augusta's Daughter."

ISBN-13: 9781932043815
Library of Congress Control Number: 2012945380
©2012 Judit Martin   Printed in the USA

To Pia
(who gave me the idea)

About the Author

Judit Martin, whose ancestors were early English and Scottish immigrants, grew up in Franklin, Michigan. After high school in nearby Birmingham, she attended Beloit College in Beloit, Wisconsin, and in 1961 graduated from Washington State University in Pullman, Washington, with a degree in English and a teaching certificate. She taught for several years before setting out to fulfill her childhood dream of spending two years travelling in Europe. Captivated by the experience, she extended her stay with a job teaching English in a Turkish girls' school in Izmir, Turkey, followed by a job at the American School in London. When she finally came to Sweden in 1969 she fell in love with the countryside, with its remnants of the old peasant culture, and settled there.

As a single mother, she raised her two Swedish-born daughters out in the country near the mining village of Zinkgruvan, where she still lives in her slightly primitive old house. For many years she worked as a weather observer for the Swedish weather bureau, going outside every three hours, day and night, to observe and report the weather, a job which left her much free time in which to write. She has had several short stories published in Scottish literary magazines and two documentary books published in Swedish. "Augusta's Daughter" is her first published novel. "Although I have dual citizenship," Judit says, "after over forty years in Sweden, I don't feel like an American, nor am I a Swede. I am just myself, which suits me perfectly."

CONTENTS

INTRODUCTION

Many years ago, I made a promise to my great-grandmother, Elsa-Carolina. Over a period of ten days aboard a boat to Sweden, I encouraged her to tell me the story of her life. In exchange, she asked me, a little awkwardly, if perhaps I could write down some of what she told me, in case her great-great- grandchildren one day wondered about their ancestors. I promised wholeheartedly, and each evening made detailed notes of what she had told me during the day. In fact, I became so absorbed in her story that after her death, I returned to the old country and immersed myself in its dying peasant culture, putting aside my promise. There would be plenty of time for that later. Half a century passed.

One morning when I looked in the mirror, instead of seeing my own face, it was Elsa-Carolina who stared back at me. In the same instant, I could feel her hand squeezing mine as I had made my promise all those years ago. And, for the first time, I realized that I was the sole keeper of a story that was not mine to hoard, and certainly not mine to take to the grave with me. It is a story that belongs to my great-great-grand-mother and to my own great-grandchildren, and to all of us inbetween. And, in many ways, it is a story that belongs to anyone who comes from a similar background.

How I became keeper of the story began one rainy day in the spring of my senior year in college, a few years after the end of the Second World War.

PROLOGUE

The March wind propelled me along the sidewalk, pelting my back with huge raindrops determined to force their way through my coat. Hunching my shoulders and pulling in my head like a turtle, I clutched my books to my chest and hurried toward the student boarding house.

By the time I reached the front steps, my feet were soaked, for it had been impossible to avoid all the puddles. I gave them a cursory wipe on the doormat, then crossed the hall to my mailbox. Way in the back was a small envelope. Immediately I recognized my great-grandmother's handwriting. Usually she only wrote on special occasions, such as my birthday or Christmas.

Why now, I wondered? She was my favorite of all my relatives—the only one who wasn't boring and bigoted. We always had long interesting talks when we met, but we never corresponded. I continued up to my room, kicked off my shoes, draped my coat over the radiator, and flopped down on the bed. Turning the envelope over curiously, I slipped my thumb under the flap. It loosened willingly, and I pulled out a small piece of writing paper with flowers across the top.

March 16, 1948

My Dear Carrie,
As you perhaps know, your great-grandfather Erik and I had one unfulfilled dream—to return to our homeland after all these years in America. Oh, how we scrimped and saved! Then, just when our dream was about to come true, it was killed by the Nazis, who made travel too risky. In a way, the Nazis killed Grandpa Erik also. His heart couldn't take the disappointment. But my heart is still strong and my will even stronger. Only one thing is missing, and I am hoping you can help me with that.

I understand from your mother that you will be finished with your teacher's training at the end of May and that you have a teaching job lined up for September. Could you think to give me your June, July, and August and go home to Sweden with me?

I am ninety-four years old and, even though I can still get around on my own with no problem, I would rather not travel alone. There is money for two, so you needn't worry about that. You would simply take Grandpa Erik's place. It would make me so happy!

Oh, do say yes! It would be a perfect end to my days.

Love,

Great Granny Elsa-Carolina

I read the letter over three times before daring to believe what I was reading. "Could you think to?" If only she knew how much I longed to go to Sweden, to see the places she had talked about when I was a child. I had often wondered if I would even be able to find them once I finally got a chance to go there, let alone connect her half-forgotten stories to them properly. Yet it wasn't the details that were important. It was the atmosphere around them that pulled at me, made me feel that I belonged there somehow.

I shook the rain out of my coat and put it on again, tucking the letter as far down as I could in one of the pockets, and hurried the few blocks to the Western Union office. Why didn't she have a telephone! That was part of her old-fashioned Swedishness.

"What do I need a telephone for?" she would argue. "We never had one at home. Besides, all my friends are dead now, so who would I call?"

The waiting room was empty, so I went directly to the window instead of first filling out the telegram blank. I was out of breath and my hair dripped onto the counter in front of me.

"What do you wish to send for the message?" the telegrapher asked once I had given Granny's name and address.

"Just write, 'Yes! Yes! Yes!'" I told him. "And sign it, 'Your namesake.'"

He did as I requested, but not without giving me a very strange, questioning look.

The next day I received the following telegram in return:

"Wonderful stop So happy stop Come here at Easter to discuss stop."

I went. We discussed. And that was how it all began.

We sailed the second week of June 1948, with gifts of coffee, chocolate, cigarettes, nylon stockings, and other post-war scarcities packed with our clothes. In an attempt to make our ten days on board pass more quickly, we decided to take an hour-long walk around the ship twice daily. Hopefully it would help keep us in shape for all the walking we planned to do in Sweden. Granny had no trouble getting around and although she had a cane, I never saw her lean on it. Mostly she used it as a pointer or to tap the ground when she was impatient.

"It was Grandpa Erik's," she explained, showing me the beautifully carved handle. "His grandfather made it in the winter of 1801 when he was convalescing from having lost a couple of toes to frostbite. Just before he died, he gave it to Erik's father, who in turn gave it to Erik. I carry it because it was Erik's, but also because it commands respect. You know, 'watch out for the little old lady with the cane.' It's a pretty good weapon, too," she added, waving it above her head.

She had a point about the little old lady part. She was barely five feet tall and had never broken a hundred pounds, except when pregnant. As for being old, it was impossible to guess her age. Her face had the softness that comes with years, but it was almost entirely devoid of wrinkles, aside from the laugh lines radiating from the corners of her bright blue eyes. She wore her still-thick gray hair in a braid wound around her head, which gave her an almost girlish appearance. And she had all her own teeth. Only her gnarled, misshapen hands betrayed the secret of her hard life. Those she kept hidden beneath her apron when they weren't busy with some task. The only time she was without an apron was when she was out in public. Then she often wore gloves. Even at her age she had a strong sense of pride. She had come up in the world since immigrating to America and had always felt a sense of shame concerning the poverty of her past.

Only her immediate family was aware of the fact that she had suffered hardships in her younger years. And even they knew few details. Nor were they interested. Of all her descendants in America—a daughter (deceased), a granddaughter (my mother), a great-granddaughter (me), and three great-grandsons (my younger brothers)—I was the only one who, as a child, had begged her to tell me stories about her life in the old country. And, what she told me had left an idyllic glow in my memory. I had no idea that she had omitted most of her story, judging it unfit for a child's ears. Nor did I realize that this journey, which had begun as the fulfillment of the dream she and Erik had had, was going to awaken memories she had purposely left locked away in her old wooden *America chest* after she had emptied it of the few belongings she brought with her to the New World.

She had let seventy-five years pass without a backward glance. It wasn't until she was sailing back toward her past that she dared to reopen that chest and take a look at the memories she had always felt were better left forgotten. And as she looked and remembered, she shared with me what she found.

For many years afterwards, I simply lived in the shadow of Elsa-Carolina's life. But with the approach of my own old age, I suddenly realized it was time to fulfill my long-ago promise to her. Here, at last, is Elsa-Carolina's story.

GRANKULLEN

January 1854 was so cold that often the mercury curled up in the bulb of the thermometer and refused to budge upwards. Over an *aln** of snow covered the ground, with drifts three *alnar* high. And on this particular night, the north wind howled through the forest, bending the slender birches and swaying the rigid pines blocking its path. When it reached the little cottage in the clearing at the top of the hill, rather than veering off and passing on either side of it, it pressed its way straight in between the moss-caulked timber walls, leaving a dust-like layer of powdered snow on the floor. The insides of the two windows had long since been covered with *tum*-thick ice, blocking what little light the short winter days gave.

Augusta was awakened by a sharp pain announcing that the child she had carried for so long was soon to make its appearance. She slipped out from under the covers carefully so as not to wake Olov, pulled aside the curtain hanging across the front of the built-in cupboard bed and, searching for the stepping bench with her foot, climbed out into the blackness of the cottage's main room. Her breath formed a thick cloud in front of her face.

Pulling her shawl from the peg by the door, she went out into the even colder entrance way. Out of habit, her stockinged feet found her wooden shoes where she had left them by the wood basket. Drawing her shawl tighter around her heavy body, she jerked the outside door open, causing it to cry out shrilly on its iron hinges. In the moonlight she saw that the previous day's snowfall had been rearranged by the night wind, swept off the open places and piled in great drifts against the buildings as well as on the cottage doorstep. She had no choice but to wade through it, filling her shoes with snow, which quickly melted, soaking her only pair of woolen stockings. But there was no time to bemoan her bad luck.

In the first clear place she came to, she pulled up her coarsely woven nightgown and squatted down to urinate. The wind whipped her sleep-loosened hair across her face mercilessly. She shivered, not from the cold so much as from fear. Think if there were a wolf hiding on the edge of the forest, waiting to rip her child from her. Ever since the day she had overheard two old women talking about such a thing happening in a nearby village she had hardly dared go outside. Letting her nightgown fall down around her ankles, she hurried back to the shelter of the

*See glossary for definitions of Swedish words.

cottage and the comforting sound of Olov's soft snoring in the darkened kitchen. On the far side of the room his ten-year-old sister, Helga, was still asleep in the *utdragssoffa*. As a maid, it was her job to get up first and make the fire and boil the coffee, but Augusta hadn't the heart to wake her.

Carefully she brushed away the night's ashes on the raised hearth until she found glowing coals. She laid a few pieces of peeled birch bark and some twigs over them and blew gently until the fire crackled to life, replacing the darkness with dancing light. Pulling aside the curtain across the front of the bed, she studied Olov's sleeping face. The long blond lashes of his closed eyelids curled up from his cheek bones, making him look young and innocent, while his shaggy beard and even shaggier straw-colored hair gave him a wild, uncontrolled appearance. Together they revealed the extremes in his being.

Augusta Torsdotter and Olov Aronsson had met while they were both working at Ekefors Manor, she as a housemaid and he as a farmhand, the only jobs available to the sons and daughters of landless peasants. Such was their lot in life. Neither of them had hopes of ever rising above that status, since all other doors were closed to them from birth. Nor had their marriage been the result of a romantic attraction. In those days most marriages, especially in the so-called better classes, were arranged by the couple's parents, to the advantage of one or both of the families. And even among the poorer classes, a couple was not entirely free to marry without parental approval, as well as that of the church. If the local priest felt that a man would not be a good provider or that a woman would be a poor householder, he could refuse to let them marry for the sake of the parish welfare system. Or permission could be refused if one of the partners had an incurable illness, particularly epilepsy, which was believed to be passed on genetically. It even happened that a person was not allowed to get married if he or she could not read, for such a person didn't have the proper knowledge of the *Catechism* required by the church for marriage.

For Augusta and Olov, there had been no such hinders, however, nor had parental approval been necessary. It was their master, Baron Ekefors, who had taken the parental role—to his own advantage, of course. He simply told each of them to come to his office after the noon meal one day.

When Olov showed up in the manor house kitchen that afternoon, he was surprised to find Augusta already waiting there. Neither spoke.

Obediently they followed the parlor maid who led them down a long dark hallway to the other end of the house and left them standing in front of a closed door. Olov looked at Augusta for an explanation. But she just shrugged her shoulders slightly. Not knowing what else to do, Olov took a deep breath and knocked, hoping he wasn't being disrespectful towards the baron.

"Come in!" came a gruff command from inside the room.

They entered. Like the hallway, the room was unlit, and everything about it was heavy: the dark paneled walls, the dark green velvet draperies shrouding the windows, the overstuffed leather armchairs, and the thick Persian rug on the floor. Ekefors sat behind a massive oak desk, which seemed to double his authority. Olov stood before him, hat in hand, while Augusta remained in the doorway, eyes downcast, afraid to go farther.

"I assume Aronsson is familiar with Grankullen, the *torp* on the northern edge of the manor," the baron began, without introduction.

"Grankullen? Does Baron Ekefors mean Ulfskullen?" Olov asked. He had never heard it referred to as anything other than Ulfskullen after Ulf Hansson, who had lived there all his life. Although it belonged to Ekefors Manor, Ulf and his wife had spent every free minute clearing fields and improving the place, hoping that one of their children would take it over after them. But, alas, they were blessed with five daughters, all of whom married and moved away.

"That's the one. It's vacant now. The cottage is in passable condition, and there is already a large potato patch dug, as well as two fenced pastures, a cowshed, and pig sty. I need a strong young couple to take it over. If Aronsson and Torsdotter were to get married, they could live up there and work at the manor in the usual way to pay the rent."

"But what about Hansson and his wife?" Olov couldn't help asking.

"Hansson is too disabled to work any longer, so they had to leave the cottage. They have probably gone to live with one of their children, or else to the poorhouse," the baron told him matter-of-factly.

Olov started to speak, but a cold look from Ekefors made him swallow his words. It was common knowledge that Ulf Hansson was disabled because of negligence on the part of Baron Ekefors.

"I can't have people here who don't pay their way. That's how life is. And it will be the same for Aronsson when he can no longer work," Ekefors assured him.

"Yes, Baron, I know," Olov conceded.

"So what does Aronsson say about Grankullen?"

"May I look at it first?"

"Yes, of course."

He opened a desk drawer, pulled out a large iron key, and handed it to Olov.

"Aronsson will owe me 250 days of work a year. And his wife will be expected to do what is asked of her from time to time," he added, looking past Olov towards the door where Augusta stood still staring at the floor. "Let me know by tomorrow."

"Yes, Baron," Olov replied with a slight bow before leaving the room. Augusta curtsied and followed after him without looking up.

Olov and Augusta were casual acquaintances and each knew the other to be a hard worker, as well as honest and God-fearing. And while Olov took a drink with the other men now and then, he never let himself become drunk. It was those qualities that were important in a marriage. The rest was immaterial; it was assumed that they would grow together in time. No matter what their personal feelings might be, both knew, each for their own reasons, that such an opportunity would not pass their way again.

That afternoon they made their way through the forest up to the *torp*. The path was narrow, giving Augusta an excuse to walk behind Olov, who in turn was glad to note that she kept a few paces behind him. Like most men, he had disdain for women who didn't know their place in respect to menfolk. But most of all, walking single file made it unnecessary to talk. Augusta felt like chattel—an animal being led home after having been purchased at an open market—whose life had been bargained away by others. Her sense of degradation was such that she couldn't even lift her head high enough to see the heels of Olov's boots ahead of her.

Presently, the forest gave way to a clearing on the top of a hill. On the far side was a cluster of low wooden buildings, their grass-covered roofs edged in white from the layer of birch bark underneath the sod. Olov tugged at a bit of it above the cottage door, hoping that the whole roof was sufficiently water-proofed with birch bark to keep out the rain.

Then, inserting the key in the lock, he pushed the door open and went in. Even though it had only stood empty a short time, it had already taken on a musty, closed-up smell. In the center of the back wall of the main room was an ordinary *aln*-high hearth below a huge stone chimney. Placed around the other walls were an old table with benches on either side, a wooden *utdragssoffa* that could be pulled out into a box bed, and in the far corner, a bed built onto the wall like a cupboard, with a curtain across the front and a cupboard built into the foot end.

Two small windows let in the little light that managed to push its way through the treetops barricading the sky. On the end wall, a door led to what was known as the best room which was only used for special occasions. It contained an *utdragssoffa* and a large table.

Olov straddled one of the benches and looked around the room, then at Augusta, who was standing by the hearth poking at the dead ashes with a stick. Although he had seen her many times before, it was the first time he had really looked at her. He tried to imagine coming home at the end of the day to find her standing as she was now, stirring his evening porridge. Around the edge of her face, her dark hair had loosened from the single braid lying down her back, as though she had been working hard. He let his eyes slide down her body. She was of sturdy build, with large hands, firm breasts, and wide hips.

"Is it agreed that Augusta shall become my wife?" he asked finally. "Or does she dream of someone else?"

Until recently she had, indeed, dreamed of someone else. But she also knew that, under the circumstances, she must be thankful for that which was being offered her now.

"There is no one else," she answered, barely above a whisper.

"Will she bear my children?"

"If it be God's will," she replied. Her throat was so tight she could hardly speak.

"And be an obedient wife to me?"

"I shall do my best."

"And perhaps grow to care for me?"

"Perhaps."

"Shall I accept Ekefors' offer then?"

"As Olov wishes."

As a woman, she hadn't anything to say in the matter. Therefore she felt honored that he wondered if she dreamed of someone else, as well as his asking if he should accept the offer. At the same time, that which was unsaid frightened her. But Olov seemed not to notice her discomfort.

Having agreed, he locked the door and they returned to the manor to inform Baron Ekefors of their decision.

"Good. Aronsson can move into Grankullen as soon as he wishes," he told Olov. "The banns must be read aloud in church the next three Sundays before the wedding ceremony can take place. But now that

Aronsson has made clear his intention to marry Augusta, he is free, as is customary, to take his fiancée into his home and bed as his wife. And when Augusta moves from the Manor house, she will be released from her duties as a maid and compensated for the first half of this work year, which is to say, she will receive half of her yearly pay, both in cash and kind. The cash amounts to twenty-five crowns. But since it would be silly to give her half a pair of shoes, she can have two aprons, instead of one, as well as an extra yard of cloth."

Augusta said nothing, even though she was badly in need of a new pair of shoes. She knew that Ekefors had purposely traded her shoes for an apron and that she was in no position to complain. He was always quick to rub salt in another's misfortune.

With that he dismissed them. Olov still had the key in his pocket. Thus within a few short hours both of their lives had changed in ways that neither of them could have imagined when they had awakened that morning.

Immediately they set about turning the cottage into a home. Like every peasant girl, Augusta had long ago begun filling her bride's chest with her handwork: sheets, pillowcases, towels, quilts, bolster covers to be filled with bed straw, nightgowns, and aprons, all hand-woven, sewn with neat, even stitches, and decorated with her embroidered monogram. In his spare time, Olov, similarly, had been making tools and implements in the hope of one day acquiring a little *torp*. True, Grankullen didn't actually belong to him, but he had certainly come a good step above that of a farmhand living like an animal in a stall in the corner of a barn with three other men.

Although custom permitted Olov and Augusta to live together, neither of them seemed ready for such a move. Quite simply, they were strangers, shy in each other's presence. Each night Olov returned to his straw-filled farmhand's bunk in Ekefors' barn and Augusta to the *utdragssoffa* bed in the kitchen of the manor house, where she had slept for the past two years. Then one evening there was a new farmhand sitting on Olov's bunk when he came in from work. Without a word, he gathered his few possessions and set off through the forest to Grankullen. In his mind's eye, he imagined Augusta standing by the hearth waiting for him. But the cottage was cold and empty when he stepped inside. He almost felt afraid, for, like most peasants, he was used to always having people around him. Never in his life had he spent a night completely alone. As he looked around the room, a feeling of helplessness overtook him. He needed to start a fire on the hearth in order to get rid of the dampness and warm the boiled potatoes he had taken with him from breakfast, but such tasks were women's work. He had never had to start the fire himself. He must convince Augusta to move in as soon as possible.

After several futile attempts, he finally succeeded in getting a small fire going. Pulling the potatoes from his jacket pocket, he sliced them into a three-legged cast iron pan and set it over the flames. While they warmed, he fetched a basket of wood from the shed and a pail of water from the well. That done, he sat on the edge of the hearth and began spearing pieces of half-warm potato and eating them off the point of his knife.

He wondered what it was going to be like having his own place and a woman in his bed. Such a life had always been his dream, yet he had never believed in its reality. He had been sent from home to work as a farmhand at the age of ten and now, twenty years later, he was still only a farmhand, who had spent his best years living like an animal, slaving for others, with nothing to show for it. He had become an old man before his time. He could hardly believe the turn of events that had not only given him a *torp*, but a young wife along with it.

The hooting of an owl woke him from his reverie. It was getting late and the night air was creeping into the cottage between the timbers. He laid more wood on the fire and looked around for a place to sleep. Augusta's chest was standing under the window where he had set it the day they had brought it from her father's house. In the light from the fire, he could see the intricate swirls of her initials painted below the giant keyhole. Hesitantly, he turned the iron key and lifted the lid, as though it held some secret insight into the woman with whom he was going to share his life. He hoped she wouldn't mind if he took out a quilt, for the night was already chilly. Lying on top of all the linen was her bridal quilt. Gently he lifted the corner of it and looked at the row of tiny stitches holding the border in place. Even he, who knew so little of womanly things, could see that it was exceptionally well made.

Suddenly, he was filled with pride over having such a wife. He only wished he had had the foresight to choose her himself. He laid the corner of the quilt carefully back in place and closed the chest. Even if Augusta was his, he could not bring himself to take her quilt from her chest.

Out in the shed, he found a few empty grain sacks that would have to do for the night. He placed an armload of straw on the floor in the corner of the room, laid a grain sack on top of it, and curled up with the other two sacks over him. He was so tired that he fell asleep immediately.

The next morning he sought out Augusta.

"The time has come to move to Grankullen," he told her.

She nodded.

That evening she followed him through the forest to their new home. Olov had laid a fire before leaving that morning and after a couple of strikes with the flint, the bits of birch bark blazed to life. As the flames ate hungrily through the dry wood, lighting the room, she noticed that he had also fetched a pail of water from the nearby spring and set it on a stool at the end of the hearth, even though both tasks were women's work.

Glancing beyond it, she saw a pile of straw in the corner, with three coarsely woven grain sacks folded neatly on top of it. The cupboard bed had not been used. Quickly Olov scooped up the straw and added it to the straw in the bed. His thoughtfulness made Augusta wish she could run out the door and never come back.

But instead, she opened her chest, pulled out a newly woven linen mattress bag and stuffed the straw into it. On top of it she spread her bridal quilt, whose elaborate design implied a joy she certainly did not feel, and smoothed it out with the palm of her shaking hand. Neither looked at the other.

Silently, they ate the potatoes and dry bread she had brought from the manor house kitchen. Augusta felt time slipping away from her, and she took smaller and smaller bites to prolong the inevitable, while Olov ate greedily in anticipation. By the time they had finished their meal, it was almost dark inside the cottage and the leaping flames from the fire cast nervous shadows on the walls. Olov wiped his mouth with the back of his hand and stood up. Augusta jumped to her feet obediently, before realizing he was only going outside to relieve himself around the corner of the cottage. Seeing her chance, she pulled her nightgown over her head like a tent and undressed quickly underneath it.

Olov returned just as she was getting into bed. He kicked off his heavy leather boots, pulled off his trousers, drew his tunic over his head, and slid under Augusta's bridal quilt, dressed only in a long homespun shirt. Without warning, he rolled on top of her and ran his cold hand up under her nightgown, forcing her legs apart.

"No!" she cried spontaneously, struggling to free herself from the weight of his body as he moved on top of her. He paid no heed to her protest. Suddenly he was like a wild animal, pushing, groaning, pumping. And then just as suddenly, his whole body went limp and he rolled off her.

Presently the evenness of his breathing told her he was asleep. For a long time she lay on her back just as he had left her, mulling over her situation. In those brief minutes everything had supposedly righted itself. She had officially left her girlhood behind forever and become a woman. The days of wearing her hair down her back in a long braid were gone, although she was not yet entitled to wear a married woman's kerchief. Nor did she any longer belong to the group of young housemaids who had been her friends, nor to a group of married women whom she hardly knew. All at once she felt very alone, not knowing what was expected of her.

The only thing she knew for sure was that her life had taken a false turn, and she didn't know how to set it right again.

While she waited for the fire to take, Augusta thought back to those first days which seemed so long ago, even though less than a year had passed since then.

Like many women, she was already with child when the actual wedding ceremony took place. Although such a condition was frowned upon by the church, it was nonetheless perfectly acceptable socially. Since one of the main functions of marriage was procreation and childlessness a source of shame, an engaged couple often preferred to be sure they could reproduce before marrying. Children were needed to help with the work, as well as being their parents' old age insurance. An old couple without children to look after them often ended their days in the poorhouse. But not only that; it was necessary to have many children, for infant and childhood deaths were common.

Augusta didn't tell Olov that she was pregnant. Men and women didn't talk about such things. In the mornings she was always in the barn milking, with the dung pile near at hand, when the sickness overtook her. Afterwards she tossed a little fresh dung over it and got on with her chores. The months passed. Now and then she slid her hands underneath her apron, pressing them against her belly in the hope that it was still flat—that it had only been a dream. But her hands refused to deny the truth; her belly was becoming rounder. She couldn't bring herself to look at it. As a child she had been taught to hide her body, even from her own eyes, and the changes taking place in it embarrassed and upset her.

Like most married couples, she and Olov never saw each other naked. Bodies and bodily functions were something one kept for oneself and anything to do with sex or the sexual organs was considered to be dirty and sinful.

One afternoon, when her thickening waist and enlarged breasts had finally forced her to accept that a child was on the way, she took out a pile of her mother's old clothes, which she had saved after her mother's death, and searched for material she could turn into baby clothes. Closing her eyes, she rubbed each bit of hand-woven linen between her fingertips until she found several pieces which were satiny smooth from long wear. Not only would they be gentlest against a baby's skin, but clothes sewn from old material would keep the child from becoming vain.

Several days later, Olov discovered her secret. It wasn't that he noticed the shape of her belly, but rather that he came upon her sewing small nightgowns when he returned from the manor earlier than usual one evening.

"Is it time to make a cradle?" he asked.

"Yes," she replied, looking down at her hands nervously.

"How soon?"

"Sometime after the new year."

"That gives me plenty of time then," he said, satisfied.

That was the only time the subject was mentioned. Pregnancy was a natural part of life and women carried on with their duties until it was time for the baby to come. Yet Augusta could see by the way he worked on the cradle that Olov was pleased. Like most men, she knew he hoped for a son.

Olov was pleased, while Augusta was scared. If only God would let everything go well. At the same time, she knew that much lay in her own hands. There were so many things one had to watch out for during pregnancy. And then there was the birth itself. That she tried not to think about, for it only reminded her of her mother's death in childbirth. She had never been able to reconcile herself with a God who let—or perhaps even caused—such things to happen.

One day toward the end of September Olov was told to bring Augusta with him to the manor, where she was needed to help with the potato harvest. They had hoped to harvest their own potatoes that same week, but now they would have to wait. It was an unwritten law that the manor's needs always came before those of the people working on it. It had been so as far back as anyone could remember. Peasants were born into their niche in society and lived out their lives under its rules and customs. The manor was their home and its master and mistress served as their parents, with the right to give orders, punish for misdemeanors, and reward good work. The first two comprised daily life; the third occurred seldom. One obeyed without question. Thus, although neither of them wished it, Augusta followed Olov to the manor the next day.

Taking up potatoes was back-breaking work. The men did the initial digging, turning up the undersides of the plants. Behind them came the women, bending over to grub through the heavy damp earth with half-frozen fingers in search of the tubers that lay hidden from sight. Each one, no matter how small, was to be harvested. The best were for human consumption, while the others were divided into seedlings or pig food. And to make sure the job was done properly, inspectors patrolled the rows, with their eyes on those who reached the end of a row too quickly, as well as those who lagged too far behind.

Augusta had helped harvest potatoes ever since she was old enough to walk in the furrows between the rows. Her long fingers, which were used to burrowing through the earth like moles, worked quickly and never mistook a smooth stone for a potato. But this year her back quickly rebelled at holding up her bent-over weight. At first she tried hunkering down, taking short awkward steps, but soon she was reduced to creeping along the rows on her hands and knees, muddying her ankle-length skirt. The women in the rows on either side of her exchanged curious looks and slowed their paces to hers. Within minutes an inspector was straddling the row just ahead of her, blocking her way. Augusta was unaware of his presence until she nearly put her hand on his leather boot. She sat back on her heels and looked up. Inspector Persson looked down at her, hands on his hips and his lips pulled back in a sarcastic smile. If there was one person on the manor she despised, it was Inspector Persson. When she had been a housemaid, he had taken every opportunity he could to fondle her breasts. In the end, she had gone to the baron and complained.

"Women's bodies were created for men's pleasure," Ekefors had laughed. "Don't wave the merchandise in Persson's face if Augusta doesn't want it handled."

But now she was a married woman. Surely he wouldn't touch her, especially not with so many other people nearby.

"Augusta used to be such a good picker," Persson mocked, looking at her stomach. "But now it looks like her fun is interfering with her work." He grinned at her.

Out of habit she bowed her head to her superior and, without stopping to consider the consequences, spit on his boot.

"Augusta will pay for that!" he hissed between clinched teeth, then turned on his heal and marched off down the row.

Augusta stood up, arching backwards to straighten her aching back, and watched him continue his rounds as if nothing had happened. But the look in his eyes made her regret her action. Sooner or later, he would get even with her.

Some of the women continued to follow her slower pace, full of respect for her daring to stand up to the man they all feared and loathed.

Others, afraid of the consequences of such disrespectful behavior, once again worked at their former paces. But they were all in agreement on one point: Olov's Augusta was with child.

As Augusta was getting ready to leave the field at the end of the day, a voice behind her spoke her name. She turned to find Simon's-Stina, an old woman who lived alone in a primitive little shack since her husband Simon's death. She patted Augusta's arm gently.

"When Augusta's time comes, send her Olov to fetch old Stina. She doesn't remember it, but I brought both Augusta and Olov into the world, and many more before and since."

Augusta looked at the tiny woman standing in front of her. She had but one tooth, and that one loose, and her face was as deeply furrowed as the potato field where they stood. She looked well over a hundred, except for her twinkling sky-blue eyes. It was said that in her youth Stina had extracted a frog from a snake without killing either one, and thus was credited with having magical powers.

"I will send him," she answered. "Thank you."

With her secret out, Augusta was suddenly accepted into the company of married women who, until now, had all but ignored her. A married woman's fulfillment came not with putting up her hair and wearing a kerchief on her head; it came with the bearing of her husband's child. Women who had never spoken to her previously now offered advice when they chanced to meet. For a pregnant woman, the world was filled with danger.

"Don't go past the churchyard on the way to church on Sunday. If there happens to be an open grave, the dead person's spirit will pass into Augusta's unborn baby," she was warned by one.

"Augusta must be careful not to step over any rope or string that might be lying about, for it will cause a difficult birth," she was told by another.

"Stay in the house as much as possible. That way Augusta will avoid accidentally seeing a fire, which could mark her child," she was advised by a third.

"Watching an animal being slaughtered can cause 'falling sickness' [epilepsy] in an unborn child," she was informed.

There was no end to the horrible misfortunes which could befall one who was ignorant or careless. Another bit of advice she received from a number of people was that it was high time she had a maid. To have a maid was not a luxury; it was a part of everyday life even for the poorest, for it didn't cost more than a little food. Peasant families were large, and it was often difficult to feed and clothe all the children. Therefore, when a child turned thirteen—or in many cases, ten or even seven—it was time to leave home and make one's way in the world. For boys, this meant becoming a farmhand; for girls, a housemaid.

There was no shortage of eligible children. During the first years they were paid in kind—a set of hand-me-down clothes or shoes at the end of each year—as well as being fed and given a place to sleep. That the food consisted mainly of potatoes, salted herring, and porridge day after day didn't matter. The master and mistress and their children ate the same thing. That was what there was, and no one knew anything different. Nor was there any privacy. The maids, and often the farmer and his entire family, slept in pull-out box-beds in the kitchen during the winter half of the year. Seldom did a maid have an entire box-bed to herself. If the household had more than one maid, they shared the bed; otherwise she shared a bed with one of the children in the family. Such was everyday life.

Realizing that having to care for a baby was going to make it harder for her to do all that needed to be done, Augusta approached Olov on the subject of a maid. She didn't need to use any of the arguments she had prepared ahead of time. He agreed immediately, suggesting that they take his youngest sister, seven-year-old Helga. Although the law of 1842 had made it mandatory for all children to attend school, the poorer peasants still considered it unimportant for a girl to be educated. And many people were against schooling altogether. What did the poor have to gain from it? It only served to entice children away from the family farms where their help was needed.

As far as Olov's parents were concerned, they felt that until the day Helga was forced to go to school, it was better that she learn how to take care of household chores and small children, which would be her lot later in life.

As for reading, most women were able to read Luther's Catechism and the psalm book, which comprised the only reading material found in peasant homes. Augusta could teach Helga that much. In short, Olov's parents were glad for the chance to place Helga with relatives, where she would receive better treatment than at the hands of strangers. A housemaid's life was hard enough, and all too often they were mercilessly taken advantage of by those for whom they worked.

And so it was that Helga came walking the three *fjärdingsvägar* from home through the forest to Grankullen one October Sunday just after the first frost. In a neatly wrapped package she carried her belongings: a hand-me-down dress that her mother had "turned" so that the unfaded back side of the material was on the outside, an apron, and long wool stockings knitted from coarse homespun yarn. She wore her heavy sweater under her shawl and her hand-me-down shoes hung over her shoulder by the tied-together laces. She was only allowed to wear them when there was snow, for the soles were almost worn through. Although the ground was still frosty in the middle of the day, the bottoms of her feet were so calloused from going barefoot that she hardly felt the cold. It was the fear of being attacked by wild animals or carried off by a troll that made her shiver. She walked as fast as she could, glancing behind her from time to time. Even grown-ups feared the forest. For a small child alone, it was a nightmare that made her heart beat like a drum. It wasn't until she spotted the cottage in the middle of the clearing that she managed to slow down and catch her breath.

Augusta welcomed her warmly. Helga was a cheerful soul and took things in stride. She was just as glad to come to Aunt Gusta as Augusta was to have her.

"Helga can hang her shawl on this peg here," Augusta told her, indicating an empty peg by the door. "Now come and sit down and have some warm milk." She filled a wooden bowl with milk and added a spoonful of red lingonberries from a crock in the cupboard, then sat down across the table from her.

"Now tell me, how was the walk through the forest? Was it Helga's first time alone?"

Helga nodded, while chasing lingonberries through the milk with her spoon.

"Was it frightening?"

Helga nodded vigorously. "I had to keep looking behind me."

"It's not pleasant to be frightened, but it shows that Helga is intelligent and can take care of herself in the forest."

Helga glanced up at her aunt shyly. She rarely received any praise from adults and Augusta's words warmed her.

Once she had finished her milk and berries, Augusta helped her raise the wooden lid of the *utdragssoffa* she had been sitting on and fasten it in an upright position with a peg. Together they pulled out the box-like portion underneath. Two-thirds of its length contained a straw bolster, which served as a mattress, and several sheepskins for covers. In the remaining third they placed her clothes.

That night Helga lay awake long after Olov and Augusta had fallen asleep. She had never slept by herself and she was both cold and lonely in such a large empty bed. The next night she opened the lid, but didn't bother to pull out the bottom section. It was more comforting to sleep in a narrow space almost entirely filled by her own body.

Helga proved to be a great help to Augusta. She learned quickly and was eager to please, while at the same time keeping herself in the background and showing respect for her older brother and his wife. Augusta sensed that she was curious about the coming birth. She was the youngest in her family and thus had never experienced the birth of another child. Nor did Augusta know what role she should play in the event.

A sharp pain brought Augusta back to the present. The fire had begun to take the chill from the air, and the coffee was boiling. She heard Olov turn over on the bed straw.

"It's time for Olov to get up," she said. "His coffee is ready."

She took down his heavy woolen stockings from the clothes line over the fire and handed them to him. Swinging his legs over the high wooden edge of the bed, he pulled them on, then reached for his trousers. While the hot coffee brought him slowly to life, Augusta put some leftover potatoes in the three-legged frying pan and set it over the fire. From a crock she took three salted herrings, placed them in the frying pan for a few moments, then cut off a part of one to save for Helga before setting the pan on the table. With his sheath knife Olov speared one potato after another along with bits of herring, eating them from the knife tip, while Augusta picked hers up with her fingers. There was nothing to indicate that it wasn't going to be a day like every other day. Not knowing how to tell Olov that the child was on its way, she said nothing.

As soon as Olov left for the manor Augusta woke Helga and they set to work. This was no time for laziness—it would only make the birth more difficult, as well as causing her child to be lazy later in life. There were many last minute things to be taken care of. The cow must be milked and firewood brought in. Lots of firewood. Not only must the cottage be kept warmer than usual when the time came, but even more important, the fire must burn day and night to keep away evil spirits. They also needed as much water as possible, which meant several trips to the spring to fill every available container. When those tasks were completed, they carried in armload after armload of straw, for it was customary that women gave birth on a bed of straw placed on the floor so as to avoid staining their few hand-woven sheets.

On top of the straw she lay the three grain sacks that she had scrubbed thoroughly during the summer. Lastly, she took her birthing gown out of her chest. It was part of her trousseau; a white, long-sleeved gown with a lace collar and embroidery on the sleeves, which was only worn while giving birth. It seemed so long ago that she had sewn it. At that time she had had no idea what pregnancy and giving birth entailed. Likewise, she hadn't been much more than a child when her youngest brother was born. All she remembered was that she and her brothers and sisters were sent outside and the door locked behind them. When they were finally let back in again, there was a new baby in a basket by the fire and her mother was dead.

It was afternoon by the time they had completed all the necessary preparations. Augusta looked around the room, trying to see it through the eyes of the women who would be coming to help during her confinement. Everything must be in order. Peasant women had sharp eyes that never missed even the smallest details, and they were quick to gossip about anything that was not as it should be. That it was the first time some of them would enter her home, as well as it being her transition from wife to mother, made it especially important. What others saw now would determine how she would be looked upon in the future. Above all, she must not be an embarrassment to Olov. His honor depended on her.

Without warning, she felt something warm and wet running down her legs. Frightened, she turned to Helga.

"It's time for Helga to go down to the big house and find Olov," she said. "Tell him he must go after Simon's-Stina. Quickly!"

"Is Aunt Gusta going to have the baby now?" she asked, wide-eyed.

"Yes. Quite soon, I think. If Helga can't find Olov, tell one of the other adults that Augusta needs Stina as soon as possible. Hurry now, before it is dark. Ask if Helga can sleep there in the big kitchen tonight," she added as an afterthought.

Not long after Helga disappeared down the path, the sky began to redden.

The next pain that came seared through her like lightning, forcing her to sit down on the bench. Suddenly, she felt alone and frightened. She could no longer keep at bay the questions she had for so long been pushing out of her mind. What was it like, this giving birth? It had cost her mother her life. What would she do if the baby started to come before Simon's-Stina got there? She had no idea what to expect—even less, what to do. She opened the door and looked out. There was no sign of Olov or Stina on the path. The last light was leaving the sky and soon all the evil beings in the forest would begin to creep nearer the cottage under the cover of darkness. What if one of them made her lose control of herself during the birth and utter that which must not be said? Augusta slammed the door, hoping the noise would drive such creatures back to the depths of the forest.

She knew she must keep busy. From her chest she took out all the clean rags she had gathered, as well as the long swaddling bands her grandmother had woven, which had been wrapped around all the newborn babies in the family for the past two generations. She was just about to go after a loaf of bread when another pain came, doubling her over. She eased herself down onto the bench. It was only by sheer willpower that she managed to get to her feet again once it ceased. Her fear began to take over. Had she done something wrong while carrying the child, something of which she was unaware? Or was she being punished?

"Dear God in heaven," she beseeched, "please send Simon's-Stina before it's too late. Pleeeease. I'm sorry. I repent. I know I have sinned. Please forgive me. I promise to do whatever God asks of me, if He will only send her in time."

With each new pain she wept, beating her fist on the table and crying out to God, then collapsing almost into unconsciousness until it subsided. Over and over she repented, begged, and promised, repented, begged, and promised.

The fire was beginning to die down by the time she heard the sound of stamping feet in the entranceway. The door opened and Simon's-Stina came in. Behind her was Blind-Ola's Berta, a large rather stern woman whose presence commanded respect, followed by Anna-vid-Bäcken (Anna-by-the-Creek, so called to distinguish her from several other women named Anna), a tall wiry woman who often assisted Stina with deliveries. Last came Halta-Maja (Maja-the-Cripple), a little warm soul whose gentle motherliness counteracted the somewhat more practical-minded efficiency of the others. Each of them had a basket or pot of food. One never attended a birth empty-handed.

"Olov?" Augusta questioned weakly when the door closed behind the four of them.

"He is staying with Blind-Ola for the night," Berta told her. "And Helga is at the big house."

Without further discussion, they slipped the birthing gown over her head and peeled off her clothes from underneath it. It embarrassed her to feel these women's hands on her naked body, but it was the least of her worries at that moment. The worst was when they laid her on the feed sacks and Simon's-Stina reached up under the gown, spread her legs apart, and began poking with her bony fingers. Instinctively she tried to close her legs.

"This is no time for shyness," Stina told her. "This is how women have babies. All of us here have been through the same thing. Augusta will get used to it."

After Stina's examination, they unpinned Augusta's long hair, as well as their own, and loosened any clothes they had on which were tight, all the while chanting, "All which is bound shall be loosened. All which is bound shall be loosened."

By this time Augusta's pains were coming closer together, but she felt calmer, soothed and secure with Stina there. When the pains came, Stina placed one hand in the small of her back and the other hand at the bottom of her stomach. Augusta could feel a wave of heat flowing between her two hands, immediately lessening the intensity of the pain.

Although none of the women had ever been in the cottage, they moved around as if they lived there. Berta brought in a large basin from the entrance way in which to bathe the baby. Then she removed the unspun wool from Augusta's spinning basket and replaced it with several layers of old cloths. Between the last two layers, as a form of protection from evil forces, she placed a small piece of steel that had been passed down through her family just for that purpose. Then she spread the blankets from the cradle on top of the makeshift bed. At one end she set a small psalm book. To lay an unbaptized child directly in a cradle was dangerous. With so much going on, a troll could easily creep into the cottage when no one was paying attention and snatch a newborn baby from its cradle, replacing it with a troll child. But it would never look for the child in a spinning basket.

At the same time, Anna blew life into the fire. Once it was blazing and the water was boiling, she opened the little bundle of herbs Stina had given her. First she made a drink from some bits of cinnamon to help strengthen the contractions. Then she put fennel, anise, and caraway into a separate pot, added a few rags, and let them boil several minutes. When they were barely cool enough to handle, Stina lay them on Augusta's stomach.

Now the contractions came closer together, each one a little stronger than the previous one. While Stina's hands still lessened the pain, they could not obliterate it. For Augusta, who had never known pain, it was becoming unbearable. Blind-Ola's Berta tried to comfort her as best she could.

"This is how it has to be," she explained. "The Bible says that we shall bring forth our children in pain, and not to do so is a sin."

"B-but how much pain?" wept Augusta.

Halta-Maja handed her a bottle.

"Blow the pain into this," she said and demonstrated how to blow short, quick breaths into the empty bottle. Much to Augusta's surprise, it seemed to lessen the next pain.

Time passed. Augusta was becoming exhausted. More than once she was on the verge of making Stina her confessor, in an attempt to find relief, but each time she opened her mouth to speak, no sound came out. And each time Stina looked at her curiously, but said nothing, although small worry lines showed between her eyebrows. Then, at last, in the middle of the night, the baby's head began to show. Stina's face lightened ever so slightly.

"It's best that we take it standing," she said to the others when the time drew near.

Together they helped Augusta to her feet in the straw and placed a chair on either side of her.

"Bend over and put your hands on the chairs for support," Stina told her.

Anna and Berta stood on each side of her to hold her arms when she pushed. Maja warmed a wrapping cloth by the fire while Stina knelt in the straw, ready to receive the child when it came. Now it was up to Augusta to do the rest. Helpers at a birth never interfered with the actual delivery. If possible, any contact with a woman's sexual organs was to be avoided. Only if a serious problem arose would Stina intervene.

Augusta bent over, her birthing gown lifted up over her back and, while Stina gave her instructions as when to push and when not to, Maja held the bottle for her to blow the pain into. Slowly the head emerged, followed by the shoulders; then suddenly Stina was holding a girl-child in her hands. The three helpers shouted their praise, while Stina's face remained serious. She never showed her satisfaction ahead of time, for the job was not complete until the afterbirth had come.

In the meantime, she held the child up to her mouth and sucked its nose clear. Then she passed her scissors clock-wise through a candle flame and cut the cord, which she had tied with a linen thread. The cord itself was set aside to be dried and saved. There would be many medicinal uses for it later. Dried and pulverized, it could be taken for stomach problems, put on birthmarks, taken as a protection against epilepsy, or made into a broth to cure bed-wetting. As soon as the afterbirth came, it was put into the fire. Once it had burned, the ashes must be saved and later given to the child in its milk so it would have a healthy stomach.

And now began the time of vigilance. Not only was the unbaptized baby a heathen, but in her unclean state, Augusta, too, was regarded as a heathen until her churching ceremony in six weeks' time. Both risked being carried off to a cave in the mountains by a troll. To guard against such a fate, Augusta must keep a piece of steel close to her body at all times, as well as a page from a psalm book. For the unbaptized child, the danger was much greater and the protection more complex.

One form of protection was the ritual surrounding the child's first bath. Berta prepared for it by scraping a glowing coal from the fire and, holding it between two sticks, dropping it into the basin of bath water waiting by the hearth. From her pocket she fished up the silver coin which Olov had entrusted to her, which also must be put into the water, both as protection and as Stina's payment. It was the job of the woman who had acted as midwife to give the baby its first bath. Stina carried out this ceremony with the same tenderness with which she would have bathed her own child. Meanwhile, Berta and Anna helped Augusta up into the cupboard bed, slipped her scissors and psalm book under the pillow to safeguard her, and brought her a *kaffekask*, a cup of strong coffee laced with vodka-like *brännvin*, which for centuries had been Sweden's main alcoholic drink.

Once the baby was dry, the stump of the cord was folded upwards against her stomach to prevent her from becoming a bed-wetter, and a piece of cloth covered with candle wax was put on top of it, held in place by a large copper coin, which in turn was held in place by strips of linen. Then, beginning at the baby's feet, Berta and Anna wrapped the swaddling bands around her clockwise to ensure that her legs would be straight. For the first few days her arms must also be swaddled against her chest, the right hand over the left to prevent left handedness. Lastly, Berta pressed the head gently between her hands to round it a bit more before winding the ends of the swaddling bands around it to hold the shape. Only then was the child placed in Augusta's arms.

She studied the little wrinkled face beside her, a face that looked almost as old as it did new. She knew Olov would be disappointed because it wasn't a boy-child, but secretly she was relieved. Girl-children were not so important and perhaps he wouldn't look at her as he would a boy. She herself was pleased to have a daughter who would be a help to her and to whom she could teach womanly things. A son would never really be hers, for he would follow after his father as soon as he could walk. She wondered what life would hold for this tiny being.

The next thing she knew, Anna was shaking her gently.

"Time to wake up. Augusta must be hungry after all that hard work."

As Augusta floated upward from the depths of her sleep, she smelled the rye flour porridge Anna was holding out to her. An indentation in the center of it was filled with melted butter and a moat of cream separated it from the edge of the wooden bowl. Sticking straight up in it was a wooden spoon, which Olov had carved as a welcome gift for the child. Augusta scooped up a tiny bit of porridge with it, dipped it in the butter, then the cream, and touched it to the baby's lips. Instinctively they opened ever so slightly and she slipped the tip of the spoon between them. The three women standing by the bed clapped their hands gaily, not only to voice their approval, but also to accustom the child to loud noises. At last the baby was placed in the spinning basket and the spoon wiped off and hung in the spoon rack on the wall, whereupon Augusta was given her own spoon with which to eat the rest of the porridge.

All the precautions concerning trolls and evil forces made Augusta nervous. She wanted to have the baby baptized as soon as possible.

"The priest?" she tried to ask. "The baby..."

"Augusta needn't worry," Stina assured her. "She's strong and healthy, so there is no need to rush to the priest with her. But Augusta must be very careful. No stranger must see her nursing the child or come upon it naked, for they can have the evil eye or evil tongue with them. In fact, no strangers should be allowed to enter the cottage at all. Nor must the child be left alone even for a minute. There are many evil forces around us that we cannot see, which makes them so much more dangerous."

"Yes, I know. That's what frightens me," Augusta replied.

Stina patted her hand comfortingly.

"Now Augusta is learning what it is to be a mother. They say that a woman's work is never done, nor does a mother's worry ever end."

A light knocking on the outside door brought everyone to life the next morning. Stina went out into the entranceway.

"Who is it?" she asked through the closed door.

"Olov."

"Who else is with Olov?"

"Only Smed-Johan's Moa." (Blacksmith Johan's Moa)

Stina turned the large iron key and opened the door.

"Come in quickly," she told them, hustling them into the entrance-way and closing the door on their heels.

"Has it come yet?" Olov whispered hesitantly.

"Oh, yes. Olov can be proud of his Augusta. She did well."

"Is it a s..." he began.

"Sh-h-h-h," Stina said, shaking her head. "Olov has a healthy, well-formed daughter. Go in and have a look at her, but don't forget to 'take the fire' first, to burn up any evil creatures that might have followed Moa and Olov in."

They went directly to the hearth and held their hands over the flames before even taking off their outdoor clothes. The women gathered around Moa and the basket of food she had with her to see if she had made beer soup. It was a simple soup of barley flour, fresh milk and beer, sweetened with syrup, but no one could make it like Moa. Nor did she disappoint them. Also in her basket was some fresh crisp bread, as well as several kinds of small cookies for their coffee.

While the women were busy setting out the food, Olov took the stool from under the water pail and set it beside the bed. Glancing behind him to make sure none of the women were watching, he laid his hand over Augusta's.

"How has Augusta had it during this night?" he inquired a little formally, not knowing how one asked about such things.

"As most women have it, I guess. I'm sorry that I haven't managed to give Olov a son, but perhaps he will accept a strong healthy girl this time?" she said, her voice raising to a question at the end.

"There will be many children. It doesn't matter which sort comes first. The important thing is that it is strong and healthy," he told her.

She felt his hand tighten ever so slightly over hers and she knew that he meant what he said. She took a deep breath.

"Will Olov look at the child?" she asked cautiously.

He nodded, glancing at the cradle, only to find it was empty. He turned back to her with a look on his face that made her smile.

"Come," she said, turning back the quilt and getting out of bed on shaking legs. She led him across the room to the bureau and indicated the spinning basket on top of it.

"No troll would think to look there for a heathen child," she said in a whisper, in case one should be close enough to hear. She was terrified that a troll might sneak in and snatch the child, leaving a troll child in its place. She had seen such a child once. It had a very big head and cried all the time. Then one day it died. She was afraid the same thing might happen to her as a punishment. But she kept her fear to herself.

Olov lifted the basket down gently and looked at the sleeping face, so small and so beautiful. He thought of the nights when his lust had exploded inside Augusta and he could still remember the feel of her growing stomach when he had dared to touch it under the quilt. But he was unable to connect that to the human being lying in the basket in front of him. He knew how it happened, but the mystery of it was beyond his comprehension.

"What does Olov think?" Augusta asked timidly.

He had no words for his joy. He looked at his wife. Nineteen years old, she was, and he an old man of almost thirty. And between them they had produced this being. Augusta looked up, wondering at his silence, and their eyes met. There was no need for words. The answer was written clearly on his face. She grasped his arm for support, and he helped her back to bed.

That night Augusta was still awake when Olov crept into the cupboard bed and pulled the curtain across the front. She continued to toss and turn, unable to find any peace.

"Olov," she said finally, "we must get the child to the priest and have her baptized as soon as possible."

"As soon as possible?" he questioned.

"Yes. I cannot rest until she is protected by the holy sacrament."

"But we must choose a name first."

Some time ago they had discussed names for a son, but concluded that perhaps it was a bad omen to decide on a name for a person not yet born, so they had never gone on to consider girls' names.

"We mustn't name her after someone who is still living," Augusta said, "for that is to speed that person's death. If I should name her after the person who had the most honorable qualities I can think of, I would name her after my mother, who died so young. It would be an honor to let her granddaughter bear her name and thus keep her memory alive."

"Augusta is right," Olov remarked. "I would be proud to have a daughter like Augusta's mother."

"But what about Olov's grandmother?" Augusta added. "She was so kind and such a strong, hard-working, God-fearing woman."

"Then why not a double name," Olov suggested.

They each tried the names silently in their two possible combinations, for the name must not be spoken aloud until it is given to the child by the priest at baptism. They both agreed that they only fit together one way.

Although they had not discussed godparents, they were quickly in agreement. Olov was in favor of having his brother Gustaf as godfather, for he was the most successful male in either of their families. Not only had he qualities of thrift that would be positive for the child to inherit, but should anything happen to Olov, he was the person who had the best possibility of helping to support a godchild. However, his wife Greta was with child, and for her to be godmother was to risk losing their unborn child or having a difficult birth. Augusta was secretly glad, since she had someone else in mind; someone who, beyond all others, had qualities she would wish her child—especially a girl-child—to develop. That person was Simon's-Stina. When she mentioned Stina's name, Olov agreed immediately and wholeheartedly.

"Yes, by all means, do ask her," he said. "She would be a true godmother."

Once it was decided, Olov set out for Gustav's farm, taking with him the white walking stick that by tradition served as a warning. To be asked to be a godparent was an honor and to refuse that honor was to bring shame upon oneself, as well as to harm the child by causing it to become negative or even sick. Consequently, if a person did not want to be a godparent, they had a chance to hide when a new father was seen approaching with a white stick, and thus avoid being asked and refusing.

But there was no risk of Gustaf refusing. He had seen Olov coming across the field and was sitting at the kitchen table with two small glasses and a square cut-glass decanter of *brännvin* in front of him when his younger brother came in.

"Congratulations!" he said. "Word has it that Olov and his Augusta have gotten a girl-child. All is well, I hope." He nodded in the direction of the bench, and Olov sat down.

"Thank you. Yes, all went well. Simon's-Stina was there."

Gustaf filled both glasses, replaced the stopper in the decanter, and raised his glass.

"*Skål!*"

Olov raised his in response, whereupon each emptied his glass in a single gulp.

"Has the child a name yet?" Gustaf asked.

"She shall have a double name, after our grandmother and Augusta's mother."

Gustaf rolled the names silently through his mouth.

"Yes. Good," he concluded. "May she grow up to be like both of them."

They said nothing for a few moments, while Olov tapped the floor lightly with the tip of the walking stick, wondering if it was time to get to the point of his visit. He cleared his throat.

"Could Gustaf take it upon himself to be godfather to the lass?" he asked.

"It would be an honor," he replied. "But Olov is not thinking about asking my Greta, is he?"

"No. That will have to be another time. I am thinking to ask Simon's-Stina."

Suddenly he was unsure. Could Gustaf and Stina agree, if need be? He hadn't considered that possibility until just now.

"Can Gustaf and Stina..." he began

"Yes, I should think so. Stina is a sensible woman."

And with that settled, Gustaf drew the stopper from the decanter again and refilled their glasses with crystal clear *brännvin*. This time it was Olov who raised his glass first.

"*Skål* and thank you," he said.

After exchanging family news and discussing the weather, Olov stood up to leave.

"Sit down, Little Brother," Gustaf said. "It's cold out, and you need one for the road."

By the time Olov set out for home, his spirit, as well has his body, was warm. Gustaf, who had always put himself above Olov and held their adult relationship on a formal level, had called him Little Brother for the first time since he was a small child and had treated him as an equal.

Olov never had a chance to pay Simon's-Stina a visit with his white walking stick. Stina herself brought up the subject the next day, never suspecting she was going to be asked.

"Has Augusta decided who she wishes to be godmother for her child and carry it to church to be baptized?" she asked while rewinding the swaddling bands after having changed the diaper.

"Yes, I have—if Stina is willing to take on that responsibility," Augusta answered spontaneously, never giving her the chance to refuse.

Stina smiled a toothless smile. "It would gladden me to carry the child to the church," she replied. "And, if I live to be a hundred, maybe I can deliver her first born child also."

They both laughed. There was something about that tiny woman that Augusta trusted implicitly and to know that she would care for the child, if need be, was a comfort. And even if that situation never arose, there was still so much Stina could teach her. Godparents were not just people who symbolically took responsibility for a child at the baptismal ceremony. They took their responsibility seriously and kept in close contact with their godchildren as long as they were children—and in some cases, even beyond that time.

On the day of the baptism, Simon's-Stina arrived with the sunrise, bearing a bundle wrapped in brown paper. Inside was her old black church dress, which she had worn on every special occasion as long as she or anyone else could remember. Augusta saw that she had carefully patched and mended all the worn and torn places.

"Why has Stina taken so much trouble with her old dress?" Augusta asked her. "I thought she was given a new dress by Fru Ekefors."

"Yes, that is true," Stina replied, "but don't you know that a god-mother should never wear anything new when she carries her godchild to the church? To do so will make the child grow up to be proud and conceited."

"But Stina could have borrowed a dress from someone instead."

"Does Augusta want her daughter to grow up to be a borrower?"

"Well, no," she admitted. "But Stina has gone to such an effort to make this dress look nice."

"And so shall your daughter grow up being able to make do with little, rather than needing new clothes to make herself look fine or borrowing to make herself look like someone she is not."

Augusta felt stupid and small, even though Stina had spoken matter-of-factly. What kind of a mother was she going to be when there was still so much she herself had to learn? Such knowledge was passed on from mother to daughter, yet she couldn't blame her mother. She had had enough to do just to keep clothes on the backs of her many children and a bit of food on the table. She hadn't had much time to teach them about the smaller details in life. Augusta wondered if perhaps she had chosen Stina as much for herself as for her child.

Augusta laid the newly bathed baby on the table for Stina to swaddle.

From now until they returned from church, the child was in her hands. This would be the first time it left the relative safety of the cottage, and there was no way of telling what unexpected dangers it would meet along the way. Therefore, it was necessary to protect it in every manner possible. Before starting to rewind the swaddling cloths, Stina tore a page from a psalm book, wrapped it around Augusta's sheep sheers, and laid them on the child's chest. Then as she wound the cloths around the baby's body, she slipped other things in with them: a silver coin she had saved that would both protect and ensure good economy in later life, a bit of the dried umbilical cord to protect against sickness, and a piece of bread to prevent starvation later in life. For the first time, the child's arms were left free of the swaddling bands, which seemed to please her, for she waved them in the air like a small bird trying its wings. Finally, the baptismal gown, which had been worn by Augusta and all her siblings, as well as all of their children, was pulled over the child's head, her arms pushed through the sleeves, and the long skirt pulled down over the rest of her body. Stina stood back, nodded approvingly. Picking her up, she showed her around the room.

"This is the kitchen, my child," she explained. "It is filled with things thou shall learn to use. Here is the hearth, where thy food is cooked and which gives thee light and warmth." Suddenly she lifted the child over the glowing coals of the fire and held her up in the huge chimney for a few seconds. "It may be dark up there, but thou shan't be afraid of the dark," she told her, then swung her down and stuck her head into the oven which was built into the chimney. "And here is where thou shall bake thy bread." From there she continued across the room. "Here is the spinning wheel, on which thou shall spin thy yarn. And the loom, where thou shall weave thy cloth. And the butter churn and molds for forming cheese. May thou grow up to be a clever housewife like thy mother."

"Now we must hurry," she said, wrapping a shawl around the small bundle. At the door she stopped and turned toward Olov and Augusta. "Will thee have a Christian child back?"

"Yes," they answered together, according to the ritual.

"What shall the child be named?" she asked.

"Elsa," whispered Olov.

"Carolina," whispered Augusta.

With that, Stina opened the door and stepped out into the frosty morning. Pulling the shawl up over the child's face, she walked quickly down the path.

Olov's brother Gustaf was waiting for them in front of the church. As soon as he caught sight of Stina, he hurried to meet her, anxious to see his niece for the first time. He smiled approvingly when she removed the shawl from the child's face and together they walked up the steps to the church. Before entering, Stina struck the door several times with the child's feet to make sure she would grow up to be strong and healthy. Finally the priest, who was waiting for them in the weapon house (as the foyer was called) blew twice on the baby's face.

"May the devil depart from this child, who is created in God's image, and leave room for the holy spirit!" he said, while making the sign of the cross over her head and chest. Then, laying his hand on her head, he said a prayer. After having driven out the devil, the child was worthy of entering the church, whereafter the godparents followed the priest in to the baptismal font and professed the Christian faith in her name.

"And what be the child's name?" the priest asked.

Stina stepped forward and whispered to him.

"I baptize thee, Elsa-Carolina, in the name of the Father, the Son, and the Holy Ghost," he said in a voice that echoed through the church. Stina breathed a sigh of relief.

After the service, Stina and Gustaf walked back through the forest to Grankullen, followed by friends and relatives who would partake in the baptismal feast. Olov and Augusta were waiting at the door when they arrived. Before the child was taken into the house, a piece of bread was put in her hand, to ensure once again that she would never go hungry. Stina then handed the child to Olov with the words that had been used for centuries.

"Thou gave me a heathen, and I have brought thee back a Christian. Raise her in godliness and good morals."

Olov took the child and turned to Augusta. "Will thee take this child and raise her for me?"

"There is no one else here who is better at that than I," she answered, taking her daughter.

Thereafter she handed the child to her own father, who in turn handed her to the next male relative, and she was thus passed among all the men-folk in the room so that she would one day have good luck in love and a rich marriage. Finally, when it was time to eat, she was placed in the cradle, still dressed in the baptismal gown. Before being left to sleep, she was symbolically beaten on top of the covers with a birch branch to ensure that she would be obedient and good-natured.

And now began the feast in honor of the newly baptized child. The cottage was full to overflowing with guests. All the women had something with them. There were many different kinds of porridge and rice puddings decorated with cinnamon and sugar, bread, butter, cheese, meat, potatoes, coffee, cakes, and *brännvin*. The rest of the day was spent eating, talking, and laughing, the men sitting together with their *brännvin* and the women gossiping over coffee.

Toward evening, Olov took out his violin and the familiar, slightly melancholy folk tunes pulled people to their feet. Soon the room was a whirl of color from the parish costumes. Weddings, baptisms, and funerals were the main social events in people's lives, and they made the most of every opportunity that presented itself. But not the guest of honor, little Elsa-Carolina. She showed no interest in the festivities and only woke twice for a little refreshment.

Elsa-Carolina was a contented baby. And if she cried, Augusta picked her up and held her until she stopped, even though she knew a baby should not be held, not even when nursing. Such attention would only spoil it. She could clearly remember her mother bent over the cradle in which her younger brother Gösta lay, her huge breast dangling above his face as he nursed, while she read from the Bible which lay open on a chair on the other side of the cradle. She was a God-fearing woman and, like many women, was careful to unquestioningly do things according to the dictates of tradition.

Yet another incident stood out clearly in her mind. As a child, she had often watched Gösta's tiny hands reaching wildly into the air when he cried, and she was convinced that he wanted to be picked up. Her mother assured her that his hands were simply being pulled up by elves who were sucking on his fingers, whereupon she would press his arms down and squeeze his hands into tight fists. While Augusta knew that elves did strange things, she couldn't believe they were sucking on Gösta's fingers. Finally her pity had gotten the better of her one day while her mother was out milking. As soon as Gösta started to cry, she had lifted him from the cradle and held him in her lap. As a reward, he had stopped crying and given her a huge toothless grin—and as punishment her mother had told her that if she took him out of his cradle again, Old Man Wind would come and carry her away forever.

"You will make him weak and lazy by picking him up when he cries," she said by way of explanation.

Augusta had not repeated the misdeed, but she had vowed that she would not treat her own children in the same way. But now when she had a child of her own, she was not so confident. As a young girl, she had always considered that any child she gave birth to would be hers. But she was quickly realizing that she was only one of many to whom Elsa-Carolina belonged. She may have given birth to her, but it was Olov's name—Olovsdotter—that she bore and it was he who was congratulated at her birth. Also, both of their families were quick to claim her as one of their own. Suddenly she felt that this little being wasn't hers at all; she belonged to all of them and it was simply her job to take care of her for them.

One day when Stina was visiting, Elsa-Carolina began to cry. Augusta looked at Stina hesitantly, reluctant to pick the child up in her presence. Stina smiled at her confusion.

"Do what Augusta feels is right," she told Augusta, "but use discretion so as not to attract others' attention. She knows how people can be when they think someone has dangerous ideas. I don't think Augusta wants to be called in by the priest and the parish elders and lectured about how she should raise her children."

More and more, Augusta realized she had a true friend in Stina.

The week before her churching ceremony, Augusta was awakened one night by Olov's embrace. She freed herself and sat straight up in bed.

"What is Olov doing?" she demanded.

"I want my wife," he answered.

"Doesn't he know it's a sin to lie with an unclean woman? Think if I should have a child afterwards. Everyone would know what we had done. And Olov would have to pay a rump-tax to the church for having lain with his wife."

"The rump-tax won't put me in the poorhouse. Besides, no one will know unless she is unlucky and gets pregnant."

"But the child of an unclean woman can be a werewolf."

"I don't believe that."

"But I've heard of someone it happened to," she protested.

And so it was that Augusta refused to give in to her husband and thus they had their first disagreement.

In the weeks that followed the baptism, Augusta, who was still an unclean heathen, had to stay indoors unless it was absolutely necessary to go out.

Nor would she be welcome in other people's homes anyway, for it was believed that an unclean woman brought rats in with her. But the days passed slowly and she quickly tired of being confined to the cottage. At the same time, Stina tried to impress her with the importance of not threatening people by going out.

"People will spit on Augusta if she shows herself before she has rejoined the congregation. Not long ago a woman in another parish was stoned by her neighbors for going out to look for a cow that had gone astray," she told her. "Augusta is a married woman and mother now, and she must remember that what she does affects not only herself, but also those related to her. Why doesn't she occupy herself with baking the bread to be given to the women who follow her to church for her churching ceremony?"

Stina was right. It was time to prepare for that Sunday. If she waited much longer, the bread would be too fresh and would fall apart when people dunked it in their coffee.

On the Saturday morning before her churching, Augusta cut in half each of the round flat church breads she had baked, wrapped them in a cloth, and packed them carefully into a basket. Since she herself must not go out, it was up to Helga to deliver a half to each of the neighbor women who were going to accompany her to church for the ceremony the following day.

At last Sunday morning came, bringing with it the end of her isolation. The women began arriving to help her get ready. The ceremony required a black dress. For most women this meant their wedding dress which, for practical reasons, was black. But Augusta's didn't fit as well as it had the first time she had worn it. The women fussed over her, talking and laughing as they squeezed her into it. One of them lent her a pair of black gloves and someone else wrapped a white handkerchief around her psalm book and handed it to her.

"Augusta must walk with this pressed against her breast so that her milk will not dry up," she was instructed.

They stepped back and regarded her.

"Have we forgotten anything?" one of them asked.

"Oh, yes! I must have my black silk shawl," Augusta cried. Quickly she went to her chest and took out a small package wrapped in brown paper. With trembling fingers she opened it and unfolded the shawl. She hadn't worn it since before she had gotten married. One of the women laid it over her shoulders and Augusta pulled it close around her neck, remembering the first time she had worn it.

"I'm ready now," she concluded.

Lastly, a smoldering linen rag was laid on the doorstep, over which she must step when leaving the house, letting the smoke purify her. The walk to church was filled with danger, since it was the last chance a troll or other evil power had to get at this heathen woman. Yet she felt quite safe surrounded by so many women.

When they reached the church, she was left on her own in the weapon house to be purified by the priest before being allowed to enter the building itself. The rest of the congregation walked past without so much as a word of greeting to her in her unclean state. Once everyone was seated, an assistant set a low kneeling stool in the doorway leading to the interior of the church. Then the whole congregation turned and watched the priest walk down the aisle to where Augusta knelt in the doorway. Placing his hand on her head, he said a long prayer over her, then gave her his hand and led her into the congregation, where she took her place on the women's side of the church together with the women who had accompanied her. Simon's-Stina, who sat directly behind her, tapped her lightly on the shoulder.

"Don't forget about this," she said, holding out a little wooden box that Augusta had filled with small candies before leaving home. She took it and removed the lid before passing it to Halta-Maja, who sat beside her. Silently, the box circled the prescribed three times among her fol-lowers, with each person taking one candy each time it went past. When it came back to her after the third round, it was empty. She replaced the lid and turned it over in her hand. Each half was made of a long thin strip of wood bent into an oval shape, with the overlapping ends sewn together with pieces of root, while the top and bottom pieces of wood were held in place with tiny pegs. She ran her fingers over its satiny smooth surface. Olov had made it especially for this occasion.

"Augusta will be needing this for her churching candies," he had said almost gruffly when he handed it to her. It was his way of saying what he could not put into words. For Augusta, such gestures were painful, making her feel like an unworthy recipient of his caring. Now, when she finally was allowed to return to church and take communion, she felt even more unclean than before. Realizing this, she made up her mind to unburden her heart to Simon's-Stina.

While Augusta waited for an opportunity to unburden herself to Stina, she thought back to the year before her marriage to Olov. It had been a carefree time, full of excitement, with high hopes for the future. It was the happiest time in her short life.

The sun was already high in the June sky when Augusta was awakened by the voices of the other girls. She turned over heavily. At first she couldn't figure out where she was, for she obviously was not in her usual bed in the manor house kitchen. Then she remembered. The entire household of Ekefors Manor had moved out to their summer quarters in the loft rooms above several small timbered storage buildings, as Scandinavian country-dwellers had done since the Middle Ages.

Throughout the long winter, the darkness and chill drew people together, as though they derived warmth from one another. The large manor house kitchen became the center point in all their lives. They ate together and at night everyone—the housemaids, the older farmhands, and any visitors or travelers who happened to be passing by, as well as the baron and his wife and children—slept there in various *utdragssoffa* beds in order to take advantage of what little heat the banked-up fire gave. Privacy was non-existent, nor was it something one sought. People were used to living close to one another and never imagined any other way of life. Children were conceived and born and people died in the midst of all else that went on in the kitchen. It was all a part of life.

But with the light and warmth of summer, people became expansive and craved breathing space. The sleeping lofts—one for the housemaids and another for the farmhands—offered just that. And for those few months, the baron and his wife were left to sleep by themselves in a room in another outbuilding, while their children shared beds with the hired help.

The housemaids' loft was reached by an outside stairway leading up to a roofed balcony that ran the length of the building. The room itself was empty, except for the skeletons of five primitive bunk beds fastened to the walls, with box bottoms to hold the bed straw in place. Rather than real windows, square holes had been fashioned in the timber walls, to be left wide open all summer and covered by shutters the rest of the year. The age of the building could be reckoned by the width of the pine floor boards, cut in the days when there were still huge trees, and worn smooth by more than a century of summer feet. During the months that it was inhabited, the room was cluttered with the wooden chests where the girls kept their clothes and other belongings. The rest of the year it was left to the mice and rats, who nested in the remains of the straw.

"What time is it?" Augusta mumbled sleepily.

One of the older housemaids looked over at the door, where the sun struck a series of hack marks in the frame. One could tell the time according to which mark the light had reached. She squinted as she counted.

"A little before 3:00," she reported.

Augusta sat up, rubbing her eyes free from sleep. Through the open window she could see that it was a perfect day for making hay. Lisa, her bed-mate, was already up and dressed. Hurriedly she pulled on her dark ankle-length skirt and white long-sleeved blouse with embroidered collar and cuffs, over which she laced up her red felted bodice. This was the extent of her clothing, for underwear was unheard of in those days, and shoes were only worn during the winter months, when the summer calluses on one's feet failed to shield against the cold.

By 3 a.m. everyone was gathered in the field, the men with their newly sharpened scythes and the women carrying their wooden rakes. Although the sun was already high in the sky, the lush grass was still wet with dew, making it easier to cut. As always, each cutter was to be followed by a raker. Many relationships had their beginnings in the hay fields, when the choosing of work partners took place. There was nothing official about this choosing. Sometimes it was the man who openly chose his raker; other times it was the woman who more subtly made it known to a certain man that she wished to rake the grass as he cut it. And, of course, there were also the leftovers, those who neither chose nor were chosen, but were simply thrown together to do a job.

A number of the cutter/raker twosomes had already been formed by the time Baron Ekefors' son, Erling, joined them. After a quick glance at the remaining girls, Erling nodded towards Augusta and motioned her to follow him. Although she knew it was simply because she was the youngest and most attractive of the leftovers, she was nonetheless thrilled by the honor of raking for the young master of Ekefors Manor. Not only was he good looking with his slightly too-long straw-blond hair, deep blue eyes, and finely chiseled features, but he had no airs, in spite of being the sole heir to a well-to-do estate. He worked as hard as any of the men and was a better cutter than most of them. Although not a word passed between them, at the end of the day she could see that he was pleased by her ability to keep up with his pace and still rake thoroughly. To her surprise, he chose her again the next day, long before she had become a part of the leftover group. And like many of the other first- day pairs, they continued to work together throughout the week. By the time the field was lined with rows of small drying haystacks, Augusta was so used to working with Erling that she felt quite comfortable in his presence. Now and then he would turn around and let his eyes silently search hers until she felt her face and neck redden. But he never spoke. For her, it was enough just watching the muscles in his back work beneath his sweat-soaked shirt as he swung his scythe in rhythmic half circles ahead of her.

A couple of weeks passed while the hay dried in the June heat, during which other work was done. Augusta's days were filled from early morning until late evening. Sometimes she woke up so happy that she wanted to shout; other times she felt like a great empty flour sack. Both of these feelings were tied to Erling Ekefors and the memory of his sweaty back and deep blue eyes.

At the same time, she warned herself not to become enchanted by him. It was common knowledge that, even though landowners' sons often socialized freely with the hired help, they only played with servant girls, flattering them with whatever attention was necessary in order to have their way with them. Then, when a girl became pregnant, the boy no longer recognized her when they chanced to meet. And if she had the nerve to name him as the father of her child, he would, of course, deny it, while threatening to sue her for slandering his family's good name. If such a case actually did end in the local court, there was no question as to who would be believed and who was seen to be a liar. No judge would dare rule against a rich family in the parish—especially not in favor of a mere servant girl. Augusta did all she could to put Erling Ekefors out of her mind.

When the hay was dry, Augusta was among those sent out to the fields to help load it onto wagons to be hauled to the barn. As usual, the men forked it up onto the wagon for the girls to tramp down. One of these men was Erling. Another was Olov.

Augusta and several other girls climbed onto the empty wagon and, while they waited for the men to build up the first thick layer of hay on the bottom, she glanced at Erling. He was watching her. She felt the same attraction that she had experienced when they had worked together. It was so strong that she had to force herself to turn away.

Quickly, she began stomping on the little hay that had already been loaded, ignoring the loaders. Yet all the while she could feel Erling's eyes watching her.

As soon as the first wagon was heaped to overflowing, both Erling and Olov positioned themselves behind it in order to help the trampers back down to earth again—an act that involved sliding down the back side of the enormous load of hay and being caught before hitting the ground. Olov caught the first girl and set her down safely. The next one slid into Erling's arms, but Augusta noticed that he quickly released her onto the ground. Only she and Lisa were left.

"Be nice, and let me go next," Lisa giggled into her ear. Augusta willingly moved aside. Lisa slid into Olov's arms, and they disappeared around the side of the wagon, headed for where the others sat in the shade of a nearby tree. With no one there to see him, Erling looked up at her and smiled, holding out his arms invitingly. She jumped. He caught her, with one hand on either side of her waist, and held on to her, lingering a few seconds. Then as he set her on the ground, he grasped both her hands gently and let them slide through his own.

"Thanks," she said, looking up at him. He smiled and bowed slightly.

The rest of the day, Augusta tried her best to dampen her attraction for Erling. She let others determine whose arms she slid into from the top of the hay load. Sometimes Erling caught her, but more often than not, it was Olov or one of the other men. Nor did she sit near him in the grass when they had a coffee break. However, she quickly realized that he usually placed himself in such a position that he could watch her without it being obvious. Yet he never paid the least bit of attention to her in front of the others.

By Midsummer's Eve, the last of the hay had been collected and stowed away inside the barn. Now everyone's attention turned to the celebration of the summer solstice. Midsummer completed the long line of holidays that filled the spring, the last until Christmas. And, next to Christmas, it was the most popular holiday of the year.

The festivities began in the afternoon when a long table was set up in the yard, covered with Madame Ekefors' best hand-woven linen tablecloth and her heirloom china and silverware. Several large bouquets of wildflowers were placed along its center and the long benches on both sides made it possible to squeeze in any number of people. Everyone connected to the manor was invited, as well as all the local people in the area. And, as with all special occasions, there was no holding back when it came to food. Even during bad years, when both the rich and the poor suffered from hunger, people offered the best of what they had on holidays, as well as for weddings, baptisms, and funerals. But 1853 was no famine year, and the long table at Ekefors Manor was weighed down with food—various kinds of herring, meatballs, sausages, eggs, both hard and soft breads, butter, cheese, tiny new potatoes, cakes, cookies, coffee, home-brewed beer, and *brännvin*.

The women satisfied themselves with coffee, but the men and many of the boys, as well as a number of servant girls, preferred *brännvin*, which was distilled in almost every home, rich or poor, and without which no feast or party was complete.

The weather was perfect, and everyone was in the best of spirits. A Midsummer pole, tightly wound with small leafy branches and flowers, had been raised in the middle of the lawn like a giant cross. From each end of the cross-piece hung a large wreath consisting entirely of wild-flowers bound together. The children and young unmarried housemaids also wore crowns of intertwined flowers on their heads. Everyone talked and ate and laughed until their sides were ready to split.

Finally, after much begging and *brännvin*, old Lars-i-Kröken (Lars-in-the-Curve of the road) took out his fiddle, wiped it off carefully, and fitted it under his chin. People joined hands and whirled around the pole to the well-known folk dance tunes that belonged to Midsummer. Everyone danced, from the youngest toddler to old Baroness Ekefors. Now and then Lars sagged down into a chair, only to be revived by more drink. Eventually he was so drunk that the bow began to screech across the strings. Rather than protest when he was led away, he willingly handed his fiddle to his grandson, Nål-Nisse (Needle-Nisse), the village tailor, who picked up where he had left off. The majority of old dances were group or line dances, where one changed partners often. Thus, Augusta found herself passing through Erling's arms many times that evening. And each time he took her hand, he held it firmly, as if it belonged to him and he didn't want to let it go; or was Augusta simply imagining it? No, she was sure it was so. None of the other men took her hand in that way.

The twilight of midnight passed, and the sky began to brighten again. Soon the sun would be up. Nål-Nisse was tiring, but still the younger people danced. Finally, he announced that he had had enough.

"Just one more song!" everyone begged.

"All right," he answered finally. "This is the last one. Take a partner."

The men chose quickly, and Augusta found herself still on the sidelines when Nål-Nisse drew the bow across the first string. Just as she turned to leave, someone took her hand from behind and pulled her around. It was Erling. He held her hand even more tightly than before. When the dance was over, he hastily plucked a daisy from her now wilted crown of flowers and stuck it through the top button hole of his blouse.

"Thank you for tonight," he said and gave her hand a little squeeze. And then he was gone, hurrying to catch up with several of the other farmhands.

"Augusta! Are you coming?" Lisa called from the edge of the yard. "We have to pick our flowers."

Augusta smiled to herself. Yes, of course. As always on Midsummer's Eve, every girl must pick nine different kinds of wildflowers and put them under her pillow so she would dream about the man she was going to marry. She and Lisa walked out into the meadow across from the big house with several other girls and began picking silently: daisy, forget-me-not, bluebell, lily of the valley, buttercup, cowslip, snapdragon, Queen Anne's lace, almond blossom. Up in the loft, each of them placed a tiny bouquet under her pillow and quickly fell into an exhausted sleep.

When Augusta awoke the next morning, she could feel the presence of a man from her dream hovering close to her. But when she closed her eyes to come nearer him, she realized to her disappointment that it was Olov. Asch! She should have known better than to believe in such silly old superstitions. Tossing the flattened flowers out the window of the loft, she went out to do the milking.

But while the man in her dream was Olov, the man in her life continued to be Erling. And she also dreamed about him—hours of whimsical day dreams—but always against a background of gray hopelessness. They met often in the company of others, for life was a community enterprise. Erling was careful not to betray his interest in Augusta. Instead, he was quick to return the flirting gestures the other girls sent his way, although Augusta noticed that he himself never initiated them. At the same time, he sent her messages so subtle that they could only be seen by one who was on the lookout for them. Augusta was looking, and she caught them. And during the long summer days when people spent so much of their time outdoors, Erling took advantage of every chance he could to cross paths with her when she was alone. It made her both glad and afraid.

"What is it Master Ekefors wants with me?" she finally asked him one day when he found her in the hayloft. It was the first time they had been alone in such a secluded place, and she realized that the thing all the older girls whispered about was about to happen to her.

"Can't Augusta call me by my name—Erling," he said, taking her hand. "I don't want anything particular. I only want to see Augusta. I'm not going to seduce her."

She gave him a puzzled look.

"Isn't that what Master Erling followed me here for?"

"No," he laughed, collapsing in the hay and pulling her down beside him. "I like Augusta too much to do that. But I would like to kiss her, if I may."

Augusta looked down, blushing. She had never been kissed before.

"If he wishes," she replied shyly.

She was still convinced that he wanted much more than that. But to her surprise, he kissed her and then backed away again.

"Does Augusta mind that we meet in secret?" he asked.

"What does Master Erling mean?"

"I mean that I would court Augusta openly if I could, but my father would put a quick end to it if I did. However, next May I come of age and then I am free to do as I wish."

Augusta swallowed. "And what is it that he wishes to do?"

"I wish to take a wife and settle down to raise a family."

"And play with me in the meantime."

"Don't be silly!" he declared. "If I just wanted to play with Augusta, I would have rolled her in the hay long ago. But I have more serious wishes concerning her. But I have to wait until I come of age."

All that autumn they continued to meet secretly, yet Augusta remained suspicious of Erling's motives. But when he continued to show her the highest respect, never pressing himself on her, her mistrust gradually withered and died. At Christmas time, they became secretly engaged. As was customary, he gave her a simple gold ring.

"When Augusta returns from visiting her family on Christmas Day, she can wear this on her right hand," he told her. "She can tell those who ask that it belonged to her mother. No one will ask more."

And Erling proved to be right. When Lisa asked where she got the ring, Augusta said that her father had given it to her because he knew her mother had wanted her oldest daughter to have it. Apparently Lisa passed on the information. No one else mentioned it.

As soon as the excitement of Christmas was past, the New Year rung in, and the Thirteenth Day was celebrated, people began to look forward to the next exciting event of the year: the spring market. Unlike the winter holidays, whose preparations brought everyone to the edge of exhaustion, the market was a time of freedom.

For housemaids and farmhands, life in the countryside was filled with repetitious daily tasks and devoid of any sort of social life beyond the confines of the manor. One saw the same faces day after day. Only on rare occasions did a new one appear. Nor was there any nearby town, much less a city, to visit. In fact, there wasn't even a general store where one could be sent on an errand. Only certain larger towns were allowed by law to have shops, and no sort of commerce was permitted to take place in the small villages. A village was simply a cluster of farms and estates, all of which were self-sufficient. Those things which they could not produce were purchased at the spring or autumn outdoor markets.

Aside from having one free Sunday a month, those who worked for the big farmers and landowners were given time off to go to the two yearly markets. This was their only chance to meet freely with old friends and others of their own station; a time when unattached young people found new faces to consider. The market town lay the better part of a two-day journey from Ekefors Manor and its activities extended over several days. Every person had to take enough food with him to last the entire time they were away from the manor and also enough sheep skins to serve as bedding. A change of clothes wasn't really necessary; the heavy homespun cloth of peasant clothes could stand many days' wear before showing the dirt.

On the morning of their departure, everyone was up and ready to go long before dawn. The air was cold from the night frost and small drifts of snow still lay in sheltered places. But the sky was clear, sprinkled with millions of stars which the sun would drive away in an hour or two. A number of farm wagons stood waiting in front of the barn. One was loaded with beaver, fox, moose, and deer skins to be sold or traded for spring necessities. Another contained Cooper-Wilhelm's wooden barrels and casks of all shapes and sizes for the storage of everything from salted herring and meat to lingonberries. And along with them were Smed-Johan's nails and horse shoes. Still another wagon was loaded with copper pans and containers made by a coppersmith who lived in a shack on the edge of the manor grounds, as well as a number of baskets Blind-Ola had woven from the roots and saplings his wife Berta had gathered. Packed among these wares were various wooden cheese forms, milk troughs, mangle boards, bowls, and spoons of all sizes carved by idle hands during the long dark winter evenings. The last wagon was filled with hay for the horses and oxen, as well as each person's food basket and bedding.

Among the fifteen to twenty people going were all the housemaids and farmhands, who gladly left the running of the manor to the few people who were too old to care about the market. It was a time of unusual freedom, when rules and regulations, titles, and one's place seemed to be forgotten. The group from Ekefors Manor set out walking in close formation, but before long there were stragglers and a few couples disappeared completely. No one paid them any heed. They all met up again in the evening when everyone reached Nysäter, where they always spent the night on market journeys. The village consisted of several farms, each with its dwelling house and outbuildings placed along the rutted wagon road, making it a convenient overnight stop. Nor did the farm families mind, for not only did travelers bring news of faraway places, but more important, the few pennies they paid to sleep on the kitchen floor were a welcome income for those who rarely felt the weight of a coin in their pockets.

Although Erling was among the market-bound farmhands, he was careful to ignore Augusta. And that evening, he made sure that they did not sleep in the same farm kitchen. But before everyone turned in for the night, he managed to get her aside for a few moments.

"Try to lie close to the door and when the others are asleep, sneak out and meet me behind the barn," he whispered. He gave her hand a quick squeeze and disappeared.

While the fires on the various kitchen hearths burned down, the market-bound travelers curled up on the floor between their sheepskins and gradually let go of the day as sleep overtook them. All except for Augusta. She lay wide awake, filled with both desire and fear. She knew that this time Erling would want more than just kisses, and once again she was afraid that perhaps he was simply playing with her. Why would a landowner's son want a peasant girl like her as a wife? At the same time, she longed to believe in his intentions. Why would he have otherwise given her the ring? Her head spun with unanswerable questions. Nor did it matter right now. All she wanted was to be with him.

When the room was filled with the even breathing of sleep, she sat up cautiously. No one stirred. Slowly she got to her feet and opened the door. Still no one's breathing changed. She stepped outside, closing the door silently behind her. Erling was waiting behind the barn.

"At last!" he exclaimed. "I was afraid Augusta had fallen asleep."

He pulled her tight against him, kissing the top of her head, her forehead, and finally her mouth. She could feel him hard against her stomach. And for the first time in her life, she experienced the overwhelming power of desire.

"Come," he whispered and, taking her by the hand, he led her into the barn. Up in the loft he had already laid a sheepskin in the hay. He pulled her down onto it and lay beside her. To her surprise, he didn't jump on her like a rooster on a hen, as she had expected. Instead, he moved hesitantly, making sure she was willing. And when she gave herself to him, she understood that he was not playing with her. To be secretly engaged had defined their relationship, but now they had made an unbreakable commitment to each other. But still it must remain a secret.

As they neared the market town the next day, the road began to fill with groups of people headed in the same direction. Some rode in loaded wagons, while others struggled on foot under heavy burdens. A few prodded oxen or other livestock along the rutted road, secure in the fact that the market would be swarming with prospective buyers. The winter had been hard, and many people had been forced to slaughter their animals for lack of fodder. Even though it was a long way to drive such creatures, it was believed that one could get much higher prices for them at the market than by selling to one's neighbors. Yet many a time, a man's ox was bought at the market by his neighbor and driven back home along the same road it had come that morning.

The spirit of the crowd increased to a boisterous procession as it grew. Consequently, Augusta had no need to stifle her own private joy, for everyone was light-headed and gay. For his part, Erling made a point of keeping the young workers of Ekefors Manor gathered about him so as to have her innocently close by. And when they reached the journey's usual resting place, a circle of stones left by their Stone Age ancestors, they were careful to place themselves opposite each other within the group while they ate. As much as Augusta longed to declare her feelings before everyone by sitting beside Erling as his fiancée, she was more concerned with not risking what she had. When the autumn market came, they would be able to go together openly.

Late that afternoon, they at last reached the tollhouse at the entrance to the town. A boom over the road prevented them from going farther without first declaring and paying a tax on the saleable goods in their wagons. After much unloading and reloading, accompanied by grumbling directed towards the king and his way of filling his coffers, they were allowed to proceed through the town to the marketplace on the far side. Just beyond there lay the church village, two long rows of tiny wooden cabins, each with a door and a small shuttered window on the front side. Inside were built-in benches along three windowless walls and an open hearth in the center of the room, above which a hole in the roof could be uncovered to act as a chimney. The cabins were used by people who came from great distances to attend church services and markets. Ekefors Manor leased several of them and while they provided the hired help with a place to stay, people were forced to double up on the sleeping benches as usual. They certainly offered no opportunity for Augusta and Erling to be alone together.

The market began the following morning. Augusta and several of the other girls were up with the sun, eager to not miss a thing. But most of all, Augusta hoped to meet Lisa, whom she hadn't seen since October when she had left Ekefors Manor for a new job at Björkhöjden Manor. She made her way along the path between the two rows of cabins, wondering which held the Björkhöjden people. Suddenly she heard Lisa's laughter coming from an open door. She knocked on the door post.

"Lisa?" she called.

There was a scrambling within the darkness of the cabin and Lisa appeared in the doorway.

"Augusta!" she cried. "Oh, I'd so hoped to meet Augusta today!"

They embraced each other in a girlish hug, from which Augusta pulled back and glanced at her friend's stomach curiously. Nothing showed under Lisa's long full skirt, but she was sure she had felt a bulge there. She linked her arm through Lisa's and led her along the path.

"Is Lisa...?" she began.

Lisa nodded.

"But who? I thought she was sweet on Olov."

"I was—last summer. But then I met up with Ox-Olle when I moved to Björkhöjden. Augusta remembers him, doesn't she? We're going to have the banns read next Sunday, when he gets back from visiting his father. We're hoping he will let Olle have a bit of his inheritance ahead of time so we can get our own place."

"Just think!" Augusta giggled. "Lisa is going to be a mother!"

"But what about Augusta? Isn't there anyone in her life?"

All of a sudden she realized how much she had missed Lisa. They had shared so much more than just a box-bed when they had worked together at Ekefors Manor. This past winter there had been no one with whom she could share her secrets. For an instant she wanted to tell her about Erling, yet she dared not. Instead, she squeezed Lisa's arm against her side.

"Come on, let's celebrate the last market trip as maidens!" she cried.

The marketplace was lined by several rows of weather-grayed log stands separated by wide dirt paths. Each stand had shutters that folded down to form a wide counter on which wares lay for sale and above which the turf-clad roof extended to protect customers and goods from rain. From inside the stands, sellers leaned out across the counters, chatting with passersby.

Augusta and Lisa sauntered from one stand to the next, overwhelmed by all that was available. In one stand, an old woman and her daughter had small cheeses stacked on the counter beside crocks of well-salted butter. In the stall next to them, a red-faced man in a leather apron stood behind piles of nails, all with irregular heads and squared shafts, which he had made during the winter.

Across from him was a candy stand which they found irresistible. The woman behind the counter twisted a piece of paper around her fingers to form a cone, folded up the bottom, and filled it with a penny's worth of freshly made sweets. Nibbling them sparingly, they proceeded on their way.

They passed a stand with dried meat and fish hanging above the counter and wooden barrels of salted herring lined up behind it. In another stand, a shoemaker was resoling a pair of boots while a farmhand waited on a bench outside, his bare feet black with winter dirt. On the counter stood a selection of men's, women's, and children's high-buttoned shoes together with a couple of shoe lasts. Next door, a young man sold various grades of leather, as well as bridles and harnesses. They passed these stands with only mild interest. But when they came to a stand selling trinkets, they stood for a long time admiring the shawls, gloves, hair ribbons, handkerchiefs, small painted boxes, and even engagement and wedding rings. Augusta watched several young couples trying on rings, jealous of their freedom to do so openly. Finally, she pulled at Lisa impatiently and they continued on their way.

In an area beyond the stands, people were selling directly from their wagons or from the ground in front of them. They offered everything from wooden casks, rope, shovels, plows, and grindstones to looms, baskets, and copper pots and pans, most of them handmade. In a handcart sat a old woman winding string around bunches of clean-stripped birch twigs to make whisks. Coming closer, Augusta recognized

Blind-Beda, who lived with her grown son, Beda's-Boy, in a hut built into the side of a hill near Ekefors Manor. She had been blind since shortly after Boy's birth, the story being that the Lord had struck her blind for refusing to reveal the father's name. Consequently, the people in the parish had turned their backs on her. But Blind-Beda was a fighter. She had refused to give up on life, in spite of being an outcast. And now in her old age and crippled by rheumatism, she was reduced to making whisks, brushes, and brooms, which Boy, who had become an old man, peddled in order to earn a few copper coins toward their scanty needs.

Augusta took the old woman by the hand.

"How nice to see Aunt Beda!" she exclaimed.

Beda's wrinkled face broke into a smile.

"Is it Tor's daughter Augusta?" she asked confidently.

"It is. How did Beda manage to come all the way to the market?"

"I rode in this cart," she answered, patting its bottom.

"Has Boy gotten a horse?" Augusta asked, wondering if their fortune had turned at last.

Beda laughed. "Oh, no, Child. Boy is my horse. It only took us three days."

Augusta looked at the bent figure of Boy standing some distance away with a basket full of whisks and brushes for sale. She thought of the rutted road which went up and down countless hills between Beda's hut and the market town. And of Boy, whose entire life had been spent helping his mother, who had sinned by bringing him into the world. Why did God place such burdens on some people while others went free? It didn't seem fair. She took several of the coins she had intended to spend on herself and bought a whisk and a hearth brush from Beda. As they walked away, she handed the brush to Lisa.

"Use this to keep the hearth clean. And this," she continued, handing her the whisk, "to stir the porridge for Olle and the child. And may Lisa's life be brighter than Blind-Beda's."

Just then two ragged children approached them.

"Please, Miss, do you have a copper for us? Our mother is sick and there is nothing to eat at home."

They were skinny and dirty, with runny noses, and their clothes consisted mostly of half sewn-on patches. From the looks of their feet, they didn't own any shoes. Before Augusta could open her purse, a man ran toward the children waving a stick.

"I thought I told you brats to keep away from here!" he yelled.

The children began to run, but he was able to grab one of them by the hair, whereupon he beat him several times with his stick before shoving him out of his way.

"They're from town, and they have no right to be begging here," he said to excuse his behavior before strutting off.

"Rich swine!" Augusta mumbled to Lisa. "He's certainly never been hungry."

She looked around for the children, but they had disappeared.

As the afternoon progressed, the market became livelier. Most of the older men had concluded their more important business with a handshake and a shot or two of *brännvin* and, as usual, the younger men had gotten drunk as quickly as possible on the one day they had the freedom to do so. Now men who would otherwise never dare approach girls from outside their own parishes found the courage to strike up conversations with any lass who caught their fancy. And so it was that Titus, from the parish beyond Ekefors Manor, placed himself in Augusta's path.

"Well, if it isn't Ekefors-Augusta!" he declared, tipping his hat as he fell into step beside her. Both she and Lisa ignored him. "Shall we go and look at the dancing bear over there?"

The girls glanced at each other, wondering how to get rid of him. But they needn't have worried. When Olov and several others had heard someone say "Ekefors-Augusta," they had immediately recognized Titus's voice. It was an unwritten law that lads were not allowed to have anything to do with girls outside their own parishes. Everyone knew that, especially Titus, who always seemed to be looking for trouble. This breach of acceptable behavior angered Olov. Seeing that, the other farmhands gave him a shove toward Titus. Olov was known as the best fighter in the parish. Even before the first blows were exchanged, a crowd had begun to gather. Fights were an accepted, and even welcomed, part of market life. Those involved claimed to be fighting for any number of reasons, but in reality, these brawls were often just an excuse for impoverished farmhands to vent their pent-up frustrations, for they had no way to strike out at the real, intangible cause of their misery. For men of better means, fighting gave them a chance to publicly prove their manhood. Others fought for the sheer excitement of it. No market, no matter how small, escaped this form of entertainment, for entertainment it was. Fights were far more popular with the crowds than the sideshows, where one had to pay to look at freaks who did nothing but stand on a stage.

Augusta stood beside Lisa in the growing circle of onlookers, flattered to have been the cause of such a spectacle. By now both Olov and Titus were struggling on the ground, slugging and bleeding, their Sunday clothes torn and dirty. People from both parishes egged on their respective man, while outsiders cheered the fight in general. No one tried to stop it. Not even the women.

Beside Augusta, an old man was hopping up and down, tearing his hair. Tears rolled down the weathered lines in his face.

"What's the matter?" someone asked him. "Are you ill?"

"No," he sniffed. "It's just that I used to be able to fight like that, but now I'm too old and good for nothing," he wailed. Several older men nearby nodded in silent agreement.

When Titus at last gave in to defeat, Olov helped him to his feet and handed him his hat, which had been flattened in the fray.

"Stay away from our girls from now on, do you hear!" he told him. "Otherwise it'll be worse next time."

Titus lifted his right arm weakly and they shook hands. Part of the crowd surrounded Olov, cheering and pounding him on the back before leading him away to celebrate his victory. A small group of people helped the groaning Titus over to a mossy place under a tree and a couple of girls set about washing his wounds while his comrades poured *brännvin* into him to ease his pain and humiliation. When he was too drunk to stand up, they left him to sleep it off and went in search of more excitement. The next fight had already begun.

Everyone was in good spirits on the way back to Ekefors Manor the following day. Almost everything they had taken to market had been sold and now the wagons were loaded with necessary purchases for the coming year. In order to protect those people who had sold their own wares and pocketed the money, they walked together in a tight group. After every market there was always someone who was attacked by bandits and robbed on the way home. Olov had become the housemaids' hero and they jostled each other to have a chance to walk at his side. It made him feel embarrassed and shy. He was no hero. If he hadn't been there, someone else would have put Titus in his place. It happened all the time. Either one followed the longstanding customs or one paid the price. Nonetheless, never having been much of a lady's man, he warmed to the attention and was soon walking with his arms around the waists of those beside him.

"My rescuer," Augusta said jokingly when they stopped to rest by the stone ring.

"My pleasure," Olov replied with a bow.

That night Augusta and Erling again met in the hayloft.

"I hope Augusta is not turning sweet on Olov now, after today's heroic deed," Erling remarked half questioningly.

"Don't be silly! Of course not! Besides, it had nothing to do with me. I just happened to be handy, giving him an excuse to carry on the age-old feud between parishes."

Before they parted that night, Erling pulled a package out of his pocket and handed it to her.

"Everyone was buying engagement presents, as they always do at markets, so when no one was looking, I bought one too."

"What is it?" she asked curiously. "I can't see a thing in the dark."

"Well, it's best I tell Augusta. That way she can pretend she bought it herself and no one will know the difference—except for Lisa. But she's not here now."

"But what is it?"

"Do you remember the black silk shawls in the trinket stand?"

"Oh! I wanted one so badly, but I didn't have enough money." She opened one end of the package and ran her fingers over the soft silk. "Oh, thank you, Erling!"

Just before the spring planting, Augusta understood that she was with child. She hadn't given much thought to such a possibility during those nights in the hay with Erling, when the power of desiring and being desired had obliterated her common sense. And when her regular bleeding had failed to come with the full moon, she had told herself it was because she was no longer a virgin. But when she had unexpectedly vomited one morning, she saw reality lying at her feet. It was as if she had been whirling dizzily around a dance floor, princess of the ball for months, and that the musicians had stopped playing abruptly in the middle of a song. She, too, stopped abruptly and looked around, only to find herself completely alone. Her ball gown was nothing but a tattered and dirty homespun peasant dress, with a stream of vomit running down the skirt towards her bare feet.

She was frightened beyond words. All at once, Erling's past assurances of love seemed as thin as famine porridge, completely without substance. In the blindness of her bliss, she had walked into the very trap that every housemaid tried to avoid. It was bad enough to get into "circumstances" with a farmhand who might possibly marry her. But her master's son! And a baron on top of it! Whatever had she been thinking? It was painful to remember how she had devoured every one of his soft words and had been so happy for his gifts. And what now? Oh, if only Lisa were still at Ekefors Manor. She was the only person Augusta could imagine confiding in. All the other girls were too childish and silly, and the women stiff and proper. They had certainly never been young and in love.

That day was an eternity in which Augusta burned in hell. She was hardly aware of what she was doing as she moved from one task to the next. The few solutions open to her went round and round in her head. Telling Erling was not one of them. She must retain at least a scrap of pride, if nothing else. Nor did she know any old woman who could rid her of the unwanted child growing inside her. And to ask anyone for advice was too dangerous. It was going to be hard enough to keep her condition secret while living together with so many people in the manor house kitchen. Once it became known, she would lose her job. Nor could she go back to her family. She had left home because she and her stepmother couldn't tolerate each other even under normal circumstances. She knew no one who would take her in. Nor could she run away to the city. As soon as she was seen outside her own parish, questions would be asked by the authorities. Some girls managed to keep their pregnancies secret, give birth in a shed or under open sky, and then leave the baby on the church steps—or even take its life. But in the end, they were always caught and punished. To murder a newborn child carried the death sentence. To let nature take its course and accept the consequences was hardly a solution, either. Life as an unwed mother was no life at all. Such a woman was referred to as a whore, even to her face, and unwelcome wherever she went. No one would employ a whore with a child, forcing her to resort to vagrancy, which was against the law. At best, she would end up in the poorhouse, living in a room with the parish's outcasts: the old, poor, sick, weak-minded, insane, as well as the parentless children. Augusta couldn't envision such a life.

Evening came at last. The milking took longer than usual. The cows sensed her unrest, stamping their feet and swishing their tails, while their noses tossed the fodder from side to side in the crib in search of a few bits of hay among the dried leaves and straw which must sustain them until the new grass came. Augusta pressed her face against Stjerna's side, seeking that sense of peace and well-being the cows always gave her. But all she found was her own anxiety. Even Stjerna was anxious. After she had squeezed the last drops from the cow's teat, she patted her rump gently and got to her feet. Her mind was made up.

Mechanically she strained the warm milk through a few pine boughs, then poured it into the low wooden separating troughs and slid them like drawers into the cooling cupboard. The cream would rise during the night, but someone else would have to skim it off and churn it the next morning.

When the evening meal was finished, Augusta slipped out the side door into the twilight. Pulling her shawl closer around her shoulders, she set out through the woods toward the mill. As she approached it, she could see that the door was closed and that the huge iron key was hanging on its nail beside the window. Kvarn-Anders had gone home. She continued across the clearing, careful to avoid the numerous manure piles left behind by the horses waiting for their wagonloads of grain to be ground. Between the old millstone step and the wall of the building the first coltsfoots had pushed their way up, their yellow blossoms closed and bowed for the night. Ordinarily the sight would have delighted her, but now she walked past without seeing them. Behind the building a narrow path made its way along the edge of the millrun up to the pond above. In the steepest parts there were moss-covered stone steps, put in by Kvarn-Anders' great grandfather, the first miller at Ekefors Manor. Lifting her skirts so as not to trip on them, she climbed slowly, the tiny weightless child weighing her down inside as though she were already carrying it in her arms. How many young girls had climbed these steps ahead of her? She knew she was far from the first. The mill stream rushed downwards past her, playfully casting a spray of droplets at her skirt. It intrigued her that the water could be so gay.

The mill pond was surrounded by ancient trees, their thick roots crawling across the ground toward the water. On both sides of the flood gates large flat stones formed a walkway across the run. At the moment the gates were partially open, so that the surface of the water in the pond was well below the level of the stones. Augusta walked out toward the gates, where she knew the water was deepest, moving closer to the edge with each step. Bending over, she tried to see the bottom of the pond, but the water was muddy from the spring rains. Small whirlpools glided like shadows around the surface and water beetles skated to the music of the falling water. It made her dizzy. She backed away from the edge and sat down, leaning against the gate frame with her feet out in front of her. She looked at her shoes. They were quite new. Someone else could wear them. She untied the laces. At the same time, she couldn't stop thinking about a scene she had witnessed when she first came to the manor.

Malin, one of the young housemaids, had failed to show up for supper. Questions were asked, but no one knew where she could be. When she hadn't appeared by the end of the meal, the farmhands were sent to look for her. But no one was overly concerned. Meals were missed now and then. The other girls took care of their chores in the kitchen as usual, talking and laughing over the dish pans. Suddenly one of the men rushed into the kitchen.

"The mill pond!" he panted. "Hurry! She's in the mill pond!"

Leaving the pans of dish water by the fire, they all ran through the woods towards the mill. The hem of Malin's skirt was floating on the surface and her head was visible underwater, pressed against the flood gates by the current. A couple of men were grappling frantically with boat hooks, trying to pull her out, even though they knew it was too late. Horrified, Augusta watched them drag the lifeless body up over the edge of the stones. The wet clothes clinging to her belly answered the question as to why she had turned to the pond. The bystanders speculated among themselves in hushed tones.

"Was it yours, Hasse?" one of the stall hands ventured, turning to Hasse, who had been the most successful of her several suitors.

Hasse shook his head without looking up.

"Funny she didn't blame it on anyone. Wonder if it's old man Ekefors'?" someone else mused.

"I wouldn't be surprised," ventured one of the housemaids in a whisper. Malin's braid had loosened so that her long hair stuck to the side of her face and neck. Her eyes were wide open, silently screaming in terror! No one dared touch her.

Finally one of the men went after the wooden seat from an *utdragssoffa* and they managed to roll her onto it by pulling on her clothes.

By the time the procession reached the manor house, the baron and his wife had already been informed.

"Take a good look at her, housemaids," Ekefors admonished. "This is the result of a girl failing to obey God's laws. Then, rather than accept responsibility for her sin, she has cast herself and her unborn child into hell, as well as soiling the honor of Ekefors Manor."

The housemaids and farmhands stood in a half circle around the unfortunate girl, heads bowed before their master and mistress, and let the words rain over them.

"Why hasn't someone at least closed her eyes?" Baroness Ekefors demanded. "Olivia! See to it!"

Olivia, who was the oldest and in charge of the other girls, was unable to even look at Malin.

She turned to Augusta, who was the youngest.

"Augusta," she ordered, "close the eyes."

Augusta was horrified. Everyone looked at her, waiting. Gingerly she stepped forward and placed her thumb and forefinger on Malin's eyelids and drew them downwards over her lifeless eyes, as she had seen her mother do when her grandmother died. It wasn't as bad as she had expected. Just sad.

"All right, back to work everyone," Ekefors directed. "Lars and Hasse, put the body in the woodshed until tomorrow."

The girls trooped back to the kitchen where they finished the dishes silently, each lost in her own private thoughts. Such a thing could happen to any of them. Even though Malin had had other suitors, they all knew that it was Hasse she had been sweet on. That she should have given herself to him was quite natural; most girls did the same. But she had kept well hidden the fact that she was in a family way.

"I heard them arguing last night," one of the girls said finally, barely above a whisper. "I couldn't hear what they were saying, but it sounded as if he was angry and she was crying."

It's always the same, Augusta thought. Everything is fine until the girl gets pregnant. Then she becomes a whore, while the boy goes free, even when everyone knows he is the father. He must be caught in the act before the blame can be laid on him. And even then he is never ostracized socially. The girl must bear the consequences and social stigma entirely on her own.

Because she had taken her own life, Malin was buried outside the churchyard wall to the north. There was no priest, no ceremony, no one in attendance. And the grave bore no marker. But the mound of bare earth was clearly visible to all who attended church that next Sunday. And to make certain that everyone understood the seriousness of what had happened, Reverend Holmgren's entire sermon dealt with the sins of whoring, of taking one's life, and of murdering an unborn child. Everyone from Ekefors Manor was present. The women and girls listened with politely bowed heads, the married women smugly proud that they had escaped such a fate and the housemaids promising themselves they would be more careful. The men and boys were even more restless than usual, anxious to get out into the open again. The sermon was clearly aimed at the womenfolk and had nothing to do with them. Reverend Holmgren never once implied that another person besides Malin was in any way to blame.

Now, as Augusta sat on the same stones in front of the flood gates where Malin had been pulled from the water, she could not face the thought of sharing the same fate. Slowly she put on her shoes again. She had no idea what she was going to do, only what she was not going to do. She loved life too much to die.

On her way back from the mill, she began to toy with the thought that perhaps Erling did care about her and would not turn his back on her. But how to tell him? What if his parents turned her out of Ekefors Manor? She had nowhere to go. No one employed a pregnant girl or an unwed mother. She would become an outcast.

Days passed. She managed to hide her morning sickness, but she couldn't bring herself to tell Erling. As much as possible, she avoided him. And when they did chance to meet, she couldn't look at him. Finally one day he sought her out when she was alone.

"What is the matter with Augusta?" he asked. "She seems to avoid me and no longer looks me in the face. Is there someone else who is important to her now?"

The only answer he got was her sniffling.

"What is it?" he asked again. "Augusta must tell me."

Augusta took a deep breath.

"I-I-I'm with child," she said.

"So that's it!" he exclaimed. "I'll go and talk to Father tonight. Augusta must wipe her tears now, so that no one sees her crying and wonders what is going on."

Augusta never knew what was said between father and son that night. When she met Erling the following day, it was clear that Baron Ekefors had not given his blessing to the situation.

"He said that since I am planning to one day take over the manor, it is about time I learn something about how to run it. Inspector Persson was to go on a business errand to my uncle in Norway, but Father has decided to send me instead. He said we will discuss our situation when I get back. In the meantime, we are to keep it to ourselves."

"But when is Erling leaving?"

"Tonight. I have to get to Kristiania in time to catch the boat up the coast."

"And when will he be back?" she asked.

"In about a month, if the weather is on my side."

"A month?" she repeated, bewildered. "Such a long time."

"Don't worry. It will fly past. Then we will have the rest of our lives together."

The next day Baron Ekefors called Augusta into his office. It wasn't the visit she had expected.

"Is it true that Augusta is with child and is calling my son the father in hopes of one day becoming mistress of Ekefors Manor?" he began in a friendly tone.

"Yes, Baron, it is true that Master Erling is the father of the child I bear. But I am not interested in Ekefors Manor. I love Master Erling. Nothing more."

"You servant girls are all alike. Any man will roll a girl in the hay if she makes herself available to him. That doesn't mean he wants to take her for his wife. Nor can she catch him by becoming pregnant."

"But, Sir, I didn't make myself available to Master Erling. It was he who sought me out."

Baron Ekefors laughed cynically. "I seem to remember Augusta flaunting herself in front of Inspector Persson a while back," he reminded her. "But never mind how it came about. I can easily understand that my son wouldn't say no to a fling with a servant girl like Augusta. But he has no intention of marrying her, so she can put that idea out of her head once and for all."

Augusta was dumbfounded, unable to take in the baron's unexpected words.

"But he said that he wants to marry me," she offered meekly, forgetting her position before her superior.

"A man will say anything a woman wants to hear when his balls rule his brain. Augusta can forget about Erling. He has assured me he doesn't want her," he told her. "So, the question is, what shall we do about this situation?"

Augusta was silent a long while. She couldn't believe that Erling didn't want her— and yet she had always lived with the tiny fear that perhaps he really was just playing with her. She didn't know what to believe. The only thing she knew for sure was that she was caught in a situation which was out of her hands.

"Ekefors Manor has a good reputation," he went on finally, "and I cannot employ whores—for that is what pregnant girls like Augusta are: whores. Augusta knows that as well as everyone else does. So it looks like there are only a couple of choices. I can dismiss Augusta and leave her to survive as best she can as a vagrant, but I am sure she is aware of the fact that no one will give food or lodging—much less work—to a whore. Not to mention that vagrancy is against the law. Or she can go back to her family, although I don't imagine her stepmother wants to have a whore living in the same house as her children."

His words were like whip-lashes across Augusta's face. She hung her head like a beaten dog, unable to say another word.

"Or shall I make other arrangements?" he asked.

Augusta nodded, without bothering to ask what other arrangements he had in mind. If she couldn't be with Erling, then she didn't care. Anything would be better than becoming a vagrant.

And so it was that Baron Ekefors called Augusta and Olov into his office the following afternoon.

By the time Erling came home a month later, the banns had been read three Sundays in a row and his parents had given Augusta and Olov a simple wedding immediately afterwards. When he heard the news, Erling left Ekefors Manor without even seeing his father and joined the army as a simple foot soldier. In return, Baron Ekefors disowned his only son.

OLOV'S GIRL

When he was offered Grankullen, and thus, to a certain degree, the chance to become his own master, Olov had jumped at the opportunity. He never stopped to consider whether he was getting anything else in the bargain. He was glad to get Augusta. She was clever, thrifty, industrious, and obedient. In the two years they had been married, they had worked hard to improve the cottage and sheds, cleared more land, and managed to save enough of what little cash came their way to purchase a cow. And even though she hadn't given him the son he had hoped for, the girl-child she had produced was strong and healthy. That was, indeed, a blessing in an era when many children never reached their first birthday. In fact, he had become so fond of Elsa-Carolina that he wondered why he had ever wanted a son. As he watched her grow, it gladdened him to see in her a miniature of the woman he had come to appreciate and respect. In his heart he was grateful to Baron Ekefors for having chosen such a wife for him. When he thought back to his reckless days as a poor farmhand who owned nothing and lived like an animal in a corner of a barn, he could hardly believe the turn his life had taken.

Life was by no means so straightforward for Augusta, however. She, too, watched Elsa-Carolina grow, while anxiously keeping an eye open for any betraying likeness to Erling, simultaneously longing for some visible connection to him and praying she would find none. Nor had her confession to Stina relieved her sense of guilt. Stina had advised her not to confess to Olov unless he should ask. She said simply that what was done could not be undone and that Augusta had more to lose than to gain by telling him. Since the birth of the child, Olov had become more attentive and protective. But instead of being able to appreciate his attentions, they made her feel more guilty. Her only salvation was that she was too busy to have time to brood over her situation.

One afternoon, Simon's-Stina stopped in unexpectedly, bringing a little apron she had sewn for her goddaughter and some herbs for Augusta, who was expecting another child. She saw at once that Augusta was troubled, but she said nothing. It was better to let it come on its own.

"Where is Elsalina?" she asked, looking around the room. "Auntie Stina has something for her."

Elsa-Carolina dropped the pine cone she had been playing with and ran toward her godmother with outstretched arms, something she did with no other adult. Stina swung her into the air, then onto her hip.

"Auntie Stina made something for her special girl," she told her. Although the child hadn't yet begun to talk, it was clear that she understood what was said to her. She grasped the little package and shook it.

"No, no, not like that," Stina prompted.

She set her down on the floor and together removed the string and brown paper. Elsa-Carolina pulled out the little apron with a squeal of delight.

"Shall we try it on, Elsalina?" Stina asked.

Elsa-Carolina stood up while Stina fitted it over her *kolt*.

"There!" she exclaimed. "Now Elsalina looks just like Mamma Augusta. Just wait until Papa Olov sees how big his girl is now."

Elsa-Carolina strutted around the room several times, then toddled back to her pine cone. Stina turned to Augusta, who sat at the table with her head in her hands.

"What is the matter, Child?" she asked. "Augusta looks so sad today. Has something happened?"

"I feel so unfair, so evil," she whispered. "Olov is so fond of her. He doesn't even suspect she isn't his. And I go here keeping that secret from him, lying to him with my silence. It's not right."

"Hush, hush," Stina soothed. "No, it's not right. But what choice does Augusta have now?"

"I could tell him the truth."

"It is too late for that. One either confesses such things right from the beginning or else one keeps quiet. At least, with your Olov."

"What does Stina mean? Why shouldn't I tell him—even if he does get angry? He has a right to be angry."

"I will tell Augusta why. Because he has a dark side to him, which Augusta has yet to see. Does she know why her Olov never gets drunk, like the rest of the men?"

Augusta shook her head.

"Because when he is drunk, he loses control of himself. Before Augusta knew him, he was constantly in fights—most of which he won because he is strong as an ox. He very nearly killed a man several years ago. A man who lied to him about something. Baron Ekefors' sudden appearance was all that prevented Olov from crushing his skull. I know, because I was called to tend to the man's wounds. The whole affair was hushed up, but the baron gave Olov a stern warning. I imagine he matched Augusta and Olov up as a way to keep him in line, although I must say that, under the circumstances, I think it was an unfair and dangerous thing to do to Augusta. He should have told him the whole truth behind his offer. I can't help but wonder if Ekefors was trying to get back at Augusta for having been together with his son."

Augusta stared at Stina in disbelief. Suddenly she felt afraid.

"What would he do if he found out the truth?" she asked.

"I don't know. Olov is a proud and righteous man, but I'm not sure he is a forgiving one. He guards his honor jealously and could well throw Augusta out of the house with what he would call her 'whore-child.'"

"But how am I to ever have a clean conscience if I cannot tell him the truth?" Augusta sniffed, wiping her nose on the back of her hand.

"Sometimes we cannot make life all clean and orderly as we would wish to have it. Even if Augusta cannot have Olov's forgiveness, I think God has forgiven her."

"How does Stina know that?"

"Because He has protected Augusta by giving the child its mother's looks rather than its father's. He has done the best He could, and now it is up to Augusta to accept His grace and let the matter rest."

"Does Stina really think so?"

"Yes."

Stina's words comforted Augusta and she was able to put her anxiety out of her mind for a while. Summer had come and her days were filled with the many tasks of housekeeping, as well as the making of as much cheese and butter as possible in order to earn a few coins at the autumn market. She worked automatically, rarely having to think about what she was doing, leaving her thoughts to wander freely. Married life saddened her. It was not at all as she had imagined it would be. True, she had come to like Olov well enough; it wasn't that. It was the lie which darkened her life, the turmoil of her guilt. She prayed that the baby she was carrying would be a boy-child and thus replace Elsa-Carolina in Olov's affections. Perhaps then it wouldn't matter so much, should he discover the truth. She felt as though she had become old in the few years she had been married. Certainly the youthful light-heartedness and sense of fun she had possessed as a housemaid had disappeared. Still, she knew that Olov cared for her, even though she kept a distance from him. Maybe he was just as glad. He was awkward in his affection, finding it much easier to spill his feelings over onto Elsa-Carolina, who gladly accepted them. Whenever he had a chance, he took her with him, holding her hand while she traipsed at his side or carrying her on his shoulders when her small legs tired. He showed her the nest of newly hatched baby birds in the tree behind the cottage, a "V" of geese flying south in the autumn, moose and lynx tracks in the new-fallen snow, the first anemones in the spring. And each time they returned to the house, both of them bubbled with enthusiasm over what they had seen. Augusta had never known him to derive so much enjoyment from the company of another person. He referred to the child always as "my Elsa-Carolina" and glowed with pride when people noticed her beauty. Rather than being called Olov's-Elsa among the manor folk, as she normally would have been, she was known as Olov's-Girl.

By August, the long, light-filled days of summer were gradually starting to darken at either end. As if to compensate, nature covered the forest floor with a carpet of blueberries interspersed with tight clusters of red lingonberries. While everyone looked forward to the fresh blueberries, it was the lingonberries that were most sought. In the peasants' monotonous diet of salted herring, potatoes, dry bread, and porridge they comprised a welcomed bright spot. Because sugar was expensive and only bought in small quantities, the sour lingonberries were simply cooked and stored in wooden casks or ceramic crocks. It wasn't until they were served with porridge that they were finally sweetened with a tiny bit of precious sugar. To Augusta, they were just as precious as the sugar, for they were the only source of fruit available during the long winter.

Late summer was a busy time. There were so many things that must be done before the snow fell and freezing temperatures dominated, not the least of which was storing enough food to last through the coming winter. But this year it was especially difficult for Augusta. Not only did she have to hurry to get everything finished before her approaching confinement, but worse, her large, heavy body made it uncomfortable for her to work bent over, while standing caused her back to ache. Be that as it may, the lingonberries were ripe and must be picked.

The day was sunny and warm with a slight breeze playing in the tree tops. Augusta grasped the edge of a herring barrel and pulled herself up from the newly scrubbed floor of the storage shed. Lifting the wooden pail of rinse water, she cast its contents out across the floor. Most of the water immediately disappeared through the wide cracks between the boards, while the rest ran towards the sagging back corner of the building. With a broom of bound twigs she guided its flow to the fist-sized hole at the base of the wall and listened to the splattering sound as it ran out onto the stones under the shed. When the splashing ceased, she bent over and replaced the wooden plug. To forget the plug was to invite a hoard of rats and mice to make short work of the family's winter rations. Lastly, she took in the wooden lingon casks that Helga had washed and lined them up beside the bread bin to air without their lids. Satisfied that everything was in its place, she went out, leaving the door open so the floor would dry more quickly.

Elsa-Carolina and Helga came toward her hand in hand, each swinging a small basket.

"I thought we were going to go after Elsalina has had her nap," Augusta said to Helga.

"She couldn't sleep," Helga replied. "She just lay there saying 'berries, berries, Elsa pick berries.'"

"Well, all right," Augusta conceded. "It is too nice a day to be inside anyway."

The three of them followed the deer path from behind the cottage into the forest until they came to where the undergrowth thinned and both lingon and blueberries took over. Helga continued on the path a ways before kneeling in a large patch. Elsa-Carolina squatted down among the first berries she saw and began picking. The lingon she placed in her basket and the blueberries went directly into her mouth. Augusta watched her for a minute, fascinated to see how gently she handled them, removing any leaves and twigs that landed in the basket. She was certainly going to grow up to be an industrious and capable housewife.

Satisfied that the child was content to pick and eat, Augusta hunched down awkwardly nearby. Quickly she set about pulling the clumps of ripe lingonberries from their branches and sifting them through her fingers before letting them cascade into her basket. She loved berry picking, silently taking that which nature offered, while the birds conversed overhead and the wind sang in the trees. Being in the forest always reminded her of Erling, of their secret meetings under the trees. She still longed for him. Think if Baron Ekefors had given them his blessing. How she wished he could see his daughter. She imagined him one day coming back to Ekefors Manor, of meeting him by chance. What would they do? What could they do? The church and the community held all doors closed for them. And yet…

Now and then Helga's or Elsa's voice broke into her wandering thoughts. But it wasn't until she stood up to stretch that she realized that she must have been daydreaming a long time. Her basket was nearly full. She turned around to see how Elsa was doing, but the child was nowhere in sight.

"Helga!" she called. "Is Elsalina still picking berries?"

"I don't know. Isn't she with Augusta?"

"No, I thought she was with Helga. Elsalina!" she yelled. "Where is Elsalina? Come and show Mamma how many berries she has picked." Her voice rang through the trees, then faded into silence.

Both she and Helga ran to the place where the child had first hunkered down to pick, but there was no sign of her. Augusta's heart began to pound.

"Elsalina!" she screamed. "Where is Elsalina? Come!" But her cries went unanswered.

Frantically, they combed the area, calling her name over and over. They knew she couldn't have been dragged away by a bear or a wolf or they would have heard her scream. No, the child must have been *bergtagen:* lured away to a secret cave by a forest nymph posing as a beautiful fairy-like woman. She had heard stories about people and animals being *bergtagen.* Some were only held a short time, but others were never seen again. Such was the danger for everyone who went into the forest alone.

Stumbling and falling over dead branches and half decayed stumps had quickly exhausted Augusta. She leaned against a tree to catch her breath, which was coming in great sobbing gasps. Her hands were shaking so violently that she could hardly hold the corner of her apron up to her face to wipe away her tears. Before she could think of what to do next, a dry branch snapped behind her.

"What has happened?" she heard Olov's voice say. "I heard a lot of shouting when I came up to the cottage. Where is Elsa-Carolina?"

"S-s-she's been b-b-*bergtagen,*" Augusta stammered.

"Bergtagen?" Olov had always scoffed at such superstitions, considering them to be one of those silly things womenfolk dreamed up.

"It's more likely that she just wandered off somewhere," he interrupted. "Don't just stand there! We have to look for her!" he added impatiently.

"We have already looked in every possible place," she told him. But he didn't hear her; he was already searching wildly while calling out Elsa-Carolina's name. His impatience quickly grew to desperation and finally fear. By the time he rejoined Augusta and Helga, he was shaking.

"Augusta and Helga must continue searching while I run down to the manor and get more people to help us."

Long before he reached the manor, *bergtagning* had ceased to be a superstition. For Olov as well as Augusta, it was a reality.

Coming out of the forest, he saw a group of farmhands leave the barn and walk toward the big house.

"Wait!" he yelled, running even harder in order to catch up with them. They turned around and looked at him curiously.

"Everyone must come and help search for Elsa-Carolina. She has been *bergtagen!*"

"*Bergtagen?*" one of them called back half jokingly, while the others snickered.

But when he came abreast of them they fell serious. Olov was weeping.

"Run up to the big house and fetch Simon's-Stina," one of the men ordered the youngest of the group, a boy of ten. "I just saw her go past with a basket of herbs for the baroness. She's good at finding things."

Within minutes, a group of six or seven men and Simon's-Stina were on their way up to Grankullen behind Olov.

When they reached the cottage, Stina let the others go on ahead of her. Her intuition told her that there must be a simple explanation to what had happened. First she went into the cottage to check Elsalina's favorite nooks. Finding them empty, she returned to the yard from where she could hear a faint chorus of voices calling Elsalina's name. She was not convinced that the child had been *bergtagen,* yet she could not entirely rule out the possibility. She had to admit to herself that she was not quite sure where she stood in relation to the many superstitions that surrounded people's lives. She only knew that she was not ready to accept such a possibility until she had exhausted all other explanations.

She closed her eyes, trying to slip back into a child's way of seeing the world. What would she do if she got tired of picking berries? Without being aware of it, her feet were already taking her towards the shed where Augusta stored their provisions. The door was open, lighting the windowless room. Against one wall was a double bin with hinged lids, one side for flour and the other for storing round flat loaves of dried bread. Stina lifted the lids one at a time. Both were nearly empty. What bread was left was covered with mold. From the beams above her head hung a rat-proof cheese rack, each of its four shelves crowded with small round cheeses wrapped in cloth. Along the back wall stood a row of barrels of various sizes, used for the storage of salted herring and, now and then, salted pork. The potato bin, as well as the butter churn, were empty. The wooden casks beside the bread bin were open and ready to be filled with lingon. In the bottom of one were scattered a few berries, both blueberries and lingon, and an empty basket lay on the floor. On the nearby pile of uncleaned wool lay Elsa-Carolina, curled up like a cat and sound asleep. Stina lifted her up gently. She yawned and rubbed her eyes, then opened them.

"Auntie Stina?" she murmured, puzzled, then caught sight of the lingon casks behind them.

"Look!" she said excitedly, leaning out of Stina's arms, pointing. "See Elsalina's berries."

"Yes, Elsalina picked many berries. Look at Auntie Stina now. Elsalina must always stay with her mother or Helga! She is not to walk in the forest all by herself! There are many dangerous things in the forest that can hurt her!" Her tone was unquestionably harsh.

Although she was not yet three, Elsa knew she had done something wrong. Auntie Stina had never before been angry with her.

Without another word, Stina set her down, and they walked silently in the direction of the calling voices. The pride Elsa had derived from having helped her mother and Helga pick berries was crushed by Stina's reprimand.

The search party had gathered in the clearing to discuss what to do next. When Olov saw Stina and Elsalina coming toward them, he stood rooted to the ground in disbelief. He had been sure she had been *bergtagen.*

"Papa!" she cried. She ran to him, glad to escape Stina's anger.

Swooping her up, Olov hugged her tightly against his sweat-drenched body. He didn't even try to hide his tears.

It wasn't Elsa-Carolina's disappearance that caused people at Ekefors Manor to gossip; it was not unusual that children disappeared in one manner or another. Most were found, but some were never seen again and were assumed to have been *bergtagen.* Such things were a part of life, and in times of famine even welcomed as one less mouth to feed.

No, it was Olov's tears that caused the gossip, for it was highly uncommon that a grown man cried, and especially not openly in front of others. Few fathers paid much heed to a young child. The death rate was high among children and attachment opened the way for greater loss. While everyone was aware of Olov's attachment for Elsa-Carolina, many were surprised to see how deep it went. Even Augusta was surprised. The realization caused her to clutch her secret even more tightly, while her guilt pressed heavier than ever.

That autumn Augusta gave birth to another girl-child, whom they named Märta Elisabeth. There could be no question of who her father was; she looked as much like Olov as a baby can look like an adult. Olov himself was indifferent to the fact that he had not gotten a son. For him, there was no one but Elsa-Carolina.

Shortly after Märta Elisabeth's baptism and Augusta's readmittance to the congregation came the annual *husförhör*, where the priest quizzed every member of the parish, from small children to the old and feeble, to determine whether they could read and how knowledgeable they were concerning Luther's *Catechism*.

More than any other single aspect of life, this cross-examination terrified people the most. The Lutheran Church was the only church allowed, and it exerted power equal to—and in some cases beyond—that of the government. Everyone automatically belonged to it, whether they wished to or not. Attendance at the Sunday service was mandatory, unless one was bedridden or too old to leave home. Taking communion was compulsory for those who had been confirmed. Truants were called upon to explain their absence and risked being fined.

Nor were the priests known for showing compassion toward their parishioners. Rather, they set themselves above their flocks, whom they looked upon as wayward children to be punished when necessary. The fact that they lived in fine houses, had more than enough food even in bad years, thanks to taking a tenth of every parishioner's produce, and rode in carriages didn't add to their popularity among the poor peasants. Yet priests were always met with the deepest outward respect by their parishioners.

On the *husförhör* Sunday, all those belonging to Ekefors Manor gathered at one of the cottages on the estate. It was one of the few times that everyone came together, thus making it a social event as well. Yet the gaiety was tainted by each person's private fear of the questioning to which he or she would be subjected. But once it was over, people relaxed and enjoyed the food and coffee the women supplied.

Helga was especially nervous, for she had difficulty reading aloud in spite of Augusta's efforts to teach her. In order to make out the words at all, she had to hold the book close to her face. She could read Luther's *Little Catechism* well enough since she had long ago learned all the questions and answers by heart. But now she had reached the age when she would be required to read a passage from the Bible, whose words were so small that she couldn't make them out, no matter how close she held the book. But that was not something she could explain to Reverend Holmgren. One did not speak to him unless spoken to, and then one only answered his questions. One never spoke of anything personal with those in a higher social position.

When her turn came to stand before Reverend Holmgren, she reluctantly let go of Augusta's hand, which had given her what little courage she had. Augusta, too, was ill at ease.

"Is this Helga Maria Aronsdotter?" Holmgren asked, removing his glasses as he looked up from the record book on the desk in front of him. On the edge of the table closest to her lay a large leather-bound Bible, closed except for its unfastened brass clasp. The sight of it made her knees weak.

Helga curtsied. "Yes, Sir," she replied scarcely above a whisper.

"And she lives with her brother, Olov Aronsson, and his wife Augusta Torsdotter?"

Helga nodded.

"Speak up, Child!" he said curtly.

"Yes, Sir," she answered quietly, staring at her feet.

He then asked several questions from Luther's *Little Catechism*. Although she knew the answers perfectly, her throat tightened and her mind became muddled, causing her to forget whole phrases. All she could think about was the Bible waiting for her.

"That was a very poor showing for a girl Helga's age," Holmgren concluded gruffly.

Helga bowed her head in shame, as if he had struck her.

"Open the Bible at random with your left hand and read from the right hand page," he commanded.

Helga's hands were shaking so badly that she could hardly lift the leather-bound cover and the pages slipped out from under her grasp. When it was at last lying open in front of her, the text was only a black blur. Gingerly she reached for the book to lift it to her face, but the priest's angry voice stopped her.

"Don't touch it! Leave it lying as it is!" he ordered.

Helga's hands dropped to her sides and instead, she bent over the book.

"Stand up straight, Girl! Have you no respect? Read!" Holmgren shouted.

By now people had stopped talking among themselves and were watching Helga, sympathizing with the helpless child. But no one dared to address Reverend Holmgren in her defense. Such a thing simply was not done.

"I-I-I can't read it, Sir," she whispered.

"Helga means, she can't read!" he snapped.

Helga shook her head. Reading and reading the Bible were one and the same. That was all there was to read.

"Hasn't Augusta taught Helga to read, as she promised to do when Helga became to them?"

"She has tried, Sir. But I cannot read, Sir," she stammered, doing her best to hold back her tears. Suddenly her bladder let go and she found herself standing in a warm, reeking puddle.

Reverend Holmgren sniffed, then bent around the edge of the table to look at her feet.

"Ush!" he bellowed. "Is Helga an uncivilized heathen, also? Get out of here and beg thy Savior's forgiveness!" He was so angry that his face had turned bright red.

Augusta stepped forward to take Helga by the hand, just in time to see him write the word "idiot" in the church book as his evaluation of her intelligence. She was so angry that she forgot her place.

"The child can't see properly," she said quietly.

"Fiddlesticks!" he retorted. "How many fingers am I holding up, Child?" he demanded.

Helga looked up at the giant of a man before her with his arm raised above his head.

"Two, Sir," she answered confidently, for she could see big things like arms and fingers.

"See! There is nothing wrong with her sight," Reverend Holmgren declared. "She is just uneducable. Augusta has not even been able to train her to go 'around the corner.' Clean up this disgraceful mess and take her out of here!"

Augusta led the weeping child out of the cottage and together they walked home, taking turns carrying Märta Elisabeth. Halfway there, Olov caught up to them, with Elsa-Carolina on his shoulders.

"I didn't feel like staying and socializing after that horrible scene," he said.

"I agree. He should understand that Helga can't see properly. He himself has to wear eyeglasses in order to read. Why don't they make them for young children?"

"I don't know. But next time we have *husförhör*, Helga can stay at home or go and visit our parents," Olov concluded, patting his sister's head to comfort her.

Olov kept his word: Helga never again attended a *husförhör* until she was forced to as an adult. By that time she had a pair of glasses.

Life took an unexpected turn for Augusta one summer day when Elsa-Carolina was three and a half. In addition to the semi-annual open markets, there was one other form of commerce in the countryside: the Västgöta *knallar*. These were men from the province of Västergötland who had been granted the right to wander on foot as traveling salesmen. Most of them carried their goods over their shoulders in large double sacks, with one part hanging down the back and the other over the chest. Because Västergötland was the textile center of Sweden, these *knallar* carried a large variety of cloth, as well as ribbons, satin shawls that women wore to church, buttons, needles, thread, and even soap, pencils, coffee, sugar cubes, spices, candy, and other odds and ends that were otherwise hard to come by. Most of them followed the same routes year after year and were eagerly awaited and welcomed by their customers, whom they knew by name as well as their economic circumstances. Occasionally their arrival was not so welcome, as, for example, when an article had been left on credit on a previous visit and there was still no money to pay off the debt. On the other hand, unlike visits paid by one's landlord, which could result in another mouth to feed, these *knallar* were upright men whose livelihoods depended on their reputations. News traveled fast, and one wrong move could make a man unwelcome within a large area. An unfamiliar *knalle* was looked upon with suspicion and caution.

And so it was that day when Elsa-Carolina ran to her mother and announced that a strange man with a sack was coming up the path from the forest. Augusta hurried to the window. It was hard to get a good look at him, for he had his hat pulled down low on his forehead. He was too tall to be Wandering Jon, who wasn't due for another month. Unconsciously, she smoothed her apron and straightened up around the hearth. These men were quick to size up the state of a home and pass the information on in the next home they visited.

There was the sound of footsteps on the porch, then the cry of the hinges as the door opened. The man stepped into the room cautiously and, after a simple "Good day," let his sack slide down his arm to the floor. He stood for a minute, letting his glance take in the room and its occupants.

"Welcome," Augusta said hesitantly, drying her hands on her apron. "Is he new to this area? I have never seen his face before."

"Yes, one might say so," the man replied. "Has the missus time to look at the contents of my sack?"

"A few minutes, yes. Let me see what he has today," Augusta answered.

The man untwisted the narrow section between the two sacks and opened the long slit in the cloth joining the two parts.

"Is the missus alone?" he asked quietly.

Augusta jumped nervously, regretting that she had let him in. At the same time, she nodded.

"She needn't be afraid," he told her. "Is the missus married to a Norwegian?"

"How so?" she asked.

"Her wedding ring—on her right hand, as in Norway."

"Oh, no," she laughed. "That was my mother's ring, which she left to me when she died."

"Oh, I see."

He began pulling things out of the sack: ribbons, buttons, spools of thread, a few bits of cloth. All the while, Elsa-Carolina stood behind her mother's skirt, hiding from the strange man. But when he pulled out a little cardboard picture of Jesus surrounded by small children, she forgot her shyness. She stepped toward the open sack.

"And this fair maid," the man said, looking at her, "is she the missus' firstborn?"

"Yes," Augusta said proudly.

He held out the card to Elsa. "Perhaps the princess has some use for this," he said.

The child's eyes grew wide as she took the card from his outstretched hand.

"What do you say when someone gives you something?" Augusta reminded her.

"Thank you," she peeped, while making a little curtsy.

"Now run along and play," her mother told her.

Elsa could hardly believe her good luck! She had no toys, except for a few pine cone animals on stick legs that her father had made. The only books in the house were Luther's *Catechism* and a little book of sermons, and the only picture they had was of King Oskar the First and the Royal Family, which hung over the bench. And now, a picture all her very own! She stared at it, examining each of the children with Jesus; their hair and faces, their clothes. And Jesus, who looked so friendly and inviting. He reminded her of her father, except that his hair was longer and darker. But such a strange place he sat, with only a few funny looking trees behind him instead of a whole forest.

As Elsa-Carolina lost herself in the picture, the man continued to pluck things from his sack.

"And how old might the child be?" he questioned casually.

"Three and a half—four in January."

"Ah," he replied knowingly. He reached into his pocket and pulled out a small object that he handed to Augusta.

"The missus is right, I am not from this area. I usually travel in the south. But a few months ago I ran into a soldier there who asked if I were going northward. I said I was. (It's all the same to me which road I travel. There are possible customers everywhere.) He became excited, and he asked if I could visit the cottages surrounding Ekefors Manor. But before we had a chance to pass a few words, his mates began to yell at him to hurry up. He looked around helplessly, then ripped a brass button from his uniform and gave it to me. 'If you find a woman there who wears her mother's wedding ring on her right hand and whose first-born will be four in January, give this to her. Tell her I haven't even a copper coin to send, but that she shall give this to the child as a memento when it is older.' Though he was a foot soldier, he spoke not like a peasant."

"Did he tell you his name?" Augusta asked. Her heart was thumping so hard that it must be visible beneath the bib of her apron.

"No. He said names were unnecessary when I asked his."

"Yes, he was right," she mused, turning the button over in her hand. Suddenly she began rummaging through her sewing basket and pulled out a white square of material that she had hemmed as a kerchief for Elsa-Carolina. She had only finished embroidering the first letter of the child's monogram.

"Here, take this. If he ever meets the foot soldier again, give this to him and tell him that the child's name is Elsa-Carolina and that she is strong and healthy."

"I shall do so," he promised. "And the missus can be sure that I shan't speak of this to anyone. Such things, though not as uncommon as she might imagine, are to be kept private. I am but a message bearer."

When he saw her eyes fill with tears, he packed up his sack without his usual sales talk, bowed slightly and bid her goodbye. On his way out he patted Elsa-Carolina on the head. "I shall also tell him she is beautiful," he remarked, closing the door.

The winter that Elsa-Carolina turned five was exceptionally cold. It was dark in the mornings when Olov made his way down to the manor through the deep snow and dark when he returned in the evenings. Yet no matter how tired and cold he was when he got home, he never failed to greet Elsa cheerfully, asking her what she had done during the day. Then one day, it was still light when he came through the door. He walked past Elsa without a word.

"A terrible thing has happened," Olov said, shaking the snow off his jacket. His beard and eyebrows were stiff with ice.

Augusta stopped what she was doing and looked at him.

"What?" she asked, at the same time sensing that she didn't want to know.

"A military delegation came to the manor this morning with a wooden coffin. It seems that Master Ekefors was killed accidentally in a training maneuver. He had been serving as a foot soldier in the south of Sweden under an assumed name, but after his death, his real identity was discovered. Ordinarily they don't bother so much with foot soldiers, but because of his social position, they have sent the body home to be buried. The baroness is hysterical with grief, while the baron is raving about how it was his own damn fault for joining up at the bottom of the ranks. We were given the rest of the day off. Tomorrow is the viewing and the day after that, the funeral. Everyone connected to the manor is expected to attend both events."

Stunned speechless, Augusta grasped the edge of the table to keep herself from collapsing.

In the same instant, Märta fell and began to cry. She rushed to pick her up.

"There, there," she soothed, rocking back and forth with her. "It's all right, it's all right. Things like that happen now and then, but the hurt will pass. Don't cry now."

As she said the words, she knew they were for herself, rather than for Märta. She continued rocking the child long after her crying had ceased. Even though it was relatively warm in the cottage, she was shaking as if she were frozen to the bone. It was impossible to take in Olov's words. Erling couldn't be dead. Not he who was so full of life. Surely in another minute Märta would run and play again and the world would right itself and go on from where it had gone awry a couple of minutes earlier. It must just be a bad dream.

Having delivered the news, Olov sat on a stool beside the fire and, pulling off his boots, began rubbing bear grease into them. The unexpected free hours suited him fine. It was too cold to be working outside. He thought about Erling while he worked the grease into the well-worn leather. The news didn't surprise him. He had liked Erling well enough, but a soldier's life was often predestined to end badly. Death was nothing unusual; they all lived in its proximity every day. To him, the death of a small child who had never had a chance to live seemed worse than that of a soldier who consciously risked his life by joining up.

Neither of them spoke of Erling the rest of the day. Augusta was terrified by the thought of having to attend the viewing and the funeral without exposing the depth of her grief.

The following day, Augusta dressed in her warmest clothes, with her black silk shawl over she shoulders. She bundled Elsa-Carolina up in her only dress, a heavy sweater, a shawl that covered her head and hung down almost to the ground in back, and long woolen stockings she had knitted from coarse, homespun yarn. But when she tried to put the child's boots on her she discovered that, due to the thickness of the new stockings, she could hardly squeeze her feet into them. Part way down the path, Elsa's feet began to freeze and she could hardly walk. Seeing her discomfort, Olov lifted her up onto his shoulders and held onto her feet with his big mittened hands to warm them. Once they came out of the forest onto the plowed road to the manor he set her down again.

The whole length of the roadway was cleared past the various barns, blacksmith and harness shops, storage sheds, and other buildings, and the banks of snow along the edges were covered with pine boughs. In front of the gate to the big house was a long wooden box resting on a low platform. At one end of it stood Inspector Persson dressed in a long black coat. Many people from the small cottages belonging to Ekefors Manor were there, talking quietly in little groups or standing beside the box looking into it. Elsa was immediately curious to see what was in the box that was of such great interest to everyone. At the same time, Augusta, who had lagged behind, held her tightly by the hand, reluctant to go closer. When Olov realized they weren't close behind him, he turned and signaled to them to hurry and catch up. Augusta shook her head, nodding toward the child. Seeing his opportunity, Inspector Persson left his post and went toward them. Taking Elsa's free hand, he pulled her, along with her mother, who was still holding her other hand, up to where Olov was already standing beside the coffin. Still grasping her hand, he bent down between Olov and Elsa-Carolina.

"Take a good look at your father, little Missy," he said loudly enough for those around them to hear.

Elsa felt Olov's body stiffen with a jerk, but her only reaction was bewilderment. A man was lying in the box, dressed in a fancy uniform and holding a psalm book in his hands. What she didn't see as a five year old was that around the psalm book was wrapped a white handkerchief with an "E" embroidered on it. Augusta saw it and broke down. Olov saw it and recognized the special way in which his wife embroidered the initial "E" on the child's clothes, but he held himself together.

Suddenly, without a word of explanation, they were on their way home again. This time Olov walked behind Augusta and her daughter, shoving them along whenever they slowed down, while Helga followed after him carrying Märta. By the time they stumbled through the cottage door, Elsa was so cold she could hardly move. The fire had gone out, except for a few coals under the banked ashes, leaving the room so chilly that they could see their breaths. Augusta had just taken off her coat and was about to blow life into the fire when Olov grabbed her from behind and threw her against the wall.

"You whore! All these years Augusta has lied to me! Lied right in my face! When everyone at the manor knew the truth! How could Augusta do such a thing!"

At that point, words failed him, and he let his fists talk instead. Elsa was petrified, watching while the father she worshipped beat her mother mercilessly. There was no stopping him. Both she and Helga tried to go between them, but they hadn't a chance against his raging strength. Nor did Augusta fight back or try to escape. She took his anger. For her, it was the punishment she felt she had deserved for so long. By the time she slumped unconscious to the floor, he had knocked out several of her teeth and pulled handfuls of hair from her head. After kicking her a couple of times, he walked out, slamming the door behind him.

In the eternity of those minutes, a door also slammed permanently between Elsa and Olov. She continued to regard him as her father, for Inspector Persson's revelation had gone over her head completely, but she hated him for what he had done to her mother. Likewise, she quickly understood that he no longer liked her. And on a level that had no words, she grew up feeling that what had happened was her fault. That day changed all their lives forever.

To vindicate himself and restore his honor, Olov forced Augusta to go to Erling's funeral the following day. Few would have recognized her when she appeared at the graveside, had she not been with him. Her face was so swollen that her eyes were only tiny slits and her nose seemed flattened into her cheeks. People stared at her, some of the women with pity in their eyes, but no one dared approach her as long as Olov was nearby. Most of the men simply shrugged their shoulders and hoped that she would serve as a warning to their wives and fiancées, so that they themselves would never need to take such action. As the man of the house, Olov had every right to physically punish his wife. That was life.

The only person at the funeral who defied the invisible barrier Olov had put up between the congregation and Augusta was Simon's-Stina. The first chance she got, she pulled Augusta aside and asked her what had happened, for she had not been present at the viewing the previous day.

Augusta looked behind her to see where Olov was, then twisted the ring from her right hand.

"Take this," she said quickly, holding it out to Stina. "Give it to Elsalina when she is grown up and tell her the whole story behind it."

Stina began to protest, but Augusta interrupted her. "He will rip it from my finger when he remembers it. Besides, he is going to drive me to my death long before the child reaches adulthood. Thank God she has Stina to watch out for her!"

"Don't say such a thing!" Stina scolded, shocked by Augusta's bluntness.

Hurriedly, Augusta related what had happened. Stina took the ring without further argument.

"I will see that it is given to her ," she promised.

As the group of mourners squeezed together to pass through the churchyard gate and out into the road after the funeral service, Reverend Holmgren put his arm out to block Augusta's way. It was not a friendly gesture, but rather one that expressed his reluctance to touch his battered parishioner.

"Augusta shall present herself at the rectory at 3:00 o'clock this afternoon," he ordered.

She looked at him questioningly.

"Don't be late!" he ordered.

Suddenly Augusta felt exhausted. It was more than enough with all that had happened in the past two days, without also having to answer to Holmgren. But she had no choice. His orders were law within the community.

Several hours later, she was admitted to the rectory and ushered through double doors into a large room. At a long table in front of her sat Reverend Holmgren, dressed in his vestments and flanked by the parish clerk and three church elders chosen from among the largest landowners. One of them was Baron Ekefors. Although there were several chairs on her side of the table, she was not asked to sit down.

Holmgren cleared his throat.

"Does Augusta realize the seriousness of publicly accusing the late Erling Ekefors of having fathered her child? And after his untimely death, no less, when he had no chance to defend himself. Dragging the Ekefors family through the mud like that is slander, for which Augusta can be punished."

"His Holiness Reverend Holmgren," Augusta began respectfully, "it was not I who said Master Ekefors was the father of my child. It was Inspector Persson, Sir. I never told a living soul except for Master Ekefors. We were already secretly engaged and planned to be married as soon as he came of age that spring and became his own master. Baron Ekefors knows that Master Ekefors is the child's father, Sir."

"I know of no such thing!" the baron interrupted. "My son came to me and said that this slut here before us was chasing after him and accusing him of having fathered her child, even though they never had any sort of relationship. He certainly had no intention of marrying her. If he were to stoop so low as to take a common peasant girl for a wife, there were plenty of prettier ones to choose."

Augusta became so upset that she forgot her place.

"That's not true," she wept, staring at the floor. "Baron Ekefors pushed me off on Olov Aronsson in order to keep Master Erling and me apart. 'Other arrangements,' he called it."

The men in front of her were so shocked by her unethical behavior that for a moment none of them knew what to say. Then Reverend Holmgren's arm flew up, his finger pointing toward the door. His voice quivered in rage.

"I hereby sentence Augusta Torsdotter to sit in the stocks outside the church door next Sunday for her disrespectful behavior!" he roared. "Now get out!"

And so it was that Augusta found herself caught between two opposing forces: her husband, who was punishing her for not having told the truth, and the priest, who was punishing her for telling the truth.

Sunday morning at breakfast Olov announced that he was taking Helga and Märta to visit his family for the day.

"But Elsa…" Augusta began meekly.

"That is Augusta's problem," he snapped. "Wrap the child well, Helga. It's cold out."

Helga wound an extra shawl around Märta while glancing at Augusta helplessly, afraid to speak.

The door closed behind them and Augusta slumped down onto the bench. She hadn't much time to figure out what to do with Elsa. Had it been summer, she could have put her in the empty wooden storage bin in the shed, whose sides were too high for the child to climb over—a not entirely uncommon practice when a child must be left alone. But it was too cold; she might freeze to death. Yet the thought of letting her see her mother publicly degraded was unthinkable after all the child had recently witnessed. Perhaps she could tie her to something indoors, although the cottage would quickly become ice cold once the fire was untended.

A few minutes later, a knock on the door interrupted her pondering.

"Who is it?" she called nervously.

"Stina."

Hastily she opened the door.

"I was on my way home from looking in on Blind-Beda just now when I met Olov and the girls on their way to his parents' place. So I figured you must need someone to take care of Elsalina."

"Thank God for godmothers!" Augusta laughed in relief. The strangeness of the sound coming from her mouth made her realize that she couldn't remember when she had last laughed. But as quickly as the laugh had left her, she was serious again.

"I don't know how I am going to be able to go though this humiliation," she said. "I am not ashamed of what I said, for it was the truth. But no one else knows that and they will all think that I have done something terrible. Why is life so cruel? I can't help that Erling and I loved each other. Why must I suffer for that? It's not fair."

"No, it's not fair," Stina agreed. "There is much in this life that is not fair. What is most unfair is that we women are hardly looked upon as human beings. But Augusta knows in her heart that she was right and that Baron Ekefors lied, and she has to let that be the only thing that matters now. Even though Augusta is forced to pay their price, she can do it knowing the truth and with her head held high. Don't be late now."

The morning was cold and gray, the air tight with tiny snowflakes. Augusta dressed in her warmest clothes and wrapped herself in her heavy shawl.

"Here, take this one, too," Stina said, wrapping her own shawl around Augusta's shoulders on top of all her other clothes. "It will give Augusta strength. Hurry back, and I will have some soup waiting to warm her."

Outside the church, the curate stood stamping his feet in the cold while waiting for Augusta, his breath forming white steam clouds above his head. With a short nod, he indicated a bench outside the weapon house. It was covered with a foot of snow. Rather than helping her, he grew impatient with her fumbling attempt to clear it herself with the corner of her shawl. When she was at last seated, he fastened the wooden stocks over her ankles and locked them, then left her to her fate.

Stina's words were foremost in her mind. As the congregation filed past her into the church, she tried to hold her head high and look at each person. She knew every one of them, and they knew her. But most of them looked straight ahead, refusing to acknowledge her presence. On the faces of those few who dared to meet her gaze, she read a mixture of pity and contempt. The last to pass her was Inspector Persson. He stopped directly in front of her, trying to humiliate her with his glare. But Augusta refused to look down. To cover his defeat, he bent forward and spit in her face.

"Now we're even," he sneered and, righting his jacket with a haughty jerk, he entered the building. She could feel the heat of his contempt in the saliva that slowly ran down her cheek.

Rather than bringing about repentance, sitting in the stocks fueled Augusta's hatred. But only a small portion of it was directed at Inspector Persson. The majority of it was hatred toward the church that preached the love of God and then treated its members so cruelly, hatred toward the pompous priests who looked down their noses at the members of their flocks, hatred toward the rich farmers who had the right to lie when it suited them. As her sense of injustice grew with the cold, so, too, did her strength.

Eventually the service ended and the restless male members of the congregation poured out the door much more quickly than they had entered it, leaving the womenfolk inside to drink their coffee. Everywhere small groups of men and youths gathered and immediately one could hear the sound of popping corks and see heads tipped back swigging *brännvin*. In no time, voices became louder and occasionally angry, followed by a jabbing shove at someone's shoulder. As usual at gatherings, a few fights broke out, bringing Reverend Holmgren to the door.

"This is the Sabbath!" he yelled above the din. "Show some respect for God's temple!"

Cheers went up from some of the groups, but the noise did not decrease. By the time the women had drunk their coffee, most of the men were well on their way to being drunk. None of them paid the least bit of attention to Augusta shivering in the stocks. Few had known why she sat there when they had entered the church, but now as groups of women emerged, it was obvious from their contemptuous looks that she had been the subject of their coffee hour discussions. For the first time, Augusta saw the congregation itself from a new perspective. People spent an hour and a half sitting bolt upright on uncomfortable pews in a cold church listening to the priest preach about God and Jesus and how to love one's neighbor and live a righteous life. But no sooner had they stepped out the door than the men set about getting drunk and the women became nasty and judgmental. They were all sinners, just as she was. It was only that they didn't have to pay for their sins.

When the curate finally came out to free Augusta, she was so cold and stiff that she could hardly stand up straight.

"Augusta is to go into Reverend Holmgren so that he can accept her apology and readmit her to the congregation," he told her.

At first she thought she had heard wrong.

"Hurry up," he urged. "Don't keep him waiting."

Her anger boiled over.

"Tell Reverend Holmgren that Augusta Torsdotter shall never again set foot in his church," she answered hastily, trying not to cry. Shaking the snow from Stina's shawl, she hurried past him and out of the church grounds. By the time she reached home, her rage had burned away her chill.

"Augusta is going to get herself into a lot of trouble by turning her back on the parish church," Stina warned her. "Think of all the things tied up with the church: Baptism, readmittance after childbirth, *husförhör*, weddings, funerals, not to mention being required to go to Sunday services and take communion."

"I don't care. I have paid my debt now, and I am finished with the church," she wept in desperation like an angry child.

Stina smiled just enough to wrinkle the little lines around her eyes. Secretly, she was proud of Augusta's daring but felt that it would be wrong of her to encourage it. The parish church ruled the parish, and to reject it was to make life difficult for oneself.

The exposure of the lie upon which their marriage had been grounded was like an earthquake, opening a giant chasm between Augusta and Olov. No bridges existed that could take either of them over to the other, nor could they meet half way. Olov had been wronged and had exercised his right to inflict punishment. But he was unable to go on from there. Forgiveness was not a word he knew. His pride would not allow it.

Augusta had let him make a fool of himself with his shows of affection for a child that wasn't his. Everyone must be laughing behind his back.

Those few days brought to an end any semblance of family life in Grankullen. After that, nothing was as it had been. Olov turned his back on the family and took up his old bachelor habits: drinking and playing cards, not with the manor's farmhands, of course. He avoided them as much as possible. Instead, he spent his free time with a couple of heavy-drinking unmarried brothers who lived in a cave-like hut out in the forest. Many was the time he came home drunk, stumbling and swearing in the darkness.

"Please, not tonight," Augusta would whisper. "I'm in my unclean days."

"A man can have his wife anytime he wishes," he would shout. "It's her duty."

She was afraid to argue with him. Not only was a woman her husband's property, but he had the right to beat her if she failed to obey him.

Elsa-Carolina couldn't understand what had happened. In the course of an afternoon she had gone from being Olov's-Girl to ceasing to exist for him. He went so far as to have her last name, Olovsdotter, changed to Augustasdotter in the church records. She had no idea what she had done to earn his dislike, only that it had to do with both her and her mother, for he treated them both the same way. She longed for him to once again take her on his shoulders when he went out, yet at the same time, she was afraid to go near him. Whenever he was at home, she kept close to Augusta's side, in order to protect and be protected by her. But even she rejected Elsa in some way. When they were alone, she was as she had always been. But as soon as Olov came home, she only paid attention to Märta, and Elsa ceased to exist for her. The only person who was unchanged was Helga. Elsa was always glad when night came and she could creep close to her in the *utdragssoffa* they shared. There she felt safe, because she knew that Helga liked her all the time, not just sometimes.

Gradually the memories of the good times faded, leaving only a heavy sorrow that hung over them all like a black cloak. For Elsa-Carolina, it was the beginning of the lifelong guilt she bore for having destroyed her mother's life. And although she knew intellectually, as an adult, that it wasn't her fault, she was never able to dislodge her sense of guilt about Augusta's fate. At the same time, she always felt there was more to it, something of which she was unaware.

Although Olov still exercised his husbandly rights with Augusta whenever it pleased him, he had divorced himself from her in every other way possible. Only the legal tie remained. He treated her worse than the lowest housemaid, giving orders and slapping her when she didn't follow them quickly enough. And almost every night he forced himself on her, filling her with his contempt.

When Elsa was six, Augusta gave birth to a boy-child. Simon's-Stina was the only adult present. Some of the neighboring women made excuses for not coming; others didn't even feel the need to excuse themselves. Augusta's behavior had placed her outside society's bounds. Thus it fell to Helga and Elsa to assist Stina. The labor was long and difficult. For two days, Elsa watched her mother writhe and cry in pain, each of her screams cutting like the knife of death through her. All she understood was that there was a baby in her mother's stomach that was trying to get out. But how? And where? And when she finally saw her mother's wide open legs with a bloody, slimy baby coming out from between them, she was sick to her stomach. If that was how one got a baby, she was never going to have one!

Olov stayed away for a week, having left the day Stina arrived. When he did return, he was drunk. He took a few aggressive steps toward the bed where Augusta was nursing the child.

"It's a boy," Augusta said quickly, hoping to appease him.

Without a word, he pulled the child from her breast and unwound the swaddling cloths to see if she was telling the truth.

"Has he been named?" he wanted to know.

"No. Olov can name his son," Augusta answered.

"What about his baptism?"

"That is up to Olov."

Several days later, Helga carried her nephew to his baptism and returned to present him as Aron Peder Olovsson. There was no baptismal feast.

Around the time of Peder's birth, the flame of religious revival, which had been sweeping across the Swedish countryside for over a decade, finally made its way to the isolated parishes surrounding Ekefors Manor. Lay preachers appeared, preaching their down-to-earth hellfire and damnation religion in the peasants' own everyday language, rather than the esoteric language of the church. This more personal approach to religion appealed to the common people, many of whom disliked the aloof, upper-class priesthood. And thus, in spite of the law of 1726 forbidding private religious gatherings and preaching by anyone but ordained Lutheran priests, people began to attend secret revival meetings, disregarding threats of flogging, fines, imprisonment on bread and water, or even exile. Often it was the women who were drawn to these lay preachers. Augusta's sister, Tilda, was one of them.

With the coming of autumn, the days were shortening rapidly. Augusta was impatient to set out while the sun was still above the trees, for she had a two- hour walk through the forest ahead of her. The forest was frightening even in daylight, for there could be trolls or wolves or other creatures lurking just out of sight behind bushes and trees. Hastily, she placed a few items in a basket: a small round cheese she had made during the summer, a flat bread, half of their last homemade sausage, and a bottle of *svagdricka,* a weak beer brewed in every peasant household. She had looked forward to this day ever since a passing tramp had come with the message from Tilda, asking if she could pay her a visit the following week. She had heard rumors that her sister had become a follower of a certain Brother Axelsson, for which she could be severely punished should it become known to the church fathers. She was both surprised that Tilda dared to defy the church's authority and teachings, and curious to hear about this Brother Axelsson.

Carefully she re-wound her long braid around her head, fastening it with her brass comb, then pinned her mother's broach at the neck of her best blouse. Lastly, she wrapped the fringed church shawl Erling had given her around her shoulders, once again feeling the warmth of his embrace. After a couple of last-minute instructions to Helga, she set out. She had asked Olov's permission to be gone overnight, to which he had had no objections. For the most part, he ignored her, not caring what she did, as long as she did not further disgrace his name.

As soon as Augusta entered the forest, rather than being afraid, a sense of freedom and well-being came over her. The sky was a deep blue, without a cloud or a breath of wind. As she walked, the sun flickered through the few leaves still clinging to the trees. The path was narrow, in some places disappearing completely, while in other places well-travelled by moose and deer and perhaps a tramp or two. Now and then a yellow birch leaf gave up its hold on the bygone summer and floated silently to the ground. Not a sound was heard, except for Augusta's muted footsteps on the damp leaves strewn along the path. It was as if she had returned to her childhood and the past seven years had never occurred. For a few moments she felt happy again.

It was late afternoon by the time she came into the clearing surrounding Tilda's cottage. It looked the same as always, yet different somehow. As she came nearer, she noticed that the huge rose bushes on either side of the door were gone. For years, they had been Tilda's pride and joy, growing clear up to the eaves. And the two front windows stood empty of their usual curtains and potted plants, giving the cottage a somber, unlived-in look. Just when she began to wonder if Tilda and her family had moved away, the door opened. The woman who came out onto the step was dressed in a simple gray homespun skirt and blouse, without collar or cuffs or pleats. The body of the blouse was cut so large that it completely hid the bulge of her bosom. Her hair hung straight down over her shoulders in a style Augusta had never seen on a grown woman, or even a young girl. It wasn't until she was almost to the open door that she realized that the woman was her sister.

"Come in, with God's blessing," Tilda said, stepping aside to let her enter. Augusta hardly recognized the cottage's single room. The floor, which was ordinarily covered with Tilda's hand-woven rag rugs, was completely bare, as was the long table that had always had an embroidered runner down its center. None of the windows had curtains, and all the house plants were gone, as was Tilda's beautiful patchwork bridal quilt that had always covered the bed. In its place was an old, coarsely woven gray cover. Her two small children were dressed in colorless *koltar,* from which the collars had been removed.

"Tilda, what has happened?" she asked as she set her basket on the table. The whole atmosphere made her uneasy.

But rather than answer, Tilda lifted the bottle of *svagdricka* from Augusta's basket, went out onto the step, and emptied it into the earth where one of the rosebushes had once grown.

"We don't tolerate the devil's drink in this house," she said.

"The devil's drink?" Augusta repeated. "It was just *svagdricka* that I made myself. Even the children drink it."

"Yes, it always starts that way. And now Augusta's husband is drinking *brännvin* again!"

"And how does Tilda know that?" snapped Augusta.

"News travels," her sister remarked dryly.

"But what has happened here?" Augusta pressed, taking in the room with a sweep of her hand. "Where are the rugs, the curtains, the flowers, the bridal quilt? And what has Tilda done to herself, dressing like that and cutting off her beautiful thick braid?"

"It's all vanity, works of the devil. Only the humble can enter the kingdom of heaven," Tilda answered curtly.

"One does not become humble by cutting off one's hair or tearing out one's rose bushes," Augusta concluded.

"But one hasn't a chance of entering the kingdom of heaven as long as one has such things as beautiful rose bushes or hair that one is proud of. One must conquer vanity. Otherwise one is condemned to eternal hellfire and damnation."

"Is that why Tilda has asked me to pay her a visit? So she can condemn me for what she calls my vanity?"

"I asked Augusta to come here to listen to Brother Axelsson tonight."

"Surely Tilda knows how dangerous it is to listen to such people," Augusta remarked, forgetting her previous curiosity.

"This man speaks from the Bible. He is not self-righteous, nor fat from stuffing himself on his tenth that he takes from each of his parishioners, even as he knows them to be starving. Nor does he have unacknowledged offspring scattered across the countryside, as does Reverend Holmgren and most others like him. He is as humble as Jesus, owning almost nothing, seeking only to awaken people so that they may see that the path they are following within the church is leading them straight to hell."

Augusta could hardly argue with what Tilda was saying about the church, but she didn't know if she had the nerve to go as far astray as Tilda had. But before they could discuss it further, several neighbors arrived, all dressed in the same simple manner as Tilda. With them was a small, rather insignificant looking man who introduced himself as Brother Axelsson. He looked like he had never done a day of physical labor in his life. He could hardly be a threat to the established church.

By now darkness had fallen. Tilda pulled the blankets from the beds and hung them over the cottage's three windows and her husband locked the door against possible official intruders. Everyone sat around the table, the women on one side and the men on the other. Brother Axelsson stood at one end, examining those assembled before him. It was hard to guess his age, although the gray streaks in his beard put him well over forty. Suddenly, without any warning, his fist smashed down beside the open Bible on the table in front of him. A fire flashed in his eyes.

"We are told in 1 Timothy 2:9 that 'women shall adorn themselves in modest apparel, with shamefacedness and sobriety, not with braided hair, or gold, or pearls, or costly array,'" he thundered, looking straight at Augusta. "Away with thy damned vain clothes, thy hair combs, thy broaches! Thy garments shall be humble, made from thine own home-spun wool and without useless decoration. No pleats, no frilly collars, no cuffs, for these are the devil's works. Thou must be pure in body and soul! If thee are not, thee will go straight to hell. Likewise, the Sabbath shall be strictly observed. No work is to be done, no word is to be spoken of earthly matters, not even a flower may be picked. This is the only way to salvation and without salvation there is only burning hellfire left! And ye who have lied and sinned shall burn in everlasting hell unless ye repent! Yet repentance is not enough. One must change thy ways. Be rid of vanity and self-righteousness, and may thy dwelling place reflect thy piety. There shall be no unnecessary decorations. No rugs on the floors, nor cloths on the tables, nor curtains at the windows, nor pictures on the walls. No sinful colors anywhere! Only nature's grays and browns. Nor shall men go bearing golden watch chains across their bellies nor buckles on their shoes. One need not shiny buttons when a simple hook will do to close a garment."

And all the while he spoke, his eyes never left Augusta, for she was the only person in the room not dressed in utter simplicity. Each word stung her, as if he were flogging her with a birch rod. She stood up to leave, but Tilda's hand stopped her.

"If Augusta leaves now, she walks straight into the fires of hell forever," she hissed.

Augusta sank back down onto the bench, aware that all eyes were upon her. Brother Axelsson continued to preach, but she no longer heard his words. Then, just as suddenly as he had begun speaking, he stopped and the room fell deadly silent. It was such an intense silence that one was sucked into it and left panting for breath. One of the women stood up and began to say a prayer. Almost immediately, her words became unintelligible, slurring together and sounding like a foreign language, whereupon she began to shout. Her entire body shook, until she could no longer stand up. Even after she fell to the floor, she kept up her hysterical shouting until she was frothing at the mouth. When she was at last quiet, several women helped her to her feet, and she took her seat as if nothing had happened.

Although the woman's behavior had frightened Augusta, she found herself being carried away on Brother Axelsson's words, drawn to this strange religion. Here, perhaps, she could find relief from her torment.

Brother Axelsson continued to preach in his thundering voice for what seemed like hours. The force of his words surrounded her, pressing into her through the pores of her skin rather than through her ears. Now and then she heard him repeat the same phrase, "Confess your sins. Repent. Accept Jesus Christ as your personal savior and be saved." She felt like she was being pulled out to sea by a huge wave, unable to swim to save herself. Presently, some force beyond herself pulled her to her feet. She walked to the head of the table, her arms outstretched.

"Brother Axelsson, help me!" she cried. "I am a sinner, a liar. For five years I deceived my husband by letting him believe that he was the father to my firstborn. For all these years I have loved the child's father, not my husband. Pray for me, Brother Axelsson."

By now she was wailing, tears streaming down her face.

"Only Jesus can help thee," he told her. "But first she must place her faith in Him and accept Him as her savior. And she must promise to follow His teachings and obey His commands and go where He leads her."

He placed his hands on her shoulders, pressing her towards the floor.

"Oh, Jesus," she wept, "I lay my life in your hands! I accept you as my savior."

The words flowed from her mouth as if someone else were saying them. Finally her legs gave out, and she fell to the floor writhing. Visions of hellfire with people screaming as they burned alternated with visions of paradise, filled with white clouds and angels. And there was Jesus, looking at her and saying, "Repent and follow me, for I shall show thee the way. Sin no more."

She could hardly breathe for the fire surging through her, causing her arms and legs to jerk out of control. Her body seemed to be possessed by—by what? The Devil? The Holy Spirit? She had no idea, for she no longer belonged to herself. The force was so great that she was unable to stand against it and she surrendered.

When Augusta became calm at last, she was lifted to her feet.

"Is Augusta ready to follow Jesus from now on, no matter what happens?" Brother Axelsson asked her.

"Y-y-yes," she stammered.

"And leave her vanity behind and live humbly?"

"Yes."

"Is Augusta sure?"

"Yes."

"Bring me some scissors," Brother Axelsson commanded. "This braid is like a serpent around Augusta's head."

A pair of sheep shears were laid on the table. Brother Axelsson pulled the comb from Augusta's hair and cast it into the fire on the open hearth. She felt her heavy braid loosen from her head and uncoil down her spine like a live serpent. A hand lifted it and Brother Axelsson cut through it with the sheep shears. It, too, landed in the fire, filling the room with the smell of burning hair.

"And there ye have it!" he cried. "The stench of hellfire and brimstone!" Augusta's legs could barely hold her upright, so powerful was the glow of Jesus all around her. Yet Brother Axelsson only needed to remind her to beware of the path of sin, which leads directly to hell, whereupon the light of Jesus disappeared, leaving her in darkness, except for the eternal hellfire in front of her, its heat causing sweat to run from every pore.

Augusta was frightened, frightened of the power of Jesus, whom she felt unworthy to follow, and frightened of the threat of hell. Yet she realized that it was too late to turn back. Her hair was already shortened to shoulder length and hung straight down on either side of her face. But when she felt a hand remove her mother's broach from under her chin, she experienced a wave of regret.

"Wait!" she cried. "That was my mother's—a keepsake."

"Does Augusta want it so she can remember that her mother was proud and vain when she wore it and is now burning in hell?" Axelsson asked.

"No!" she cried. "She is not in hell!" She looked pleadingly at her sister for confirmation.

"She followed the fat priests, the church's false prophets, her whole life," Tilda replied.

Augusta heard her mother's broach clink against the stones at the back of the open fireplace, then felt the cold blade of the sheep shears slip between her neck and the collar of her blouse. The familiar sound of cloth being cut sent shivers along her spine as the collar was removed, leaving just enough cloth to be turned over and hemmed against tearing. Next, the ruffles around her wrists disappeared in the same manner. Lastly, Brother Axelsson lifted the black shawl, which had slipped from Augusta's shoulders.

"What about this?" he cried, looking at the other women.

"It's silk," one of them answered.

"Away with such arrogance!" he declared, casting it into the flames.

Augusta gasped. "Erling!" she cried, as though he had been jerked from her arms.

Brother Axelsson ignored her cry.

"When Augusta gets home, she shall undo the pleats in her garments and thereafter wear them in such a way that her womanly shape is no longer visible. And beware, she who has whored here will also whore in hell. And she might remind her husband that he who plays cards here shall play with white hot cards in hell."

Suddenly Augusta was filled with the love of Jesus. She had been reborn, given a second chance, and finally shown the right road to follow. At last she had found the peace for which she had been searching for so long.

When Olov came home from the manor the following evening, he hardly recognized the place. Every bit of hominess had vanished: curtains, rugs, the picture of the Royal Family, the colorful bridal quilt, the few house plants she had proudly grown from cuttings. Even his little shaving mirror was gone from the shelf. Nor did he recognize the figure standing by the fire, whose straight hair fell down to the shoulders of her baggy, collarless blouse. The children, too, had been transformed. Gone were the gay woven bands which had decorated their now-severe collarless frocks. Both girls' natural curls had been cut off, leaving their hair short and almost straight.

"What is going on here?" Olov blurted out. "Has Augusta gone mad?"

"I have never been more sane in my life. It is Olov who is mad, if he doesn't wake up and stop his drinking and card playing and follow Jesus instead."

"Yeah, and end up in prison, starving on bread and water, for having gone against the church," he snorted.

"Give thyself to Jesus, and He will take care of thee."

"I'll bet!"

Just then he saw his other shirt lying on the table. "What has Augusta done?" he bellowed, snatching it possessively. It, too, was without collar or cuffs.

"We are going to start living according to the Bible and follow Jesus' teachings from now on," she told him.

"Augusta and her bastard daughter can live according to whatever they wish, but leave me and my children out of it! I expect to see our clothes in their former condition when I come home tomorrow evening." He stormed out, slamming the door behind him.

For Augusta, there was no going back. Not even Olov's fists could knock her from the path she now trod. Their clothes and surroundings remained simple and unadorned. Olov drank, and Augusta prayed. And each time a revival preacher was in the area, Augusta went to hear him, never failing to fall into a trance and speak in tongues while writhing on the ground. And when she could stand again, she felt cleansed, a few steps closer to heaven or farther away from the fires of hell, depending on her state of mind.

Augusta's new religion influenced every aspect of her life, never letting her forget the hellfire that awaited sinners. Every time she relapsed into her old ways, it was the fear of the devil's pointed fork that prodded her into the path of righteousness again. Yet in her heart she knew that even her piousness was not sufficient to save her, to earn her admittance to heaven. She must win Olov over to Jesus' side. She spent every free minute reading the Bible. She prayed when she woke up and before she went to bed. She said a blessing before each meal, as well as a small "bless thee" and "may God be with thee" over the children's heads throughout the day. On Sundays, no one was allowed to lift a finger to do any tasks. They ate food prepared the previous day—cold porridge for breakfast, cold herring and cold potatoes for their midday meal, and cold soup for supper.

Even the animals were forced to follow what Olov referred to as "the holy road." They were given Sunday's ration of hay and dry leaves just before midnight on Saturday evening and the last drops of milk were squeezed from Gullan's udder at the same time. That animals could not understand if they ate all their rations at once they would go hungry on the Sabbath, did not concern Augusta. It was God's will. And she looked upon Gullan's swollen udder on Monday morning as some sort of necessary penance for the cow's eventual entrance into animal heaven. Nor could Olov rescue the animals; the barn was a woman's domain, whose threshold a man never crossed. No man would do such woman's work as milking or mucking, not even when his wife lay in childbirth. At those times, a cow could wait several days for a neighbor woman to relieve her.

For the children, Sundays were torture. They had to sit still indoors, regardless of the weather, and listen to Augusta read from the Bible, which they failed to understand, or Hoof's *Postilla*. Jacob Otto Hoof was a well-known revival leader who spoke the people's language. His *Postilla,* or book of sermons, was found in many homes, enabling his followers to read his sermons when they were unable to hear him in person. His many commandments and warnings were designed to keep people on the straight and narrow. Even the use of the simple word "good" was to exhibit the sin of pride, whereas, for example, women who curled their hair would have their hair and skull burned to a crisp in hell. His warnings for hellfire and damnation were in such vivid language that even children understood them and were frightened.

When there was a revival meeting in the vicinity, Augusta dragged Elsa along with her, while Märta and Peder got to stay home with Olov who, of course, didn't keep the Sabbath in accordance with Augusta's instructions. On the one hand, Elsa enjoyed going somewhere alone with her mother, for she was more loving and considerate when it was just the two of them. But once they reached the meeting place, Augusta became another person. The first chance she got, she would stand up to say a prayer. Halfway through it, she became possessed, screaming strange words that no one understood. Finally she would fall to the ground in convulsions, still babbling, and foaming at the mouth. Elsa was petrified of her! One day they met Simon's-Stina on their way home. Elsa's legs were shaking so badly that she could hardly walk. The nice time they had had together on their way to the meeting had disappeared when they had gotten there and she was half expecting her mother to start raving again.

"Where have Augusta and my Elsalina been?" Stina asked curiously.

"At a revival meeting," her mother replied.

Stina looked beyond her to where Elsa was lagging behind.

"Does Augusta mean that she has taken the child to witness people screaming in tongues and frothing at the mouth? Her own mother included! Look at her—she's frightened half to death. It's Augusta's business if she wants to partake of such meetings, but it is no place for a child."

She stepped past Augusta and took her godchild's hand.

"From now on she can stay with me when Augusta goes to her meetings," she declared. Elsa understood that Stina did not approve of Augusta's new religion.

Reverend Holmgren, too, expressed his disapproval of Augusta's new religion. One day he sought her out at Grankullen. Augusta was not surprised by his appearance. He had already called on several of the other wayward members of his flock, threatening them with fines if they did not return to his fold. Those who didn't acquiesce found the spectre of possible prison sentences added to their fines. Some relented, others held out.

The day Augusta caught sight of him marching up the path, she was prepared. Quickly she went into the entranceway and turned the iron key in the lock. Soon afterwards, she heard the muted click of the latch, immediately followed by the thud of a his shoulder against the door, which he had assumed would swing open to him. A few seconds later he began pounding on it angrily. When he set about yelling her name, she jerked it open.

"Will the reverend kindly refrain from making so much noise," she said in a hard voice. "The baby just went to sleep."

Automatically he placed his foot on the doorstep in order to continue into the entranceway, but Augusta's body blocked his way.

"What is it he is wanting?" she asked.

"Augusta knows perfectly well why I am here. Religious gatherings without the presence of an ordained priest are against the law," he told her. "If she doesn't mend her ways and return to the church, I will personally see to it that Augusta is locked up in the insane asylum—for anyone who behaves as she does is obviously crazy."

"Is that all the reverend has come to tell me?" she asked.

"Yes. And Augusta knows I mean what I say."

"Goodbye, then," she replied politely, closing the door in his face. Once again the key turned in the lock.

However, it wasn't that Augusta was overly brave that day. At one of the revival meetings, she had learned that the government had abolished the 1726 law forbidding private gatherings for religious purposes. Certainly Holmgren must have known that but had never reckoned with such information reaching the bottom level of society. The church was now powerless to stop the revivalist invasion and punish its participants.

Elsa-Carolina's childhood ended shortly thereafter, in her seventh year, when Helga turned fourteen. Olov had, as much as possible, tried to shield his sister from Augusta's religious fanaticism, but now that she had reached confirmation age, he felt it was imperative that she return to his family's parish and begin studying the teachings of the Lutheran Church with others her own age. Confirmation was not just the act of joining the church; it was also a coming-of-age ritual, after which one was set adrift in the adult world to make one's own way. Without saying anything, Olov had obtained a position for her as a housemaid with the parish curate. Augusta was furious when she found out Helga was leaving.

"I thought Olov had no use for the church after the way Reverend Holmgren treated Helga at the *husförhör*," she told him.

"I don't, but everyone must be confirmed. Besides, it makes more sense than that rubbish Augusta is obsessed by."

"Rubbish? I simply do not want to go to hell, that's all. But how am I going to manage without Helga?" she cried. "Olov knows that I am going to have another child in a couple of months. I need help with all there is to do around here."

"Take thy bastard daughter as a maid," he told her. "She is the same age as Helga was when she first came to us. It is about time the child began earning her keep. Why should I support her?"

Although she pleaded with him, he refused to give in. It was as if he wanted to make Elsa-Carolina pay for the fact that she existed.

When Augusta realized that they had reached a dead end, she relented—on the condition that Olov tell Elsa-Carolina himself, making it clear that it was his decision.

The next day at dinner, Olov took up the subject.

"This is the last meal Helga will be eating with us," he announced. "Tomorrow she is moving back to her own parish and shall work as a housemaid for the parish curate and prepare for her confirmation. So Elsa-Carolina shall take over Helga's job as housemaid here."

Elsa looked up at him in surprise.

"What does Papa mean?" she asked weakly.

"I mean that Elsa shall be the first one up each morning. She shall start the fire, grind and boil the coffee, as well as doing all the tasks Helga has been doing all these years. Is Elsa so stupid that she has not seen all that Helga does each day?"

Elsa felt her face redden with shame. Of course, she knew what Helga did. She was not stupid.

"Why doesn't Papa like me like he did when I was little?" she asked, barely above a whisper, while looking down into her bowl.

"I am not Elsa-Carolina's papa!" Olov shouted. He stood up so violently that Elsa ducked, expecting him to hit her. But instead, he grabbed his jacket off the peg on the wall and stormed out, slamming the door behind him. Elsa looked up cautiously.

"Why isn't he my papa?" she asked, looking at her mother.

"Elsa is too young to understand it now. I will tell her when she is Helga's age," Augusta said.

"But who is my papa?" she persisted.

Augusta said nothing for a few moments, weighing the situation.

Finally she spoke.

"Do you remember a couple of winters ago when we saw a dead man lying in a wooden box?"

"Does Mamma mean the day Papa pulled out Mamma's hair and hit her so hard that her teeth fell out?"

Augusta cringed at the clarity of her memory.

"Yes, that day," she managed to say. "The man in the box was Elsa's father."

That night she lay in bed thinking about the man who was her father. He had looked nice lying in the box with his eyes closed and his hands holding a psalm book. Her very own father. Think if he could come back. She still didn't understand why Olov should dislike her so, but now that she had her own father, it didn't matter so much.

When Elsa began working as a housemaid, she thought her life had come to an end. Most of the time her mother tried not to overwork her, but there was so much to do that she needed all the help she could get. It wasn't just a matter of taking care of the children, washing clothes, cooking meals, and keeping the house tidy. They had to card and spin wool and flax, then weave the cloth from which Augusta made all their clothes. The loom was set up in front of the south window all winter long and she spent every free minute weaving. Often Augusta worked long into the night after everyone else had to gone to sleep, while the flames from the hearth cast a faint flickering light upon her work. When she had woven the entire warp, which could be many yards long, she then cut out clothes for everyone, herself and Olov included, and sewed them by hand. Elsa-Carolina had been taught to knit at a young age and whenever she wasn't busy at some specific task, she had to knit on an unfinished stocking or mitten that she always carried in her apron pocket. She even knit while she was walking. And since there were no shops in the countryside where one could buy food, they had to grow or gather all their own food and preserve it for winter. There was more than enough to keep a woman and a child busy.

When Olov was at home, he could be quite merciless with his demands. He expected the fire to be made and the cottage relatively warm when he got up in the morning. His coffee cup was to be on the table and beside it his *brännvin* glass. Every man started the day with a shot or two of this strong intoxicating drink. In many families, even the children were given *brännvin* before they set off for school in the cold winter weather. And of course Olov's coffee should be boiling hot. If Elsa overslept, Olov literally dragged her out of bed and tossed her onto the floor amidst a barrage of nasty words.

As time went on, Augusta retreated into herself more and more. Elsa could no longer depend on her kindness when Olov wasn't home. Sometimes she was easy-going, but then she could suddenly straighten up and turn hard for no reason. When her newly won peace of mind began to desert her, she became increasingly fanatical in her religious devotion. Perhaps things would have been better had Olov forgiven her, but instead, he never let her forget that she had lied to him and humiliated him in front of everyone at Ekefors Manor. And she, for her part, continually tried to get him to stop drinking and accept Jesus as his savior. When he refused to even listen to her pleading, she became obsessed with the idea that it was her fault that he wasn't saved and that her own salvation lay in bringing him to Jesus.

In the midst of all this, she gave birth to a boy-child, whom they named Per-Hugo. Sadly, he brought no joy into the family. He was simply another mouth to feed and body to clothe. After his birth, Augusta's voice could often be heard in the darkness begging Olov, "Please don't. I don't want any more babies." His reply was always the same: "Augusta is my wife, and I can take her whenever I wish." And in spite of her pleas, when Hugo was just over a year old, she gave birth prematurely to twin girls, whom they named Moa and Hilma. Both were small and weak and Augusta didn't have ample milk for two. Hilma lived less than a week. But even with all the milk for herself, Moa failed to thrive. Before the warm days of summer arrived, she had joined her twin in the parish cemetery. Although childhood deaths were very common, Augusta was convinced that she was being punished by God.

And less than a year after the birth of the twins, Augusta realized she was once more with child.

Huge autumn raindrops pelted the roof of the cowshed, quickly soaking through the sod to the layer of birch bark underneath, before running down to the eaves and cascading to the ground like a waterfall. It had been raining all night, forming a small lake in front of the door. Inside, Augusta had just finished the morning milking. When she hauled her heavy body up off the little three-legged milking stool, she discovered that the back of her long skirt was wet and stuck to her thighs. She sighed. She had been having pains off and on all night and now, finally, her water had broken. Soon she would push another human being out into the world. The thought left her joyless. At thirty, she felt old and worn out from bearing so many children.

Although she would never say it aloud, she had been relieved when the twins had died. What had life to offer them, poor females, beyond pain and toil? Better that they had gone directly to heaven and had been spared this earthly existence. At the same time, she knew it was wrong to feel that way. She also felt guilty because she didn't want this child that was about to be born. To her, it was unclean, the result of Olov's drunken lust. He had become like an animal, forcing himself on her with his huffing and jabbing. She was ashamed to have people know that she had had relations with such a drunken heathen. Thus when she had no longer been able to hide her condition, she had stopped attending revival meetings in order to avoid the judgmental eyes of the other women. Leaving the state church and embracing the new religion had not eradicated the social values that had been instilled in these peasant women since birth. In fact, many of them had become even more self-righteous than they had been previously.

Without the revival meetings to give her the strength to fight for Olov's salvation and thus win her own, Augusta fell into a pit of apathy. She went about her daily tasks mechanically and without caring. Life no longer held any meaning for her. She often thought of Erling, wishing it were his child she bore. How different her life would have been with him—to have lived without having to lie, to have wanted the children they created, to have wanted him. Such thoughts warmed her momentarily, until she remembered that Erling was dead and that the girl she had once been, had died with him—and that such longing was sinful.

The cowshed door let out a painful cry on its iron hinges when Augusta closed it behind her and stepped out into the rain. Clutching her shawl with one hand and trying to keep the milk from sloshing over the edge of the pail, she hurried toward the house, ignoring the sharpness of the pine needles under her bare feet. Inside the entranceway she quickly strained the milk through a large wooden funnel filled with pine branches.

"Elsalina, swing the cauldron of water over the fire and then pour the milk into the separating troughs and put them into the milk cupboard," she instructed. "And Märta must hurry down to the manor and find someone who can go after Simon's-Stina."

While Elsa poured the still-warm milk into the shallow wooden trays and slid them into the milk cupboard to let the cream rise, Augusta gathered the few items she needed for the birth: two pieces of linen warp to tie the cord, which she wound around her forefinger for safekeeping, a pair of scissors, some old sheets and clean rags, and the swaddling cloths. Now that there were small children in the house, she had decided to give birth in the tiny best room, leaving Elsa-Carolina to care for the household and younger children.

"Elsa must keep the fire going and the water hot. Do not come into the best room until I call for the water. Not even if she hears a lot of strange noises. Sometimes having a baby hurts. But it is nothing for a child to witness. Does Elsa understand?"

"Yes, Mother," she answered solemnly, without reminding Augusta that she had been present at Peder's birth. She was glad that she needn't witness another one.

"Simon's-Stina should be here soon."

Elsa saw her mother grimace momentarily.

"It's all right," Augusta reassured her. "It's a woman's lot in life. Elsa will experience it herself soon enough."

Elsa barely had time to worry about her mother. Four-year-old Peder stood beside her at the hearth, pulling on her skirt while she stirred their breakfast porridge.

"Peder hungry! Peder hungry!" he whined.

"Go and sit at the table," she told him. "It's almost ready."

She ladled the thin rye flour porridge into the communal wooden bowl, dropped a spoonful of cooked lingonberries in the center of it, and set it on the table. Peder immediately plunged his spoon into the little red pool of berries. In the same instant, Elsa slapped his hand so hard that his wooden spoon flew across the room.

"Shame on Peder!" she scolded. "He knows full well that the berries are for all of us! Go and pick up thy spoon and keep it to the edge of the bowl for the rest of the meal. I'm sure that Hugo will be glad to eat thy portion of berries."

Peder slid down from the bench, sniffling quietly, and retrieved the spoon. As he ate from the edge of the bowl, he watched the berry juice bleed into the porridge where Elsa's spoon scooped out mouthfuls for herself and Hugo. He knew it was fruitless to plead with her. In his short life, he had already learned that once his mother or sister said something, no amount of begging would change it. Sadly he watched Hugo greedily devouring his share of the berries, having already forgotten how his misfortune had come about.

As soon as they had finished eating, Elsa sent them off to play with their pine cone animals in a corner of the room while she tidied up and made a thicker porridge to give her mother when the time came.

From the best room, she could hear occasional moaning sounds. Once when they were particularly intense, Elsa lifted the latch gently and opened the door a crack. But before she could see anything, Augusta told her to close it.

"I'll call you if I need anything," she told her. "Don't open the door again."

Time seemed to stand still. Elsa swept the floor, then pulled some newly clipped wool from her mother's spinning basket. Carefully she placed a few curls of it on the wire cards and began carding it into long soft rolls. She liked working with wool and looked forward to the day when she would be big enough to spin. It seemed magical the way the fat rolls of lightly rolled wool stretched out into tightly twisted yarn as they passed through one's hands and onto the bobbin on the spinning wheel. When all the wool was carded, she placed the rolls in the basket and set it aside for the day when her mother would once again spend her evenings spinning in front of the fire.

By now Peder and Hugo were tired of playing and began to fuss for their mother. To distract them, Elsa took out the card with the picture of Jesus on it that she had long ago gotten from a peddler and showed them how it looked where Jesus lived.

Presently she heard her mother groaning, then panting heavily, followed by straining sounds. Her own body tensed, as if to help her. Suddenly a baby cried, only to immediately be overpowered by Augusta screaming, "No! No! No!" Elsa jumped to her feet, stuffing the picture into her apron pocket.

"Shall I bring Mamma some hot water?" she called through the closed door.

"No! No! Stay away!" Augusta screamed.

Elsa backed away from the door, shocked by the violence in her mother's voice.

"No! No! No!" Augusta wailed hysterically, over and over, until her voice gave way to sobbing.

Meanwhile, the boys had begun to cry also. Elsa-Carolina huddled with them in the far corner of the room, trying not to hear her mother's cries. If only Stina would hurry up! Augusta was still crying hysterically when Stina arrived, out of breath with Märta close behind her. When she heard the cries coming from the best room, she rushed in without stopping to ask what had happened. From behind the closed door, Elsa could hear her trying unsuccessfully to soothe her mother.

Suddenly there were footsteps tramping on the porch and two neighboring women appeared.

"We heard that Augusta's time has come and that she had sent for Simon's-Stina, so we came up to see if we could help in any way," one of them explained.

Elsa looked at them hesitatingly, unsure of what to say. She needn't have worried. Without waiting for a reply, they followed the sound of Augusta's cries into the best room. The tone of Stina's voice changed immediately.

"Thank you for coming, but we don't need any help," she said curtly, ushering them out of the room as quickly as they had entered it. Once she was sure they were on their way down the path again, Stina continued to try to calm Augusta and bring her to her senses. Eventually she got her to drink some tea made from marjoram leaves and then sat with her until she fell asleep, exhausted.

"Mamma Augusta will sleep for a while," Stina told the children. "She has had a girl-child, but there was something wrong with it, and it has gone to heaven. I will be back soon. Do not go into the best room unless Mamma Augusta wants something."

Later in the afternoon, two strange men dressed in suits appeared at the door demanding to speak with Augusta Torsdotter.

"She's sleeping, Sir," Märta replied, curtsying politely.

The other man stepped past Märta and went directly to the cupboard bed in the corner of the room. Triumphantly he jerked open the curtain hanging across it, only to find it empty.

"Where is she?" he shouted at Märta.

But before she could answer, he flung open the door to the best room.

"Here she is!" he called to his companion.

Both of them went into the best room, closing the door behind them. Elsa could hear them waking her mother and then her hysterical crying. Presently one of them came out into the main room. All four children jumped to their feet.

"Which one of you went to the manor for help today?"

"I did, Sir," Märta said.

The man turned his icy blue eyes to Elsa.

"What's your name, Child?"

"Elsa-Carolina," she replied, curtsying timidly.

"So Elsa-Carolina stayed here and took care of the younger children," he concluded.

"Yes, Sir," she replied, twisting the corner of her apron around her finger nervously. His aggressiveness frightened her.

"Did Elsa-Carolina go into her mother in the other room at any time?"

"No, Sir. I was not allowed to go in unless she called me."

"But Elsa-Carolina knew she was having a baby, didn't she?"

"Yes, Sir."

"And she heard the baby cry when it was born, didn't she?"

"Yes, Sir," she replied. She knew that all babies cried when they were born.

He gave a snort of satisfaction and returned to the best room. Soon Augusta could be heard screaming even more hysterically than before. Then the door opened again and she stood in the doorway, supported between the two men. She was babbling in the same manner as when she spoke in tongues at revival meetings, and at the same time trying to jerk her arms free. Her hair was damp and matted, sticking to the side of her face, and she still had on the white birthing gown, the lower part of which was covered with blood.

"Mamma!" Elsa cried, taking several steps toward her. But Augusta's wild eyes stopped her. She neither heard her daughter's voice nor saw the child in front of her.

"Is this her shawl?" one of the men asked, pulling down a shawl from the clothesline stretched above the hearth.

Märta nodded, unable to speak.

"What about her shoes?" he wanted to know.

"She doesn't have any this time of year. She only has winter ones," Elsa told him.

"Fetch them!" he barked.

Elsa did as she was told, even though none of them except Olov ever wore shoes before the ground was covered with frost. But when they tried to get Augusta to put her feet into them, she kicked them off again. Finally they wound the shawl around her and led her out the door barefoot.

One of the men carried a bundle wrapped in rags tucked under his free arm.

When Stina returned an hour later, she was horrified by Elsa's account of what had taken place. She did her best to comfort the children, saying that the baby had died and that their mother was sick and had had to go to the hospital. But Elsa could see on her face and by her evasive manner that something much worse had happened.

Because Simon's-Stina was anxious to find out what had happened to Augusta and to speak in her behalf, she left Elsa to take care of the other children until Olov came home.

"Elsa can make some supper and then Märta can help put the boys to bed. Don't worry if papa Olov doesn't come home until late. He has probably already heard what happened and..." She paused, not knowing what more to say. "Well, don't wait up for him," she concluded lamely.

Once Stina had gone, Elsa cooked a few potatoes for the four of them. As an afterthought, she fished a salted herring out of the wooden keg in the storehouse and divided it among them. They never ate herring for supper, but she felt they needed something special to take their minds off the disappearance of their mother.

Instead of the usual grace that Augusta said before each meal, Märta bowed her head and said, "Thanks to thee, God, for the herring, and please bring our mother back soon."

Elsa set two small potatoes and a piece of herring in the slightly hollowed-out places on the table top in front of Märta and the boys. She was cutting up Hugo's potato when Olov appeared, reeking of *brännvin*. He tossed his jacket onto the bench and took his place at the head of the table. Without a word, he reached into the bowl and plucked up the last two potatoes, which Elsa had intended for herself. In doing so, he noticed the frying pan with a bit of herring still in it. His gaze turned to the food in front of the children.

"So Elsa thinks she can take from the herring keg when her mother isn't here!" he bellowed, slapping her so hard that her head hit the wall. "Well, now that her mother is no longer here, there is no reason for her to be here either! As of tomorrow, the parish can take care of Augusta's bastard."

He stabbed the last piece of herring with the tip of his hunting knife and stuck it directly into his mouth.

It wasn't the first time Olov had hit her, but his blows always came as a shock. Jumping up from the table she ran outside, determined not to let him see her cry. Knowing she was safe in the women's domain of the cowshed, she threw herself in a pile of straw and tried to make sense of the day's events while her body jerked in gulping sobs. Everything had been as usual until her mother had begun screaming. After that nothing made sense. Who were the two men who came? Where did they come from, and why had they taken her mother away? And what did Olov mean when he referred to her as Augusta's bastard?

In the middle of the night she awoke to find herself still huddled in the straw, stiff and freezing cold. Quietly, she crept back into the cottage and, feeling her way in the darkness, crawled into the sofa bed between Märta and Peder. Olov's heavy breathing filled the room from behind the curtains of the cupboard bed.

The next morning, she failed to wake up before the others to start the fire. It wasn't the first time Olov had dragged her out of bed, but this time he was angrier than usual.

"Elsa has overslept for the last time!" he yelled at her. "Go down to the manor and tell them that Olov Aronsson is no longer taking care of Augusta Torsdotter's bastard."

He tossed her shawl at her and directed her towards the door. Once outside, she turned back towards the house. Olov stood on the little porch.

"Go!" he ordered. "Do as she is told for once."

Stunned and only half awake, Elsa made her way down the path. Dawn had not yet broken, and the wind was cold. She pulled her woolen shawl tight around her thin body, glad that she hadn't taken off her sweater when she had crawled into bed the night before. The stars were starting to disappear, but once she entered the forest, it was still almost impossible to see the path. Nor had she ever been in the forest by herself in the dark. Stories she had heard about people being carried away by trolls or killed by wolves filled her head. She was afraid to keep walking in the dark, yet she didn't dare stop either. Her legs kept moving forward, her bare feet oblivious to the roots and stones in the path. When she finally reached the manor, her heart was pounding so hard that she could hardly breathe.

The first person she met was Blind-Ola's Berta coming from the milkhouse.

"My, isn't Elsa out early," she commented matter-of-factly, then looked at the child closely.

"What ever is the matter?" she asked.

"W-w-where is Simon's-Stina?" she managed to ask between gasps for air.

"They have taken her along with Elsa's mother. I heard someone say they are on their way to Gothenburg, but I don't know if that is true or not. At any rate, Stina is not here. Why is Elsa looking for her?"

Elsa hesitated.

"Ah, ah, Mamma's Olov sent me away. He says that he is no longer going to take care of Augusta's bastard."

"Oh, so that's how it is," Berta mused to herself. "Best that Elsa goes up to the big house. There must be someone in the kitchen who can do something. Has Elsa eaten breakfast?"

"No," she answered, realizing how hungry she was. "Not supper, either. He took my potatoes," she couldn't help saying before beginning to cry.

"Run along now and tell the cook that Elsa has eaten neither supper nor breakfast."

Elsa curtsied and continued towards the big house, wiping her eyes on the ends of her shawl as she went.

Pushing open the door to the servants' entrance, she stepped into the warmth of the manor house kitchen. It never ceased to overwhelm her. One wall was covered with china plates leaning forward against the slats of their simple racks. On the mantel above the huge open hearth, the lids to the many copper cooking pots were lined up according to size. Their smooth polished surfaces gleamed like small suns against the whitewashed chimney. And across the ceiling, loaves of round flat hole-bread were strung on poles to dry in the heat from the fires before being stored. Only the stone floor was cold, forcing her to hop from one foot to the other.

A kitchen maid was pouring *brännvin* into a bottle containing a sprig of wormwood, while now and then stirring a pot of porridge hanging over the fire. The cook herself was nowhere to be seen. Instead, Baroness Ekefors stood in the middle of the room issuing orders. Too late, Elsa drew back towards the door.

"And what may Augusta's Elsa be doing here at this hour of the morning?" the baroness wanted to know.

Elsa curtsied. "Blind-Ola's Berta sent me here to say that I am hungry."

"And why may that be?"

"Mamma's Olov sent me away. He says he is no longer going to take care of Augusta's bastard."

"Yes, I can understand how he feels," the baroness said coldly, looking down her nose at the child before her. "And certainly we at Ekefors Manor are not going to take care of her either. Her mother has brought shame upon the manor by her outrageous behavior." She turned to the kitchen maid. "Agnes, thin out a ladleful of porridge to a gruel for the child. In the meantime, I shall speak with the baron concerning what is to be done with her."

Agnes looked her up and down.

"When did Elsa eat last?" she asked once the baroness had left the room. She herself was without parents or family and Elsa's situation was familiar to her.

"Yesterday noon," she replied.

Agnes dished out two ladlefuls of porridge into a bowl and set a cup of water beside it. "Eat this as it is. But if Elsa hears the baroness's footsteps, pour the water into it and stir it to a gruel."

By the time Baroness Ekefors returned, Elsa had managed to eat two helpings of undiluted porridge and was feeling somewhat better.

"The baron and I have decided that it is best for Augusta's Elsa to go to her mother's family in the next parish," she stated. "I assume Elsa has been to visit Augusta's stepmother at some time?"

"N-n-no, Ma'am," Elsa said meekly. "I have never met her. But is not Baroness Ekefors my father's mother?" she added innocently.

"No, Baroness Ekefors is not Elsa's grandmother!" The baroness shouted. "Elsa might as well forget that idea right now!"

Elsa was confused, nor had she any idea that she was ill thought of at the manor. She backed towards the door, curtsying on her way.

"Does Elsa know the way to her mother's family's cottage?" the baroness called after her.

"No, Ma'am."

"Follow the road leading away from the manor. At the end of it, go to the right." She pointed with her right arm to make sure Elsa knew which way was right. "If she walks along that road at a good pace, she should come to the village of Stenbro by evening. There she can ask after Tor Knutsson."

Elsa continued backing up until she bumped into the door behind her. All the while, Baroness Ekefors watched her disgustedly. It never occurred to her to accept the girl as her own flesh and blood. All she saw before her was a dirty, barefoot child in tattered clothes. Her pride would not let her see Erling beneath the outer poverty. Instead, she threw her head back arrogantly and strutted out of the kitchen, swinging her long skirt behind her.

Elsa walked slowly around the manor house to the driveway that led from the front door through a long, tree-lined avenue to the road. Part way along it, she heard someone call her name.

"Wait!" Agnes yelled, running to catch up with her. "Take this." Standing so that her body blocked any curious eyes from the house, she thrust a half-dry hole-bread into Elsa's hands.

Elsa walked all day long. Even though the soles of her feet were leather-hard after the summer, they still began to blister by the middle of the afternoon. Now and then she broke off a piece of bread and let her saliva soften it in her mouth.

The road was nothing more than two dirt tracks with grass growing between them. Nor was it straight; it wound like a snake along the edges of fields and around outcroppings of bedrock, following the contours of the land through forests and beside lakes, while climbing and descending the many hills. Often when she reached the top of one hill, she could see several *fjärdingsväg* of road winding through the valley ahead of her. It seemed endless. There were few farms along the way, and almost no travelers, except for a few tramps or an occasional farmer dutifully driving a well-to-do traveler from one inn to the next, as required by law. Local people stayed within their own parishes, except on market days. Elsa walked as if in a trance, her hand in her apron pocket, her fingertips resting against the little picture of Jesus and the children.

It was late afternoon by the time she reached Stenbro. Never had she walked so far. She was exhausted. Gathering her courage, she knocked on the door of the first cottage she came to and asked where Tor Knutsson lived.

"And who might this lassie be?" asked the woman who came to the door.

"I am his granddaughter, Augusta's Elsa-Carolina, Ma'am," she answered, curtsying.

"Oh, the whore-child," the woman said, spitting on the ground three times, as when a black cat crossed one's path, and then pulling the door toward herself until Elsa could only see half her face. "Keep going down the road about a *fjärdingsväg*, until she comes to a path leading to a derelict barn. The cottage lies behind it."

The door closed and Elsa heard the key turn. It made her feel as though she were carrying a deadly disease.

Dusk was falling when she finally reached the old barn. From behind it came the sound of voices. She hurried up the path, relieved to have arrived at last. Much to her surprise, the cottage was even smaller than the one at Grankullen. The door was level with the ground, without any entranceway or even a porch, and the single window had only three panes of glass, the missing fourth replaced by greased paper. Moss covered the unpainted siding up to the window sill, leaving the half-rotten planks jagged near the ground, and the sod roof sagged. A woman was hauling a pail of water up from a well in the front yard, while two older children carried a potato basket of wood toward the cottage, followed by a child about Elsa's age with an armload of twigs. All were dressed in rags.

Elsa hesitated by the corner of the barn, both attracted and repulsed by the scene before her. Finally the cold dampness of evening forced her to approach the cottage.

"And who might this be?" the woman wondered when she caught sight of Elsa.

"It's Augusta's Elsa-Carolina," she answered. "I have been sent to live with my mother's father, Tor Knutsson. Is this were he lives?"

"Yes. But the child cannot live here. We don't have enough to feed and clothe ourselves and certainly nothing for one more, no matter how small."

Just then a man emerged from the barn. He was slightly bent, with gray hair and was clearly much older than the woman.

"Who is here, Anna?" he called.

"She says she is Augusta's Elsa-Carolina," the woman answered. "And that she has been sent to live with her mother's father."

"And where is thy mother, Child?"

"Two men came and took her away yesterday. Then Mamma's Olov sent me away and Baroness Ekefors said I must go to my mother's family."

"Oh my lord! So it is true what I have heard about Augusta! But what about Elsa's godmother, Simon's-Stina?"

"She is gone, too. With Mamma."

"But Elsa's godfather?" the woman suggested.

"'Tis Olov's brother," the man told her, "so there's no help there." He turned to Elsa. "It is not possible for Elsa to live here. Augusta's step-mother and I have small children to feed, as well as Elsa's mother's two youngest brothers. We don't have enough to eat ourselves."

Elsa was so tired and hungry that she started to cry.

"Well, Elsa can stay here until we can work out something else," he concluded. "Perhaps she can be boarded out as a maid. If not, there is always the poorhouse. They have to take her there."

His talk worried Elsa. She was used to being with members of her family and had never been alone among strangers. Even though she didn't know Tor Knutsson, the fact that he was her grandfather was com-forting. But after an evening meal of one potato with salt and a few spoonfuls of skimmed milk, followed by a night on the floor rolled in a moose hide, his alternatives didn't sound so frightening. Other places must at least have beds. And food.

Two days later, Elsa-Carolina went to church with her grandfather and his family. The service was long and boring and her head fell towards her chest on more than one occasion. At the end of the sermon, much to her surprise, the priest looked down at her and said, "We have a ten-year-old girl-child with us today who is homeless. Anyone who is interested in taking her can wait outside the church for the parish auction, which will be held in a quarter of an hour." He almost smiled at her.

Elsa looked up at her grandfather questioningly as they were leaving the church, but he stared straight ahead and said nothing. When they came out onto the steps, the priest pulled her from among members of the Knutsson family. She tried to jerk free of him, but he gripped her arm to prevent her from following them.

"Grandpa!" she shouted. "Grandpa! Don't go!" But her grandfather kept walking without turning around. Meanwhile, a group of people had gathered at the bottom of the steps. They jostled each other to get a closer look at the child, while calling out questions.

"Can she read?"

"Can she write?"

"Is she clean?"

"Does she have lice?"

"Is she obedient?"

"Is she God-fearing?"

"Is she lazy?"

"Is she in good health?"

Elsa stood before them, paralyzed with fear. She had no idea what was going on; only that her grandfather had left her alone in a sea of strangers who seemed to want to tear her apart.

"Mamma!" she cried. "Where is my mother?"

The priest shook her by the arm. "The child must behave herself! Otherwise no one will want to take her."

Take her! Was she going to be *bergtagen,* taken away to a cave in the mountain by a troll, never to return home again? Everything was suddenly too much for her. She closed her eyes, waiting for her mother— or even Olov—to come and get her before it was too late.

Once the crowd was satisfied as to her merits, the bidding began. Unlike an ordinary auction, where the goods went to the highest bidder, people who were auctioned off went to whoever requested the least amount of compensation from the parish for taking them. People didn't take in the homeless because they were charitable, but rather, as a means of acquiring free labor.

There was no rush with the bidding. The men (for it was they who bid) discussed the child on the steps among themselves or, in a few cases, with their wives. Many thought she was too small for her age and too thin. Those who were interested in possibly bidding on her moved even nearer in order to examine her more closely. The priest turned her around so they could view her from all angles. The whole process was like a cattle auction.

"Is this Erling Ekefors' bastard?" someone called out.

"It is said to be so," the priest answered, "although I see little likeness."

Elsa still did not know what a bastard was, but she had long ago understood that it was something bad. Desperately she searched the crowd for her grandfather and his family, but they were nowhere in sight. All she saw were the scornful faces of well-dressed men and women staring up at her where she stood on the steps. Slowly her hand made its way into her apron pocket seeking the picture of Jesus and the children.

The bidding began.

"Who will take this child for five *riksdaler* in silver coin from the parish?"

No one took the offer, but there was a wave of mumbling in the crowd.

"I would like to remind parish members that the child's mother, Augusta Torsdotter, was an exceptionally hard worker as a child," the churchwarden put in.

"Yeah, and look at her now," added a voice from the crowd.

"What possessions does she have with her?" someone else asked.

The priest bent down and whispered, "Does Elsa-Carolina have any other clothes with her? Any shoes?"

She shook her head.

"No shoes?" someone in the crowded called out.

The priest straightened up slowly, looking out across the up-turned faces below him.

"There is nothing beyond what my parishioners see before them," he said finally.

There was mumbled dissatisfaction. Elsa kept her head down, ashamed of her situation; ashamed of the fact that she had nothing, ashamed of the fact that she was so worthless that no one wanted her. She wanted to run from all those people who gazed at her, run until she found her mother or Simon's-Stina. But it was as if the priest could read her thoughts, for his grip on her arm tightened. Yet he needn't have worried; she wouldn't have known which direction to run. She fingered the little picture of Jesus and the children in her pocket, wishing that she were sitting at His feet along with the other children.

"I'll take her for seven *riksdaler* if the parish can find an old pair of shoes for her," a voice said.

"I'll take her for five and she can wear the shoes left from the last maid," volunteered a large red-faced man with a gold watch chain across his bulging stomach.

"Any other bids?" the priest asked. People shook their heads.

"Sold for five *riksdaler* silver-coin to Pehr Nyqvist from Lunna Gård," the priest declared, pushing Elsa in the direction of the red-faced man.

Pehr Nyqvist owned a large farm. Although not a member of the nobility, he was well-off—as well as miserly. It was not so much the thought of acquiring a hard-working maid that made him take Elsa for five *riksdaler,* as it was a way of making use of a pair of unused shoes. He was also a strong-willed man, whose word was law. His wife, on the other hand, was weak-willed and submissive, yet her heart would have been big, had her husband allowed it to be. As it was, she simply obeyed his orders, knowing it was in her best interest not to antagonize him. Secretly, she felt unworthy of Nyqvist, as she called him, because she had failed to bear him any sons. However, he doted on the two daughters she had given him. Nothing was too good for them. But his generosity began and ended there. When the previous housemaid, a girl of ten, had recently become ill, he had reluctantly sent for an old woman who was said to have healing powers. She treated the girl with various herbal remedies, but urged that she be taken to town to the doctor. But Pehr Nyqvist was convinced that such action was an unnecessary bother and expense. And besides, it was a well-known fact that peasants did not believe in doctors. The girl died two days later. It was her shoes that Elsa-Carolina was about to step into.

Although people were concerned about what was to be done with Elsa, for them she was only a child, devoid of feelings. No one had said a word to her about the auction, much less its consequences. That Olov didn't want her at Grankullen was the only thing she could grasp. Everything else was one long nightmare filled with questions for which she had no answers. Where was her mother? Was it her fault that she was taken away? What if she came back and found Elsa gone? How would she find her again? And what about Simon's-Stina? She remembered being told once that she was like an extra mother, who would take care of her if something happened to her mother. But Stina had disappeared, too. And why hadn't the baroness wanted her at Ekefors Manor? Not even her own grandfather wanted her. What had she done to turn everyone against her? And now the priest, who at first had seemed to be friendly, didn't want her either. Instead, he was shoving her towards a strange man who was yelling at her to hurry up. She looked around. The churchyard was crowded, but there was not one face she recognized. No one even looked at her, aside from a couple of well-dressed children her own age walking beside their mother. Even though she was only ten, she could read contempt on their faces when they saw her bare feet.

It was then that she remembered the man's remark about how she could have the shoes his last maid had had. She hurried to catch up so as not to anger him. She didn't want him to hit her, as Olov did when he was angry. On the road below the church a woman and two young girls had already climbed into the front seat of a waiting trap. A boy held the restless horse by the bridle while the man hoisted himself up into the driver's seat and picked up the reins.

"Karlsson can show the new maid the way home," he told the boy.

With a slap of the reins, the horse lurched into a trot and the trap pulled away from them. Karlsson shoved his hands into his pockets and started off down the road. Elsa followed three paces behind him. Her legs moved mechanically, set in motion by the frosty ground against the soles of her feet, forcing her to lift them as soon as she had set them down. A low humming sound escaped from within her. "Mamma, Mamma, Mamma," she wept tearlessly as she felt herself moving farther and farther from all that was familiar.

Pehr Nyqvist's estate was not as large as Ekefors Manor. The household was run by three women: a cook, a kitchen maid, and the parlor maid. Several farmhands took care of the livestock and lived in the barn, among them Karlsson, who was the stable boy. There were two milk maids, whose job it was to take care of the cows and do the milking, as well as keeping the dairy barn clean. Elsa was informed that she was to help them, that they would teach her how to milk.

As was the custom during the winter half of the year, everyone except the farmhands slept in box beds that pulled out from the kitchen benches. But since each bed already had two occupants and there were no small children to squeeze in with (for the two daughters in the family could not share their bed with a poor "parish urchin," as Elsa was labeled), she was given a moose hide and a sheepskin and told to sleep on the floor in a corner of the room. The first night she pulled the sheepskin around herself as tightly as she could, but still she was cold—and lonely. Never in her life had she slept alone. When Märta was born, Elsa had been moved from the cradle into Helga's bed, and in time, Märta, and then Peder, joined them. After Helga left, Hugo took her place. There was always someone to creep close to, to make her feel secure and with whom to share the warmth. She tightened herself into a ball under the sheepskin.

"Mamma, Mamma," she cried softly, over and over into the silent room.

"Stop that bellowing over there!" Pehr Nyqvist shouted. "Otherwise she can sleep in the barn."

Elsa pulled the sheepskin over her head, but could not stop crying.

It was still dark when Elsa was awakened by something prodding her in the ribs. At first she thought it was Olov and braced herself against his angry blows. But it was a strange woman's voice that called her name. She opened her eyes slightly. In front of her was a long gray skirt from under which a foot protruded. It nudged her again.

"Get up, Child," the voice said. "The others have already gone out to begin milking."

Elsa opened her eyes wider and looked up into the face of an older woman. Like all grown women, her hair was pulled back tightly into a bun at the nape of her neck, giving her a stern appearance. But her light blue eyes betrayed an inner softness. Elsa sat up.

"I'm Ebba," the woman said. "Kitchen maid and assistant to Cook Sigrid. It's best that Elsa gets out to the barn as quickly as possible before Squire Nyqvist comes in."

Elsa folded back the sheepskin and stood up. She was already dressed, having slept in her clothes with her shawl wrapped around her for extra warmth.

Outside the morning sky was still filled with stars and the moon hung low above the treetops, ready to disappear. Its dying light cast a shimmer over the frost-frozen grass, making it look sharp as glass. Elsa stood in the doorway, shifting her weight from one foot to the other, reluctant to step into it in her bare feet, yet afraid not to. Feeling the draft from the open door, Ebba appeared behind her.

"What's the matter, Child?" she asked.

Elsa continued lifting one foot, then the other, without answering. Ebba looked down at her moving feet.

"I shall speak to Squire Nyqvist about some shoes for Elsa, but for today she will have to manage without. Run quickly now." She gave Elsa a gentle shove.

Elsa ran across the grass, lifting her feet as high as possible with each step. Pulling the heavy dairy barn door open, she stepped inside. In front of her stood a row of ten or twelve cows separated from one another by short fence-like dividers. From somewhere among them came the sound of girlish laughter. Behind her, the door banged shut, and the barn fell silent. Elsa made her way cautiously along the walkway behind the cows, ducking away from their swishing tails. The stone floor was so cold that it made her feet ache. Part way down the row she found two girls sitting back to back on low three-legged stools between two of the cows. They were older than Elsa and had already studied with the priest and had been confirmed. Thus they belonged to the adult world, even though they were not more than fourteen or fifteen years old. Elsa stood before them shyly, waiting to be told what to do.

"Take the shovel and load all the cow pies into the wheelbarrow," one of them told her.

However, the wooden shovel with its iron edge was too heavy for her to maneuver and she quickly lost her balance and stepped into a fresh cow pie. The shock of the warm oozing mass on her feet was so soothing that it mesmerized her. She stepped from one cow pie to next. For the first time since leaving home, her feet ceased to ache from the cold. It took her a long time to fill the wheelbarrow.

"All the dung gets tossed out through that hole in the wall," one of the girls added as she walked past with a full milk pail. She pointed to a hole about an *aln* above the floor with a board covering it. For Elsa, who was small and thin, this proved to be exhausting, and while her efforts warmed the rest of her body, her feet once again froze on the stone floor. Little did she suspect that, having found a way to avoid the unpleasant mucking, the girls would never teach her to milk.

Ebba kept her word and that evening Elsa was given the high leather shoes her predecessor had had. One of the soles was worn through and patched, and they were still lined with shoe straw, with which most peasants insulated their shoes instead of wearing out their hand-knit stockings. As usual, there was no right or left shoe, yet no matter which way she tried them on, she could barely squeeze her feet into them.

"She will just have to wear them without shoe straw," was Squire Nyqvist's solution.

But even without the chopped straw, they were too small. She walked awkwardly across the room to her bed in the corner, her toes cramped painfully against the ends of the shoes. Squire Nyqvist saw her discomfort, but to him she was only a child—and a girl-child at that—an expendable commodity, and not worth bothering about. His wife also saw Elsa's discomfort, but she never dared to oppose her husband. Ebba saw it, too, but she knew from experience that she would be made to pay for her lack of respect for her employer if she interfered with his dealings. She found it humiliating to be beaten. And so the matter was closed. Elsa had been given a pair of shoes; it was up to her to manage as best she could.

Elsa had not spoken since she had been auctioned off to Squire Nyqvist, nor did she utter a sound now. The prospect of a pair of shoes had been all she had had to look forward to. She no longer cared about anything. Without bothering to take the shoes off, she lay down in her corner and drew the sheepskin up over her head. The next morning when Ebba tried to wake her, Elsa stared at her unseeingly and could not be roused. Her feet were so swollen that Ebba could hardly pull off her shoes.

For several days she lay curled up in the corner of the kitchen, semi-conscious. Ebba did her best to spoon warm gruel into her, talking gently all the while, but the words drifted past, unheard. And when she finally did come back to life, it was only physically. She felt as though she were inside a glass jar sealed off from everyone, as if people couldn't see her. And there she stayed.

She had never in her life been so cold as she was that winter. It was a wonder she didn't die from pneumonia. She only had the clothes she had been wearing when Olov had driven her from home: a shift, a woolen dress, a heavy sweater, and a woolen shawl. That the Nyqvists could have given her a few old clothes their daughters had outgrown was out of the question. It was unthinkable for a parish urchin—and especially an illegitimate one—to wear such nice clothes. It didn't matter that she was freezing; one must uphold the distinction between classes. Rules and traditions must be followed.

Autumn chilled into winter and snow had already covered the ground by November. Elsa froze. She had no choice but to cram her feet into the high leather shoes, but it was not possible to lace them. Snow funneled down around her ankles and up through the hole in the bottom. Often her feet were so cold that they were numb. Nor were her sweater and shawl thick enough to keep out the cold, and certainly not the wind. Yet she never complained. She had been taught that a woman's lot in life was hard and that it was just as well to get used to it at an early age.

And although she froze, it was not that which dominated her life. The worst was that of waiting for Augusta or Stina to come and take her home again. She would even have welcomed Olov, had he come. She often thought about running away to Grankullen, but she had no idea how to get there. And she was afraid. Maids and farmhands and people who were wards of the parish were brought back by the police and physically punished if they tried to run away. So she waited. She did the tasks given her, and she did them well, but she lived in her own world, neither speaking nor responding to people's attempts to reach her. Each night she fell asleep believing that her mother was going to come to get her the following day. And each day she waited in vain, while withdrawing farther into herself, oblivious to those around her.

With the coming of Advent, the hectic Christmas preparations began.

One night Elsa was awakened just as the clock was striking two.

"Get up!" Ebba called, shaking her gently. "We have to begin boiling water to scald the pig after it's been slaughtered."

Elsa sat up unwillingly, rubbing the sleep from her eyes. She always dreaded this grim aspect of the onset of the Christmas season. Although she had never had to witness Olov actually cutting a pig's throat, the joy of Christmas dinner was destroyed by the animal's shrill death cries, which never failed to reach her ears, even when she covered them with her hands. And now, to her horror, she realized she was to be part of the killing and dismembering ritual.

Outside the sky was still filled with stars and a three-quarter moon hung low on the horizon. The snow glittered like millions of earthbound stars dancing through the misty veil of her breath. Elsa lifted her shawl over her head and pulled it tighter around her frail body, but it was unable to keep out the icy cold. She stood shivering while the largest of the pigs was dragged from the barn, tossing its head and shrieking, struggling to get free of the men on either side of it. It was obviously aware of its fate. Someone shoved a pail into Elsa's hands. In it was a whisk made of dried twigs.

"As soon as Johansson has stuck the pig, Elsa must catch all the blood in the pail, stirring it constantly so that no clots form," she was instructed.

As a knife flashed in the light from the flaming torches, the pig let out a long, high-pitched scream, and Elsa was shoved toward it until the pail was under the fountain of blood.

"Stir! Stir!" shouted angry voices, but she couldn't move.

Suddenly the flat of a hand stung the side of her head.

"Stir!"

Automatically her hand began to move in a circular motion. She could feel the warm sticky blood flowing over her fingers. So this was where blood pudding and the dumpling-like palt came from! All at once, everything around her began to spin. She managed to turn her head just in time to avoid vomiting into the pail of blood, after which someone pushed her aside with such force that she fell into a snow bank. It wasn't until she was needed to help carry scalding water that Ebba found her, half frozen and barely conscious.

By then a couple of neighbors had arrived to help with the women's part of the process. First, the hide had to be scalded and the bristles scraped off with sharp-edged blocks of wood. Elsa's task was to keep them supplied with scalding water from the iron washtub over the fire in the wash house. By the time the carcass was scraped smooth, her back ached from having tramped back and forth countless times with heavy wooden pails of hot water that splashed over her feet and the hem of her skirt. When they finally took a pause for breakfast, she couldn't remember gruel ever tasting so good.

The next task was to clean out and rinse the intestines. Elsa was relieved to see two older women take care of the cleaning, for the very smell threatened to bring up her newly eaten gruel. Once the long snake-like intestines had been rinsed, she was able to hold the cowhorn funnel in the opening while one of the other women pushed a mixture of finely chopped meat and organs into what was now a sausage casing. Some of the sausages would be eaten at Christmas, while others would be smoked and hung in the storehouse for the future.

Lastly, the pig itself had to be cut up and salted in preparation for smoking or storage, and head cheese had to be made from scraps of meat picked from the head and feet. While Elsa had long known that a pig was responsible for these Christmas delicacies, this was the first time she had witnessed the transformation in all its rawness. For days afterwards, the snow outside the woodshed remained blood red. Finally, new snow fell, hiding it as if nothing had happened there. But no amount of snow could cover the pictures that remained in Elsa's head, pictures that forever took the glow off the sight of the food-laden Christmas table.

The week before Christmas, the baking began. Aside from great quantities of cakes and pastries, huge batches of dough were set for the white breads and luxury breads made with milk or brewers' wort, which were only eaten during the Christmas holidays. At the same time, a supply of everyday rye and barley breads, as well as sourdough loaves, was baked for the coming half year. Most of these were baked with a hole in the middle so they could be hung from the ceiling poles to dry before being stored in huge bins. It was only at Christmas that bread was eaten fresh.

Aside from the baking and other food preparation before Christmas, there were three other events that took place in every country household during December, all of them in the wash house.

The first was dipping the coming year's supply of candles. All the women gathered in the wash house, where a large container of tallow was set to melt in an even larger container of hot water. It was Elsa's job to cut the wicks to the right length and loop them over sticks, after which the women dipped them into the melted tallow and hung them to harden on a rack laid between two chair backs. And thus they were dipped again and again until they had grown to candle thickness. The atmosphere was relaxed, and the women joked and laughed, treating Elsa more like one of them than they otherwise did, yet she appeared not to notice.

Next came the winter washing, which consisted of all the dirty laundry that had accumulated since the last washing the previous spring. Not only did people not change clothes very often, but they often slept in them at night. Consequently, the hand-woven linen sheets were nearly black, not to mention the clothes themselves. Elsa had had to help her mother do the washing for their family, but it was nothing compared to the piles of dirty linen at Lunna Gård. It was a job that would take a whole week, in spite of the peasant women who were hired to help for a few copper coins or a bit of flour.

First, all the dirty clothes and linen had to be soaked a few days before being scrubbed by hand in lye water. After that, everything was put in a huge wooden tub that stood on a platform above a second tub. A cloth bag full of birch ashes was added to produce more lye, and hot water was poured over it with a scoop until the tub was full. Then the plug in the bottom was pulled out, letting the hot lye water run into the lower tub to be reheated. This process was repeated a dozen times, after which came the first rinsing with clean hot water. There was not much that Elsa could help with during this part of the process. She was instructed to pay close attention, but to stay out of the way. The horror stories she had heard about children who had gotten in the way and were accidentally burned with hot lye water were enough to make her willingly obey.

As soon as the women were finished with the lye water, Elsa was called to come and help.

"Stand here by the tub and help load the sheets onto the sleds so we can haul them down to the lake," she was instructed.

Alma, the head maid who was in charge of the wash house as well as the main house, fed the sopping sheets down to her from the platform, while Elsa did her best to keep them from touching the stone floor. Hot water ran down her up-raised arms and under her dress. As soon as Alma let go of the end of a sheet, it flopped down on her, soaking her clothes. Immediately, the next sheet was coming towards her. By the time all six sleds were loaded and on their way down to the lake, Elsa was dripping wet. She had no choice but to wrap her shawl around herself and follow the others to the lake, with her wet dress clinging to her body.

The day was bitter cold, and they were forced to hack rinsing holes in the thin ice around the washing dock. Elsa was given smaller things—hand towels, pillow cases, stockings—to rinse. She knelt down with the others and sloshed them around in the ice-cold water, then laid them on a slanted beating board and beat the water out of them with a wooden paddle. By the time she was finished, her hands were bright red and numb. Once again she pulled her shawl around herself and hurried through the snow up to the kitchen, her teeth chattering. Seeing her plight, Ebba made a place for her to sit on the raised hearth beside the open fire. But it was a long time before she could stop shivering.

Several days before Christmas, there was a timid knock on the kitchen door. Elsa was sent to open it. Before her stood a boy and a girl about her own age. They were barefoot in the snow and dressed in such tattered rags that she could see parts of their naked bodies through them. Each carried a cloth sack over one shoulder. She gave them a puzzled look, then stepped aside to let them enter.

Ebba set down her rolling pin. "Come, Children. Sit down by the hearth and get warm," she invited, taking their sacks. "Elsa, pour up a little hot coffee for them."

While they warmed themselves Ebba laid a couple of specially baked beggar loaves in each sack, along with some smoked hard sausages, a few potatoes, and a bit of cheese.

"How is your mother?" she asked when she was finished.

"She can no longer get out of bed," answered the boy.

Turning around to see that Alma was nowhere in sight, Ebba went into the pantry and took a handful of coffee beans from the coffee tin. Quickly she wrapped them in a little bit of brown paper and handed them to the girl.

"Is there a coffee bean crusher at home?"

The girl nodded, then curtsied.

"Crush a couple of beans at a time and make some coffee for your mother," she instructed.

"Thank you, Ma'am," the boy said with a slight bow.

"Go straight home now and make something to eat before continuing around the parish," Ebba told them. "It is better to beg with an empty sack. People are more likely to give more to those who have nothing in their sack."

When they had gone, Ebba turned to Elsa.

"Let us hope that Elsa never gets so desperate that she must go begging. And in such rags! It is one thing to beg at Christmas when the rich are obliged to give to the poor, but one has a hard time filling one's beggar's sack the rest of the year, not to mention obtaining permission from the authorities to beg in the first place."

In the days that followed, Elsa opened the door to a number of holiday beggars, both men and women, as well as children, all of whom looked as miserable as the first two she had let into the kitchen. She couldn't get these ragged people out of her mind. It was her first experience with such a means of survival, for no beggars had ever found their way to Grankullen. Suddenly, life at Lunna Gård didn't seem quite so bad.

After having seen the size of the washtub, Elsa fearfully awaited the day before Christmas. As was the custom in the countryside, on that day, as well as at Midsummer, the giant washtub was again filled with hot water. This time every member of the household, starting with the squire and progressing downward in rank to the youngest housemaid, took his or her turn bathing in it.

The kitchen maids were, of course, last. By now it was evening. While she waited her turn, Elsa watched as Ebba climbed out of the tub onto the wooden bench and then onto the floor, her wet skin shining in the candle light. She had never before seen a woman's naked body with its slightly sagging middle-aged breasts and triangle of curly dark hair. Was that how she was going to look one day? Before her thoughts could wander further, Alma grabbed her by the arm and steered her up onto the bench.

"Dirty little urchin, get into the tub!" she commanded.

Elsa looked down into the water. A thick gray scum covered its surface. "Hurry up!" Alma told her.

When Elsa failed to move, Alma gave her a shove and the now-cold water closed around her. Terrified, she sank until it covered her head. In the same instant, her feet touched the bottom of the tub and instinctively she pushed herself up to the surface again, gasping for air. Alma grabbed her by the upper arm and immediately began scrubbing her vigorously with a soapy swine-bristle brush. By the time she was finished, Elsa's skin was raw and she felt like the newlyscraped Christmas pig. She promised herself that, when the time came for her Midsummer bath next summer, she would not utter the smallest complaint at the way her mother's gentle hands scrubbed her.

Christmas had its brighter sides, also. The Christmas table was loaded with food that one never ate any other time of year, some of which Elsa had never before seen: ham and pork, headcheese, fresh fish, stockfish, sausages, thick porridge, cheese, various sorts of bread and pastries, rice pudding, as well as newly brewed beer and *brännvin*. In the very middle of the table stood a huge mound of butter, its rich yellow glow almost as bright as the candlelight. Elsa was quickly informed that it was not there to be eaten; it was a sign of wealth to possess so much butter and was just there to impress anyone who might visit.

The few days that comprised the holiday season were the one time during the year when even servants could eat their fill of delicacies that they otherwise never tasted. Elsa could hardly believe her ears when she was instructed to place a pile of white bread, rather than the everyday black bread, at each person's place at the table on Christmas Eve. White flour was a luxury that had to be bought. At Grankullen, any money that her parents might have had was needed for more important things. Augusta had always maintained that one should be thankful that one had bread at all and not wish for the rich man's white bread. After her religious conversion, she went one step further and declared that eating white bread was sinful. The last few times Elsa had been at Ekefors Manor on special occasions, Augusta had forbidden her to eat such bread. But now her mother was not there, and she could not resist the temptation. But it was not without a sense of guilt that she indulged in the forbidden luxury. That night, she dreamed that Augusta had seen her putting a thick slice of the still-soft bread into her mouth, and she awoke with such stomach pains that she had to vomit.

To Elsa-Carolina, the winter seemed endless. Locked in her own world, she knew no future. Nothing existed beyond the cold and hunger of the present, day after day. She was too young and too miserable to notice that the sun was coming up earlier and setting later each day. It was just as well, for the work day also lengthened with the lengthening hours of daylight.

By the end of March, the sun was riding high above the horizon, its rays clearing the way for the coming spring. Small streams of melted snow ran off the rooftops and trickled toward lower ground, while colts-foot and snowdrops pushed their way through last autumn's soggy leaves. Life was waking up after the long winter.

Still, Elsa remained buried in her own misery, blind to nature's awakening. All she noticed was that she was not quite as cold as she had been. Or perhaps she was just becoming used to it. It didn't really matter. She simply did as she was told and tried to stay out of the way. She never spoke, and people had ceased speaking to her, except to give her orders.

As soon as the new blades of grass were a few inches high, the horses were let out into the pasture. They were every landowner's pride and joy and had been fed the best hay and regularly taken out for exercise all winter long. The cows, on the other hand, had been given a mixture of hay, straw, and dried leaves, with less and less hay as the winter wore on. By spring, many of them had to be propped up in their boxes with wooden frames because they were too weak to stand on their own. Cows were considered to be dispensable and would remain indoors almost until the summer solstice in the middle of June. Then, together with the sheep, they were sent out into the forest to graze, since the grass in the fields near the estate must be cut for hay. One of the younger children was sent along with the animals to see that they were not attacked by bears or wolves. The lot fell to Elsa, the youngest on the estate. She was petrified. The forest around Lunna Gård was unfamiliar to her and rumored to contain bears. That it housed wolves was no idle rumor. Elsa had often heard them howling during the cold winter nights.

The first day, Anders, the boy who had had the job the previous summer, went along to show her where to go and what to do. As soon as the gate was opened onto the path to the summer grazing area, Bella, the lead cow, set off at a run, her huge bell clanging rhythmically from side to side under her chin. The others followed her trustingly, as if bewitched. She was the oldest cow and no other creature would dare challenge her position. Even the sheep knew their place, trotting on their short legs behind the line of cows. Anders and Elsa brought up the rear. Bella led them to the outskirts of the estate where a log causeway crossed a stretch of marshy land. The half-rotten logs were damp and slimy under Elsa's bare feet and she began to half run behind Anders to get over them as quickly as possible. Suddenly she slipped and found herself waist-deep in the murky marsh water. Her mouth opened in a silent scream, but it was her splashing that Anders heard.

"Don't run on the logs," he told her as he helped her up onto the causeway again. "Elsa will soon get used to their sliminess."

She brushed what mud she could off her dress and they hurried to catch up with the animals.

On the far side of the marsh, they entered a dense primeval forest, with rock cliffs and huge moss-covered boulders, where the undergrowth hid the mouths of numerous caves. Such a troll forest was more frightening than Elsa's wildest nightmares.

"Elsa can let them graze here for the rest of the week," Anders told her. "Next week she must take them deeper into the forest."

He opened his shoulder bag and handed her a worn leather pouch.

"Here is the salt bag, which Elsa will need in order to coax them into following her. And the horn," he continued, handing her a little curved horn made from the horn of a cow. "Elsa can blow it so the cows know where she is, but also to scare away a wolf or a bear. She can also blow it if something happens and she needs help, but in that case she must blow it as loudly as possible and hope that someone hears it. She doesn't need to worry about getting lost, though. Bella knows the way home." He reached into his shoulder bag again.

"And here is Elsa's lunch," he said, handing her a piece of dried bread and a small bottle of skimmed milk. "Remember to get it from Ebba every morning."

Having passed on the necessary instructions, he said goodbye and disappeared in the direction from which they had come, leaving Elsa alone in a strange forest. She sat down on a rock and looked around cautiously. Although it was too early in the year, Bella and the others wandered off in search of mushrooms. The sheep, however, flocked nearby, watching Elsa suspiciously with their slitted, marble-like eyes. It was as if they, too, were scared, looking to her for protection. She pulled out the knitting she always carried in her apron pocket. Next winter's stockings. Hopefully, she would have another pair of boots by then. Otherwise her knitting would be in vain. She slipped the tip of the knitting needle into a stitch, but her hands were shaking so badly that she dropped both the stitch and the needle.

The forest was silent, except for a few curious birds calling warnings to one another and the gentle breeze playing in the newly-unfolded leaves. She was sure hungry bears and wolves were lurking behind every tree, waiting for a chance to attack her. And what about the wood nymph? She had heard people talk about how she would suddenly appear in the form of a beautiful young maiden, enticing people to follow her. Her charm was so great that even grown men and women succumbed to her power, forgetting all warnings, and followed her into a cave and were never seen again. Elsa had been told that it was easy to recognize the wood nymph because her back was hollow like a rotten tree trunk, but that by the time she turned her back on her victim it was already too late. It was all too much for Elsa. She let her gaze fall to her knitting, closing out everything around her, and awaited her fate, be it wild animals or the wood nymph. The only bright spot in the day was when hunger got the better of her, and she slowly chewed the dry bread between swallows of so-called blue milk.

The pre-summer days passed uneventfully one after the other. Although her fear never left her, Elsa became used to the long lonely days in the forest. She let Bella take the cows wherever she wished and with time the sheep, too, dared to leave her side. The first rainy day, Ebba had sent her off with a cape made from large sheets of birch bark crudely sewn together with bits of string. She crept under the low-hanging branches of a tree and tried to cover as much of her body as possible with the birch bark, curling her bare feet under her already-wet skirt. She sat there, letting the animals wander as they pleased, until the rain let up late in the afternoon. That evening when the foreman counted the sheep, he discovered that one was missing. Squire Nyqvist flew into a rage when he was told.

"Get back out there and don't return until it has been found!" he yelled at Elsa. "What in the hell does she think she is there for—to pick flowers?"

Elsa dared not protest, even though she was cold, wet, and hungry. She turned around and hurried toward the forest again. The summer twilight had fallen by the time she got to where the animals had grazed last. She listened for the bleating of the lost sheep, but the forest was absolutely silent. Even the birds seemed to have disappeared, leaving behind an uneasy emptiness. She fought off the urge to turn around and run. Instead, she forced herself to go beyond the tree under which she had sat most of the day. Suddenly the silence was broken by the sound of twigs snapping under running feet. Elsa froze. Not far from where she stood lay the head, ribcage, and front legs of the lost sheep. Around it were strewn the remains of the innards, together with great tufts of bloody wool. She gagged, her empty stomach heaving up bile. All she could think about was how to get out of the forest before whatever had killed the sheep came after her. But surely she would be beaten if she went back to the estate. Instead of crossing the log causeway to the meadow, she hurried along the edge of the forest, determined to find her way back to Grankullen. Once she came out onto the road she turned toward the church steeple in the distance, ready to run and hide in the reeds along the ditch if she heard anyone coming. But no one seemed to be looking for her. Not along the road, at least.

She reached the village in the middle of the night. Not a soul was about. The sky was covered with thick, low clouds, which blocked out the Midsummer light, allowing her to pass unnoticed. Just beyond the last house, the road split. As she stood trying to decide which way to go, a hay shed some distance from the road caught her eye. Stumbling across the field to it, she pulled open the rickety door and collapsed into the hay.

She slept so deeply that she failed to hear the mounted police galloping across the field the next morning. Suddenly the door to the shed flew open and the sunlight blinded her. A man with a pointed helmet stood silhouetted in the doorway.

"Here she is!" he shouted.

Another man appeared behind him. Together they stepped into the shed, grabbed her by the arms, and hauled her outside.

"What in the hell does Nyqvist's maid think she's doing?" one of them yelled at her. "People have spent the whole night searching the forest for her!"

Elsa slumped limply between them, unable to hold herself upright. She no longer cared what happened to her.

One of the men threw her over his horse like a sack of grain, head hanging down one side and legs down the other, and climbed into the saddle behind her. They set off across the field, her breath rhythmically knocked out of her in short huffs by the horse's trot.

Squire Nyqvist was waiting when they rode into the yard, the tip of his riding crop flicking impatiently against the side of his boot. As soon as the policeman dismounted, he let his whip fly against the backs of her bare legs.

"That's what the lazy, good-for-nothing whore-child deserves for trying to run away! Doesn't she know that it is against the law to leave her guardian?"

When the horse began to dance nervously to get away from the sound of the whip whizzing above his back, Nyqvist pulled her down and carried her over his shoulder toward the barn.

"And now she is going to pay for not having taken proper care of the sheep," he told her.

The next thing she knew, she was lying on her stomach on her sheep-skin in the corner of the kitchen, her entire backside burning. Once again, Ebba cared for her like a mother.

That autumn she was auctioned off once more, this time to a farmer even farther away from home.

A Short Respite

October came. It was the time when common laborers, who had been employed under one-year contracts they were not free to terminate, usually moved on in the hope of finding a better situation elsewhere.

For parish urchins, it was the humiliation of another auction and the fear of a new overlord. The very thought petrified Elsa. Not because she wanted to stay at Nyqvist's, but because there was no guarantee that the next place might not be even worse. At Nyqvist's, she at least had Ebba.

The Sunday she was to leave Nyqvist's, Ebba helped her tie her few belongings into a little bundle: the extra dress she had made for her by "turning" the well-worn dress her predecessor had left behind when she died, an extra apron, and the wool stockings Elsa had knitted while she watched the cows grazing in the forest. Ebba held up the shoes she had been given when she came to Lunna Gård, but Elsa shook her head. They had been too small from the day she had gotten them a year ago. She had gone barefoot ever since the snow had melted last spring and the bottoms of her feet were like leather.

"I pray Elsa is given a larger pair next time," Ebba said, casting them aside.

Lastly, Ebba tucked a good sized piece of bread, half a hard sausage, and a wedge of cheese in amongst her clothes. At the same time, Elsa slipped her hand into the pocket of her old sweater to make sure her picture of Jesus and the children was still there, then pinned her shawl together under her chin. She was ready.

"Now Elsa must go into the best room and formally take leave of the Nyqvists," Ebba informed her. "She shall shake hands with each member of the family and curtsy to show her appreciation for their having taken her in."

Elsa looked up at her in disbelief. That she should thank them for the way she had been treated made no sense to her. Ebba shrugged her shoulders slightly.

"It's called etiquette," she said, "which means the way things are done, even though it sometimes has no meaning."

She opened the door to the best room slightly, gave Elsa a gentle push through it, and closed it behind her.

Fru Nyqvist and her two daughters were gathered around a table listening to Squire Nyqvist read from the family Bible. His deep voice boomed through the room like Reverend Holmgren's when he preached about hell and damnation. Elsa stood in the doorway, afraid to interrupt him. Finally, he closed the book and fastened the brass clasps over its golden edge, then cleared his throat.

"The family shall not be attending the church service today, so Elsa-Carolina will have to make her way to the auction on her own."

He held out a letter sealed with red wax.

"Give this to the priest as soon as Elsa-Carolina reaches the church," he told her.

She took the letter, then cautiously offered him her hand. He grasped it and she curtsied, head bowed.

Nyqvist dropped her hand without a word and she moved on to the other members of the family, shaking hands and curtsying before each of them. Not one of them said goodbye. By the time she backed out of the room, they had already forgotten her presence, except for the oldest daughter, who was busy wiping her hand on her handkerchief.

In the kitchen, Alma and Sigrid said goodbye and half-heartedly wished her good luck before returning to their work. Only Ebba followed her outside. The October sun lay low in the sky, powerless to warm the chilly wind out of the north. Glancing around to see that no one was watching, Ebba pulled her woolen shawl from her shoulders, wrapped it around Elsa, and gave her a quick hug.

"Go well, my little friend. And may the next people be kinder to thee."

"Th-th-thank you, Eb-ba-ba," she stammered, barely above a whisper. They were the first and last words she spoke at Lunna Gård.

And thus she began the long walk back to the church and the unknown. Although the weather was frosty, the sky was deep blue and yellow leaves still clung to the birches along the roadside. She pulled both shawls tighter, feeling Ebba's warmth enfolding her. Only her feet were cold, in spite of their leather-like soles.

People were already milling around in front of the church when she arrived.

"Hurry up, Child!" the priest yelled when he caught sight of her. "Everyone is waiting."

He snatched Nyqvist's letter from her hand, sliding his thumb under the flap to break the seal. Quickly he glanced through it, then cleared his throat, and began to read aloud.

"Pehr Nyqvist has written as follows," he said, holding the letter at arm's length. 'This child, Elsa-Carolina Augustasdotter, has been my ward since October of the previous year. She is not particularly intelligent, made worse by the fact that she refuses to speak. Nor is she dependable. Not only is she incapable of shepherding the livestock, but when a sheep was killed right under her nose, she hid in a hay shed and let a dozen men search the night for her. In short, one gets more problems than work from this child.'"

Elsa's head hung in shame. No one would take her now. People stared up at her where she stood on the church steps, but no one bothered to ask the usual questions. For them, Nyqvist's letter had summed up her character sufficiently.

"Have we no takers?" the priest asked finally.

There was another long silence.

"What is the parish willing to pay for her?" came a man's voice from the middle of the crowd.

"Nyqvist took her for five *riksdalar* in silver coin, but obviously she is not worth that," answered the priest.

"I'll take her for four and a half," the voice concluded.

"Any other takers?" the priest asked.

Silence.

"Sold to Magnus Engström for four and a half *riksdalar* silver coin!" the priest exclaimed with relief. He gave Elsa a shove towards the crowd. Magnus Engström pushed his way toward her.

"Come," he said, grasping her by the shoulder and pushing her gently ahead of him toward the far edge of the crowd where his wife and children waited.

"This is my wife, Sofia, and my children, Walter, Anna, Dora, and Erik," he said, placing his hand on each child's head as he spoke their names. Erik appeared to be about her own age, Walter and Anna older, and Dora younger. "And this is Elsa-Carolina," he continued, letting his hand rest lightly on her head. "Let us go home now."

Herr Engström walked past the line of carriages where the drivers stood at attention by their horses' heads and continued down the road, followed by his wife and children. Elsa stayed a few paces behind them.

Engström's farm was a two-hour walk from the church. Though she was tired and hungry, Elsa dared not stop to take out a bit of bread from her bundle.

As soon as she saw the farm, she understood that the Engströms were not rich like the Ekefors or Nyqvists. The house was built of squared timbers turned silver-gray by the weather and without siding. The barn was surrounded by various outbuildings, beyond which stood a smaller house with a thatched roof.

"See that little house over there," Erik said, turning to Elsa. "That's where Aunt Edit and Aunt Ester live. They're my grandfather's sisters. Aunt Edit's husband is dead and Aunt Ester never had one."

Elsa smiled in acknowledgment.

To her surprise, they went past the front door and in by way of the kitchen. There was no fire burning on the hearth. The room was cold and devoid of maids or servants. Suddenly she understood: She was to be both maid and servant here.

Anna set about making a fire on the raised hearth, while the boys helped their father fetch wood. Fru Engström began taking food from the pantry—salted herring, bread, and potatoes—and Dora placed wooden bowls on the table, then removed the wooden spoons from the rack on the wall.

"Mamma, there is no spoon for Elsa-Carolina," she remarked.

"She can use this one for now," Fru Engström answered, handing Dora one of her cooking spoons.

She turned to Elsa.

"Elsa can cut the potatoes into that pan there," she said, handing her a knife and indicating a three-legged iron frying pan standing beside the fire. In no time the meal was on the table and the children were making room for Elsa on the bench.

When they had finished eating, Fru Engström took Elsa to meet her husband's mother who lived upstairs, as was common when the son took over the farm from his parents. She occupied a little room, with an open hearth at one end and an *utdragssoffa* bed at the other. In front of the single window stood a table and three chairs. The only other furnishings were a couple of freestanding cupboards and a washstand. Grandma Engström was sitting in front of the fire when they came in.

"*Farmor,* this is Elsa-Carolina," Fru Engström told her. "The child was being auctioned off after church today, but no one wanted to take her. She looked so small and frightened that I simply could not think of letting them send her to the poorhouse."

Without being told, Elsa stepped forward and curtsied, holding out her hand to the old woman without looking at her. She flinched when the thin, bony, arthritis-bent fingers grasped hers.

"These are not witch's hands," Grandma Engström said kindly, sensing her repulsion. "They are simply victims of hard work." She smiled, releasing Elsa's hand. "I hope Elsa will feel free to come up to visit any time," she continued. "It's lonely since my husband passed away. I'm always happy to have company."

Elsa curtsied again. Something about Grandma Engström reminded her of Simon's-Stina. She was glad for the invitation to visit her.

Before going back downstairs, Fru Engström disappeared into the attic, returning with an old pair of leather boots.

"Elsa can take these. They are probably a bit large, but better too large than too small. She can fill the toes with shoe straw."

"T-t-thank you, F-F-Fru Engström," she stammered, curtsying gratefully.

"Elsa can call me Aunt Sofia," Fru Engström told her. "Go ahead, try them on."

Her feet slipped into them easily, with plenty of room to grow. She laced them up and stood wiggling her toes wildly, giggling quietly to herself. First Ebba's shawl and now a pair of boots!

That night she slept in the kitchen with the rest of the family, head-to-foot between Anna and Dora in an *utdragssoffa* instead of on the floor. As she quickly understood, she had not been taken in as a housemaid. She was treated like the other children. All of them helped with the work.

The first time Elsa had a little free time, she pointed towards the stairs questioningly, indicating that she would like to go up to visit Grandma Engström.

"Of course Elsa can go up," Aunt Sofia replied. *"Farmor* will be pleased for sure. The other children don't go up so often, and I know she is lonely. She has a hard time walking, so she rarely comes down, nor is she able to help out with any of the farm work."

And indeed, Grandma Engström was delighted when Elsa appeared.

"Sit down," she invited. "I just boiled a bit of coffee. Would Elsa like some?"

Like all children her age, Elsa had begun to drink coffee with the grown-ups now and then. Although she didn't really like the taste, she nodded.

Grandma Engström poured coffee into china cups, taking the one with the broken ear for herself, and sat down opposite her. As they sipped in silence, Elsa realized that she was really no company for the old woman, since she was unable to speak. But it didn't seem to matter.

"Elsa can call me *Farmor* like the other children do," she began, then stopped. "Oh, I'm sorry. I forgot that Elsa can't talk."

Elsa looked up from her coffee cup. The woman's eyes were sky-blue and friendly. No one had ever apologized for having mentioned that she couldn't talk.

"F-f-far m-m-mor," she managed to stammer.

Grandma Engström smiled.

"When I was about Elsa's age, my mother died while giving birth to my sister. I had been very attached to her, and it was the most terrible thing that ever happened to me as a child. For many years I hated my sister and refused to have anything to do with her because it was her fault that I no longer had my mother. But my refusal still did not bring my mother back. Finally I gave in and started to like her and suddenly I felt a lot happier."

Strangely moved by the old woman's words, Elsa stared into her cup silently. In an effort to prolong her visit, *Farmor* pointed to her potted plants on the windowsill and told her what they were called, who gave them to her, and how long she had had them, as well as how one took proper care of them. Elsa remembered that her mother had also had some potted plants in the windows, but that she had thrown them all out when she had become a follower of Brother Axelsson. She had never understood her mother's actions and had missed the joy that the flowers brought into the house.

Finally, Elsa felt it was time to go and stood up, curtsied, and offered her hand to Grandma Engström.

The next Sunday she went upstairs again and was once more offered coffee.

"Can Elsa read?" Grandma Engström asked when they had finished.

Elsa nodded.

"Could Elsa read to me from the Bible? I used to always read from it when I was no longer able to go to church on Sunday, but now my eyesight is so poor that I can't see those tiny words."

Elsa was at a loss. Had *Farmor* forgotten that she couldn't speak? She felt sorry for her sitting there all alone and not even being able to read. Slowly she pulled the Bible toward her and opened it at random. The pages separated at the twenty-third psalm. Elsa knew it by heart.

"T-t-the L-lord is my shepherd," she began, then took a deep breath and continued, "I shall not want. He maketh me to lie down in green pastures: he leadeth me beside still waters..."

She could hear her own voice filling the tiny room, and although the words were not hers, they came strong and clear, without hesitation, as though someone else were saying them. She finished the psalm.

"Thank you, my dear. That was beautiful!" *Farmor* exclaimed.

Although she was able to read to *Farmor* from the Bible, she still was unable to express her own thoughts aloud. But she quickly grew fond of the old woman and began reading to her every afternoon. In time she became able to continue speaking after she had finished reading, and eventually she no longer needed the Bible as a crutch.

The Engströms were poor and humble, and the few pennies they got for taking Elsa in meant a lot to them. Somehow she sensed this and did her best to be of help rather than an extra burden. She was truly grateful to them. That winter she didn't freeze, she had boots that didn't hurt her feet, and she got to sleep in a bed rather than on the floor. And go to school. Aunt Sofia treated her as Augusta had treated Helga, like a relative. Unfortunately, neither of the girls were her age, so they didn't play together, but they didn't treat her with disdain as the Nyqvist girls had. Anna was fourteen and was going to begin studying for her confirmation as soon as the school year ended. After that, she would leave home and enter the world as an adult. Dora was only seven and no fun to play with. The two boys were in the middle. Erik was twelve and Walter had just turned ten. They were inseparable and had no time for girls, but they treated her as they treated their sisters.

The first day Elsa went to school, a gang of children gathered around her and began chanting "parish urchin, parish urchin." Suddenly Erik burst into their midst.

"Leave her alone!" he shouted. "She's our cousin, and I'll beat up anyone who teases her!"

The children scattered, for everyone looked up to Erik, who was the oldest in the school. No one teased her again.

As summer approached, Aunt Sofia and other female relatives began to prepare for the move up to the family's *fäbod,* or summer pasture, with all the animals, as peasants had done since the Middle Ages. Elsa had never been to a *fäbod,* but she had heard women and older girls talk about how they loved the long summer days spent there, away from the needs and demands of their homes and menfolk. Even though the work was hard, the atmosphere was much more relaxed than that of village life. It was a time of freedom and, for many, the high point of the year. Elsa-Carolina was captured by their excitement.

Finally one morning, several weeks before the summer solstice, Aunt Sofia woke Elsa and the others earlier than usual. The sun was just above the treetops, which meant that it couldn't be later than 3. Elsa sat up and rubbed her still-sleepy eyes.

"Everyone up!" Sofia cried, clapping her hands. "We have a long walk ahead of us today."

There was much commotion outside. A group of relatives and neighbors had gathered. Horses whinnied impatiently while Uncle Magnus and the other men shouted instructions to each other. The children dressed quickly and began to carry out the many things that needed to be transported to the *fäbod,* where all the women and children would spend the summer making cheese and other milk products, while the animals grazed freely in the forest.

She watched as the horses were fitted with saddle-like wooden frames from which were hung baskets, containers made from strips of birch bark, and coarsely woven sacks. These were filled with food, bedding, and clothes, as well as the copper pots and pans and iron cauldrons used for cheese-making. There were also wooden pails, separating troughs, butter churns, cheese forms, and bowls of all sizes. When the horses were loaded, Aunt Sofia helped Elsa strap a small birch bark container on her back. Inside were her few clothes, a Bible, her knitting, her wooden porridge bowl and spoon, a number of wooden cooking spoons, and some medicinal herbs. Lastly, she was given a wooden hay rake that also could be used as a walking stick in rough terrain.

Once everything was loaded, Flora, the lead cow, was brought from the barn. While everyone watched, her bell was ceremoniously removed and a larger one, with wildflowers and yarn tassels twisted into its rope collar, was tied around her neck. Flora had been the bell cow for many summers, and Elsa could see that she was aware of her status. Her bell, which could be heard far across the hills, was the others cows' lifeline in the forest. Finally, the rest of the animals were let out, and Flora set out proudly along the path with a trail of cows, sheep, and goats behind her.

Not only was the path up to the *fäbod* long, but it was also steep and rough. Parts of it were strewn with rocks and roots, while other stretches crossed great marshy areas, where they had to make their way carefully over slippery log causeways. None of the animals would willingly step onto the half-rotten logs, even though the men pulled on their lead ropes and the boys went behind, swatting them with birch-branch whips. And for Elsa, walking barefoot across the slimy logs brought back memories of the previous summer's shepherding, which had culminated in being beaten for a dead sheep. She prayed they would send one of the other children out to shepherd. She would gladly do any other task instead.

Late in the afternoon, just when Elsa was sure she couldn't take another step, the path suddenly emerged from the forest onto the crest of the hill. In a clearing ahead stood a cluster of old unpainted log buildings that had nearly weathered into the landscape. In the valley far below, the dense forest sheltered several deep blue lakes. But what held Elsa's fascination was the horizon formed by the dark line of hills in the distance. Slowly she turned around. She could see the horizon in every direction. Never had she imagined the world was so huge! She stood gazing in awe at the horizon, wondering what lay beyond it, while the others made their way past her to the buildings.

"Come along, now," Aunt Sofia called cheerfully. "Elsa will have plenty of time to gaze at the horizon this summer."

Elsa turned around one more time, then followed the others.

Aunt Sofia stopped in front of the main cottage and called the children to her.

"One thing we must all remember," she told them, "is that this *fäbod* does not only belong to us. When we are not here, it is used by the small folk, the invisible ones. We must be respectful and remain on friendly terms with them. Otherwise, they will do all sorts of things for revenge. They can cause animals to get sick or disappear, or even die, and they can lead children into their caves and keep them there forever. So whenever anyone is going to do something such as throw out hot water onto the ground, one must always call out a warning to them first, so they can get out of the way. If we watch out for them, they will watch out for us. They have been known to wake people in the middle of the night when a cow is about to calf, or in the morning if one has overslept. As long as one is considerate of them, they will also be considerate.

"So what I want all the children to do now is to go to each building, open the door, and say, 'Hello. May we borrow this house for the summer?' Perhaps they have already moved out, but it's good to be on the safe side, since we can't see them. And another thing: they do not like to be made fun of. Remember, one may need their help one day."

While the children went from one building to the next, the men unloaded the horses, and the women settled the animals in the barn and did the milking. When Aunt Sofia came in for supper, she brought the lead cow's bell with her and set it on the mantel.

After they had eaten, she took out the lovage plant and some of the other herbs Elsa had carried in her back pack. First, she grated the lovage root, then blended in the other herbs and some flour, and lastly, some groats. Next, she took down the cow bell and filled it with some of the mixture and, taking a sharp knife, stirred it in such a way that bits of metal were scraped into it from the inside of the bell. She repeated the process over and over until she had used all of the mixture.

"For the next three days," Aunt Sofia instructed, "we shall give each of the cows a pinch of this mixture morning and evening so that they will recognize the sound of the lead cow's bell, and also so that they will be able to find their way back to the barn on their own in the evening. If a cow doesn't return after having eaten this, it is a sure sign that the invisible people have taken her. They have even been known to take over the barn on occasion. Such a situation calls for more drastic measures to be taken. But we needn't worry about that now."

She set aside the bowl with the bell-scraping mixture and got to her feet.

"And now it's time for bed. It's been a long hard day, and we have much to do tomorrow. Elsa can sleep out in the cookhouse with the other children. She and Dora can share one bed, Erik and Walter another, and Anna and Cousin Emma the third. Cousin Sara can have the other bed for herself since she is the oldest."

The cookhouse was a low building with a door at one end, no windows, and a dirt floor. In the center of the floor, a circle of large stones formed a fireplace, over which a black cauldron hung on a chain from a rafter. Above it was an opening in the roof which let the smoke escape. Along both long walls were simple built-in box beds filled with straw. That was all. To Elsa, it felt almost like sleeping outdoors and she was glad she was not alone there. Most of all, she wondered if the small folk were living in the cookhouse with them. Up until then they had always frightened her, for everyone talked about how evil they were. Aunt Sofia was the first person she had ever heard say that they could also be helpful and that one should be considerate of them. Think if that were really so. But before she could consider it further, she fell into a deep dreamless sleep.

The next morning it was the birds, rather than Aunt Sofia, who woke her, their songs lifting her from the depths of sleep. When she stepped outside the cookhouse door, the sun shone and the air was thick with the scent of pine sap and tiny new dwarf birch leaves. Aunt Sofia was on her way to the milkhouse with two pails of fresh milk to be cooled. Much to her relief, Elsa saw Erik and Walter driving the cows along the path towards the forest with the sheep and goats following behind.

After breakfast, Anna and Dora went to help their aunts and cousins, whom they hadn't seen all winter.

"Come with me," Aunt Sofia said. "I need some help cleaning up in the main cottage. The men use it in the winter when they come up to get the hay we have gathered during the summer. It is much easier to take it home when there is snow and they can use the big sled. But they are quite blind when it comes to housekeeping—not to mention all the dust and mouse droppings that accumulate during the winter. And I suspect that the little people have a hand in it, too."

They spent the morning sweeping and dusting and scrubbing. Aunt Sofia whitewashed the hood over the open fireplace while Elsa painted the edge of the raised hearth. While it was drying, they polished the lids to the copper cooking pots and stood them on their edges along the mantel, leaning against the hood. Next, they filled several mattress bags with straw and piled them on the single bed in the corner of the cottage. After that they took out the new linen sheets Aunt Sofia had woven during the winter. To Elsa it had seemed like an endless job, passing the shuttle back and forth between hundreds and hundreds of warp threads. When Sofia had completed four lengths, as well as a bit for a pillow case, she had shown Elsa how to sew them together with tiny stitches to make two wide sheets. As a finishing touch, *Farmor* had made a strip of lace that was sewed across the top before the folded edges were sewed on. Then the sheets had been laid out in the sun to bleach. And now they were spread on top of the straw-filled mattress bags. Lastly, they spread a quilt over the bed, folding the edge of the top sheet over it a good bit to show off the lace.

"Who sleeps in this bed?" Elsa asked.

"No one, unless we have a very special guest. In fact, no one is even allowed to sit on it."

"Why not?"

"I don't really know. It's just a part of *fäbod* life. Not only at our *fäbod*, but everywhere. Every woman puts her newest and best sheets on the bed so that everyone who comes in can appreciate what a good weaver and housekeeper she is. It's like the mound of butter on the Christmas table that no one is allowed to eat. It is just to show others how well-off a household is."

Elsa looked around the room curiously, wondering where the other women slept.

"We sleep together in the *utdragssoffor*, just like at home," Aunt Sofia said. "So none of us gets spoiled."

Next, they unpacked the dish towels. Elsa saw that the two on the top of the pile were the new ones that Aunt Sofia had also woven that winter and on which she had embroidered her initials. She handed them to Elsa.

—133

"Elsa can hang these up on the towel rack there," she instructed. "As with the bed, these are only for decoration and not to be used. We use older towels, which go on the rack with the little curtain over it to hide them from sight."

So it was that social pressure even pressed its way into the freedom of *fäbod* life. Failure to conform could have a price, for people were always in need of scapegoats for their bad luck, whereupon they turned to someone who was not like everyone else.

The main task of *fäbod* life was to preserve the milk from a dozen or more cows and goats in the form of hard cheese, soft whey cheese, butter, and *långmjölk. Långmjölk* was easiest to make. A bacteria was added to the raw milk to cause it to thicken and to keep it fresher longer. Then it was poured into low bowls and simply left in a warm place for several days until it had become firm.

Hard cheese was made by using rennet made from the stomach of a newborn calf whose only nourishment had been its mother's milk. The stomach was dried and salted, then cut into pieces and stored in salt water. Once the rennet had caused the warmed milk to curdle, the curds were put into a cloth bag and the whey was squeezed out. Then salt and caraway were kneaded into the curd-mass before it was wrapped in a cloth and pressed into a cheese mold.

There were two kinds of molds. One was a basket woven from roots with a hole in the bottom, and the other was a small wooden box whose sides were held together with pegs so it could be taken apart to remove the cheese. The bottom usually had a carved design, with holes for the whey to run out. This latter type was often made by a young man as a gift for his fiancée, with their initials and the date carved on it.

The worst job was making cheese out of the whey that was left over. The thin whey had to be stirred constantly in a huge cauldron over the open fire until it was very thick. Standing in the heat of the fire for hours on end, stirring and stirring, was pure torture. And of course, that job went to one of the children. But their discomfort was forgotten when they were given a bit of the brown cheese with their supper.

The majority of milk products was preserved in some way and taken home at the end of the summer. The butter was sold, since money was almost impossible to come by, but most of the other products were kept and eaten during the winter.

Fäbod life was by no means all work, however. The women and girls worked hard and long, but there were many of them—aunts and cousins and neighbors. They laughed and joked together as they worked, in the way that women can do only when there are no men around, and which made the hardest tasks seem easy. And then there were the weekends.

One evening the week before Midsummer, Aunt Sofia's sister's daughter, Sara, the oldest of the housemaids, took the *fäbod's* three-foot-long horn made of rolled-up birch bark and went out to the edge of the hill. Lifting it to her lips, she blew a series of crystal-clear tones that echoed out across the valley. Soon after they faded, away similar horn messages could be heard answering from *fäbodar* in the distance. After a few exchanges, she returned to the group of women in the cookhouse.

"Everyone has accepted our invitation to the Midsummer fest," she announced.

During the days that followed, other activities became interspersed with the daily tasks. All the copper pots and pans were scoured until they shone like gold in the sunlight, wooden floors were scrubbed thoroughly, and earthen floors in the outbuildings were swept with twig brooms until they were almost as hard as stone. Finally, fresh leaves were strewn over all the floors, and on Friday morning, wildflowers were picked and stuck in the cracks between the wall timbers. Long tables, consisting of boards laid across sawhorses, were set up outdoors, and a tall tree was cut for a Midsummer pole.

Early Friday afternoon, people began to arrive from the surrounding *fäbodar*. Everyone was dressed in their Sunday best and the women all carried baskets filled with Midsummer food and their best coffee cups. From the farms in the valleys came the menfolk, both farmers and farmhands. Only the old people were left behind to look after things at home, the long walk being too hard on their tired legs.

The air was summer-warm with only the slightest breeze under a clear blue sky. Everyone was in the best of spirits, some of the men already staggering a little. But after all, it was Midsummer, and only the few who were deeply religious turned their backs on alcohol. Once everyone had finished their coffee (the men having laced theirs with *brännvin)*, contests of strength began: tug-of-war, weight lifting, wrestling, and stone casting. As was to be expected, the latter quickly degenerated into a serious fight between two drunken farmhands who disagreed about which of them had cast his stone the farthest.

In the meantime, the others managed to raise the Midsummer pole. An old man strapped on his accordion, and people of all ages joined hands and danced to the age-old melodies filling the air. Elsa watched them from a distance, longing to join in but afraid to intrude. Even though she felt accepted by the Engström family, she was unsure where she stood with the others. She was still a parish urchin, whose place was even below that of a housemaid.

"Come on! Everyone has to dance on Midsummer's Eve!" a voice called out and someone grabbed her by the hand, pulling her into the whirling circle.

It was Erik. He swung her around in time with the music, his free hand resting gently on her back. Elsa's face grew hot. It was only Erik, but she felt something she had never experienced before. Suddenly she felt shy before him.

The music stopped.

"Thanks," he said simply. He dropped her hand, bowed before her, and disappeared into the crowd.

Elsa stood where he had left her, staring at the ground.

Later that evening, even though she was only twelve, she followed the other girls when they went to pick their nine different wildflowers to put under their pillows. Fleetingly she wondered if she would dream about Erik, but pushed the thought away.

The next morning she awoke feeling more lighthearted than she could ever remember having felt. But she couldn't recall having dreamt at all—or perhaps the previous night had been nothing but a dream.

Just after Midsummer, Flora, the lead cow, got sick. Aunt Sofia was known for her herbal cures, but no matter what she tried, Flora just continued to get sicker. Finally she could no longer walk and had to be left in the barn all day. One evening, Elsa was sent out to the barn with a bunch of herbs and grasses to give the poor creature. As she pulled the barn door open, she sensed that there was someone inside. As her eyes gradually adjusted to the darkness in the windowless room, she could barely make out a little man standing beside the cow. Coming closer, she saw that he was angry.

"This animal has been pissing and shitting on our home all summer! If you don't move her, she is going to die!" he declared.

Petrified, Elsa dropped the herbs and ran screaming from the barn.

"A-A-Aunt Sofia!" she cried breathlessly.

Sofia dropped what she was doing and looked up.

"What ever is the matter, Child?"

"A-A man i-is g-g-going to k-kill Flora," she stammered.

"What kind of a man?" Sofia wanted to know.

"A l-l-little man. H-h-he says F-Flora is p-p-pissing an' sh-shitting on his h-home an' that wwe have to m-move her."

"So that's why she isn't getting better," she said with a sigh of relief.

"W-what does Aunt Sofia mean?"

"It's the small folk. They must live under the floor in the barn. You wait and see. Come. Let's go and move Flora."

Together they went out to the barn. The little man was nowhere in sight. They pulled Flora to her feet and coaxed her to the other side of the room, then cleaned the floor where she had been standing, covering it with fresh grass afterwards.

The next morning, Flora was standing up pulling at her rope, anxious to go outside.

Coming of Age

Elsa-Carolina loved the Engström family. No one had been so kind to her since her mother had disappeared. But nothing ever stayed the same for long. Especially not happiness. Or at least so it seemed to her as a child. Misery always seemed to be endless, whereas happiness was fleeting.

At the beginning of September, the women packed all the equipment they had hauled up to the *fäbod* a few months earlier, together with the various cheeses they had produced, the stockings they had knitted in their spare time, and the cherished memories of the comradeship they had shared during those soft summer days. An air of melancholy hung over them as they started down the long path leading to the village. No one spoke. For Elsa, it had been the most wonderful summer she had ever experienced.

The Wednesday after they returned, the autumn animal market was held in the nearby town. Uncle Magnus, as Elsa had learned to call Herr Engström, left early that morning to look for a new plow horse. He never returned. Late the same afternoon, the town constable rode up to the farm, inquiring after Magnus Engström's wife.

"There has been an accident at the market today," he told her, not caring that the children were standing about. "Fru Engström's husband was bent over examining the back hoof of a horse he was thinking of buying. Suddenly something scared the animal and it jerked its foot out of his grip and kicked backwards, catching him in the head. I'm sorry to have to tell Fru Engström that he died almost instantly."

"Wh-wh-what is the constable saying?" Aunt Sofia gasped. "Is Engström dead? My Engström?"

"I'm afraid so," the constable replied, holding a small leather pouch out to her. "Here is his purse and his wedding ring."

She took them mechanically, glancing unbelievably inside the ring where Magnus's and her initials were engraved side by side. Then her fingers closed around it and she turned away. The children stood around her, stunned.

"I guess I had better go up and tell *Farmor,*" she mumbled at last.

From that day onward, *Farmor* refused to eat or let anyone into her room. Magnus was the only one of her six children who had lived into adulthood and he was her world. A week later, overcome by her grief, she died in her sleep.

Elsa felt the loss of Uncle Magnus as though he had been her own father. Since Sofia had no way to pay the yearly rent for the farm, much less work it, she was cast out by the landowner. The rich had no mercy when dealing with the less fortunate. In fact, they could be unnaturally cruel. Anna was sent out to find a job as a housemaid, Walter became a farmhand, and Erik was sent to relatives who agreed to let him work for his keep. Aunt Sofia took little Dora with her to Stockholm to look for work. And because Elsa wasn't a member of their family, the parish elders sent her to the poorhouse.

Life in the poorhouse was far beyond the worst imaginable. Not only did it house the poor, but also people who were crazy, senile, or mentally retarded, as well as orphans and people with long-term illnesses.

Everyone shared the same room. The building itself was an old dilapidated timber cottage. The rough boards that covered the floor lay directly on the ground, causing it to be both cold and damp. None of its three small windows fit tightly in their frames, creating a constant draft both winter and summer.

Of the two rooms, the smaller was a kitchen, with an open fireplace on a raised hearth, and the larger one contained a dozen or so wooden beds with straw-filled sacks for mattresses. What heat there was came from a small hearth on the back wall.

There was no order to how people slept. The men and women were intermingled, and any woman with children shared her bed with them. Should a husband and wife land in the poorhouse together, they, too, had to share a bed, unless there happened to be an extra one empty. On the door was posted a notice with the house rules: No swearing or foul language was allowed, no one was to leave the premises without permission from the matron, no *brännvin* or other alcoholic drinks were allowed, everyone must attend the weekly prayer meetings, and the inmates must respect and obey the person in charge and carry out the duties assigned them.

Elsa was welcomed by the matron in charge and assigned the bed nearest the door. A sack for the mattress straw lay folded on top of it.

"She will have to go to one of the nearby farms and beg for some straw," the matron told her when she noticed Elsa eying the empty bag. "The old man who had this bed died two days ago. During his last weeks he made a thorough mess of both his mattress and the bed."

She then began counting out Elsa's quarterly allowance of parish-supplied food: twelve quarts of oats, eight of barley, and four of rye, as well as a few coins. Having done this, she immediately began taking back small portions of the grain.

"Everyone received their quarterly rations last week. Since Elsa was not here then, she doesn't need that week's ration," Matron explained. "With the money she can buy what other food that she wants from nearby farms, such as potatoes and herring. Elsa must keep her food locked in the chest assigned to her," she continued. "And see to it that she rations it out so that it lasts, because there won't be more for three more months. When it's gone, one must go out and beg from the farmers. And I can say ahead of time that they usually turn a deaf ear to poorhouse beggars. They feel they have already done their duty by supplying the amount of food required by the parish. They don't like giving free hand-outs."

Elsa looked around, wondering what she should do with so much grain. The matron saw her bewilderment.

"Tomorrow Elsa must take the grain to the mill down the road and have it ground to flour. Everyone cooks their own food here. Most people mix their grains together and make porridge or bread. Stor-Alfred's Agda, who lies next to Elsa, is too old and sick to get out of bed anymore. I'm sure that if Elsa offers to cook her porridge for her, she will gladly lend out her cooking pan. She needs someone to take care of her."

By the end of the week, Elsa was not only cooking Stor-Alfred's Agda's porridge, but she was also feeding the old woman, and then changing the rags that passed for diapers.

Agda had been a woman of means until her husband died, leaving enormous debts. Because she had no children to take her in, she had had no choice but to sell everything they had owned to pay his debts and then move into the poorhouse. As the years went by, she had become more and more bitter, while at the same time ordering others about as though they were her servants. None of the other women felt like catering to her and only did so when forced. Elsa's arrival freed them. Now there was a child in the poorhouse to do the tasks that no one else wanted to do. Soon Elsa was everyone's slave.

The only reprieve from the stench of the poorhouse and the demands of its inhabitants was the few hours Elsa spent in school every day that winter. She had several *fjärdingsvägar* to walk in the morning darkness, with only her two shawls over her sweater and a pair of welfare-issue wooden shoes on her feet, since those Sofia had given her had been stolen when the family was evicted. Such shoes were recognizable everywhere and caused taunts from the other children, without keeping her feet the least bit warm.

On her way home one cold afternoon, a horse and sled came up behind her on the double track that passed for a road. Elsa stepped off onto the side to let it pass, but instead, it stopped.

"Does the lassie want a ride home?" the driver asked. "I'm passing the poorhouse, so she might as well hop up and follow along."

T-t-t-thank you, S-S-Sir," she said. She took his outstretched hand and he drew her up onto the driver's seat. Behind them, an old woman was bedded down in the straw-filled sled. Seeing Elsa look at her curiously, he hastened to explain.

"That's One-Eyed Sigrid. She's one of those rotating folks." He paused when he saw that Elsa didn't understand. "Some poor people end up in the poorhouse and others rotate. Those who rotate move from farm to farm. Sometimes they only stay in a place a couple a days, sometimes a week. It depends on how well-to-do the farm is. It's the duty of the people they stay with to take care of them, give them food and a place to sleep. But I can tell, Missy, the farmers don't like being forced to take them in. No one goes out a their way to be nice to those poor folks. They're treated worse than animals. Some places they have to sleep in the barn or a shed, even in the winter, and only get scraps and leftovers to eat. The slops farmers give to their pigs are better than what they give to rotating folk. It's often up to me to drive them between farms when it's time for them to move. Old One-Eyed Sigrid here is sick with a fever. But it was time for her to move to the next farm, so they packed her up and told me where to take her. Nobody keeps a rotator longer than they have to, especially if they're sick. I hope old Sigrid doesn't pass away in the wagon from the cold."

Elsa glanced back at Sigrid. Her one eye stared up at the sky and her toothless mouth formed a cavern in her wrinkled face. Suddenly it struck her that this old woman must have one day been a young girl like herself. Was this how she, too, was going to end her days—being moved from farm to farm, alone, with no one who cared about her? She turned back around and concentrated on the track ahead of them.

That evening, Stor-Alfred's Agda took her last breath after a hard death-struggle in the darkness. Elsa lay in the next bed, listening to the sounds emitting from the old woman. No one else in the room seemed to pay any attention. They were used to people dying. They were all awaiting the same fate sooner or later. For most of them it would be a relief. But for Elsa, it was something new and horrifying. When she couldn't stand it any longer, she took her blanket and huddled in the far corner of the room, as far from Agda's death rattles as possible. Slowly she rocked back and forth, whispering "Mamma, Mamma," yet knowing that her mother could never find her. Eventually she heard a voice call her name. It was Per's-Hanna.

"Come here, Child," she said. "Bring your blanket and crawl into my bed."

Elsa stood up on shaky legs.

"Spread your blanket on top of mine," Hanna told her. "That way we will both be warmer and Elsa won't be so alone."

She lifted the covers and pulled Elsa underneath, tight against her body. For the first time since coming to the poorhouse, Elsa fell asleep without shivering.

From that night on, they shared the same bed, not only for the physical warmth it offered, but also because of the caring warmth that had grown between them. Hanna, who had long been a widow, had lost her only child to pneumonia when the girl was Elsa's age. Now, due to an injury that made it impossible for her to live alone, Hanna had been forced to move into the poorhouse. Elsa cared for her tenderly, as though she were her own mother. And every day she read aloud to her from the Bible. In return, Hanna helped her prepare for her confirmation the following year.

It was an unusually cold winter that year, and a number of the older people died, either from illness, malnutrition, or the cold. But with each death, someone new arrived to take over the empty bed, as well as the dead person's clothes, for most people came to the poorhouse with only the tattered and patched clothes they had on their backs. Often the women would fight over a skirt or sweater or shawl that death had left behind and with time petty vendettas built up. Those who didn't take part took sides. It was the only form of entertainment available.

The three men living there were all rather taciturn and kept their distance from the women, as well as from each other. Dansband-Harry sat out in the shed and played his fiddle for hours whenever someone died. Svarta-Björn, who had worked in the forest his whole life, took charge of the woodshed, carrying in wood each morning before going out to collect new fall-wood. And lastly there was Skräddare-Emmerik, a tailor by trade, who liked to take long walks, a habit he had developed after spending hours sitting cross-legged on his sewing table. For him, it was degrading to have to ask permission to go for a walk and he refused to do so. Most of all, he liked to return to the forest near his old home, where he knew every tree and rock. But Matron was convinced that he was running away whenever he set out in that direction and she invariably sent someone after him. With time, he became more and more depressed over his lack of freedom. Finally one day he managed to escape when no one saw him. After hours of searching, they finally found him, hanging from the limb of a tree in his beloved forest. Matron called it an accident, claiming that he hadn't known what he was doing, but those who knew him knew he had literally come to the end of his rope. He was buried outside the churchyard wall with the suicides.

Elsa never got used to life in the poorhouse with its stench, the senile jabbering of many of its inmates, the bedridden people who had to be nursed and cleaned up, and the continuous procession of deaths. She especially hated to be sent up to the attic to see after Tok-Siri and Blind-Emma. Blind-Emma sat in bed all day with a washbasin full of water on her lap, rinsing her hands and wiping her blind eyes with a wet rag, soaking both herself and her bed. It was said that as a child, she had been told that she went blind because she was always rubbing her eyes with her dirty hands. Ever since then, she had been obsessed with washing herself. When she ran out of water, she would lean over the side of the bed and thump her cane on the floor until someone came up with more. Tok-Siri was either strapped down in her bed or tied to the wall like a prisoner in a dungeon. Years ago when she had been living downstairs, she suddenly went crazy and attacked another woman with a poker. After that, to protect the others, she was locked in the attic with Döv-Anna, who was too deaf to hear her banging on the door and screaming to be let out. But when Anna died from heart failure after Siri had attacked her, it was decided that she must be restrained day and night. From that day on, she lived in her own private world, beyond human contact, laughing constantly. When she soiled herself, she played in her feces and fought violently when anyone tried to clean her up. The two women seemed oblivious to each other's existence and didn't appear to be bothered by sharing the attic. For Elsa, it was a living nightmare to have to go up to them with food or Emma's water, for Siri was like a mad dog trying to break free from her chains whenever anyone entered the room. Elsa was able to force herself to refill Emma's basin or shovel food into her mouth at mealtimes, but that was the limit of her compassion. As for Siri, she merely slid a bowl across the floor to her and ran downstairs as fast as she could.

The only thing that made life in the poorhouse bearable was the comfort of Hanna's presence. But that was to be short-lived. Toward the end of the winter, an epidemic of diphtheria broke out. Those who showed the slightest signs of fever and sore throat were immediately put into quarantine, Per's-Hanna was among them. When Elsa came back from school one day, Hanna and four of the others were gone, and their beds were standing in the yard airing. The rest of the people had been temporarily moved to the parish hall while the entire building was being smoked to drive out any trace of the illness. Eventually those who were not sick moved back to their old places. Elsa waited for Hanna, but she didn't return with the others. Finally, she sought out Matron and asked where Hanna was.

"She's dead," Matron answered simply.

Elsa looked down at the floor, a lump rising in her throat. As soon as Matron left the room, she sank into a corner, pulling her shawl tightly around herself and her knees up to her chest, and began to rock back and forth slowly.

With the loss of Hanna, Elsa once again stopped speaking and became apathetic like the people around her. She understood Skräddare-Emmerik. What was the point in living? Life was only pain, over and over again.

Eventually the winter solstice passed and the sun began its climb back up into the sky. Every day became lighter and brighter than the one before. The meter-deep snow packed together, crusting over at night, then shrinking as the sun beat down on it during the day. At last March came, and the birds began to sing again. But Elsa didn't even notice.

At that point, every person who had meant anything to her had vanished, one after the other. First her mother and Simon's-Stina disappeared. Then Ebba, followed by Aunt Sofia. Then Hanna took her under her wing like a mother bird, only to disappear forever one day shortly after, leaving her deeply depressed. She probably would have taken Skräddare-Emmerik's way out had not Reverend Holmgren and Brother Axelsson instilled the fear of the eternal flames of hell and damnation in her. Consequently, she was too frightened to risk killing herself. Instead, she withdrew into her shell like a snail and shut out the rest of the world. She simply didn't allow herself to care about anyone.

Most of all, she turned her back on anyone who was nice to her. She had to, in order to avoid letting them become important to her. And because she couldn't speak properly, people left her to herself. She continued to go to school, simply to get away from the demands of the poorhouse, but she didn't learn anything. Her body was there, but not her soul. Sometimes she was punished for not knowing the lesson, but even that didn't touch her. Her life had reached a new low point.

One morning, several weeks after Hanna's death, Elsa woke earlier than usual. Sharp pains stabbed through her stomach, and she could hardly keep from crying out. Strangely, her bed felt wet and her clothes, which she had slept in for the sake of their warmth, were stuck to her legs. She slid her hand cautiously under the blanket to investigate, unable to believe that she had wet the bed. When she held her hand up to the dim light from the window, she saw it was covered in blood. She remembered her mother giving birth, her obvious pain, the blood. Yet she couldn't be having a baby. Her stomach wasn't big like Augusta's had been. Suddenly, she was very frightened. Maybe she was dying. Even if life was hard, she didn't want to die. She pulled the blanket over her head.

"Dear God, I've tried to be good, even though I've failed," she cried silently. "If only I could live a little longer, I would do better. I'm not ready to die."

When Matron came in an hour later, she found Elsa still in bed.

"Get up!" she demanded. "Elsa is going to be late for school."

When she got no response, she jerked the blanket off to find Elsa curled in pain, the bed soaked in blood.

"So that's it," she remarked nonchalantly. "Get out of bed and get going."

Elsa whimpered but didn't move.

"Elsa might as well learn right now that no one cares that a woman has her days. Life goes on as usual. Only the weak and feeble-minded lie around and complain about the pain. Now get up and go to school. The bed will dry."

Elsa did her best to get up, but she could barely stand upright. She looked down at her bloodstained skirt.

"Put her other skirt on over it," Matron told her. "Hurry up now."

Still without an explanation as to what had happened to her, Elsa made her way to school. No one paid the least bit of attention to the blood which seeped through the back of her skirt.

By the time she went to bed that night, the blood on the coarse cloth of the mattress sack had dried, as had the blood on her skirt. She lay awake for a long time, wondering where all the blood was coming from and why. If only Hanna had been there, she could have told her, but now there was no one she could talk to. Her only comfort was the fact that apparently it was normal for girls and women to bleed. But she was to have a few more periods before discovering what function they served.

In those days, no one talked about menstruation, even though a woman could hardly keep her days a secret when everyone could see blood on her clothes. There were no such things as sanitary napkins. In fact, women and girls didn't even wear underwear. When a woman had her period, her blood ran free. It wasn't until the end of the 1800s that women began to knit napkins that could be filled with cotton or some other absorbent material, such as shredded peat or white moss, which they washed rather than threw away. But no one gave a second thought to the blood on a woman's or girl's skirt. And for the most part, women didn't even bother to wash the blood off their legs or bodies. People didn't wash themselves every day, and especially not when there were many people living in the same room and thus no privacy. Also, one had to be very careful when one washed away blood, for if the supernatural beings got hold of it, one fell under their power. They could draw the blood out of a menstruating woman, causing her to become sick or even die.

In general, people were not concerned with hygiene. Everyone wore the same clothes day after day, week after week. They worked in them, often slept in them, spilled things on them, wiped their hands on them. Also, there was no such a thing as toilet paper. People used their fingers or a shirt-tail or the hem of a skirt. No one paid any attention to how things looked or smelled. That was simply how life was, and no one knew anything different. Soap, which had to be made at home, was a luxury, water had to be carried from a well, and hot water heated over the fire. Thus washing only took place on special occasions. Also, to make an effort to keep oneself clean was looked upon as vanity, an attempt to be better than everyone else.

As was the custom, at the age of fourteen, Elsa's school days were over and she began to "read with the priest," as it was called, in preparation for her confirmation. It was decided by those who had power over her life that she should live in the rectory and be employed as a maid while studying. The vicar's wife, who wasn't well, was in need of help, and it was as good a way as any to prepare herself for her future as a housemaid. The thought of living in the rectory was akin to going to heaven. Or so she thought.

It was still dark when Elsa woke up on the morning of the day she had been looking forward to for so long. She could hardly believe she was going to the rectory. Hurriedly she pulled on her skirt, buttoned her blouse over her swelling breasts, and pinned her sweater together in case the buttons should give way. The night before she had made watered-down porridge from the last of her ration of flour, setting it aside in a bowl for breakfast. When she took it down from the shelf, there was a thin layer of ice across the top, and on top of the ice were rat droppings. Her first reaction was one of revulsion, until she realized that it would have been far worse if it hadn't frozen and she had found the rat droppings when she had gotten to the bottom of the bowl. Carefully she removed them with a spoon, then closed her eyes and choked down the watery porridge.

Just as she was about to go out the door, Matron appeared bearing a package wrapped in brown paper.

"Here. Elsa will be needing some other clothes," she said, thrusting it at her.

Tucking the package under her arm, Elsa stepped out into the chilly dawn, closing the poorhouse door behind her for the last time.

The ground was covered with frost. Along the edges of the path the last of the wildflowers waited stiffly for the sun to rise above the treetops and free them. Elsa, too, waited for what warmth the sun would bring. She had five *fjärdingsvägar* to walk on a breakfast of a little cold watery porridge. But she was free of the poorhouse at last.

It was afternoon by the time she could make out a church steeple in the distance. Presently, a large yellow house came into view. By now her feet were red with cold, and Ebba's shawl no longer kept her emaciated body warm. She hurried the last half mile to the church and then along the treelined carriageway leading to the rectory. Timidly, she lifted the knocker on the side door, and let it fall.

"And who is this?" asked the maid who opened the door.

"E-E-Elsa-C-C-Carolina."

"Oh, is she the urchin from the poorhouse?"

Elsa nodded.

"Come in," she said, stepping aside so Elsa could enter the kitchen.

"She just missed afternoon coffee."

Elsa waited for her to offer her something to eat anyway, but soon understood that what was missed was missed. Although she felt sick from hunger, she dared not say anything.

"Reverend Stenbom has been waiting all afternoon," she was told. "Change into something presentable before going in to him."

Elsa laid her package on the table and untied the string. Just as the brown paper fell open, several insects—whether they were lice or fleas she never saw—darted into the folds of Fru Hansson's dress, which had been hanging on a peg in the poorhouse since her death.

"Get those rags out of here!" the maid screamed, wrapping the paper around the bundle quickly before casting the whole thing out into the yard. "How dare she bring such vermin into the rectory! Get outside before she spreads them all over the kitchen!"

She gave Elsa a rough shove out the door.

"Gudrun!" the maid called. "Take that urchin out to the wash house and scrub her from head to toe and then find some clothes for her. She is covered with vermin!"

A woman appeared and, taking her by the arm, led her to the wash house where she was ordered to strip. Taking a stick, she shoved the pile of clothes out the door. Then, without bothering to make a fire and warm the water, she made Elsa stand in a tub and set about scrubbing every inch of her body with a potato brush.

"Wait here," she commanded when she had finished. She tossed an old rag at Elsa. "Here. Dry off."

Presently she returned with some old, but clean, clothes.

"She can wash her own clothes in the lake and present them to me for inspection before bringing them into the house."

Once dressed in hand-me-downs, the maid directed her to the drawing room where Reverend Stenbom awaited her.

"Come in," he said coldly, closing his book in his lap. "I am Nathan Stenbom. I have been waiting all day for Elsa-Carolina to show up." He turned to the maid. "Asta can go now."

Elsa stood before him, eyes downcast, still shivering with cold.

"So Elsa has come to work in the household while she prepares for her confirmation," he continued, letting his eyes glide over her. "I hope she is as willing a worker as she is said to be. She will be paid thirty crowns for the year, but from that sum she will be required to pay for the clothing she has just received, as well as for a pair of shoes and another change of clothes. She will also receive food and a place to sleep, in return for which she will do all that is required of her, without question or complaint. Is that understood?"

Elsa nodded, wondering what would be required of her.

"And she will show respect for her master and mistress, as well as the other maids, at all times."

"Y-y-yes, S-S-Sir," she managed to answer.

"She can go back to the kitchen now. Asta will give her instructions."

He opened his book, and Elsa no longer existed for him.

All things considered, life at the rectory was not at all bad after the past year in the poorhouse. Because Reverend Stenbom was a respected man in the community and ranked among the highest socially, he was obligated to treat his servants decently. Thus Elsa was warm, reasonably well-fed, and slept in an *utdragssoffa* bed in the kitchen along with the other servants. She was also given time off to attend confirmation lessons, which Reverend Stenbom held for the parish's youths, and time to study her *Catechism* in the evenings. Nor were her household duties excessive.

Best of all, in the afternoons she was required to read aloud to the rector's wife, who spent much of the day in bed. Just what was wrong with her, Elsa never discovered. Undefined illnesses were quite common among upper-class women. At first, Elsa had assumed she would have to read to her from the Bible, but she quickly discovered that Fru Stenbom was not at all interested in Bible stories. Instead, Elsa was at liberty to choose whatever books she wished from the rectory library. It was the act of being read aloud to that pleased Fru Stenbom, not what was being read to her.

Although Reverend Stenbom treated Elsa kindly, she was afraid of him. He was a large, tall man with a protruding stomach over which his vest and watch chain stretched. His voice was rather gruff, and he never smiled, being completely without humor.

"Because I have no children of my own, God has sent Elsa-Carolina to me to care for," he told her one evening when they said good-night. He put his arm around her shoulders and pulled her against him briefly. "Elsa can think of me as her father."

"T-t-thank you, Sir," she replied, keeping her eyes downcast. Olov had never put his arm around her. It was a pleasant feeling to know that someone cared about her. Her fear began to dissipate.

The weeks passed. Elsa studied her *Catechism* and became the best in the confirmation class. It was clear to everyone that she was Reverend Stenbom's pet, which both embarrassed her and made her proud.

When spring came, and it was no longer necessary for the servants to sleep in the warmth of the kitchen, Stenbom suggested to Agnes that Elsa be moved to a little room in the attic where she could be alone to study in the evenings. Elsa was overjoyed. Never had she had a room of her own.

"Elsa-Carolina mustn't let it go to her head," Stenbom warned her. "No matter where she sleeps, she is still a servant here and obligated to fulfill her duties, whatever they may be."

"Y-yes, Sir," she answered solemnly.

Asta took her upstairs after dinner and showed her the room. There was an *utdragssoffa,* a table, a chair, and a washstand. White curtains framed the window, turning the view across the surrounding fields into a picture.

"Keep the door locked at night," Asta told her dryly.

After Elsa had moved up to the attic, she sometimes bumped into Reverend Stenbom in the back hall on her way up to bed.

"Goodnight," he said politely. "Sleep well."

"G-g-goodnight, S-Sir," she replied and hurried up the stairs.

Then one night he grabbed her arm, stopping her in the hallway.

"Not so fast, my daughter. Let Father give thee a good-night kiss."

Before she could pull away, he had planted a light kiss on her forehead.

"There, that wasn't so painful, was it?" he said.

"N-n-no, Sir," she answered dutifully.

Several nights later, he was waiting for her at the top of the stairs. This time he put his arms around her and hugged her against his body. She tried to struggle free.

"I'm not going to hurt Elsa," he cooed. "I just thought she would like to show me the room that I was kind enough to arrange for her."

Obediently, she stepped aside and let him enter. He looked around the room, pleased. The bed was made, her clothes hung on pegs, and her Bible was open on the table. Nothing was out of place.

"I can see that Elsa-Carolina is a very tidy person," he remarked. "I like to see that in a woman." With that he bid her goodnight and left.

She sank down into the box-bed with a sigh. How impolite she had been! After all he had done for her, he must think she was just a silly little child.

The next time he met her at the top of the stairs, he simply pushed her into the room, closing the door behind them with his foot. He was no longer the man who had put his arm around her shoulders or had given her a fatherly goodnight kiss on the forehead. He had become hard, almost evil.

"I want to show Elsa something," he told her, catching his breath as though he had been running.

She was too scared to protest. Quickly, he unbuttoned his fly, then grabbed her hand and shoved it into his open pants. When she felt his swollen organ, she jerked her hand away.

"Take it out," he told her hoarsely.

She shook her head.

"Remember, Elsa agreed to do what is required of her, without questioning or complaining. This is something she must learn. It's part of growing up."

He tipped her back into the bed and ran his hands up under her blouse, pinching her tender nipples.

"N-no!" she cried, trying to push him away.

"Yes! Hush now. We don't want the others to hear, do we?"

Quickly, he pulled her skirt up, separated her legs with his knee, and forced himself into her. Her mouth opened in a scream at the sudden and intense pain, but before the sound could rise from within her, he had covered it with his hand.

"Hush, I said!" He jammed himself into her over and over, smashing her head against the end of the bed, while she tried to push him off. Then suddenly, with a few jerks, he was finished. She struggled out from under him.

"L-L-Leave m-m-me alone," she cried.

"She'll get used to it," he told her.

"N-No!"

"It's a woman's lot in life. It is God's intention that it should be so. That is the role He has given women."

She shook her head.

"Elsa has a good life here," he told her, "certainly better than any-where else she has been these past years. She wouldn't like to go back to the poorhouse, would she? One must do what is required of one and show gratitude by repaying kindnesses. Isn't that so?"

She couldn't argue with him. He was the priest, and one was obliged to do as he said. Even grown men bowed before him and obeyed. The priest had more power in the village than the king. And she certainly

—151

did not want to go back to the poorhouse.

He got up and stuffed his collapsed member back into his pants.

"Not a word now. This is our little secret. Agreed?"

"I-I-I don't want a b-b-baby," she stammered.

"Do not fear. If God should choose to give thee a child, I promise I shall treat Elsa as if she were my own daughter."

She realized too late that she was ensnared in a trap from which she could not free herself.

After that night, Reverend Stenbom regularly visited Elsa's room once or twice a week before retiring. When he was finished, he always reminded her of how lucky she, a poor orphan, was to be living in such luxury, that her parents would be relieved to know that he was following God's will and preparing her for life. Elsa didn't know what to believe. She was disgusted by what he was doing, sure that it was sinful.

But if she couldn't trust her confirmation priest, who could she trust? Perhaps it was God's will. Who was she to know things like that? Yet even if it were God's will, she still found it disgusting the way Reverend Stenbom huffed and puffed and grunted as he unfeelingly drove himself deep into her body, oblivious to the fact that he was hurting her. It must have been the wrathful Old Testament God who had created women for such a purpose, not the loving God Jesus spoke about.

One morning it was not the singing of the birds outside her window that woke Elsa, but rather sharp pains in her stomach and last night's supper pushing itself up into her throat. She reached the chamber pot just in time, then dressed quickly and crept down the back stairs to empty it. Just as she opened the back door Asta stuck her head out into the hall.

"Elsa is up early today," she noted. "Ush! It smells of vomit out here. Is she sick?"

"No, Ma'am, s-s-something I-I-I ate."

"Humph! I hope Elsa realizes she is playing with fire."

Elsa looked at her questioningly, but Asta withdrew her head and closed the kitchen door with a bang. Elsa held her fear at bay by convincing herself that it was the evening porridge that was causing her to be sick every morning.

Finally, Asta confided in Gudrun.

"Can't Gudrun find out what is the matter with Elsa-Carolina? She is sick every morning, and I suspect the worst. Gudrun saw her naked the day she arrived and can easily determine whether there has been any change in her breasts."

Gudrun agreed to inspect her, waiting until evening to talk to her alone in her room.

"Asta says Elsa is sick every morning," she remarked. "Is that so?"

"It's t-the p-p-porridge…" she began.

"When did she last have her days?" Gudrun interrupted.

Elsa thought for a moment. "At Whitsuntide," she concluded.

"Not since then? That was over four months ago."

Elsa didn't answer. She could feel the blood draining from her face causing her to become light-headed. The fear that she had held pressed down for so long began to make its way to the surface. She steadied herself against the washstand.

"Has she been together with any boys?"

Elsa shook her head. The only boys she knew were the ones who were in her confirmation class, but she had never had anything to do with any of them.

"Let me see Elsa's breasts," Gudrun said. She lifted up her blouse and inspected them carefully. They were certainly fuller than the day she had bathed the girl.

"And now thy belly," she continued, pulling up her skirt and running her hand over its ever so slight roundness.

"Now, tell me what boy has had his thing up between Elsa's legs," she said, her voice becoming a little harder.

Frightened, Elsa shook her head decidedly. "N-n-no one," she said.

"Look at me, Elsa-Carolina. Who?"

Elsa glanced at her and shook her head again. "N-no one," she repeated.

"Have it Elsa's way. Time will bring the truth. Loose girls like Elsa end up crying out the father's name when their labor pains become unbearable during childbirth."

"C-Child b-b-birth?" Elsa repeated.

"Elsa is going to have a baby," Gudrun told her.

"A b-baby?" So it was true. The word had been spoken.

"Yes, a baby. If the Reverend should find out, Elsa will be sent back to the poorhouse. Does Elsa understand?"

Elsa nodded and the conversation came to an end.

Gudrun went straight to Asta and confirmed her suspicions.

"Who do you suppose the father is?" she wondered aloud. "The girl denies that she has been together with anyone."

Asta shrugged her shoulders. "They always do. It's a shame. She's a nice girl. Hopefully, she will be able to hide her condition as long as she is living here."

For a long time, she was able to hide her condition from Reverend Stenbom, for he simply pulled her skirt up to her hips before ramming into her. Then one evening, he appeared unexpectedly and found her about to pull on her nightgown over her rounded belly.

"And who, may I ask, has given Elsa that belly?" he demanded, grabbing her by the arm. "I thought she was grateful for what she has here. Has she been together with one of the boys in the confirmation class?"

"N-n-no, S-Sir."

"Who, then?"

"'Tis Reverend S-S-Stenbom who has d-d-done it, S-S-Sir."

The flat of his hand stung her face.

"Have some respect, girl!" he shouted. "False accusations can get one into a lot of trouble. Pack up thy belongings and get thee off from here first thing tomorrow! I cannot have such sinfulness contaminating the rectory!"

Elsa stared at him unbelievingly. "R-R-Reverend S-Stenbom promised h-h-he would t-t-take care of m-me as if I were h-h-his own..." Her voice died away. How could she have been so naïve.

The next morning, Elsa came into the kitchen with her few belongings wrapped in her extra skirt. Everything was as usual. Gudrun was washing dishes while Asta scraped leftover scraps from the previous day into a container for the beggar woman who waited on a bench by the door every morning. All three of them stopped talking and looked at her.

"I warned Elsa to hide her condition from Reverend Stenbom," Asta said. "He doesn't tolerate having girls here who are in the family way."

"T-t-tis Reverend S-S-Stenbom who d-did it to me!" Elsa said almost in a whisper.

Asta handed the container to the beggar woman, closing the door after her.

"Keep thy mouth shut. No one ever believes the servant girl. The Reverend will beat Elsa for daring to drag his reputation down into the mud," she told Elsa. "Get thee off before he comes in." She thrust a chunk of dry bread and an envelope into Elsa's hand. "Her wages," she said.

Elsa stuffed the envelope into her pocket and walked out the door without saying goodbye. The beggar woman was already on her way down the road.

The weather was mild for September. A few birch leaves had turned yellow and fallen, but most of them were still clinging to their branches in hope of an Indian summer that would offer a reprieve from their fate. For Elsa, there was no reprieve; her fate had been dealt to her and she had no choice but to accept it. She opened the rectory gate and walked though it out into the world. She had no idea where to go. The only thing she knew was that if she turned to the right on the road, she would eventually come back to the poorhouse. Therefore, she turned to the left.

She walked all day, putting one foot in front of the other mechanically. She was in no hurry, for she had no place to go. Now and then, she broke off a bit of bread and chewed it absently. The longer she walked, the more clearly reality appeared before her, like an emerging landscape sharpening as the surrounding fog dissipated. How blind she had been to let herself believe Reverend Stenbom's promise to treat her as his own daughter. She had been easy prey, for she had longed for the kindness he had shown her at first. Of course, she had heard tales of housemaids being seduced or raped by their employers. House fathers, as they were called, had absolute power over everyone in their households—wives, children, maids, and farmhands—and could treat them however they wished, including beating them for misbehavior. But she had assumed that the parish priest was an honorable man. And when it was too late, she had no choice, unless she wanted to return to the poorhouse. Slowly she began to realize that her fate had been sealed from the day she had been sent as a maid at the rectory.

And now here she was, walking aimlessly, with Reverend Stenbom's child in her belly. And she was the one who must bear the blame and shame, stigmatized for the rest of her life, while his life went on as always, with his parishioners bowing to him respectfully in his role as the right hand of God. And each time she would look at the child, she would be forced to remember the pain and humiliation of it being rammed into her.

Later that afternoon, she slumped down on a rock, too exhausted to go on. Now she understood why many girls found their solution in the lake. One way or another, her life was over. Even if a baby was stillborn or died on its own, the girl was automatically accused of having murdered it, a crime punishable by death. And if one did succeed in getting rid of a dead baby, people often maintained that they could hear it crying from its hiding place. Any girl who was suspected of having secretly given birth to a child and then gotten rid of it immediately had her breasts checked for milk. No, the lake was the least painful solution. Presently, she heard women's voices coming along the road. When they came abreast of her, she recognized Ester, Gunhild, and Hilma—mother, daughter, and grandmother—from her home parish. Gunhild was carrying an infant. Elsa looked up and smiled, happy to see familiar faces at last.

"Why if it isn't Augusta's Elsa-Carolina," Ester remarked, her voice icy with disgust. "Look at her! 'Tis true what the old beggar woman told us."

Gunhild spat three times—tvee! tvee! tvee!—to ward off the evil that threatened her child in the presence of an unwed mother.

"Tie up thy hair!" Hilma ordered. "Only untainted maidens are allowed to go with their hair loose. And cover thy head with the whore's cap to warn people that they are in the presence of an evil sinner. If this child gets rickets, we will know who is to blame! Now get off the road!"

"'T'was R-R-Reverend S-S-Stenbom w-who…" Elsa began, but they turned their backs on her.

"What can one expect with a mother like Augusta!" Ester remarked. "First, it's a baron's son who is to blame and now a priest! Such vanity!"

Although Elsa had heard women speak in such a manner about society's outcasts, she had never imagined that she herself would be treated that way by people she had known her whole life. That morning she had hoped to find her way back to her own parish, and the familiar voices had told her that she was going in the right direction. But they also told her that she was likely to be treated worse by her own people than by strangers. The lake called to her more strongly than ever. There were many along the way to chose from. She began walking once again.

After about a *fjärdingsväg*, she came to a small pond surrounded by forest. She made her way to its edge, where she stood for a long time. Evening was coming on. The air was perfectly still, except for a couple of birds calling goodnight to each other across the water. Time was running out. Her bread was gone. It was getting chilly. She was tired, with no place to sleep but a bed of pine needles beneath one of the many evergreens.

She set her bundle of belongings down by a rock and walked toward the pond, intending to keep going until she was in over her head. But her feet refused to carry her into the water. She looked up. On the far side of the lake, a giant harvest moon was climbing up from the forest to have a look at its reflection in the water. A voice from within forbade her to contaminate the holiness of the scene with her selfish desire to destroy herself and her child. She was sure it was God speaking to her. She backed away from the water's edge, half expecting Him to rise like Neptune from its depths. Grabbing her bundle, she ran towards the road, almost bumping into an old woman on her way to fetch water.

"What is the matter, my Child?" she asked.

Elsa burst into tears.

Without having to be told, the old woman understood the situation.

"Come home with me," she said, leading the way.

Elsa followed willingly. Something about the woman seemed vaguely familiar. She limped, one leg being shorter than the other.

The cottage was warm and welcoming, the flickering light from the fire on the hearth dancing on the walls. The woman scraped the leftover porridge from a wooden bowl into a frying pan and set it over the fire. Once it was warm she placed it between them on the edge of the hearth and motioned to Elsa to join her. They ate in silence.

"My name is Maja," the woman said when they had finished eating. "And who may thee be?"

"Elsa-Carolina," Elsa managed to answer without stuttering.

"Augusta's Elsa-Carolina?"

Elsa nodded.

"I knew Augusta. And I was present at Elsa's birth. People call me Halta-Maja (Maja the Cripple). I needn't explain why."

"Oh! Mamma spoke of Halta-Maja when I was little," she replied, remembering how Augusta had told her of the woman's kindness.

"I suppose Elsa is on her way to her godmother," Maja continued.

"Simon's-Stina? Where is she?" Was it true what Maja had just said?

"I met her on the road a couple of days ago, walking home. She is not well, though. Tomorrow, I will explain how to find her cottage from here. But for now, it's time for a good night's sleep."

She limped across the room to the box bed in the corner and fluffed up the straw in the mattress sack.

"We can share the bed. It's warmer that way."

"One last thing," she said once they were settled. "Drowning oneself and one's child is not the solution."

Not only was Elsa free from Reverend Stenbom's frequent visits, but best of all, she was on her way to Stina! It was like coming home. She was no longer alone. She felt like a small child who creeps up into its mother's lap. But unlike her mother, whose moods toward her had been unpredictable, Stina had always been unwavering in her affection. Suddenly the burden of her life was lifted from her shoulders, and she experienced the first flicker of hope since leaving Engström's. She could hardly wait to be on her way when she awoke that morning.

Halta-Maja placed a cold potato and a piece of salted herring in front of Elsa and urged her to eat.

"But what about Maja? Isn't she going to eat?"

"I don't eat breakfast," Maja said simply.

Elsa wasn't sure if she was telling the truth, but she was too hungry to argue. When she had finished, Maja explained how to find Stina's cottage without having to go past Ekefors Manor.

"Be strong and stay away from lakes now," Maja told her when they said goodbye. "And give my greetings to Stina."

Unlike the previous day, Elsa walked along the path quickly now. She could hardly wait to see Simon's-Stina again and also learn what had happened to her mother. For the time being, the past years were forgotten. In her excitement, she even managed to forget her growing belly.

As she came into a clearing in the forest, she saw Stina's cottage hunkering low to the ground, its thatched roof green with moss, just as she remembered it. She pushed the door open without knocking. In the light from the small window she could see Stina lying in her *utdragssoffa* covered with a sheepskin. A few coals glowed on the hearth, without giving off any warmth.

"Is my godmother awake?" she asked, barely above a whisper. The words flowed smoothly, as if she had never stuttered.

"Is it Elsalina?" Stina replied, opening her eyes. "Oh, how I've longed to see my goddaughter once more!"

"Once more?" Elsa repeated. It sounded like a last wish. "Is Stina so ill?"

"I don't rightly know, my Child. Come here and let me look at you."

Elsa sat on the edge of the bed and took Stina's hand. So much had happened to each of them since that terrible day when Augusta was taken away that neither of them knew where to start.

When Elsa saw that Stina had fallen asleep again, she brought in the last of the wood from the shed and managed to blow life into the embers on the hearth. Then she looked around for something to eat. Because Stina had been away for so long—not to mention having returned in the autumn—the meat and herring she had salted five autumns ago had rotted in their barrels, as had the potatoes she had stored in the root cellar. But in a basket on the floor beside the hearth she found a little bag of rye flour, a few potatoes, and some coffee beans, which Stina must have brought home with her. She didn't dare think about the future. Winter was on its way. Stina was old and appeared to be too sick to work, while she herself would have a hard time finding anyone who would employ her with her big belly. In spite of that, she felt a great sense of security just being near her godmother.

When Stina woke up late in the afternoon, Elsa made some porridge from a little of the flour. She helped Stina to sit up and fed her a bit of the warm gruel, then ate what was left. By now the room was warmer and Stina more chipper. She watched as Elsa ground some of the coffee beans and set the three-legged coffee *kaffepetter* in a corner of the fire to boil. Finally she spoke.

"What has happened to my godchild?"

Elsa looked down at her stomach.

"Does Stina mean this?" she replied.

"Yes. Who is the father?"

"I shall explain while we drink our coffee."

And so she told Stina about Reverend Stenbom and her months at the rectory.

"The disgusting swine!" Stina declared when she had finished. "But Elsalina isn't his only victim. He has at least six bastards in his parish that I know of. But there is nothing we can do about it now. Even if one took him to court, there is no chance of winning against him. I know of one girl who tried, and it just made her life more difficult. And it's too late to abort it. We will figure out something."

"I trust my godmother to help me," she said. "But for now, please tell me what happened to my mother."

A pained expression crossed Stina's face momentarily. Then, taking a deep breath, she began.

"Well, she had given birth to a baby girl before I got to Grankullen. If Elsalina remembers, she was crying hysterically when I arrived. The baby had a very large head and no fingers on one hand. She was convinced that God was punishing her for not wanting the child in the first place, not to mention for having kept Elsa's paternity a secret from Olov. It made her crazy. When those two peasant women came—does Elsalina remember them?"

She nodded.

"Well, when they came into the room, they saw the dead baby. After I ushered them out, they must have gone down to the manor and told people we had killed it. Someone must have sent for the constable. He accused Augusta of having murdered the child. And when I came along, they arrested me, too, as an accomplice."

"Did she murder it?" Elsa asked.

"I honestly don't know. But it wouldn't have lived anyway. There was a trial of sorts in Gothenburg, but Augusta was too out of her mind to defend herself and no one believed what I said. In the end, we were both imprisoned. Unfortunately, Augusta was in a very dangerous condition, having been literally yanked out of childbed. She had lost a lot of blood, also, aside from having lost her mind. She only survived a week or two."

The news didn't really shock Elsa. She had long ago felt that her mother was dead, although she couldn't have said how she knew.

"But what about Stina?"

"I was imprisoned for four years, first in a single cell on bread and water, which they hoped would induce me to tell them what they considered to be the truth. When that failed, they finally put me in a large cell with a number of other women and I was sent to work in the spinning mill during the daytime."

"What was that like?" Elsa wondered.

"It sounds nice, but in truth, it was horrible. It was hard to breathe in there because of all the dust. And it was hot and noisy. We had to work fourteen hour shifts, and the food could hardly be called food. Well, Elsalina can see what it has done to me."

"But how did Stina get home from there?"

"Believe it or not, I walked. I was so weak that it took me nearly a month. Actually, I was lucky. Every night people took me in and gave me a bit of food and a place to sleep. Otherwise I would never have made it. But apparently crops have failed everywhere and there is talk of this being the greatest famine yet."

They were silent a few moments, each considering the situation.

"Times are bad, and we are both outcasts now," Stina concluded. "Just as people will turn their backs on Elsalina, so will they turn their backs on me and choose to believe that I was involved in the death of Augusta's child. One finds out very quickly who one's friends are."

The next morning Stina sent Elsa to Björkelund, a tiny farm in an out-of-the-way corner of the parish.

"Tell Aunt Elna that I have returned and ask if she could come to visit me as soon as she has time. Try to hide thy stomach, if possible. If she asks questions, just say that I shall explain everything. She is the one person I know whom I can trust completely. I have delivered all nine of her children and we got to know each other quite well in the process."

Aunt Elna welcomed Elsa.

"So this is Augusta's Elsa-Carolina," she said. "Stina's goddaughter, if I remember correctly. Such a tragedy! Augusta was a fine woman. Don't pay any attention to anyone who says otherwise. And how is Stina?"

"Not well," Elsa said. "She's too weak to get out of bed."

A worried look crossed Elna's face.

"Tell her I shall come this afternoon. By the way, is there anything to eat in the cottage?"

Elsa hesitated to answer.

"Never mind what Stina says. She is too proud for her own good. Just tell me the truth. Is there any salted meat or herring?"

Elsa shook her head.

"Potatoes?"

"A kilo perhaps."

"Flour?"

"Enough for thin porridge for a couple of days."

"Anything else?"

"A few coffee beans."

"Is that all?"

Elsa nodded.

Elna lifted down a basket from a hook in the ceiling and disappeared into the pantry. When she returned there was a dried hole bread, a piece of salted American bacon, a bottle with blue milk, and some dried apple rings lying in the bottom. She handed it to Elsa.

"Soak the apples in a bit of warm water for a while and then put them in the porridge," she instructed. "I will come along very soon."

When Elna came that afternoon, Stina explained the situation to her.

"As Elna must have noticed, Elsalina has had the misfortune to have been raped by Reverend Stenbom while working as a maid in the rectory. When he discovered she was pregnant and demanded to know who the father was, she told him the truth—that it was he—and of

—161

course he threw her out. He would have thrown her out anyway, even if she hadn't accused him."

"He has a goodly number of bastard children in his parish," Elna remarked. "Either he feels that no one would openly accuse him of rape or blackmail because of his position or else he is confident that he could win any court case against him for the same reason. One way or another, a girl of fifteen hasn't a chance against him, not even from the first minute he lays a hand on her."

"He's not the only old billy goat within the priesthood," Stina added. "And it is disgusting the way people side with them. Do they honestly believe that, in God's eyes, a priest can do whatever he wishes? It makes me ill to have to sit in church and listen to them pretend to be so holy!"

Eventually their conversation turned to the present problems.

"As Elna can see," Stina began, but Elna interrupted her.

"Obviously, Stina cannot stay here over the winter," she began. "She has no food stored, no wood, nothing. Nor is she capable of working, at least not at the moment. Nor can Elsa-Carolina stay here. There are only two choices, as far as I can see: the poorhouse or Björkelund. And of those two choices, there is only one logical solution. There is the little cottage behind our house, where my husband's parents lived after they sold the farm to us, as Stina must remember. They are both gone now. His mother died just last summer, so everything is still in order there, including wood for the winter. It will be perfect for Stina, and Elsa and they can eat at our table. Elsa can help out as long as she is able. And when her time comes, she will be in good hands."

Stina groped for Elna's hand.

"I am in no position to let my pride rule. I accept Elna's kind offer," she said. Her voice was thick with emotion. Although she had always been stubbornly independent, she knew when she was beaten.

"I shall repay Elna for her kindness once I am strong again," she said. "I can see hard times coming—not just for my goddaughter, but for us all. Elsalina has no one but me now. I never imagined when I promised to take upon myself the responsibilities of a godparent that it would come to this. It is both a sorrow and a joy. It's a pity that Gustav wasn't enough of a Christian to uphold his promise to act as godfather to her when she needed his support."

Of all that was said between the two women that day, one comment stuck in Elsa's mind: "I can see hard times coming…for us all." Such a statement from Stina's mouth was a prophecy to be heeded. She had a reputation for never being wrong.

Once Elna had gone, Stina instructed Elsa to gather some things to take with them: The few clothes she owned, a Bible, some dried herbs, a jar of ointment, swaddling cloths, her sewing basket, and a little wooden box that was standing on the ledge above the hearth.

The next morning, the young farmhand from Björkelund arrived with an old horse-drawn wagon full of straw. While Elsa made a bed with the sheepskins Elna had sent along, the boy went in to get Stina. Ignoring her somewhat weak protests that she could walk out to the wagon on her own, he scooped her up from the bed and carried her out the door. Just as he was about to lay her in the wagon, she looked up into his face.

"And what be thy name?" she asked.

"Tiberius Ersson," he replied.

"I thought as much," Stina said with a little laugh. "I brought Tiberius into the world and now he is carrying me out of my cottage!"

Tiberius laughed. "No disrespect meant, Ma'am," he replied. "But it feels good to repay a service!"

They made Stina as comfortable as possible in the wagon, with sheepskins under, over, and around her. Although the sun shone brightly, it offered no warmth, nor had it managed to burn away the night's frost. Overhead golden birch leaves hung motionless against the clear blue of the autumn sky. The forest was silent, except for the rhythm of the horse's gait on the hard-packed ground and the occasional crunching of the wagon wheels when they passed through ice-covered puddles in the rutted road.

Elna had readied the cottage while Tiberius was gone, filling the mattress bags with fresh straw and making up the *utdragssoffa* beds with clean hand-woven sheets. By the time Stina and Elsa arrived, the fire on the hearth had driven out the worst of the dampness. It was the cleanest, most comfortable place Stina had slept since the day Augusta gave birth to the malformed baby four years previously. After Elna left, Elsalina sat on the edge of the bed holding Stina's arthritis-twisted hand. Neither of them spoke. They were simply glad to have found each other again.

The autumn days shortened quickly into long dark nights with the approach of winter. At the beginning of November, the ground was blanketed by a layer of snow that grew almost daily until it reached the window sills. Every day Elna's husband, Elving, brought in wood for them, but the fire on the raised hearth failed to produce much heat and almost no light. In order to keep as warm as possible, Stina and Elsalina shared the bed closest to the fire. It was during those long days and nights that Stina told her goddaughter all that she knew about Augusta's life, as well as Elsalina's own earliest years.

One evening, Stina asked for the little wooden box which they had brought with them from her cottage. Opening it, she plucked out a small object that shone in the light of the fire.

"Here is the button off your father's uniform that your mother was keeping for you," she said, handing Elsalina a brass button with a military insignia on it. "Do you remember the day the peddler came to the cottage with a message from Erling?"

"I vaguely remember a man with a sack full of exciting things. And I still have the picture of Jesus and the little children that he gave me. But I didn't know anything about the button until you told me the other night."

"Erling was a fine lad. Such a pity that you never got to know him. He was honest and had a heart—two things which were unsuited for his position in life."

She tipped the remaining object into her hand and looked at it briefly.

"And here is the engagement ring he gave your mother, which she wore on her right hand, saying it had been her mother's."

She handed Elsa a plain gold band.

"Had you been older, you could have worn it and passed for a widow where you're not known."

Elsa slipped the ring onto the ring finger of her right hand and regarded it from arm's length.

"How nice to have something that connects my mother and father," she mused.

When the news of Stina's return reached the village, women began showing up in twos and threes to welcome her home. But behind their seemingly friendly visits lay the desire to look down their righteous noses at Augusta's pregnant daughter and cluck to themselves about how they had known all along that no good could come of her. They were careful to only cast disdainful looks at her behind Stina's back, but whenever Elsa went into the village alone, she was openly confronted with derogatory and often hostile comments. Before long, Herr Svartvall, the parish *sexman*, whose job it was to see to it that people's morals were kept in line, called her to the parish house.

"Why has Elsa-Carolina not been to church since her return to the parish?" he wanted to know.

She looked down at her feet, not knowing what to answer. If she told him the truth, that she could not worship a god who let her be punished for what his so-called servant had done to her, it would only make the situation worse. Thus she said nothing.

"Elsa-Carolina has brought shame on the entire parish by her behavior," he told her harshly. "It would have been better if she had not come back. But since she is here now, she will act according to the customs of this parish."

He tossed a frayed brown whore's cap at her. "From now on, she will wear this cap to warn others of the danger of her presence, for no mother wants her child, born or unborn, to come in contact with an unwed mother and risk getting rickets. And it shall also serve to remind her of her sins. And she is to appear in church every Sunday, seated in the last pew, which is reserved for people like her. She will note that there is no one else sitting there. The other members of this parish are righteous and God-fearing."

Without another word, he turned his back on her and left the room.

His present of the whore's cap didn't surprise her. She was well aware of the fact that unwed mothers must wear such headgear. What surprised her was that she hadn't been forced to do so long before that. But she couldn't face having to go to church.

Rather than bother Stina by asking her advice, she went to Elna.

"To be honest," Elna told her, "I think it would be easier for Elsa to simply go to church. Augusta fought the church, but I don't think she felt any better by doing so. Elsa already has enough against her without that. Let her body be present, as required. No one has to know that her thoughts are elsewhere. We can all go together."

On Sunday, Elsa walked to church with Elna and her family. But when she started to follow them down the aisle to their pew, she was stopped by Herr Svartvall.

"Elsa-Carolina shall sit in the last pew," he reminded her, taking her by the arm and steering her back down the aisle.

Sitting there alone, her thoughts wandered back to the summer at

Engström's *fäbod*. How she missed Aunt Sofia! So many times she had wondered what had happened to her. How could God be so cruel to someone like Sofia, while letting people like Reverend Stenbom and Reverend Holmgren act as His holy servants? It made no sense. And all the while behind her thoughts Holmgren's voice raved on about the wages of sin. By the time the service ended, Elsa was finished with God.

She hurried out to wait for Elna, who had been cornered by a couple of the older women. As usual, people stood around outside in front of the church gossiping. No one spoke to her, neither the married women nor the girls her own age with whom she had grown up. Instead, she could hear their disparaging remarks whispered loudly from behind half-shielding hands, accompanied by disapproving sidelong glances. The small children who were present were held tightly by the hand to prevent them from getting close to her for fear she would infect them with some illness. She felt as though she were being stoned by an angry crowd. Without waiting for Elna, she hurried across the churchyard and out through the gate to the road.

Although she reluctantly wore the whore's cap when she had to go out where she might meet people, she avoided going to church as much as possible, claiming she was ill.

That winter proved to be much harder than either Stina or Elsalina had expected. They had, each in her own way, been isolated from the events that had taken place in the countryside since the previous spring—Stina in her prison cell and Elsa in the prison of wealth at the rectory. Outside each of those prisons, unbeknownst to them, raged the Great Famine.

Famines had come and gone throughout Swedish history, but the latter half of the 1860s had contained a string of unusually poor harvests, culminating in the worst famine ever. The summer had been unusually hot and dry. For the farmers, who were completely dependent on the weather, rain was the only means of watering their fields. Most crops had sprouted during the spring, but failed to grow in the dry, hard-packed earth. Then when harvest time came, the sky opened up and dumped torrents of rain on the earth day after day, destroying what little had managed to survive the summer drought. But in the rectory, people had hardly been aware of the situation, for Reverend Stenbom had made sure that each of his parishioners came with the tenth of their income and the portion of their harvest that was due him. There had always been plenty of food on his table and in his pantry.

Realizing what was coming, Elna had gathered and stored everything that nature had to offer. But even the blueberries and lingonberries were scarce, having been victimized by the weather along with everything else. She had gathered and prepared bark for bark flour, as well as various lichens and crabgrass. Like bark, crabgrass had to be prepared before it could be used: rinsed, dried, chopped, re-dried, and then ground and mixed with a little flour. And during the summer months she had made hard cheese out of the little milk their cow gave. By autumn, she had done everything possible to be prepared for the coming winter.

As the winter progressed, the already depleted parish storehouses were quickly emptied by the needy. Soon a stream of beggars began to appear on Elna's doorstep—small groups of barefoot children dressed in rags barely covering their emaciated bodies, weary mothers bearing whimpering babies, old people shuffling haltingly with the help of walking sticks. All of them carried tattered gunnysacks in which they hoped to gather a few crusts of dry *barkbröd,* or perhaps a potato or a salted herring, or, with luck, even a scoop of coarse rye flour mixed with ground bark. At first, Elna did her best to give a something to each of them, but before long she was forced to save what little was left for those closest to her.

Elsalina and Stina continued to eat with Elna's family, but the amount of food on the table became less and less. Eventually Stina remained in the cottage, maintaining that she wasn't hungry. When Elsalina realized that Stina was, in fact, too weak to walk over to Elna's cottage, she became alarmed.

"Stina must eat!" she told her. "She must be strong enough to deliver my child in a few months. She promised to help me."

Reluctantly, Stina gave in and ate the few morsels Elsalina brought from Elna's kitchen every day. But her strength failed to return, and she spent much of her time in bed.

One evening, as Elving and Elna were discussing the pros and cons of Elving's plan to ski to Norway to buy much-needed flour, their neighbor, Nils Nilsson, appeared in the doorway.

"I just came by to inform Elving that a shipload of Russian rye flour is rumored to have reached the east coast. It is said that the Queen is giving it away to the needy."

Elving shrugged. "Rumors are but rumors. And even if it is true, and there is enough to feed those who are starving between the coast and here, there are many greedy hands along the way. Mark my words: We will never even see an empty sack from it. Methinks it wiser to ski over to Norway and buy flour. We know for a fact that the Norwegians have plenty to sell. My brother's son, Torleif, is going to accompany me. Why not join us?"

Nils Nilsson was hesitant. "I shall think about it," he answered.

"We are setting out at dawn the day after tomorrow," Elving told him. "We must go while we still have a little to take with us to eat during the journey. We cannot reckon with being able to replenish our supplies at the few isolated farmsteads along the way. They may well be worse off than we are."

"How long does Elving plan to be gone?"

"I don't rightly know. Two weeks, at least. Even though it is cold enough to travel on the frozen rivers and lakes, rather than fighting our way through the forests, it is not going to be easy in such deep snow. And coming back will be even worse when we are laden with all the flour we can carry on our backs. But I don't see that we have any choice. I can't sit here and watch my family starve."

Those were Elving's last words on the matter. Two days later, he and Torleif set out at dawn as planned, disappearing down the path leading from the farm. Nils Nilsson had declined to go with them, feeling that he was not a good enough skier. Instead, he promised to see that Elving's family received their share of the Russian flour, should it materialize while he was gone.

The days passed slowly for the three women at Björkelund. Rather than keeping two households going, Stina and Elsalina moved in with Elna and her four youngest children, who were still at home. Elna took the smallest children into her bed in the corner of the kitchen, and Stina and Elsalina slept in the vacated bed closest to the hearth.

Each night before going to bed, Elna marked the passing of the day on the wall by the door. For the first two weeks, she managed to keep her eyes from the path to the farm. But on the fifteenth day, she began her vigil. At the same time, she also watched their food supply shrink. When Elving had been gone a little over three weeks, Elna became visibly anxious, not just about her husband, but also about how she was going to feed everyone. There had been no further word of the Russian flour and her own supply was almost gone. And what was left in the salted herring barrel was extremely salty and half rotten, making it difficult to choke down. The only other thing they had to eat was the last of the dried bread, which was thick with mold that was almost impossible to scrape away, and a thin gruel made mainly with ground bark and a tiny bit of rye flour. The winter forest had nothing to offer: no berries nor grasses or tender young pine shoots which people usually ate to stave off their hunger in times of famine. There were only lichens, which made a bitter-tasting flour when ground and gave almost no nourishment. The children constantly cried out in hunger. When Elna realized that there would be no spring for any of them if they didn't get something to eat during the winter, she gave in and cooked the few seed potatoes she had been saving.

One afternoon, Elna sent Elsa to the storehouse to fetch a few pieces of salted herring for supper. The little log storage building was cold and depressing. The shelves, which had once held rows of cheeses, were empty, the poles in the ceiling where sausages and other dried and smoked meats usually hung were also empty, as was the flour bin. All that was left was a little dried bread in the bread bin and the herring in a barrel by the door.

Elsa lifted off the wooden lid and dipped the long-handled scoop gently into the brine, letting it blindly search for pieces of fish. But it found nothing. Her breath caught in her throat. Surely... She began stirring the brownish brine vigorously, watching for scraps of fish to swirl upwards. But nothing appeared. Her heart began to pound. Pushing up her sleeves, she leaned over the edge of the wooden barrel and plunged her arms into the icy brine. She felt around the bottom of the barrel slowly. There weren't even any tiny scraps left. Drying her arms on her skirt, she replaced the lid and went back to the house. She didn't need to say anything. Everyone understood when they saw her face.

The next day, Elsa and two of Elna's children, Axel and Emilie, joined the ever-increasing stream of beggars. Rather than face their neighbors, they took a little-used path through the forest to the next parish where they were relatively unknown. The path ended on the edge of a meadow, across which they could see a small farmhouse. They hesitated, looking from one to the other nervously.

"Come now," Elsa urged. "Walk in my footsteps."

She led them across the field single file, trudging through snow drifts which reached well above her knees and even higher on the younger children. The house grew more formidable with every step. When they reached the side door, Axel and Emilie held back, not daring to go further. Elsa would have gladly turned and run back into the forest, but her hunger drove her forward. Although it was customary to simply walk into a house and stand inside the kitchen door until one was noticed, Elsa could not let herself take the liberty of doing so. Instead she knocked timidly. The children hovered a short distance away, afraid to leave her side, yet afraid to come closer to the house. Presently the door opened and a woman looked down on them.

"And what brings these children to my door?" she asked coldly.

"W-w-we have nothing t-t-to eat at h-h-home, Ma'am," Elsa stammered.

The woman glanced down at her.

"Is she not Augusta's whore-child?" she remarked disgustedly, glancing down at Elsa's belly. Without another word, she backed into the house and closed the door.

Elsa saw that Emilie, who was twelve, understood the situation, but ten-year-old Axel was clearly puzzled. Many times he had seen their mother share what little they had with strangers who came begging. He assumed that was how things were done.

"Why?" he began, still holding the empty sack open in front of him, ready to extend it toward whatever would be offered them.

"Come," Elsa said, ignoring his unfinished question. She took him by the hand and led him along the wagon tracks away from the house.

"Maybe they don't have anything to eat either," she added, hoping to satisfy him.

When they met with the same reaction at the next two cottages, Emilie suggested shyly that perhaps she and Axel should try going to the door by themselves. Elsa agreed, staying out of sight when they came to the next cottage. A woman clothed in scanty rags, with a whimpering baby in her arms, opened to them.

"I'm sorry, Children," she said kindly. "Has no one informed thee that we in this parish have only empty storehouses these days? A number of people have already died from hunger, including small children. The only people who are not out begging are those who are too weak to leave their beds. However, word has it that things are better near the coast, but who can walk that far on an empty stomach! Let alone with only a few rags to keep out the cold."

Dejected, the three of them made their way home again, the empty beggar's sack hanging limply over Axel's shoulder.

Emilie repeated the woman's words to their mother.

"Yes, I have heard the same from people here—that things are better along the coast. If Father doesn't return in the next day or two I shall set out in that direction, for I cannot sit here and await flour to rain down from heaven."

When Elving failed to return, Elna made her decision.

"I'll take Axel and Benjamin with me," she told them. "It is better that Emilie stays here, for she can be the most help to Stina and Elsa. And I'm afraid I must leave Selma, also. She is too young to walk so far. And, God willing, perhaps Elving will have returned by the time I'm back."

At dawn the next morning the three of them set out. Each carried a woven sack, although Elna had no illusions about returning with them filled. But they could at least be used at night against the cold.

Not long after Elna had set out, those at home came to the bottom of the dry bread bin. Elsa did her best to ration out what was left of the flour and bark mixture, making a thin gruel of it morning and evening. Stina ate only a few spoonfuls each time, claiming that she didn't need much since she was confined to her bed. Little Selma whimpered from hunger almost constantly. Emilie did her best to hide her pangs of hunger, as did Elsa. Stina encouraged Elsa to eat more, explaining that the baby was taking almost everything she was eating.

"Elsa won't kill the baby by not eating; it will kill Elsa instead," she told her.

The week after Elna left, a neighbor came by to ask if Elving had come home yet. She needed him to make a small coffin for their youngest child. He had been so hungry that he had eaten handfuls of sawdust from in front of the woodshed when no one was watching him. Nor had he been the first to do so. Several adults had met the same fate by eating porridge they had cooked from sawdust. And in another village, an elderly couple had been found dead with their mouths stuffed with mattress straw. Elsa was convinced that she, too, was going to die, for she was unbearably hungry. Only Stina seemed untouched by hunger.

The existence of the baby kicking in her stomach awoke mixed feelings in Elsalina. In time she thought less and less about Reverend Stenbom's part in it. Instead, she looked upon it as her baby. All hers. She began to look forward to having it, perhaps as a replacement for the family she had lost. She made tiny clothes from scraps of cloth Elna had given her. She considered various names. She imagined teaching it to read. Then suddenly the request for a small coffin had thrown reality in her face. She saw it as a sign that the child was going to die. And even if it did survive, it would always be a bastard like herself, a social outcast.

And how could she support the two of them? She would be forced to let someone else care for it while she worked. Every morning she woke up to a living nightmare. And when her hunger became too great, she prayed that she wouldn't wake up.

One afternoon, just as the winter sun was sinking behind the edge of the forest, there was the sound of footsteps on the porch. The door opened and a snow-covered figure stumbled into the room and collapsed. At first they took him for yet another beggar.

"And who might this be?" Emilie asked.

"E-E-Elna?" stammered a hoarse voice.

"Papa!" Emilie cried.

His beard and eyebrows were caked with ice and he was stiff from the cold. Gently they began removing his outer clothing. But when they tried to take off his boots, he cried out in pain.

"Be careful," Stina warned from her bed. "He may well have frostbite."

When they were unable to get his boots off, Stina suggested they cut the stitching along the seams, making it possible to re-sew them. When they finally freed his feet, they were a waxy bright red color and freezing to the touch.

"Don't rub them," Stina cautioned. "Wrap them in a warm sheepskin and then give him something hot to drink. Hot water will do, if there's nothing else. What about his fingers?"

"They look normal," Elsa told her. "And so do his ears and nose."

Once Elving's feet were attended to, they pulled off the clothes he'd been wearing since leaving home and wrapped him in quilts which had been warmed before the fire. Finally he managed to swallow a little hot water, along with a shot of *brännvin*. It was the alcohol flowing through his chilled body that brought him back to life.

"On the porch," he said at last. "Look on the porch. It's not so much, but I couldn't carry more."

Outside the door lay a sack of rye flour.

"Cook some thin porridge for all of us," Stina said. "But make it very thin. To gorge oneself after having starved can easily bring about one's death, and a painful one, at that."

Several days after Elving's return, Elna and the boys also returned. They had reached the coast, only to discover that the much-awaited Russian flour was not only gone, but it had been damp and stale and full of clumps and stones. Disheartened, they had turned around and started for home while they still had the strength to walk. When Elna saw Elving and the sack of flour, she broke down and wept.

"One would never believe some of the things we saw along the way," she told him. "People were going in every direction, trying to get to some place they hoped was better than where they were. All of them were bone-thin. Now and then one came across a dead body by the roadside or saw parents carrying a dead child, reluctant to leave it behind. What a relief to come home! If I am going to starve to death, I don't want to die on the road."

Now that everyone was home, the cottage was crowded. But Elna and Elving would not hear of Stina and Elsalina moving back to the little cottage.

"Soon Elsalina is going to need all the help and support she can get," Elna told them. "It's better that she is here where I can keep an eye on her."

Several nights after Elna's return, Elsalina was awakened by a searing pain in her abdomen. She tried to lie still so as to not wake Stina, but she was unable to stop the groan which rose from the pit of her stomach.

"Has Elsalina's time come?" Stina wondered sleepily.

"I think so," Elsa answered apologetically.

"There's no hurry," Stina assured her. "We can wait until the pains come close together. Try to get some sleep in the meantime. Elsalina will need all the strength she can muster."

The rest of the night passed slowly. Shooting pains woke Elsa periodically, but Stina was always able to soothe them with her hands. When dawn broke, Elna and the children brought in as much wood and water as possible. Although no one said anything, everyone awaited the birth with foreboding. Even though they now had rye flour in the bin, it couldn't supply all the nutrition they lacked. Nor did Elna dare use it extravagantly, for it must last them through the remainder of the winter. Therefore she only made it into a thin porridge for breakfast and a thinner gruel for supper. They were eating just enough to keep them alive.

Elsa remembered almost nothing of the child's birth. Afterward Elna told her that she had passed out between contractions. But fate must have had a finger in it, for the baby came feet first and Stina, who had insisted on getting out of bed to deliver it, was able to grasp its legs and give a helping hand to the tiny girl-child as she emerged. Had she come head first, Elsa wouldn't have had the strength to even push the head out. Stina and Elna examined the child carefully, finding her to be well-formed, without a trace of Stenbom in her delicate features. At fifteen, Elsa-Carolina had left maidenhood behind her and become a mother.

Because of her dislike for the church, and priests especially, Elsa was against having her child baptized.

"Elsalina should think it over carefully," Stina told her. "In spite of what she may think about the church, none of us knows what happens after we die. Look at baptism as a sort of insurance. Even if it turns out to be unnecessary, it hasn't hurt anything. In these days of famine, one must be realistic. Her chances of survival are not very good. None of our chances are. Personally, I think she should be baptized—and soon. Just to be on the safe side."

After some thought, Elsa conceded. She turned to Elna.

"Would Elna be willing to take her to the church and be her godmother?"

"Yes, of course. I would be honored," Elna said. "And what shall her name be?"

"Stina-Kajsa Elsdotter."

"Kajsa?" Elna questioned.

"My mother's name was Kajsa-Augusta. And Elsdotter is short for Elsalina's daughter. If Holmgren won't accept Elsdotter, tell him to take Nathansdotter instead. Reverend Stenbom is the only Nathan around here, and it would serve him right."

And so it was. The following Sunday, Elna wrapped the child as warmly as possible and walked the short distance to the village church. There were no festivities to celebrate Stina-Kajsa Elsdotter's baptism.

Six weeks later, it was Elsalina's turn to make her way to church for her churching ceremony. But rather than a ceremony, it promised to be a public reprimand, to let her and the entire congregation know how reprehensible she was. It was a day she had dreaded after having witnessed a similar ceremony involving another unwed mother.

The girl, who was not much older than herself, had been a kitchen maid at a large estate. It was common knowledge that she had been raped by the owner, nor had she hesitated to name him as the father of her child. Not only did he deny having had anything to do with the girl, but he even threatened to sue her for having blackened his name. When she had come to church for her churching, she had been told to wait outside. Once the congregation was seated, the girl had been escorted down the center aisle between the parish clerk and the *sexman*. Everyone had turned to look at her, disgust written on their faces. She had been steered into the vestry where a group of men awaited her: the priest, two churchwardens, four men appointed as parish representatives, plus her escorts. The vestry door was left wide open so that the congregation could hear every word that was said. For a seeming eternity, those nine men had chastised and condemned the girl, not only for having sinned, but even worse, for having implicated one of the leading members of the parish.

When they had humiliated her totally, she had been forced to retrace her steps down the aisle, alone. She had been crying so hard that she could barely walk. Every head turned to follow her steps, every face a hard mask of pious disdain. Among them sat the father of her child, without a flicker of compassion on his face. She was never in her right mind after that and eventually had to be locked up in an asylum. It was then that Elsa-Carolina had made up her mind that she would never subject herself to such degrading treatment from anyone, regardless of the consequences.

When the day for her churching arrived, she refused to participate.

"I agreed to let Kajsa be baptized for her sake. But this is for my sake. I am not going to let those hypocrites tear me apart for their own sins."

Neither Stina nor Elna could argue against her.

From that day onward, Elsa had nothing to do with the church. The unfairness of being raped by the parish priest, bearing his child, and being left to take the blame while he went scot-free was more than she could forgive. Nor did Stenbom ever indicate to her that he was sorry or offer to pay for the child. Even farmhands behaved better than that when they got girls pregnant. Elsa's anger and bitterness would not have been quite so great had she been raped by Baron Ekefors or Squire Nyqvist—but a priest! God could hardly exist if He let his so-called servants behave in such a manner.

One night not long after Kajsa's birth, Stina woke up with a burning fever and pains in her chest.

"What's wrong?" Elsalina whispered anxiously when she was awakened by Stina's weak thrashing beside her in the bed.

"Pneumonia," Stina answered knowingly.

"What shall I do?" Elsa wondered.

"There is nothing that can be done. My body is too weak to fight it," Stina replied.

"Stina mustn't talk so! She mustn't just give up!"

"It's not a matter of giving up, my child. I am long past eighty, and I'm tired. I can't go on forever. I have brought Augusta, then Elsalina, and finally Elsalina's Kajsa into the world. But it is impossible for me to wait around to deliver Kajsa's child. And I have done my best to pass on all that I know about Augusta's life and Elsalina's younger years, so as not to take anything unsaid with me."

"But Stina," Elsalina began.

"There are some things over which we have no control," Stina continued. "I believe it is possible to will one's own death, but I don't think it is possible to prevent one's own death if one's time has run out."

"Stina," Elsa begged.

"My dear child, let us be thankful for the time we have shared over the years that Elsalina has been my goddaughter. Don't be sad; it is only my body that is dying. My spirit will continue to live in Elsalina's heart. And we shall meet again, together with Augusta and her Erling. In the meantime, I shall be watching over my goddaughter. But for now, let us sleep a while longer."

When dawn came, Stina was delirious with fever. Elsalina sat beside her throughout the day, bathing her sweat-drenched forehead with cold wet rags. But each time she removed them, the tiny pearls of sweat surfaced again. And all her efforts to spoon a bit of watery gruel into Stina's mouth were in vain. Elsalina understood that she had made up her mind to let her illness do what it had come to do. There was no going back, nor could she let herself think of the future without her godmother.

Stina's breathing was labored, but otherwise she appeared to be at peace. Elsalina was reminded of the Twenty-Third Psalm: "Yea, though I walk through the valley of the shadow of death, I will fear no evil, for Thou are with me..." Even though Stina had her quarrel with the church and its indoctrination, she was religious. She was just a little more pagan than Christian. One could see that she was walking in the valley of the shadow of death in the same way she had always walked through the forest—at peace with herself and her god. Now and then she mumbled something unintelligible and an occasional smile flickered momentarily across her withered face. Watching her, Elsalina felt her own fear of death softening, even though her fear of losing Stina remained. She stayed beside Stina the entire day, leaving her bedside only to nurse Kajsa and to eat a little thin porridge. She had long ago given up hope of ever being free from the gnawing hunger, which could cause her to double up in pain. She wondered if Kajsa felt the same thing. She nursed disinterestedly and rarely cried.

"Don't get too attached to her," Elna had warned. "She doesn't appear to have much of a fighting spirit. Most likely she won't make it through her first year. Perhaps it is better that way. Life is so cruel for a bastard child."

She knew Elna was right, although she didn't think of Kajsa as being a bastard child. True, she was Reverend Stenbom's bastard, but for Elsa-Carolina, Kajsa was just her child. Only hers. She was already attached to her.

Two nights later, Stina died in her sleep without ever having awakened from her delirium. Her departure was so smooth that Elsalina was unaware that Stina had gone until she woke up and found that her body was cold. While her grief was all-encompassing, at the same time she felt a joy for Stina's release from worldly pain and suffering. Hopefully, she would soon join her.

Word that Simon's-Stina had passed away spread quickly throughout the surrounding parishes. As the unofficial midwife and *wise woman* who could cure all sorts of ailments with her herbs and brews, she had been important to almost everyone at one time or another. On the day of her funeral, those who had the strength made their way to the village to pay their last respects. The church was packed, mostly by those women whose babies she had delivered over the span of more than sixty years, as well as by those whom she had brought into the world. When Elsalina and Elna arrived, the church was already full. They made their way to Elna's family's pew. Presently Reverend Holmgren appeared from the vestry. Instead of beginning the service, he climbed the few steps to the pulpit and let his gaze glide over the congregation below him.

Suddenly his eyes ceased their searching and rested on Elsa-Carolina. He cleared his throat.

"There is an unclean heathen who has crept in among us, who obviously considers it unnecessary to follow the church's laws. She is not welcome here, and we cannot begin until she has left God's house."

Elsalina felt the blood drain from her face. Reverend Holmgren continued to stare at her. Finally she tried to stand up, but her legs buckled.

"Remove her," he instructed the two church wardens.

"Stina was her godmother," Elna pleaded.

"She is unclean," Holmgren answered.

The wardens pulled Elsalina from the pew and propelled her down the aisle to the door.

"Forgive us, Stina," Elna said aloud. She got up and left the church.

She found Elsalina collapsed on the ground, weeping uncontrollably. Elna managed to pull her to her feet, but she stumbled along the road like a drunk, babbling incoherently. The only word Elna could make out was "Away! Away!" When they reached home, she fell into bed, with Kajsa in her arms, and disappeared into a deep sleep.

When Elsa finally woke up, the first word she uttered was "away," over and over again. Elna tried to talk to her, but she just gazed off into space. By the next day, she had lost interest in Kajsa. Elna began to fear for both Elsa's and Kajsa's lives. The following day, a Sunday, Elna once again made her way to the church. Apart from the religious service, church gatherings also served as a parish meeting, where news was spread, as well as official and unofficial announcements made. Elna let it be known that Elsa-Carolina's newborn baby girl needed a wet-nurse.

"She has been baptized in the church," she added, knowing that no woman would take a heathen child. She also knew that the owners of one of the larger farms in the parish had just lost a newborn child. She looked at the husband pleadingly as she spoke. Afterward, he approached her, saying he would speak with his wife, who was still bedridden after an exhausting delivery.

"There is no time to waste," Elna told him. "After what happened at Stina's funeral, Elsa-Carolina seems to have given up on life and ignores the child. She has not been in her right mind since then."

That same afternoon, a wagon drove up to Elna's cottage, and Roland Sjöström knocked on the door.

"My wife will gladly nurse the child," he told Elna.

"Oh, thank God! We can discuss the future when we see how things go, but right now the child needs to nurse properly if she is to survive."

"Yes, we can see how things go," Herr Sjöström agreed. "Excuse me for asking, but is it true what people say, that Reverend Stenbom is the father?"

"Yes, it is true."

"And," he began.

"Yes," Elna interrupted, anticipating his question, "it is also true that Elsa-Carolina's father is Baron Ekefors' son, Erling."

"So I have heard," he replied, obviously satisfied.

Elsalina was half awake when Elna took Kajsa. She had ceased to clasp the child to her, leaving her in a basket beside the bed. Although her eyes followed Elna's movements as she laid the child's few clothes in the basket and picked it up, she appeared not to comprehend what was happening. Or perhaps she no longer cared. She continued to mumble "away, away" ever since Stina's funeral.

For several weeks after Herr Sjöström had taken Kajsa, Elsalina hung between life and death. Elna did her best to get her to swallow enough thin porridge to keep her alive, but she showed no will to live.

Miraculously, just as Elna neared the last of the rye flour Elving had brought from Norway, spring began to unfold in the form of tiny nettle leaves that pushed their way to the surface in a sheltered spot behind the cowshed. Elna cooked the first ones to a watery gruel, so as not to shock her family's long-empty stomachs. The next day, she added just a pinch of flour, then a little more each day. Even Elsa responded to the vitamin-rich nettles. She began to notice life around her in a somewhat confused manner. She still didn't speak, beyond the single word "away." Then one day she sat up and felt her stomach curiously. She looked at Elna questioningly.

"Does Elsa wonder about the baby?" Elna asked.

Elsa nodded vaguely.

Elna explained what had taken place, omitting any mention of Stina for the time being.

"When Kajsa no longer needs to nurse, we shall decide what shall be done," she concluded.

Elsalina appeared unconcerned.

"Away, away," she mumbled.

One spring day, a horse and wagon drove up the road to Elna's cottage. A young farmhand jumped down from the driver's seat and lifted out a large wooden crate. Elving, whose feet had almost healed since his return from Norway, looked at it, puzzled.

"It's from Herr Sjöström," the boy told him. "And I am to say that the child is healthy and well."

Elving pried open the lid of the crate. It was filled with seed potatoes. He looked up at the boy with tears in his eyes.

"Tell Herr Sjöström that I said God bless him!" he said.

That afternoon, he and Elna planted each potato as if it were a gold nugget. The larger ones they set aside to eat in the meantime.

By the time summer finally came, Elsa was on her feet again. She spoke when necessary, but a blackness lay over her. Bit by bit, the events of the past winter came back to her: the hunger pains, Kajsa's birth, Stina's illness, her refusal to take part in the churching ceremony, Stina's death, and the humiliation of being cast out of the church at Stina's funeral. Once again it was the inhumanity of the men of God that stuck in her craw.

"I must go away from here," she told Elna one day. "I can't show my face in the parish after the way Holmgren has humiliated me. And even if I had gone through the churching ceremony, people would still look down on me as being a whore because I have a bastard child—even though I have made no secret of how she came about and who her father is. It's as if people want to believe in the holiness of the priests, even though they know they are swine. I want to go somewhere where no one knows me. Also, I miss Stina so much. There is such a great emptiness here now that she is gone. I think I would rather be somewhere that she's not been and just carry her spirit within me, as she said."

"But what about Kajsa?" Elna asked. "Elsa can't wander with a tiny child in her arms. And wherever she goes with Kajsa, she will be seen as an unwed mother and be an outcast."

"I don't know," Elsa mused. "I can't just give her up. The day Elna warned me not to become too attached to her it was already too late."

"Perhaps Elsa should go and talk with Herr and Fru Sjöström and hear what they have to say," Elna suggested.

Several days later, Elsa set out for Sjöström's farm. It lay on the far side of the parish, several hours' walk from Elna's. But the day was sunny and pleasantly warm.

When a housemaid answered the door, she presented herself.

"Good day. I am Kajsa's mother. I wonder if I might see her," she began.

The maid seemed at a loss as to how to respond.

"Who is it, Pia?" called a man's voice.

"She says she's the child's mother, Sir," the maid answered.

"Bring her in," came his reply. "I shall talk to her."

Elsa was shown into a room that served both as an office and a library. In front of the window was a large desk, behind which sat a middle-aged man dressed in what Elsa regarded as city clothes.

"Herr Sjöström?" she asked in a small voice.

"Yes. And I assume this is Elsa-Carolina. What brings her here?"

Elsa shifted from one foot to the other nervously. "I would like to see my child, Sir," she replied.

"She will awake soon," he told her. "In the meantime, may I ask what Elsa-Carolina's plans are for the future?"

She explained that she wanted to go to Stockholm in search of a job.

"What sort of job?"

"As a maid, perhaps. People say I am clever at household tasks. Or as a shop clerk. Anything but factory work, if it can be avoided."

His response was the same as Elna's: How could she work when she had a child to care for?

"At any rate," he continued, "the child is still nursing, so it isn't a question of her leaving here right now. Wouldn't it make more sense for Elsa to find a job and get her life in order first, before she thinks about bringing a child into it? At the moment she has no way to support herself and a child. Kajsa is fine here. As can be seen, we are sufficiently well off to provide for her better than Elsa can. Once she has established herself—and perhaps even found a husband—then we can come to an agreement."

He was interrupted by a cry from a nearby room.

"May I see her?" Elsa asked pleadingly.

"Yes, of course. Ester," he called. "Come with the child."

A young woman came into the room carrying Kajsa wrapped in a blanket.

"This is my wife, Ester," Herr Sjöström said.

Elsa curtsied, and they shook hands. She appeared to be not much older than Elsa. Twenty, perhaps. She was both gentle and shy. She looked at her husband nervously.

"Elsa-Carolina is just here to see how the child is doing," he told her. "She is not here to take her away."

Ester's face brightened with relief.

"Would Elsa like to hold her?" she asked, shifting the child in her arms.

"Oh, yes, please!"

She took the bundle Fru Sjöström handed her and carefully opened the blanket. How she had grown! She was no longer skin and bones, and her eyes were bright. When Kajsa's uncontrollable arms jerked and slapped her in the face, Elsa laughed for the first time in months.

"Would Elsa-Carolina care to join us for coffee?" Fru Sjöström asked.

Elsa hesitated at first. But the aroma of real coffee had already sifted into the room.

"Yes, thank you," she replied.

Presently, the housemaid appeared with a tray containing china cups and saucers, with matching creamer, sugar bowl, and coffee pot. In the middle of the tray was a plate with various sorts of cookies. Unthinkingly, Elsa began to count the different kinds. She had heard women talking about the traditional seven kinds of cookies that one offered coffee guests, but she herself had never seen more than two kinds at once.

Coffee was poured, and the plate of cookies was held out toward her. Gingerly she took one of the chocolate ones closest to her. She sipped her coffee slowly. She hadn't tasted real coffee since leaving Stenbom's. When she had finished her cookie, the plate was held out again, this time turned slightly so that a different kind of cookie was closest to her. The same ritual was repeated until she had eaten one of each kind. And as soon as her cup was empty, it was refilled with strong hot coffee. All the while she held Kajsa cradled in her left arm, unable to take her eyes off of her.

The afternoon passed quickly. By now it was getting late, and Elsa had a long walk ahead of her. She knew she should leave but was reluctant to let go of Kajsa, who had fallen asleep in her arms. She wanted to hold on to her and run out of the house, but she knew they would catch up with her and take the child. Kajsa was hers, yet she was powerless to take her.

Having finished their coffee, Herr Sjöström excused himself, saying he would be back in a minute. When he returned, he handed Elsa a leather pouch.

"Take this so that Elsa can live until she finds what she is looking for in Stockholm," he told her.

From the weight of it, she understood that there were enough coins in it to last her a long time.

"Oh, many thanks, Sir!" she replied, curtsying.

"See that she hides it securely on her body," he told her. "There are plenty of dishonest and thieving people in the world beyond the parish. Keep a few coins in a pocket to use when needed, but never let the pouch be seen by anyone."

Elsa nodded. His advice gave her the first glance of the life that awaited her.

He sent the maid out to tell the stall boy to hitch up the wagon and drive it up to the house.

"Johan will drive Elsa home," he informed her. "It's late, and it's a long way to walk."

Fru Sjöström had said almost nothing during Elsa's visit, but she had never taken her eyes off the child in Elsa's arms. Only when Elsa reluctantly handed Kajsa back to her did she relax and let a slight smile form on her lips. Elsa thanked them for their kindness and said goodbye.

Elsa was thankful for Herr Sjöström's financial help, although she didn't realize what lay behind it. She was just glad to be able to get away from the parish and its holier-than-thou people who always held their heads so high that they could only see the world by looking down their noses. She felt badly about leaving Elna, who could have used her help, but the emptiness that ate at her after losing both Kajsa and Stina was too great. She had to get away and start to live again, before she was swallowed by the huge black hole inside herself. Elna understood and, although Elsa knew she wished she would stay, she encouraged her to go.

By the time Elsa-Carolina was well enough to set out for the long walk to Stockholm, summer had arrived. Among her few belongings that she tied into a bundle were two precious books: Stina's old family Bible, containing all her ancestors' names and dates as far back as the 1500s, and her battered diary held together by a string tied around its black covers. In it Stina had written the names and dates of all the babies she had delivered, plus comments about each birth, as well as notations about other people she had tended in some way, and the noteworthy events in her own life. In the back were her herbal recipes for various ailments. Unfortunately, she had never been to school. Although she

—183

had taught herself to read, her spelling was according to her own phonetic system. But her handwriting was neat and once one caught on to her phonetic code, it was easy to read her comments. Elsa had also inherited Stina's wedding ring, which she wore on her right hand together with Augusta's engagement ring from Erling.

Luckily, the law requiring a passport for travel beyond one's home parish had been abolished a few years earlier in 1860, which made migration to the city much easier. Previously, one had had to apply for a passport, which gave one's name and destination. However, it was still necessary for the poor who were looking for work to get a letter of recommendation from their parish priest. So Elsa-Carolina was forced to present herself to Reverend Holmgren one last time.

Having resigned herself, she set out. It was an unusually warm June day. She was already sweating long before she reached the rectory, but whether it was because of the weather or because of her errand was hard to say. She fingered the little package in her pocket. She dreaded having to face Reverend Holmgren, not because she felt guilt or shame before him, but because she was repulsed by his arrogant hypocritical manner and by the fact that he had so much power over her life. She wondered how many bastard children he had in the parish besides the ones that everyone knew about.

She knocked on the outside door to the vestry, rather than giving him a chance to spew his wrath over her for entering through his church in her still-unclean state.

"Come in," he called from behind the closed door.

Elsa entered. Rather than standing humbly in the doorway with downcast eyes, she placed herself in front of his desk and looked him in the face. He cleared his throat a little nervously.

"And what has brought Elsa-Carolina to my office? Does she wish to confess her sins and repent?" he remarked half mockingly.

"I have come for the reference letter I need in order to seek work in Stockholm," she replied.

"Oh, she means a character reference," he concluded.

"Yes, Sir."

"Does she wish to confess her sins first?"

"No, Sir."

He took a blank paper from the desk drawer, opened his inkwell, and picked up his pen. After scratching a few words, he cast a bit of blotting sand over the page and handed it to her.

"I assume she can read?"

"Yes, Sir."

She looked down at the still-damp script and read: "This young woman, Elsa-Carolina Augustasdotter, refuses to confess her sins and be churched after having given birth to a bastard child."

Without a word, she folded it and tucked it into her pocket. When she withdrew her hand, it held a small parcel, wrapped in brown paper and tied with a string.

"Here is something Reverend Holmgren should have," she said, holding it out to him.

She watched his face brighten and his whole being swell with the thought that no matter how much he punished her, she still respected him.

"Many thanks," he said, untying the string.

Elsa backed toward, the door slowly, captured by the desire to see his reaction.

The paper rustled and the brown whore's cap that the *sexman* had thrown at her fell onto the desk. Reverend Holmgren's face turned an angry red.

"Why the nerve!" he cried.

His face was still red when Elsalina closed the vestry door behind her. When the day for leavetaking came, Elsa suddenly regretted her decision. She realized she had no idea what to expect. The biggest place she had ever been was the nearby market town with its 1,500 inhabitants and one main street. Stockholm was said to be a huge city with more than 100,000 inhabitants, hundreds of streets, and tens of thousands of buildings, where she knew no one. Yet she could not go on living in the parish where she was a social outcast, where people avoided her and pulled their children away when she approached. She would forever be regarded as a whore in her home parish. The unfairness of it never ceased to anger her, as did the realization that none of it touched Reverend Stenbom. He had probably long ago put her out of his mind. Sometimes, when she thought about him, she felt as if she were about to explode. She had to go away and start a new life before her anger devoured her. If she could only find a place to live and get a decent job, she could take Kajsa back. Then she could turn her back on the parish forever.

The ground was still covered with dew when Elsa went out behind Elna's cottage to urinate that last morning. The sun was already high in the sky, having only been below the horizon a couple of hours during the short June night. On her way back inside, she met Elna going towards the barn. It was the chance she was waiting for. Quickly she took the rag in which she had wrapped some of the coins from Herr Sjöström, along with a little note, and dropped it into Elna's sewing basket. By the time she found it, Elsa would be far away.

After a breakfast of watery porridge, Elsa picked up her bundle of possessions and hung it over her shoulder by the woven band that held it together. She did her best to act cheerful, but no one was fooled. Elna and the children followed her out the door.

"Oh, Elna, I don't want to leave Björkelund!" she cried.

"Elsa has made the right decision," Elna told her. "It is no life for her here. She will feel better once she is on her way. Remember to write and tell me how she is doing."

"I promise," Elsa told her.

She turned and patted each of the children on the head, then shouldered her bundle and started down the path.

"I can always go back to Elna's," she told herself. But when two women she met on the road spit on the ground three times as she passed, she knew she would never return.

Late in the afternoon as she neared Ekefors Manor on the far side of the parish, she suddenly realized that she had hardly ever thought about Olov or her half siblings since the day he had thrown her out. That life was too painful to recall. The hurt she had suffered when she had overnight gone from being the apple of Olov's eye to being the rotten apple in his basket had been hard enough to accept, but the hatred he had shown toward her was more than she could bear. As a child she could not understand what she had done to cause the father she had loved and trusted so completely to reject her. Once she had left Grankullen her only comfort had been the memory of her mother and Simon's-Stina. But now, walking through the surroundings that had once been her world, she found herself hoping she might meet her sister Märta on the road. But the only familiar face she met was Blind-Ola's Berta. She stopped the old woman.

"I am looking for Olov's Märta," she said.

"And who might thee be?" Berta asked, not recognizing Augusta's daughter.

"A relative," Elsa replied. "Is Märta still living at Grankullen?"

"Oh, yes," Berta told her. "She has been the housekeeper ever since Augusta and her whore-child disappeared."

"So Olov has not remarried?" Elsa ventured cautiously.

"No. He is still bitter about the way Augusta lied to him. He spends most of his time working to provide for his children. I just now saw him helping with the hay at the manor, if she wishes to speak with him."

"That's not necessary," she told Berta. "I'm just passing by on an errand."

They said goodbye and continued on their respective ways. As soon as Berta was out of sight, Elsa went back to the path up to Grankullen, thankful for the knowledge that Olov was not at home.

From where the path opened out below the cottage, she saw Märta hoeing potatoes. She whistled the birdcall they used to use when picking berries out of sight from each other in the forest. Märta stood up and, shading her eyes against the sun, looked down the path. In the next instant she glanced around her. Peder and Hugo were sawing wood in front of the shed. She dropped the hoe and ran down the path.

"Who's that?" called Peder.

"It's just Lina from my confirmation class," she called back. "No need to stop sawing."

She grabbed Elsa by the hand and led her back to the abandoned hoe.

"Oh, I'm so glad to see thee! I've missed thee so!" she cried.

They sat down in the grass and just looked at each other.

"Where has my sister been? What has happened to her?" Märta asked, out of breath from excitement. "I have never known what really happened that day when I ran to get Stina. I only know that Mamma had a baby and was taken away by those two men. And then Papa told Elsa to get out. Once I tried to ask him what had happened, but I got such a violent slap across the face that I never asked again. 'That lying whore and her whore-child are never again to be mentioned in this house!' he screamed at me. 'As far as we are concerned, they are dead.' I would have asked Stina, but I never saw her again. And it was not the sort of thing one asked the neighbors about. Now and then I overheard a bit of gossip, so I knew that my sister had become a parish urchin, but I never knew why."

"Does Märta know why Olov threw me out?"

"No. I was only eight at the time."

"Well then, it's a long story."

"But can't Elsa stay until tomorrow? Papa is taking the boys with him down to the manor to cut hay. We can have the whole day to ourselves."

"Wonderful! Then I will have a chance to tell Märta all that I know about our mother's life, as well as what has gone on in mine. But what

—187

about tonight?"

"Elsa can sleep in the fresh hay in the cowshed loft. I can bring her something to eat before I go to bed. Papa mustn't find out that Elsa is here. He gets crazy if he even sees something that reminds him of Mamma and Elsa."

"But how does he treat his children? Does he treat thee like his house-maid?"

"He is good to us," Märta told her. "He works hard and has become a foreman, so he earns a bit more than before. Baron Ekefors seems to favor him above everyone else."

"He should!" Elsa declared. "He is the root of all the misfortune in our lives."

Märta gave her a puzzled look.

"Tomorrow I shall tell Märta everything. For now, give me another hoe, and we can soon finish this."

Just before Olov was due home, Märta and "Lina" took a rather loud farewell of each other for the sake of the boys, who were still sawing wood. Halfway down the path, Elsa turned off into the forest and sat down on a rock to wait for Olov to pass on his way home.

Long before he came into sight she heard a mumbling sound, accompanied by his footsteps on the stones in the path. As he came closer, she realized he was singing to himself, an old folk tune he used to sing when she was small, when they were still a family. The memory of that Olov, who had been her father, had long ago been obliterated by the memory of the Olov who had rejected her and beaten her mother. But now his song took her back to the Olov she had loved and who had loved her. It was all she could do to keep from calling out to him. But she dared not. Instead, she watched him disappear up the path toward Grankullen. She vowed to herself that she would carry the singing Olov in her memory from then on, the Olov who had once been her father.

By the time Elsa left Grankullen the next afternoon, she had told Märta everything she had learned about Augusta, as well as what she herself had gone through since the day Olov had driven her away. Elsa and Märta had never really known each other until now. This shared knowledge of their mother's life created a bond between them, a closeness neither of them could feel with anyone else. More than anything, Elsa wished Märta could go with her to Stockholm, but she knew it was impossible as long as the boys were still at home.

"I promise I will come in a year from now when they are on their own," she assured Elsa. "I am not going to be Papa's housekeeper forever!"

The two of them stood at the beginning of the path, reluctant to part.

"I'll send my address as soon as I find some place to live," Elsa promised.

"Olov can't get angry if Märta gets letters from her friend Lina Ersdotter, can he?"

"Don't worry," Märta told her. "He can't read."

They laughed through their tears. Then Elsa turned and walked down the path.

It was a long way to Stockholm, a walk of many days. Although the ancient human and animal paths had simply widened with time to accommodate wagons, they continued to wind up and down hills and around corners of fields as they had always done, with each spring thaw turning them into deeply rutted quagmires. During the summer they were filled with people: beggars with empty stomachs, tramps with rolls of wire over their shoulders that they turned into whisks, trivets, rat traps, and similar devices to sell along the way, farmers going to and from markets, and a steady flow of people on the way to the big city in hopes of finding work. Among them were groups of young people from the province of Dalarna. Unlike the others, they still dressed in their brightly colored parish costumes and carried goods they had made during the winter: baskets, brooms, wooden utensils, wooden chests, hand-woven cloth, and even clocks. The girls were especially known for their hair work, beautiful broaches made from thin strands of braided hair. How one could make something so minute and delicate was a mystery.

Usually one of the young men had a fiddle or a little accordion with him. When they stopped for the evening, there would be dancing in an empty threshing barn or at a crossroads, where the crossing roads formed a larger, hard-packed dance floor. For many of those people, being on the road was a way of life.

When she started out for Stockholm, Elsa was feeling rather brave and strong, consumed by her freedom from Reverend Holmgren and the eyes of his parishioners, as well as the freedom afforded by the leather pouch tucked into her blouse, forming a third breast. The first night, she walked long after the sun had disappeared behind the hills, for June nights are never darker than twilight. She was enjoying having the road all to herself when all of a sudden she heard the sound of horse hooves coming up behind her. It was then that she realized how vulnerable she was, all alone in the middle of the night. There wasn't a house in sight—only an old hay shed on the edge of the field, half-hidden by clump of trees. Quickly, she ducked behind it, just as a man leading a horse came into view. As he came closer, she saw that he was a gypsy. Everyone feared the gypsies. There were many tales about how they cheated people, stole horses, and raped women. That the man was leading a horse with just a rope around its neck in the middle of the night was a sure sign that it was stolen. Elsa took a step backward into the shadow of the shed in case he should look around. She was shaking and her heart was pounding so hard that she was sure he could hear it. But he continued on his way, oblivious to her presence. Once the sound of the horse's hooves faded into the night, she crept into the shed and fell asleep in a pile of freshly cut hay.

The next morning, she was awakened by laughter and singing in the distance. Brushing the hay out of her hair and off her clothes, she stepped out into the sunlight, clutching her bundle of possessions. Coming toward her was a group of twenty or so young people dressed in brightly colored clothes: the girls in long striped skirts covered by aprons and white embroidered blouses under tightly-laced bodices, their heads covered with kerchiefs, and the men in dark knee-length britches met by long stockings, loose blouses, dark vests, and hats. Several of the girls stopped in front of her.

"And where might she be going?" one of them asked, glancing at her bundle.

"Stockholm," she answered.

"Has she no traveling companion?"

"No. I'm alone."

"One must never travel alone. It is too dangerous. Come with us. I can hear that she is from our neighboring province."

She linked her arm through Elsa's, and they continued down the road. But even before they had exchanged names, the girl unexpectedly pulled her into some bushes on the side of the road.

"We have to pee," she called to her friends.

Elsa's blood ran cold. She was about to be robbed!

"She mustn't carry her money up front for all to see," the girl told her, pulling out the barely hidden pouch. Quickly she unlaced her own bodice and, handing the lace to Elsa, instructed her to hang the pouch from her belt, but under her skirt, and to tie it against her thigh to keep it from swinging.

"My name's Ellus," she said as they returned to the road.

"Lina," Elsa replied without thinking.

Suddenly she had become someone whom no one knew, not even she herself. Her whole being felt lighter, less burdened. She had taken her first step towards a new life.

And Ellus was her first friend.

The journey to Stockholm seemed endless. They walked most of the way barefoot, for no one wanted to wear out their only shoes. Although Elsa's feet were already calloused from never having worn shoes except during the cold of winter, she had never walked all day every day. Sometimes not just her feet, but her entire body, ached so intensely that she was sure she couldn't take another step. But Ellus and her friends kept her going by their good spirits, sometimes literally holding her upright between them. Elsa was ashamed of her inability to keep up with the others, but she dared not tell anyone that she had recently given birth. Such a revelation could easily cause her newfound friends to turn their backs on her. She had already seen it happen with old friends. Instead, she said that she had been very sick during the winter and had almost died from starvation. However, she made no secret of the fact that both her parents were dead and that she had been in several foster homes, although she omitted saying that she had been auctioned off as a parish urchin.

"Does Lina have any relatives in Stockholm that she can stay with?" Ellus asked one day.

"No," Elsa answered hesitantly. She didn't even know anyone who had ever been in Stockholm. For people in her parish, Stockholm was as far away and unknowable as America. It was a mysterious, myth-filled place where one could escape the social pressures of village life. And it was a place where one could earn money, instead of being paid with a pair of boots or material for a skirt at the end of the year. But for most, it was just a dream.

"Then she must come with me," Ellus told her. "I always stay with my mother's sister. One more person won't make any difference."

"It would be wonderful if I could stay there until I find a place of my own," she replied.

There was no need to politely refuse and wait for the offer to be repeated. Ellus had seen her weaknesses and such self-pride would only look like what it was: self-pride. And what if Ellus didn't offer a second time?

Ellus looked sideways at her when she said "a place of my own," but she said nothing.

Passing through the city gates shocked Elsa more than she could admit even to herself. She had expected Stockholm to be like the market towns she was familiar with, only larger, where people nodded to each other in recognition when they passed in the street, where farm wagons drove at a leisurely pace, and the buildings were never more that two stories high. Instead, the streets were packed with people who rushed here and there blindly, ignoring each other, while carts, wagons, and carriages drove wildly in every direction, their drivers shouting at people to get out of the way.

And the buildings! There were half-rotten shacks as well as luxurious mansions. And rather than individual shops, there were rows of shops all connected to each other, with huge buildings three and four stories high on top of them.

But worst of all was the noise! The country sounds of leaves blowing in the trees, voices carrying across open fields, and the occasional complaints of farm animals were replaced by a sea of sounds she had never before heard. She could hardly hear what Ellus was saying. Elsa clutched her friend's arm as if she were drowning.

"Here it is," Ellus said at last, opening the door of an old wooden building. She led Elsa up a narrow dark stairway until they were three stories above the ground. She knocked on a door. It opened a crack and a small boy-child peeked out at them.

"Mamma! Mamma! It's Cousin Ellus!" he cried.

"Come in!" a voice from somewhere inside called.

From the darkness of the room emerged a woman with a small child on her hip. Her long skirt and once-white apron were soiled and loose strands of hair from the knot at the nape of her neck hung over her ears. Her hand flew up to smooth them back when she saw that Ellus was not alone.

"This is my friend Lina," Ellus told her.

They shook hands.

"Ingri," the woman said. "And this is little Amus," she continued, tussling the matted hair of the boy who clung to her skirt. She stepped aside, motioning them to come inside.

As with everything else about Stockholm, Ellus' aunt and her home were nothing like Elsa had expected. Ingri's husband worked on the docks, loading and unloading ships. On payday, he rarely had a penny in his pocket by the time he found his way home from the company tavern near the waterfront. That his wife had seven children to feed was no longer any concern of his now that his oldest son had a job.

"I've paid his way for fifteen years, so now it's his turn to bring home the paycheck," he declared every time the subject of money came up. Consequently, Ingri was forced to hold the family together as best she could by taking in rich people's dirty laundry.

"Lina can help me with the washing and ironing in return for room and board until she finds a paying job," she told Elsa. "I need all the help I can get. And Ellus can pay for her room and board out of the money she earns selling her hair work, as always. But the bed must be shared with two of the smaller children."

The thought of a bed sounded like an invitation to heaven after the recent nights sleeping in sheds or haystacks or under trees. That the bed turned out to be full of lice didn't matter. Lice were a part of life. Only at Aunt Sofia's and Stenbom's had she ever slept without their company.

Although she liked Ingri and Ellus, Elsa felt uncomfortable living there. Everyone was cramped into one room—the kitchen. Not only was it crowded at night, but worse, it provided no privacy whatsoever. Feeling Ingri's husband's eyes on her as she tried to get ready for bed brought back memories of Reverend Stenbom. She longed to find a place of her own. But she soon discovered that, because of the flow of job-seekers into the city, there was a great housing shortage. No one lived "on their own." Not even Herr Sjöström's money could buy her a place of her own. Her only hope was to get a job and thus perhaps meet some other girls to share with. After her experiences as a housemaid, she shunned the idea of a live-in job. Only as a last resort. In the meantime, she helped Ingri with the washing and often looked after the smallest children.

In her spare time, she looked for a paying job. But each time she applied for a position, she was asked to produce a letter of recommendation from her parish priest. And each time what had begun as a friendly interview suddenly turned cold and she was told that they didn't need anyone. Sometimes she said she had no letter, that it had been lost or stolen. But the answer was always the same: sorry.

Ingri began to grow suspicious. A nice girl like Lina should have no trouble finding work. At the same time, she was secretly glad, for Lina was hard-working and good company.

One evening, Ingri's son, Lassar, had someone with him when he came home from work.

"Where's Lina?" he asked Ellus. "I've brought a friend with me. He has the same dialect as Lina, and I thought she might like to meet someone from home."

Just then Elsa stepped out of the pantry with a jar of salted herring in her hand and came face to face with a tall, good looking young man with straight blond hair and deep blue eyes. She grasped the herring jar with both hands to keep from dropping it.

"Lina, this is Erik," Lassar began.

"I-I-I know," she stammered, aghast. Erik Engström looked exactly as she remembered him from the year his family had taken her in. He was just taller.

"Elsa-Carolina!" he cried in surprise.

The sight of him sent the past rushing over her. For an instant she didn't know whether she was glad to see him or hated him for having brought Elsa-Carolina back to life. But in the next instant, the warmth of his smile disarmed her. She set the jar of fish on the table with a thud.

"I see Lina and Erik already know each other," Ellus commented.

"Erik belongs to the happiest period of my life," Elsa told her.

"Sit down," Ingri invited, indicating an empty chair. She dipped the scoop into the pail of water beside the stove and added it to the old grounds in the coffee pot. "Maybe I can squeeze a couple more cups out of these grounds," she apologized.

Elsa and Erik sat down across the table from each other. Elsa stared into his open face for a long time, remembering not only his kindness, but also the kindness Uncle Magnus and Aunt Sofia had shown her.

Ingri poured the weak coffee into china cups, whose ears had long ago been broken off, and set them in front of the young people.

"What has happened to Aunt Sofia and Dora?" she asked finally.

"We are all together again," he reported. "Once Mamma was settled in Stockholm and had a job, she sent for Walter and me. She works hard, but the spark has gone out of her since Papa's death. Nor is she a city person. Elsa must come and visit her. I know it would cheer her greatly to see her foster daughter again. She often speaks longingly of that last summer when Elsa helped her at the *fäbod.*"

"I often dream of that summer," Elsa told him. "It was such a happy time!"

While Elsa and Erik brought to life a past that Elsa had never spoken of to anyone, Ingri and Ellus stared at them in disbelief. Suddenly, Lina had become a different person, a person they hardly knew.

The following Sunday, Erik came to take Elsa to visit his mother.

194—

"Oh, my dear Child!" Sofia gasped upon opening the door. "Erik said he had a surprise for me, but I had no idea!" Instead of shaking hands, she drew Elsa to her in a warm hug. "Do I dare ask what has happened in Elsa's life since we last saw her?"

Elsa shrugged, trying to act nonchalant.

"T-t-tell me about the family first," she managed to say in an unsteady voice.

"How about some coffee, for a start," Sofia said, going to the stove and starting a fire. In the meantime, Elsa tried to compose herself.

As they drank their coffee, Sofia told her about coming to Stockholm with Dora and how, once she had found work and a place to live, she had managed to find the boys and reunite them.

"But what about Anna?" Elsa asked.

"She immigrated to America. She is working as a housemaid for a rich family in Chicago."

"We're trying to save money so we can immigrate, too," Erik added. "Anna says that it is easy to get farmland there. Something called the Homestead Act, where one gets the land for free as long as one builds a house and farms it."

"I think it would be wonderful to live on the land again," Sofia said. "It feels so unnatural to live high above the ground as we do here."

"There is no future for us here," Erik continued. "I have no chance to buy my own farm in this country. One is always at the mercy of the landowners. Look what happened when Papa was killed; we were forced to leave the land my father and grandfather were born on and the farm they had built up, simply because the land belonged to an estate. And because the rich bastard who owns it has no compassion for those who are less fortunate than he happens to be. I would rather start my own farm from scratch than live like a serf on someone else's land."

"But now let me hear about Elsa's life. How long has she been in Stockholm? Where is she living?" Sofia asked.

"I've only been here a month or so. I'm staying with the family of a girl who befriended me on the road."

"But how did Erik and Elsa find each other?" she wondered.

"I work with her friend's brother," Erik explained. "He took me home to meet their lodger. He thought we must be from the same parish because we speak the same dialect."

"Where are they from?"

"Dalarna. Ellus sells her hair work, and her aunt takes in washing."

"And the father drinks too much," Erik remarked. "He works on the docks, too, and I'll be willing to bet that he drinks up most of his pay." He looked over at Elsa and saw by her reaction that he had guessed right.

"That doesn't sound like a good place for a girl Elsa's age. I suppose everyone sleeps in the same room."

Elsa nodded.

No one said anything for a while.

"Come and live with us again," Aunt Sofia said. "I've missed my foster daughter."

"That's very kind of Aunt Sofia, but I think I must explain my situation first," Elsa told her.

And so for the first time since leaving Elna's, Elsa stepped back into the past years and told Sofia and Erik all that had happened since they had last met. When she had finished, Sofia took her hand.

"Elsa is not alone, my Child," she comforted. "That sort of thing happens more than one realizes, although that doesn't make it any less painful. And it is always the girls and women who pay. But, thankfully, the harvest moon kept Elsa from paying with her life. Elsa was wise to leave the parish and make a new start in life, rather than paying for someone else's evil doings every day. Come and live with us. We can be Elsa's family again."

Just then Walter came in, dragging Dora by the hand. They stopped short when they saw that there was company. Elsa turned around to see who had come in.

"Is that our Elsa?" Walter cried.

"Yes. She's going to live with us," Sofia told him.

"Oh!" cried Dora, clapping her hands. "She can share my bed with me!"

Suddenly, Elsa had a family again and was no longer alone.

She and Ellus met often that summer, but in the autumn, Ellus went home to Dalarna. The next summer, she came to town with her fiancée, and the following summer she was married and arrived with a big stomach. After that, she disappeared from Elsa's life.

Elsa-Carolina moved in with Aunt Sofia and her children. Sofia helped her get a job with the people she worked for by presenting her as her niece. Before long, Elsa, too, caught the "America fever." She began by putting what was left of Herr Sjöström's money into the family's "America fund." After a couple of years, they had enough for the boat passage, as well as the train to Chicago, plus enough to tide them over until they got on their feet.

By that time, Erik and Elsa had realized there was more between them than just friendship. Looking back, they both agreed it had started that day when the school children were calling her a parish urchin, and he had declared that she was his cousin, threatening to beat up anyone who teased her. A few months before the family immigrated, they got married, since there was no question about their feelings and being married would make immigration much less complicated.

Their wedding was a simple occasion. Elsa-Carolina had no relatives in Stockholm, and Erik had only his mother, brother, and sister. Aside from them, there were a few friends, including Ellus, Lassar, and Ingri. Märta and Elna sent their congratulations, but neither of them had the possibility of coming to Stockholm. Regardless of its sparseness, the day was joyous and the weather beautiful.

"Is Elsa going to write that letter today?" Erik asked her the next morning.

"What makes my husband ask that?" she answered, looking up at him slyly.

"I know she has kept Kajsa in her heart these past years. And now at last she has put her life in order and married herself a loving husband," he laughed. "Write to Herr Sjöström and tell him that Kajsa's mother and stepfather are ready to come and get her and that we have saved enough money to start a new life in America."

Elsa had written that letter so many times in her head that it was just a matter of letting the words flow out through her pen and onto the paper. When she was finished, she read it aloud to Erik.

The next day they went to the post station together and sent it.

A week later came an answer. Elsa hurried home to read it with Erik.

My dear Herr and Fru Engström,
First, let me congratulate Herr and Fru Engström on their recent marriage. I trust it will be a happy and prosperous one. In regards to little Kajsa, she is healthy and happy here with my wife and me. We are both very attached to her and she to us. It would be wrong to disrupt her present life. To Kajsa we are her parents, whereas Fru Engström and the child are strangers to one another. Since Fru Engström is immigrating to America, it will be no problem for us to legally adopt

the abandoned child. I therefore consider the matter closed. I ask that Herr and Fru Engström refrain from attempting to see the child or contacting us in any way.

Sincerely, R. Sjöström

Elsa's voice was shaking by the time she reached the bottom of the page. Silently, she read it again, hoping she had misunderstood its message. It had never occurred to her that the Sjöströms might refuse to let her take Kajsa back.

"He can't do this to me!" she cried.

Aunt Sofia sighed, at a loss for words.

"I'm afraid he has already done it, my Child," she said finally. "Does Elsa have any sort of written agreement with Herr Sjöström?"

Elsa shook her head.

"So it was just a verbal agreement. Does Elsa remember exactly what he said?"

"He said that once I had established myself, and perhaps even found a husband, then we could come to an agreement. That was all. And then he gave me the leather pouch full of coins," Elsa sniffed.

"Couldn't we..." Erik began.

"Some things one is powerless to change," his mother interrupted. "Even if we went to court, there is not a chance in heaven of winning over a man like him. He has power, he has money, and his word is respected. We small people have nothing. No one listens to us. I know it sounds heartless to say this, but perhaps it is better this way. It will make it easier for Elsa to start a new life, without the constant reminder of what Reverend Stenbom did to her and how she was treated afterward."

"But Kajsa is my child!" Elsa insisted stubbornly. "It's not fair!"

"Life is not fair," Sofia told her. "Engström was my husband, and it wasn't fair that he was taken away from me, either."

Without saying anything to anyone, the next day Elsa wrote a letter to Herr Sjöström appealing to his good will. Three days later, on her way to the fish market on the waterfront, she found her unopened letter in the mailbox. Across the envelope was written "return to sender" in big, angry-looking letters. Choking back her tears, she tore it into tiny bits as she hurried along. Upon reaching the quay, she opened her hand and let the wind carry the pieces out over the water. For a long time, she stood watching them sink one by one, until there was nothing left. Slowly, she walked back to Sofia's, a kilo of herring wrapped in newspaper in her basket. She was in a quandary. Her first thought was to go to Sjöström's and demand to have her child back, yet she suspected that Aunt Sofia was right; she didn't have a chance against Herr Sjöström. Looking back, she should have understood that the day she went to see Kajsa. But she couldn't just give up, yet she knew she must. At least for the time being.

A month later, the whole family left Stockholm behind them, their destination a new life in America.

Walter and Dora settled in Chicago near Anna, and Erik and Elsa homesteaded in South Dakota. Aunt Sofia became grandmother to Erik and Elsa's daughter, Carrie's grandmother, Isabella. Although Sofia lived with them until her death at the age of eighty-six, she never really reconciled herself to life without her Engström, as she always referred to him. But she kept her sorrow to herself. Only those who had known her while her Engström was alive understood that something in her had died with him.

And like Sofia and her Engström, Elsa-Carolina always carried Kajsa quietly inside her. Several times over the years she talked about trying to find her, but Erik always dissuaded her, saying that it wasn't right to suddenly barge into her life, that she may have grown up believing that the Sjöströms were her real parents. Logically, she knew he was right. But he had no emotional bond with Kajsa as she had. Occasionally she wrote to the Sjöströms, and later, directly to Kajsa. Every letter came back marked "return to sender." Eventually a letter came back marked "not at this address," so she gave up.

After Erik's death, she took up her search once more. This time she was able to trace Kajsa through the church records with the help of the present parish priest—the first priest she had met who, in her eyes, was a decent human being. Once they found Kajsa, the same priest went to visit her and learned that she had always suspected she was adopted. Thus Elsa was able to write to her without beating around the bush.

And now, after having turned her back on her past for nearly three-quarters of her life, it was the longing to meet the daughter she had never had a chance to know that was pulling her home again. That and to see her sister Märta again before it was too late. And lastly, she wanted to find out exactly what had happened to her mother. She had never been sure whether Stina hadn't actually known any details or whether she hadn't wanted to tell her the whole story. Hopefully, the answer lay in the archives with the old court records.

Epilogue

It was sunny and warm the morning we disembarked in Gothenburg. While Granny's first reaction was the thrill of stepping onto Swedish soil once more, even if it was only a cement dock, mine was that of finally standing on solid ground without feeling the constant vibration of the ship's engines. As the crowd of passengers thinned out, I spied an older man holding a sign above his head. Coming closer, I saw that it said, "E-C. Engström." I nudged Granny.

"Look there," I said. "It seems that we're being met."

Seeing our reaction, he came toward us.

"Elsa-Carolina Engström," he said, more as a statement than a question. He held out his hand in greeting. "Vicar Gustav Grönlund. My good friend Reverend Lindblom, with whom Fru Engström has corresponded, wrote and asked me to meet Fru Engström."

We shook hands.

"Carrie," I said. "*Dotterdotters dotter*," I added, trying out some of the Swedish Granny had taught me.

"Do you speak Swedish?" he asked, surprised.

"No, not really," I laughed. "Just a couple of words."

Not only did he meet us, but he also took us to our hotel and then out to lunch. Luckily for me, he had gone to school in England and spoke the King's English. Even though she would never have admitted it, it was probably just as well for Granny, too, as her Swedish was, if not rusty, at least very old-fashioned.

When we had finished eating, Vicar Grönlund folded his napkin neatly, placed it beside his plate, and looked across the table at us.

"And what would the ladies like to do while in Gothenburg?" he asked.

"I would like to go to the archives," Granny told him.

"The archives? Is Fru Engström looking for anything specific? It's not just a matter of going in and paging through the old books like in a library. One must give relevant information to the archivist, who then finds the appropriate record books. It's usually necessary to leave the information some days in advance. What is it Fru is looking for?"

Granny hesitated, not really keen on divulging her mother's background. When she didn't answer, he continued.

"If she gives me the necessary information, I can leave it with the archivist. Unfortunately, the day after tomorrow is the beginning of the

Midsummer holidays, and everything will be closed. And I believe the archives are closed during all of July. Either we can arrange to go there when Fru Engström returns to Gothenburg or else I could make a photocopy of whatever information is found and send it to where Fru is staying."

Reluctantly, Granny told him briefly what she knew about Augusta's fate. "If it's not too much trouble, I would certainly appreciate it if the vicar could send any information that is found to my sister's address," she told him. She gave him Märta's address, as well as place names and approximate dates for Augusta's arrest and imprisonment. "I assume there must have been some sort of trial and sentencing. I would like to know the whole story, if possible."

"I promise to find everything that is documented," he assured her.

The following day, we boarded the train for Kajsa's. I could see that Granny was nervous, but when I questioned her she said simply, "Think to meet someone you haven't seen in almost eighty years!"

Considering that Kajsa had only been a baby when she last saw her, it hardly seemed like it was something to be nervous about. But I had long ago learned that Granny had her quirks.

We were met at the station by Kajsa's son-in-law Herman, a middle-aged man with huge hands coarse from farm work. Because he spoke no English, I only got the gist of the conversation from Granny's scanty translations.[1]

"Please excuse my car," he said to her as he led us toward a car parked at the curb. By American standards, it was old—pre-war, from the 1930s. On the back bumper sat a contraption that looked like a pot-bellied stove. Granny eyed it suspiciously. Seeing her expression, Herman laughed.

"It's left over from the war years, when we couldn't get gasoline. Wood is burned in this," he said, pointing to the stove, "producing a gas which powers the motor. Most people have gone back to using gasoline, but because we live out in the countryside and own some forest land, I have free access to wood."

After a few coughings and sputterings, we set off—on the wrong side of the road! Both Granny and I gasped in horror when cars came toward us in the right lane. I knew that people drove on the left in England but

[1] From here on, I have translated all conversations from Swedish to English for the sake of the reader.

there the driver sat on the right. But here, people were driving on the left, even though the drivers sat on the left.

Once again Herman laughed good-naturedly.

"Don't worry. This is how we drive here," he told Granny, patting her arm comfortingly.

After driving through a dark pine forest for a good hour, suddenly the landscape opened up into rolling farmland. On the far side of a little village, Herman turned into a gravel driveway leading to a prosperous-looking farmhouse, behind which stood a large barn surrounded by a number of sheds and outbuildings. Granny leaned forward in her seat to get a better look.

"I-i-is this Sjöström's farm?" she asked hesitantly.

"Yes," Herman told her. "As the only child, Kajsa inherited it. After her husband died, her daughter Lotti and I moved in to run the farm and look after *Mor* Kajsa."

"I'll be damned!" Granny muttered under her breath. She knew nothing of Kajsa's life. When she had located her, she had simply written and introduced herself, saying that she was coming to Sweden.

Kajsa had written back saying that Vicar Lindblom had confirmed her lifelong suspicions in regards to her origins, adding that she sincerely hoped Elsa-Carolina would come to visit. Granny had answered saying that she looked forward to their meeting and would contact her once she got to Sweden.

Herman went ahead of us to open the side door. By the time I had helped Granny up the few steps to the little porch, she was shaking like a leaf. Her nervousness was beyond me. Kajsa's letter had been so friendly and welcoming that she obviously bore her no ill will.

Once in the kitchen, I understood that little had changed since the last time Granny had been there. Kajsa's daughter Lotti was waiting for us, having set the table for the afternoon coffee, complete with fresh bread, crisp bread, butter, cheese, and cinnamon rolls.

"So welcome! So welcome!" Lotti exclaimed, the phrase being the same in both languages.

"Mamma! They're here!" she called.

Presently, the door on the far side of the kitchen, through which Kajsa had disappeared seventy-nine years earlier, opened slowly and a woman who was almost Granny's twin entered the room. Both of them stared at the floor shyly. When Granny finally lifted her gaze, I thought she was going to faint.

"Thank God!" she muttered with a sigh. "I don't know what I'd have done if she'd looked like Stenbom!"

Her nervousness evaporated and in the same instant Kajsa looked up. They both burst into laughter simultaneously, a laughter that immediately dissolved into tears.

"Mamma," Kajsa said, barely above a whisper.

To say that they fell into each other's arms sounds trite, but that is exactly what they did.

Feeling like intruders, Lotti and I went outside under the pretense of helping Herman with the luggage. Hearing our footsteps in the gravel, he quickly wiped the tears from his eyes.

"*Underbar!*" he exclaimed. "*Mor* Kajsa so glad!" he added in broken English.

That evening, Kajsa's granddaughter, Katja, arrived from a nearby town where she had just completed her first year as an English teacher. We hit it off immediately. We were about the same age, and while we both claimed Granny as our great-grandmother, neither of us could figure out what relation we were to each other. We settled for cousins.

The day after we arrived was Midsummer. The celebration was just as Granny had described it as having been in Augusta's day. People from the neighboring farms gathered at Sjöström's, as the farm was still referred to locally. A Midsummer pole in the shape of a giant cross was decorated with festoons of leaves and wildflowers before being raised in the middle of the yard, whereupon everyone, young and old, held hands and danced around it, singing traditional Midsummer songs.

From there, we moved across the lawn to the long table set with the family's best china, silverware, and crystal and loaded with food: pickled herring and new potatoes, crisp bread, newly baked white bread, cheeses, ham, salads, and ice cold schnapps as well as beer.

The meal began with a number of toasts centering around Granny's and Kajsa's reunion, each one followed by the downing of one's schnapps. By the time we got around to eating, everyone was happily tipsy.

Later that evening, Katja and I followed the sound of distant fiddle and accordion music to the village's *Folkets Park,* where an outdoor dance was underway. Katja introduced me as her American cousin, which immediately drew a crowd of young people who wanted to try out their English. Never in my life had I ever had so many dance partners!

On the way home, just as the sun was about to come up, Katja took a path across a meadow where we each picked nine different flowers to put under our pillows so we would dream about the men we were going to marry. I felt as though I had done it all before, in another time and place, that I had stepped into my great-great-grandmother Augusta's skin.

Being in Sweden, surrounded by the traditions and hearing the sing-song melody of the language gave a whole new dimension to all that Granny had told me. Listening to her talk had been just that: listening to someone else's tale. I heard the story, but I had supplied my own pictures. Granny saw her mother and Olov and Stina and Elna and all the others as she told me about them—she saw their faces, their clothes, the way they moved, and she heard their voices. I, too, saw them, but only as creations of my own fantasy. I will never know how close my visions of them came to reality, for there are no photographs of them.

It was the same with places like Grankullen, Ekefors Manor, the poor-house, the *fäbod*. Granny saw them in her mind's eye, while I had imagined them according to my own points of reference. But now my picture was becoming more three-dimensional as I actually saw the landscape and old buildings.

But no matter how much I learned about the social structure—what was right or wrong, accepted or taboo—I could never begin to feel their effects as Granny had. Nor could I begin to feel her poverty and loneliness in an uncaring world. Those things would forever extend beyond my capacity to comprehend, for it is not possible to share one's memories with another. However, I did get a chance to get a clearer picture of a few of the people and places that had colored Granny's life.

One day we visited the parish church, looking for the graves of family members. Granny was reluctant to enter the church itself with its memories of Reverend Holmgren, yet she felt bound to go in and thank Vicar Lindblom for finding Kajsa for her. He turned out to be a very pleasant old man with a big dose of humor. At the back of the church was a display of church history, including portraits of all the priests who had served the parish.

"I suppose Elsa-Carolina remembers Reverend Holmgren," he ventured, pointing to the portrait of a fat, sour-looking priest with an arrogant air about him.

Granny's face hardened. "I certainly do!" she snorted.

"We have something here that she probably also remembers," he continued, going over to a glass-covered display box. Inside was a brown cap with ties, accompanied by a text stating that women who gave birth to children out of wedlock were forced to wear such whore's caps.

"There is a story that has come down through time by word of mouth concerning this particular cap, and now that I have Elsa-Carolina here before me, I would like to learn whether it is truth or fiction."

Granny looked up at him and saw a twinkle in his eye. She burst out laughing.

"What is the popular version?" she asked.

"That a young unwed mother by the name of Elsa-Carolina gave it to Reverend Holmgren as a present when she left the parish."

"It's absolutely true!" she declared. "Everyone knew that he had a number of bastard children around the parish, but no one dared speak up. I was raped by a priest like him and then forced to take all the blame, as well as being called a liar when I told the truth. I swore I would never set foot in this church again!"

"Things did not go so well for Reverend Holmgren toward the end of his life," Lindblom said. "As the Bible says, we reap what we sow. He became very unpopular with the congregation. One of his bastard sons even confronted him and sued for compensation. Of course, he didn't win—it never would have happened in those days—but it is all recorded in the court's record books. In the end, Holmgren was forced to retire. That in itself was unusual for the times."

Granny looked at the cap. "He should have been forced to wear that," she remarked, "although it isn't big enough to cover his swollen head." She turned to me. "So now you know what Holmgren looked like, at least," she added.

Having already made one concession to churches and priests, Granny adamantly refused to go anywhere near Stenbom's church in the neighboring parish. But she did agree to go to Ekefors Manor, which she had heard still belonged to the Ekefors family.

I don't know what she expected when she knocked on the kitchen door of the manor house with Kajsa, Katja, and me standing behind her on the porch. She introduced herself as the oldest daughter of the family who had lived in Grankullen.

"Is Elsa-Carolina by any chance sister to Olov's-Märta?" she was asked.

"She is my half-sister," she replied, then turned to us. "And this is my daughter, Kajsa, and my great granddaughters, Carrie and Katja."

"Anna-Greta Ekefors-Dahl," the woman said, turning to the man who had appeared behind her, "and this is my husband, Edvind. Come in. We are just sitting down to coffee. Would the ladies care to join us?"

"Oh, that would be lovely. Thank you," Granny replied.

The others carried on polite conversation as we drank our coffee along with the regulation seven kinds of cookies. Katja did her best to translate for me.

Presently, I heard Granny say, "Ekefors-Dahl?" in a questioning tone.

"My great-grandparents built this house in 1796, and it has been inherited by the eldest male in each generation since then," Herr Ekefors-Dahl said, indicating the portrait-covered wall behind him, "except for one. Look here," he continued, getting up and pointing to one of the painted portraits of a young man. "He was the only male child in his generation, but it was his sister, whose married name was Dahl, who inherited the manor instead. I don't know why it was so. No one would ever talk about him when I was a child. I don't even know his name."

Granny stared at the portrait. "So that's what he looked like," she murmured to herself finally. Everyone turned and looked at her.

"His name was Erling," she said. "He was my father. He and my mother loved each other and had become secretly engaged, secretly because she was just a lowly housemaid. When she became pregnant with me, Erling naïvely believed that his father would allow them to marry. But instead, Baron Ekefors sent him on a so-called business trip to Norway. While he was away, the Baron forced my mother to marry one of his farmhands. Erling was so angry when he found out that he turned his back on Ekefors Manor and disgraced the family by enlisting in the army as a common foot soldier, rather than as an officer. Baron Ekefors retaliated by disowning him. Erling further disgraced the family by getting killed, not in battle, but in a training maneuver. My paternity became public at his funeral, which I remember well. My mother never tried to deny it, even though one could say that it destroyed her life, causing her years of unhappiness."

Our host whistled softly.

"So Elsa-Carolina is one of the family," he said, putting his hand on her arm.

"I have never thought of it that way," Granny replied. "Even though I am related genetically, I am certainly not related legally. Baron Ekefors emphatically maintained that Erling was not my father and the family never accepted me in any way. Quite the opposite. In the end, they drove me away."

"Well, as the present Baron of Ekefors Manor, I welcome Elsa-Carolina back!"

"What an unexpected welcome!" she remarked as we left there. "Who would ever have imagined!"

There were more people who had never met each other. After a week at Kajsa's, Granny and I, plus Kajsa and Katja, all squeezed into Herman's little car, along with our luggage and a sack of wood to power us to Märta's and get Herman home again.

"Strange," Granny mused as we drove along the dirt road from Sjöström's to Märta's, "the parish seemed so big when one walked everywhere. It took me a couple of hours to walk to Sjöström's the day I went to see Kajsa. And now it takes us less than a quarter of an hour to drive that distance. And just think, Kajsa, you had an aunt who was almost your neighbor, and you didn't even know it."

"Looking back, I realize that my parents felt it was better that I didn't know about my biological family, but it was a pity. Even though I was loved and well cared for, I was quite lonely as an only child. To have aunts and uncles and cousins nearby—and even in America—would have been wonderful!"

Märta had never made it to Stockholm. Instead, she met a man for whom it was worth giving up her dream of the city, so she stayed home, got married, and raised a family. She and her husband, Johannes, lived on a little farm that had once been part of Ekefors Manor, where they had managed to eke out a living when self-sufficiency was more important than money. After Johannes' death, Märta's son, Hannes, had taken over the farm, followed by his son, Egon. As was customary in farm families, Märta lived downstairs and the younger family—Märta's grandson Egon, his wife, and children—lived upstairs.

Although her health was poor, she was chipper and excited about our visit. She had gone through an old photo album ahead of time, anxious to surprise us with what she had discovered.

"I don't know if Elsalina remembers what Mamma looked like," she said while thumbing though the album. "I have to admit that I only have a hazy picture of her in my head. But you were enough older that perhaps you remember her more clearly. Such a pity that there are no photographs of her. But when my daughter Majken was young, people who had known Mamma swore that she looked just like her. Look at this. It's Majken's wedding photo."

She pointed to a picture of a young woman in a long black dress standing beside an uncomfortable-looking young man in a too-small suit. Granny squinted at the photo a second.

"I'll be darned!" she declared. "She's a spittin' image of Mamma!" She turned to me. "Now you can see what Augusta looked like."

It all happened so quickly and unexpectedly that I didn't have time to bring my rather diffused mental image of Augusta into focus, so I don't know how I had pictured her. Young Majken's face slipped easily onto the mother Granny had told me so much about.

When Egon wondered if there was anything special that Granny would like to do, she replied that she would love to see the *fäbod* where she had spent the summer with the Engströms. She wasn't sure where it was, but Egon was able to find the farm where the Engströms had lived by looking in the old parish records. From there we approached the present owners and asked if the *fäbod* still existed.

"Oh, yes. We cut and store a lot of hay for the winter up there," we were told. "Nowadays there is a tractor road all the way up. In fact, I am going up the day after tomorrow." He turned to Granny. "You and your family are welcome to go along, if you don't mind a little jostling."

"I can stand anything, as long as I don't have to walk the whole way," Granny declared.

The day for the trip was beautiful. The sky was a deep blue with just a few small cumulus clouds floating ever so slowly with a light breeze. As we neared the crest of the hill, Granny asked to be let down from the wagon so she could walk the last bit of the way. Linking her arm through mine and with Erik's cane in her other hand, we walked slowly, letting the tractor disappear behind the old buildings far to the right.

"Keep your eye on the top of the hill now," she told me. "Soon you will be able to see all the way over to Norway."

Suddenly, far beyond the treeless hilltop, a blueish horizon appeared in the distance across the valley. In the same instant the tractor motor stopped, letting the sound of birdsong rise out of the valley on the wind.

"Isn't it beautiful!" Granny exclaimed, squeezing my arm. "It's almost as wonderful as gazing at the stars. If paradise is like this, I'll gladly die— if I'm going to paradise, that is." She chuckled. "And listen to this: hello!" she called at the top of her lungs. Three separate echoes came singing back to us.

"When I die," she said finally, "I would like to be cremated and have my ashes cast on the wind from up here. I used to think I wanted to be buried next to Stina, since I don't know where my mother was buried, but I don't like the feeling in the parish churchyard. It's too close to the church, which makes it heavy and gloomy. Besides, I probably wouldn't be allowed to be buried there, since I have never repented. To fly freely on the wind from the hilltop feels much better."

The rest of our visit to the *fäbod* was, for Granny, of secondary importance, I realized. For me, it was interesting to see the places she had described. I had seen photographs of all the Engströms, so I had no trouble placing Aunt Sofia and the children among the *fäbod* buildings. I could almost hear them talking and laughing as they worked. It was so familiar that I felt as though I had been there with them that long ago summer. The spell of the *fäbod* fell over me. It was easy to understand why it had been the happiest time in Granny's childhood.

July passed quickly. Granny had managed to do all that she had set out to do. As she had known from the start, everyone who had played a role in her life was dead, aside from Märta and Kajsa. She had no interest in returning to places where she had been mistreated and unhappy. The only person at Nyqvist's who had been kind to her was Ebba. But she had been an old woman even then, so there was no chance that she was alive. And Stenbom's rectory held even worse memories than Nyqvist's. As for the poorhouse, it had long since been torn down, to which Granny remarked, "Good riddance!"

And, of course, Olov was gone. When he became too old to work and had to leave the cottage, Märta and Johannes took him in and cared for him. He mellowed toward the end. One day, he asked Märta what had ever happened to Elsa-Carolina, as if he had suddenly realized she was gone. Without thinking, Märta told him how she had been auctioned off, then lived in the poorhouse. In the end, she even told him about Reverend Stenbom and Kajsa. When she was finished, he had tears in his eyes.

"Tell her I'm sorry. I had no idea," he said.

Two days later he died.

According to Märta, all the buildings at Grankullen had been torn down shortly after Olov had moved from there. The weather was never kind to timber buildings, even when inhabited, and when uninhabited, they quickly returned from whence they had come. After that, the forest had moved in and made it almost impossible to even find the foundation stones. Stina's cottage, as well as Elna's, had met the same fate. Elna was dead, of course, and no one seemed to know what had happened to her children.

None of this seemed to bother Granny. She had been well aware that it would be so when planning the trip. More and more it became obvious that all she had wanted was to see the view from the *fäbod* and spend time with Märta and Kajsa. And find out what had actually happened to her mother. I had no complaints about the fact that we spent most of the summer at Märta's, along with Kajsa and Katja. Katja and I had become the best of friends. After having been steeped in Swedish peasant culture of the 1800s for the first ten days of the trip, I was now experiencing postwar Sweden of the 1940s, with Katja as my guide. And I was rapidly learning the language. Every day was new and exciting.

At the beginning of August, the letter from the archives arrived, along with apologies for it having taken so long.

"Shall I read it to you?" Märta asked when she handed it to her sister.

"No, that's not necessary," Granny replied, turning the large envelope over and over in her hands nervously. "I can manage it."

Grasping Erik's cane, she pulled herself to her feet and disappeared into our shared bedroom and closed the door. I looked at Märta. She shrugged her shoulders. All of us had dreaded the arrival of the information Granny had requested. Although she never mentioned it, it was obvious that it had been uppermost in her mind as the summer wore on.

That evening, Katja came by for our usual walk into the village to see what was going on. Thinking Granny was asleep, I tip-toed into our room to get my sweater. But she wasn't sleeping. She lay on the bed, curled into a fetal ball like a small child, mumbling to herself. The papers from the archives were scattered on the bed beside her.

"Granny, are you all right?" I asked gently.

Getting no answer, I sat down on the edge of the bed and patted her shoulder.

"What did the archive papers say?"

Her mumbling became louder now, taking on form.

"I didn't m-m-mean to...I didn't m-m-mean to...I didn't m-m-mean to..." she repeated over and over.

"Didn't mean to what?" I asked.

"It was m-m-my fault..."

It was as if she were somewhere else, out of hearing, out of reach.

Finally, I gathered up the papers and went back out to the kitchen to find out what they said. Märta read through them a couple of times before handing them to Katja. Her hands were shaking.

"Tell me in English what it says, Katja," I begged.

"It says that when the constable and his assistant came to Grankullen, they had questioned Elsa-Carolina, who had been there when the baby was born:

"'Did Elsa-Carolina know her mother was having a baby?' the constable had asked.

'Yes, Sir.'

'Was Elsa-Carolina in the room with her?'

'No, Sir. I wasn't allowed to go in unless she called me.'

'Did Elsa-Carolina hear the baby cry?'

'Yes, Sir.'

"That she had heard the baby cry was proof that it had been born alive. Augusta was convicted of having murdered it and was sent to prison." She turned to the next page. "Here it says simply that she died in prison from pneumonia."

"It's beginning to make sense now," I said. "Several times she told me that ever since she was a child she has felt guilty for having destroyed her mother's life, that it was because of her existence that Olov had turned against Augusta. At the same time, she felt that there was more to it, something she didn't know about. I don't think that she has ever connected the fact that she said she'd heard the baby cry with Augusta's arrest."

Granny remained in a comatose state for several days. On the second day, the doctor came and examined her but could do nothing. He told us to take care of her as we had been doing and to wait. Märta and I took turns sitting with her. Sometimes we talked to her or asked questions, but she was unaware of our presence, let alone our words. Now and then we were able to get her to drink a little broth or juice, but she drank like a robot. At night I slept with my arm around her, as she used to do with me when I was small and we shared a bed during her visits. Yet I don't think she noticed. She was lost somewhere inside herself. The past had become her present. There was no way to contact her.

Then one morning, a change had taken place. Although she was still in her own world, the heaviness which had surrounded her was gone. In the afternoon, Kajsa and Katja came to visit. We all sat in her room, talking and drinking coffee as if everything were normal.

All at once Granny stirred, then said something, softly, in the same way she had mumbled to herself. But now her voice was filled with joy. She smiled, her face radiant.

Suddenly, I understood that, as long as I had known her, her face had been shrouded by a veil of sadness. It was only now, when it had disappeared, that I realized it. She was still out of contact, lost in her own world, but she was happier than I had ever seen her.

I nudged Katja. "What did she say?" I asked her.

"She said, 'She's calling me. She's forgiven me. Even though she was executed, she's forgiven me!'"

"Executed?" I whispered. "I thought it was pneumonia."

Katja just shook her head, bewildered. Märta and Kajsa looked skeptical.

That evening when I opened the door to go in to bed, I understood immediately that something had happened. I called to Märta, and we went in together, both of us knowing instinctively that Granny was gone. She must have died in her sleep, for her eyes were closed and the smile etched on her face was almost angelic. Seeing how peaceful she was took the edge off my sorrow. Not only had she returned to her roots, but she had been released from the guilt that had cast its shadow over her life since childhood. I couldn't help but feel happy for her. My own sorrow would come later.

The days that followed were filled to overflowing. Everyone had been shocked by Granny's use of the word "executed." Finally Katja put through a call to the archives and asked if it was true that Augusta Torsdotter had died from pneumonia. She was told that Vicar Grönlund had been upset when it was discovered that Augusta, like all so-called "child-murderers" in those days, had been executed. He simply could not bring himself to deliver such horrible news to her daughter. So it was decided that someone should write a separate paper, supposedly copied from the death records, saying she had died from pneumonia. Of course, it was terrible to hear that Augusta had been executed (by what method none of us dared to ask), but at the same time, it validated what Granny had appeared to be experiencing during the last hours of her life. There could not have been a better way for her to die.

Feeling like a thief, I forced myself to open her suitcase and go through the things she left behind. Besides the few clothes she had brought along, there was an old shoe box with a folded piece of paper with my name on it taped to the lid. I opened it and read:

My Dearest Carrie,

In the (likely) event that I shall end my days in Sweden, I want you to have these things in the shoe box, as well as my mother's engagement ring, Stina's ring, and my ring from Erik. My last wish is to be cremated and for my ashes to be spread on the wind from the fäbod *hill. No religious service, please! There is a box at home with your name on it that contains, among other things, a lot of old letters and diaries that might be of interest to you—but you will have to learn Swedish first. And please take anything else that has meaning for you.*

My warmest thanks to you for accompanying me on my journey home.

Your Great-Granny Elsa-Carolina

Gingerly, I opened the shoe box. The things inside were familiar to me, even though I had never actually seen them: Stina's old family Bible with the well-worn picture of Jesus and the small children stuck inside, Stina's diary of deliveries and herbal recipes, the little wooden box that had contained the brass button from Erling's uniform, and the engagement ring he had given Augusta. The button was there, but the ring was still on Granny's finger, together with Stina's wedding ring. There were a few photographs that she had brought along to show people—one of her and Erik together, one of Aunt Sofia, and some of Erik and their daughter, my grandmother Isabella. Also in the box was Granny's boat ticket. When I picked it up, I saw that, unlike my round trip ticket, it was only one way.

The day we took Granny's ashes up to the *fäbod* couldn't have been more beautiful. Herman drove Kajsa, Katja, Märta, and me to the end of the road, where the original path began. Although we were offered a tractor ride, we felt it was more fitting to walk the rest of the way, as Granny had done that summer long ago. Three of us took turns carrying the urn, the coffee basket, and helping Märta climb over stones and tree roots. I was a bit concerned by the fact that there was almost no wind on which to cast the ashes. But once we emerged from the forest onto the top of the hill, a cool breeze rose out of the valley, bringing with it the sound of distant cow bells. Behind us, the birds, who had stopped singing as we passed, began calling to one another once more. Small cumulus clouds floated aimlessly above the valley as if they had nowhere to go.

Kajsa shook a white cloth out over the picnic bench in the yard, and we set out cups and saucers, along with a plate of seven kinds of cookies. Lastly, we placed Granny's urn at the head of the table. As we drank our coffee, we talked and laughed, as we had the day we drank coffee at her bedside. Now and then one of us said something that brought tears to us all, but mostly we were light-hearted.

Märta entertained us with anecdotes from their short childhood to-gether, and I added various comments that Katja had to translate for the others.

Sadly for Märta and Kajsa and Katja, the time spent with Granny had been all too short, yet all three of them were thankful for what time they had had with her. I, for my part, suddenly realized how privileged I had been to have had her my whole life—and especially for the gift of her life story that she had entrusted to me.

Finally, there was nothing left to do but what we had come to do. Strangely, by now the wind had picked up somewhat from behind us, as if getting ready to carry out Granny's last request. We set the urn on the crest of the hill where Granny had first pointed out the horizon to me.

Then one after the other, we dipped a large wooden spoon, that had once been Augusta's, into it and cast her ashes into the wind. We each said goodbye in our own way: "Goodbye, Granny!" *"Farväl, Elsalina!"* *"Adjö, Mamma!"* *"Adjö, gammel mormor!"* And each time the echo came back threefold.

Several days later, I reluctantly left the people I had grown to love and made my way back to Gothenburg alone. Vicar Grönlund met me at the station, took me to lunch, and then delivered me to the ship waiting in the harbor. At first I had dreaded the ten returning days on my own, but I soon realized what a godsend they were. Not only did they act as a transition period, but most importantly, they gave me a chance to sit undisturbed, and write down everything I could remember from our summer in Sweden.

I felt as though I were in a race with time, for already the sharpness of the past months was beginning to dull. I wanted to hold onto every little bit, to keep it alive, rather than relegate it to the back corner of my mind called memory. No other person in my life was so alive for me as Granny had been and was. I knew almost nothing about any of my other relatives, not even my own parents. Granny was the only one of them who had a past, who had roots, who was three-dimensional. The others were like cardboard cut-outs: flat and lifeless. I had to keep her essence alive.

That autumn I began teaching, but as time went on, I felt more and more out of place in America. I was unable to put down roots anywhere, for there was nothing to root myself in, nothing that said, "This is where you came from, where your ancestors came from before you. You belong here." It was as if none of my forefathers had a past. Their lives had only pressed forward, in an effort to get ahead. Where they had come from had no meaning for them. They didn't care, weren't interested. And because they had no pasts, I had none either. I was only living on the surface, as if I had come out of nowhere. The only person in the family I felt a connection with was Granny. She had given me the richness of her past, in which I could put down my roots.

Finally, I gave up trying to find my place in America and returned to Sweden, where my roots have anchored themselves firmly in both the past and the present over the last half century.

And Granny is always present in the background. Katja and I are the only ones left who remember her. Every August on the anniversary of her death, we make the trek up to the now-deserted *fäbod* with our coffee basket and drink to her memory. Then we stand on the crest of the hill and gaze out across the valley to Norway.

"Granny, it's us!" we call into the stillness. "Hello!"

"Hello, hello, hello," she answers. The last "o" rings on indefinitely.

GLOSSARY

ALN (plural ALNAR) – One aln is about two feet long.

AMERICA CHEST – A large wooden chest, often with a wreath of flowers and the date painted on the front. These were used for the storage of clothes and linens due to the lack of cupboard space. A young girl had a bridal chest, in which she kept the things she wove and sewed for her trousseau. When people immigrated to America, such chests became America chests, where people packed the things they would need in order to make a new start in "the land to the west."

BARKBRÖD – So-called bark bread was common among the poor, even in ordinary times, as a way of stretching out flour, which people couldn't afford to buy. Preparing the bark was a rather complicated procedure. Scotch pines were chosen and felled in the late spring when the sap had begun to flow. First, the bark was stripped and hung up to dry. Then the inner bark was dug out and soaked to get rid of the sap taste, and then re-dried. Finally, it was chopped into pieces small enough to fit through the hole in the grindstone and was ground to flour. In times of famine, the amount of ground bark was increased to its bakable limits. If the dough exceeded two-thirds bark flour, not only did it not stick together, but it was also almost inedible.

BERGTAGEN – It was believed that trolls or wood nymphs lured people who were alone in the forest into caves, from which they seldom or never returned. Berg means hill or mountain and tagen means taken— that one is taken into the mountain or cave.

BRÄNNVIN – *Brännvin* is a vodka-like alcoholic drink distilled from grain or potatoes, which dates back to the beginning of the 1500s. During much of its history, it has been brewed at home or readily and cheaply available. Home brew has periodically been banned, especially during famine years when the grain and potatoes that could have been eaten were distilled to *brännvin* instead. It is Sweden's most popular alcoholic drink.

DOTTERDOTTERS DOTTER – Daughter-daughter's daughter; or great-granddaughter's daughter.

FARMOR – Father's mother, paternal grandmother.

FJÄRDINGSVÄG – A unit of measure for road distance. One *fjärdingsväg* was equal to approximately one and three-fourths mile.

FOLKETS PARK – Most villages and towns had a people's park, where various community activities were held, including dances every Saturday night during the summer.

FÄBOD (pl. FÄBODAR) – Summer pastureland up in the mountains, where the cattle *(fä)* could graze in the forest and the women made cheese for the winter and to sell. A *fäbod* consisted of a number of wooden buildings.

GAMMEL MORMOR – Old grandmother.

HUSFÖRHÖR – Hus means house and a *förhör* can be an examination or an interrogation. In the case of the *husförhör,* it was definitely seen as the latter. Everyone, from young children to the elderly, was forced to stand before the parish priest and answer his questions pertaining to the church's beliefs and the Bible. He kept the parish records of births, marriages, deaths, as well as noting whether or not a person could read. He evaluated people according to their answers or lack of them. There are many examples in the old record books of people who were judged to be idiots or mentally ill. He also noted those who were blind or deaf and dumb, as well as where people lived: in the poorhouse, in a children's home, as boarders, as maids/farmhands on a farm, homeowners, and so on. The parish priest had more power locally than the government.

KAFFEPETTER – A three-legged coffee pot that stood in the fire on the open hearth.

KNALLE (pl. KNALLAR) – A peddler from the province of Västergötland, the textile center of Sweden, who traveled the countryside on foot, selling his wares as he went. These men had special permission from the government to earn their livings in this manner and were the only ones allowed to do so. To *knalla* along is to "push on."

KOLT (pl. KOLTAR) – A smock-like garment that was open down the back, worn by small children, with nothing underneath it. It was very practical for toilet training, as well as spanking.

218—

LÅNGMJÖLK – Long milk, a way of preserving milk so that it will hold a long time.

MOR – Mother.

MORMOR – Mother's mother, maternal grandmother.

POSTILLA – A book of sermons that one could read if it wasn't possible to attend a Sunday service.

RIKSDALER – The name of Swedish currency until 1873.

SEXMAN – One of six (sex) elected members of a parish who was responsible for, among other things, looking after people's morals and behavior, their church attendance, and other similar things.

SVAGDRICKA – (Literally "weak drink") A low-alcohol malt drink dating to the Middle Ages. It was drunk mainly on special occasions, such as Christmas, Easter, etc.

SKÅL – A toast, to drink to one's health. Cheers!

TORP – A cottage and a bit of land belonging to a large estate. The rent is paid by working a certain number of days on the estate per year.

TUM – The width of a thumb. Eg: Covered with *tum*-thick ice.

UNDERBAR – Wonderful.

UTDRAGSSOFFA – (Utdrag is to "pull or draw out".) This was a very common piece of furniture in peasant homes. It consisted of a long bench, or sofa, that one could sit on during the day. At night the seat was folded upwards and held in place with a peg and the box section below could be pulled out to make a double-sized bed.

WISE WOMAN – A wise woman (who was often older) acted as a midwife, as well as curing various illnesses, in the days when doctors were only found in the larger towns and cities – for those who could pay for their services.

NAMES

Döv-Anna – Deaf-Anna

Elsa-Carolina – Pronounced CARO LE' NA (Caro lee na).

Halta-Maja – Maja-the-Cripple

Kajsa – Kai'sa (Kai rhymes with fly).

Nål-Nisse – Needle-Nisse

Skräddare-Emmerik – Tailor-Emmerik

Stora Alfred – Big Alfred

Svarta Björn – Black Bear

Tok-Siri – Crazy Siri

BIBLIOGRAPHY

Conradson, Birgitta och Fredlund, Jane, Köket förr i tiden, *The Kitchen in the Old Days,* ICA förlag, Västerås, 1973.

Cronberg, Marie Lindstedt, Synd och skam, *Sin and Shame: Unwed mothers in the Swedish countryside 1680–1880,* Doctor's thesis, Lunds University, 1997.

Ejdestam, Julius, De fattigas Sverige, *Poor Folks' Sweden,* Rabén & Sjögren, Stockholm, 1969.

Ejdestam, Julius, Samling kring bordet, *Gathering Around the Table,* Rabén & Sjögren, Stockholm, 1975.

Fredlund, Jane, Så levde vi, *The Way We Lived,* ICA förlaget, Västerås, 1971.

Frykman, Jonas, Horan i bonde samhället, *The Whore [unwed mother] in Peasant Society,* Doctor's thesis, Liber Förlag, Lund University, 1977.

Höjeberg, Pia, Jordemor: Barnmorskor och barnsängskvinnor i Sverige, *Midwife: Midwives and Childbed Women in Sweden,* Carlssons Bokförlag, Malmö, 1991.

Jonsson, Karl, Fattighuset, *The Poor House, autobiographical experiences,* Jemtbokens förlag, Östersund, 1981.

Levander, Lars, Fattigtfolk och tiggare, *Poor People and Beggars,* Gidlunds förlag, Nordiska Museet & Stockholm University, 1934.

Levander, Lars, Landsväg, krog och marknad, *High Road, Tavern and Market,* Gidlunds förlag, Nordiska Museet, 1935.

Liljewall, Britt, editor, Tjära, barkbröd och vildhonung, *Tar, Barkbread, and Wild Honey,* Nordisk Museet, Stockholm, 1996.

Mas-Larsson, Sture, Troshjältar och original, *Champions of the Faith and Eccentrics,* Evangeliipress, Örebro, 1959.

Malmberg, Denise, Skammens röda blomma? Menstruationen och den menstruerande kvinnan i svensk tradition, *The Red Flower of Shame? Menstruation and the Menstruating Woman in Swedish Tradition*, Doctor's dissertation, Uppsala University, 1991.

Norlind, Tobias, Svenska Allmogens Lif, *Swedish Peasant Life*, Bohlin & Co., Stockholm, 1912.

Nothin, Torsten, En bortglömd värld, *A Forgotten World*, Norstedts, Stockholm, 1953.

Palme, Sven Ulric, Den gamla goda tiden, *The Good Old Days*, LTs förlag, Stockholm, 1970.

Persson, Boris, red, Helg och söcken, *Both Weekdays and Sundays: Life and work in the middle of the 1800s*, Bonniers förlag, Stockholm, 1973.

Rosengren, Annette, När resan var ett äventyr, *When Travelling was an Adventure*, Natur och Kultur Stockholm, 1979.

Saxon, J.L, I handelsbod på 1870-talet, *In the General Store in the 1870s*, Saxon & Lindströms förlag, Stockholm, 1932.

Sigurd, I Svenska Bondehem, *In the Swedish Farm Home*, Hugo Gebers förlag, Stockholm, 1924.

Sjöberg, Marja Taussi, Dufvans fångar, *Dufvan's Prisoners: Crime, punishment, and mankind in 19th century Sweden*, Författareförlaget, Malmö, 1986.

Sjöberg, Marja Taussi, Skiljas, *Separating: Engagement, marriage, and divorce in Norrland in the 1800s*, Författareförlaget, Malmö, 1988.

Tillhagen, Carl-Herman, Barnet i folktron, *The Child in Folklore: Conception, birth and upbringing*, LTs förlag, Stockholm, 1983.

Wiss, Roald, De gamla byarna i Tylöskogen, *The Old Villages in the Tylö Forest*, LTs förlag, Stockholm, 1978.

Wrangel, Ewert, professor, editor, Svenska Folket Genom Tiderna, nioende bandet, vid 1800-talets mitt, *The Swedish People Through the Ages: Volume nine, The Middle of the 19th Century,* Tidskriftsförlaget Allhem A.B.,Malmö, 1939.